THE
PECULIARITIES

PRAISE FOR THE PECULIARITIES

❊ ❊ ❊

"Fascinating events, surprising at first but completely believable. Characters I cared about more with each page. And best of all, it made me think, and go on thinking as one idea sprang to another, and on, and on. That is the greatest gift a writer can give."
—Anne Perry, *New York Times* bestselling author of the
Charlotte and Thomas Pitt series

"Wry, witty, twisty and tricky, *The Peculiarities* will slowly draw you into Liss's strange world of magic and monsters, and compel you to pay attention no matter how you might prefer to look away. An involving take on the mysteries of myths and mathematics that have been embedded in our collective consciousness."
—Shana Abé, *New York Times*, *USA Today*, and *Wall Street Journal* bestselling author of *The Second Mrs. Astor*

"David Liss masterfully blends rich historical fiction with terrifying supernatural body horror. He stands with Robert Louis Stevenson and Bram Stoker. Highly recommended." —Jonathan Maberry, author of *V-Wars*

"David Liss turns a new corner, and at the end of it is a splendid, unique and surprising tale of the supernatural drenched in historical atmosphere and fine characterization. You won't want to miss this one."
—Joe R. Lansdale, author of *Hap and Leonard*

"In *The Peculiarities*, David Liss brings his mastery of historical writing to bear on a Victorian tale of weird transformation. There's a strange alchemy at work in this novel where the fantastic lives alongside reality and both are truly frightening and humorous at the same time. This is a fun, horrific, engaging mystery, both for the story and for watching an accomplished writer stepping out into new territory."
—Jeffrey Ford, author of *A Natural History of Hell*

"David Liss leans into early 20th century occult thinking with the same mystical fervor as Crowley, Mathers, and Yeats—the holy trinity of the era."
—Mark Teppo, author of the *Codex of Souls* series

PRAISE FOR DAVID LISS

❄ ❄ ❄

On *A Conspiracy of Paper*
"Tremendously smart, assured, and entertaining."
—*Newsweek*

On *The Devil's Company*
"Accomplished, atmospheric and thoughtful."
—*The Washington Post*

On *The Ethical Assassin*
"[A] page-turning thriller . . . a thought-provoking and highly enjoyable yarn."
—*Baltimore Sun*

On *A Spectacle of Corruption*
"[A] wonderful book . . . easily one of the year's best."
—*The Boston Globe*

On *The Whiskey Rebels*
"Smart, page-turning fun."
—*St. Petersburg Times*

On *The Coffee Trader*
"Unusual and diverting . . . sincerity can be the greatest means of deception."
—*The New York Times Book Review*

On *The Day of Atonement*
"Enthralling . . . [a] sly, rich and swift novel of vengeance and rough justice."
—*The Seattle Times*

On *Twelfth Enchantment*
"Liss's deft touch with historical subject matter and his ability to craft tremendously appealing characters makes this a thoroughly enjoyable, satisfying read."
—Deborah Harkness, author of *A Discovery of Witches*

ALSO BY DAVID LISS

The Twelfth Enchantment (2011)
The Whiskey Rebels (2008)
The Ethical Assassin (2006)
The Coffee Trader (2003)

BENJAMIN WEAVER

The Day of Atonement (2014)
The Devil's Company (2009)
A Spectacle of Corruption (2004)
A Conspiracy of Paper (2000)

RANDOMS

Renegades (2017)
Rebels (2016)
Randoms (2015)

THE PECULIARITIES

DAVID LISS

— TACHYON —

Cover design copyright © 2021 by Elizabeth Story
Interior design copyright © 2021 by John Coulthart
Author photo copyright © Chantel Nasits

Tachyon Publications LLC
1459 18th Street #139
San Francisco, CA 94107
415.285.5615
WWW.TACHYONPUBLICATIONS.COM
TACHYON@TACHYONPUBLICATIONS.COM

Series editor: Jacob Weisman
Project editor: Jaymee Goh

Print ISBN: 978-1-61696-358-3
Digital ISBN: 978-1-61696-359-0

Printed by Versa Press, Inc.

First Edition: 2021
9 8 7 6 5 4 3 2 1

C O N T

E N T S

Hebrew Alphabet.		Alphabet of the Magi.		The Characters of Celestial Writing.	Malachim or the Writing of the Angels.	The Writing called "Passing the River."	Names of the Letters.		The Powers of the Letters.	
א	ס						Aleph	Samekh	a'	s
ב	ע						Beth	Ayin	b th v	ua ng
ג	פ						Gimel	Pe'	g gh	p ph
ד	צ						Daleth	Tzaddi	d dh th	tz
ה	ק						He'	Qoph	h'	q gh
ו	ר						Vau	Resh	vuo	r
ז	ש						...ia	Schi...	z	s sh
							...ed	Nun	l	n
מ	ף						...em	Final Pe'	m	p
נ	ץ						Nun	Final Tzaddi	n	tz

ONE

ABUNDANCE

THOMAS STANDS IN the ballroom of the massive house near Belgrave Square wishing he were somewhere else. Anywhere would do, really, except perhaps Thresher's Bank, his place of employment. It is his position at the bank, lowly though it may be, that has required him to endure this elegant and endless gathering. All his life, Thomas has been free of obligation and responsibility, but that is over now. He is a young man, and his best days are behind him.

A string quartet plays softly in one corner. Liveried servants mill about, gentle as sheep, with champagne coupes on silver trays or towel-wrapped bottles at the ready to refill empty vessels. Shifting slightly to his left, the better to be draped in shadow, Thomas seeks to make himself invisible to the few people who might condescend to speak to him. Perhaps if he can remain unseen long enough, he will simply cease to be. Though not optimistic, Thomas thinks it worth trying. He does not wish to die—not precisely—and it is an exaggeration to say Thomas has a plan to kill himself. It is not an exaggeration to say he holds such a plan in reserve. How could he not, in light of what he fears he may become?

Thomas looks up to see Mr. Walter Thresher, the governor of Thresher's Bank, and the man Thomas most blames for making his life an endless torment. It was not Walter Thresher who decreed Thomas must become a junior bank clerk. That much is true. Walter does seem determined to keep him forever in that position, however, subjecting Thomas to amounts of tedium and degradation he would have previously thought impossible.

Mr. Walter Thresher is some sixteen years older than Thomas. He has always been heavy but has grown alarmingly corpulent in the past half year since ascending to the governorship of Thresher's Bank. His hair has begun to thin and recede, as though it no longer has the strength to cling to his scalp.

Heavy bags hang under his eyes. Thomas cannot remember that Walter was ever cheerful, but there was a time when his countenance might suggest brief periods of what could reasonably be called satisfaction. No more, it seems. The responsibilities of overseeing Thresher's have settled around the new governor's middle, along his hips, and most particularly in his jowls. They have etched new lines upon his face and robbed his complexion of what little luster it once possessed. He shaved his beard some months ago, leaving side whiskers and his mustaches. It was a nod to changing fashions, though Thomas is of the opinion, one he keeps to himself, that Walter's looks improve the more his face is concealed.

"What are you doing, leaning against the wall like a street vagrant?" the governor of Thresher's Bank asks the junior clerk. "You are here to perform a task, not to lounge about uselessly."

"Of course," says Thomas. "The task. Documents to copy? Some files to be stored, perhaps?"

Walter scowls and takes a step forward, as if he is prepared to thrash this junior clerk before the guests. It is the ever-cheerful Mr. Hawke who steps forward to prevent any needless violence. He places himself between the two men, the most senior and among the most junior at the bank. "Let us not think of this task as a duty," he says to Thomas, "but rather as a delight."

Mr. Hawke—something of a professional factotum, as near as Thomas can tell—worked closely with the late Samuel Thresher for many years and now is always to be found near Samuel's heir. Unnaturally thin, not at all tall, and clean-shaven other than his bushy side whiskers, Mr. Hawke's quick, birdlike motions give him what Thomas considers to be a look of low cunning. Hawke's eyes are too blue to be masculine and unusually narrow. Hardly more than slits, really. His nose is a blade, his chin so pointy that Thomas cannot fathom why the man does not choose to hide it with a beard, fashionable or otherwise. His face appears both strangely young in firmness, yet immensely old in the toughness of wrinkles around his eyes.

Now he leans forward slightly, like a sailor atop the main mast hoping to sight land, and gazes across the ballroom. When he spies his target, he grins like a simpleton, or perhaps like a panderer. "Ah, there she is. Not an obligation, but a prize."

The woman in question stands silent and stern-faced next to her homunculus of a father. Walter Thresher has decided that Thomas must marry her, that the future of the bank, and his responsibilities to that institution, require he do so.

"I should perhaps simply walk over to her, ask her how she does, and then propose marriage?" Thomas suggests.

"Don't be a dolt," Walter snaps. "You needn't propose this evening. Converse with her. Attempt to be agreeable. I know you have little enough experience with women who require no payment for their services, but you could damn well make an effort."

"It is not so very difficult a thing to be pleasant to an attractive young lady," says Mr. Hawke in a wistful voice, as though recalling experiences of his long-ago youth.

"I cannot understand why you should want me to—"

"You are not required to understand," hisses Walter Thresher. "You are required to obey."

"One step at a time, young sir," adds Mr. Hawke in a tone that suggests he is speaking to a small child. "Your task for the evening is to be kind and attentive to this young lady. I must imagine there are less pleasant ways to pass a few hours."

Thomas does not want to marry for the good of the bank, but he supposes it may not matter. He may be dead, or something near enough to dead, long before he is made to raise the subject of marriage to a woman who can surely have as little interest in him as he has in her.

"You will do as I say," Walter Thresher tells Thomas. "You signed a contract when you came to work for the bank. You owe Thresher's your allegiance."

Thomas is slightly surprised to hear Walter reference the rumors of the curiously binding nature of contracts. In the age of the Peculiarities, many believe, only a fool breaks a binding agreement. Walter, however, is a staunch Tory and so maintains that the Peculiarities are nothing more than imaginative nonsense cooked up by disreputable newspapers. Yes, the fogs in London have become more common and thicker and, admittedly, more violent, but that is merely weather, and weather is subject to change. As for the rest—the odd occurrences and beings and transformations and, of course, the punishments meted out to those who break their promises—all a lot of rubbish. That is what Walter would say. It is what he *has* said, though, interestingly, he does not say it now.

"I confess to not reading the contract as carefully as I might," Thomas says, "but I am certain it said nothing of marriage."

"You consented to work in Thresher's best interests and conduct yourself in a manner that benefits the bank, within and without your hours of employ."

Thomas hardly thinks this amounts to a contractual obligation to marry whomever the bank governor so chooses. Walter is not a feudal lord, however much he might wish it otherwise. Even so, being no expert on contract law, Thomas isn't entirely sure about the precise wording of the document he really had no choice but to sign. It is better to say nothing and allow the absurdity of what Walter is demanding to settle around them.

Walter seems to have concluded he has reached the outer limits of what conversation can achieve. He and Mr. Hawke wander off in search of more productive conversation. Thomas, meanwhile, reflects that the handful of sentences Walter uttered were perhaps the most he has heard out of his brother's mouth, at least directed toward him, in some months—very likely since their father's funeral.

Yes, Walter Thresher and Thomas Thresher are brothers, though the former is considerably older. A stranger unfamiliar with the Thresher clan might not have observed a nearness of relation based on their conduct, though perhaps in their appearance. Thomas looks very much like a younger, leaner, more genial version of Walter.

Their relationship has always been a distant one, and Thomas living under Walter's roof for the past six months has in no way brought them closer. It was a stipulation of their late father's will, just as it was a stipulation that Thomas must immediately begin work as a junior clerk in the family bank, a task to which he must dedicate himself until Walter deems it appropriate for him to rise.

Rising, Walter has made it clear, will be impossible unless Thomas can find a way to marry himself to Miss Esther Feldstein.

Thomas, who believes himself to be dying, or perhaps something more worrying and grotesque than dying, understands none of it. With the freedom that comes from the prospect of metamorphosing out of the human condition, he cannot bring himself to care about his brother's wishes. Though why Walter should wish him to marry a Jew does, to some degree, excite his curiosity.

TWO
ADJUSTMENT

D ESPITE HIS BEST intentions, Thomas gazes across the room at the woman his brother wants him to marry. To his great relief, she demonstrates a studied determination not to meet his eye. That is encouraging. They cannot marry if they never speak to one another.

It is better not to think of Esther Feldstein. He will think of champagne. Thomas drains the contents of his flute and holds it for a servant to refill. He considers it important to repeat this process as many times as possible, to become an engine of champagne consumption. Overt drunkenness in the company of his brother is not a sound plan, but he needs armor against an evening sitting next to Esther Feldstein. Dark haired, dark eyed, and generously nosed, she is simply not the sort of woman a Thresher should be asked to marry. The idea of marrying anyone at all does not sit well with Thomas. He is only twenty-three and cannot support both a wife and his dignity on a junior clerk's income. He dislikes even more the notion of being told whom he must marry. It is 1899, and with the world poised to enter a new century, young men should no longer have such decisions made for them. That Thomas is being told to marry a Jew is beside the point. Or very nearly so.

Thomas does not share the violent dislike of Jews common among his peers. The truth is, he is largely indifferent on the subject, and he supposes Jews are no better or worse than anyone else. He even has a bit of a grudging admiration for a despised and abused people who manage to climb to success so out of proportion to their numbers. Thomas has always felt an inclination—one he has wisely suppressed—to champion Jews and Gypsies and Negroes and Irishmen when his friends disparage them. What does it say about him, he wonders, that he should feel kinship with the most wretched of the races of man?

Thomas wishes not to marry this particular Jewess for many reasons. The social stigma, the miasma of shame, that would swirl about him for the rest of his life—the rest of his existence as part of the animal kingdom, we should say—is not the whole of it, but it is certainly a hearty portion. Every invitation not received, every party at which he is snubbed, would poke the wound afresh. He supposes to a man in love, these burdens must be endurable, perhaps even sweet. *You and I stand against the world, my darling,* and all that. There is a righteous power in facing adversity for a just cause, but Thomas has spoken briefly with Miss Feldstein, and it seems unlikely he will grow to tolerate her, let alone take pleasure in copious amounts of suffering endured for her sake.

He glances around the open room as the guests mingle and laugh and tell their tedious and pointless stories. There is Walter's wife, Pearl, talking with a member of the House of Lords. Pearl is closer to Thomas's age than Walter's, and in appearance she is—well, how does one describe Pearl?

Walter is no one's idea of handsome, but a man with money needn't look like anything at all. A banker's wife, on the other hand, must be charming. Pearl may qualify on that front. She has charmed Thomas, and when he was younger, he was perhaps even a little infatuated with her, though his feelings have now matured into something closer to pity.

Pearl is not pretty. Her forehead is low, her chin weak, her dull hazel eyes too far apart. Her hair is neither brown nor blond, but a muddy and unflattering concoction. Worst of all is her nose—narrow and downturned, slightly elongated at the tip, so when she speaks it waggles over her mouth like a fishing pole held by a jittery angler. Though closer to thirty than not, she is still plagued by adolescent blemishes, which cunningly contrive to show themselves despite thickly applied pastes and powders.

On the other hand, while nature has been uncivil in forming Pearl's face, it has been more generous with her shape. Her figure aligns perfectly with the current fashion in its slender grace underpinned by womanly curves. Her dress, which is in no way immodest, makes it impossible to ignore the shocking truth that somewhere under many layers of fabric stands a naked woman. It is perhaps this to which the younger Thomas responded, though more likely it was her kindness and vulnerability. At least while in company, Walter has never shown any affection toward his wife, something that once made Thomas's heart swell with what he thought might be love but proved to be recognition of a kindred spirit.

Thomas has a most unpleasant sensation—dare we call it a Peculiar sensation?—and realizes he must discreetly make his way upstairs to tend to some extremely private needs. His brother will not notice, because Walter is having what appears to be a conversation with three of the bank's most senior directors. This is the perfect time to escape.

Just as Thomas glides by, the discussion comes to an end, but that seems to be of no moment, as Walter is now huddled close with Mr. Hawke, evidently licking his wounds. Mr. St. John, Mr. Minett, Sir Andrew Hyland, the three directors, appear no more pleased. Thomas hears them grumbling, sees them shaking their heads, and casting looks of disapprobation at one another. He hears muttered snatches of *damned foolish* and *must right the ship* and *never in his father's time*. There are rumors that Walter has stumbled since taking the helm at Thresher's. There have been whispers of large and inexplicable loans, of incoherent gambles, of a recklessness that leaves the directors confused and uneasy.

Until six months ago, when he was dragooned into junior clerking, Thomas had no intention of working for the family concern. Indeed, both his father and brother made it clear that he was not wanted at the bank. Nevertheless, these rumors trouble Thomas. Thresher's is his family's legacy, after all. He never knew his grandfather, Ulysses Thresher, the bank's founder, but his portraits suggest he was a kindly man with ready smile and sympathetic eyes. As a boy, Thomas would make up stories about his grandfather, who, in these fantasies, was reliably attentive and good-natured, always ready with a treat or toy for his favorite grandson.

Perhaps Thomas's impression of him was shaped by the knowledge that Ulysses Thresher founded his bank to serve small men. In his charter he declared his institution was to offer its services to worthy men with whom other banks would not do business. The core of Thresher's customers were meant to be Jews and Irishmen and Catholics—perhaps even, under certain circumstances, Asiatics and Negroes. If those circumstances never materialized, Thomas nevertheless believes the founder deserves credit for daring to dream. The dregs of society, Ulysses Thresher believed, could be made useful if someone would but offer a helping hand.

All of that changed under Samuel Thresher's more pragmatic leadership, which placed expansion and profit ahead of the founding principles. "Always growing" became the bank's motto. The charter was now regarded, if it was regarded at all, as a historical curiosity, the whimsical impulses of an idealist who somehow managed to succeed despite his most self-sabotaging impulses.

The bank thrived under Samuel Thresher's leadership, but Thomas worries that the venerable institution's days may now be numbered.

Much like his own.

He can no longer delay tending to the itch that has been building on his left shoulder, so Thomas slips away unseen, climbing two flights of stairs, where he disappears into his room. There is but a single, small mirror above his dressing table because Thomas does not like to be surprised by his own reflection. It is not that he considers himself unattractive. As it happens, he believes he is reasonably handsome, but of late he has had the most inexplicable notion that hidden behind the face in the mirror is the other face, the one from his dream. He has, on occasion, attempted to test this hypothesis, and of course it is all nonsense. He shuns the looking glass all the same.

The only painting upon the wall is a likeness of his mother, of whom he has no memories. The portrait shows a woman with sad eyes and hollow cheeks. The painter's efforts to flatter his subject stumbled upon an expression of unspeakable endurance. Only the hair, jauntily blond, defies the overall effect of a short-tempered school mistress.

Beatrice Thresher died giving birth to Thomas. Alternatively, she died of a fever in the weeks following childbirth. Thomas has heard both versions of the story, and he has never received an explanation for the variance. The late Samuel Thresher actively discouraged Thomas from asking questions, looking at paintings or photographs, or touching her things. Walter has always refused to discuss "my mother," as he styles her. "She is none of your concern," he declared often enough that Thomas eventually stopped asking.

Under the critical gaze of his long-dead mother, he removes his coat and vest, unties his necktie, and unbuttons his collar. He reaches around to his shoulder and finds precisely what he expects and dreads—against the paleness of his skin rests an emerald green leaf, triangular in shape, though rounded at the base like a spade on a playing card.

It snaps off from his skin painlessly. When these first started appearing a few months ago, removing the leaves left no mark, but now, where the stems have been, he develops little blemishes. They are the size of pinpricks—whiter and slightly firmer than the surrounding skin.

The leaves first grew at the rate of one a fortnight. Now they come every two or three days. Always growing, he thinks with bitter irony.

Thomas crumples the leaf and drops it into the rubbish bin under his small writing desk. He dresses once more and with slow steps, like a dog attempting to delay the end of its walk about the block, returns to the gathering. As he descends the stairs and watches the guests milling about, bankers and parliamentarians and the idle rich, he wonders if he shares something with any of them, if any among them are secretly afflicted by the Peculiarities. The more lurid newspapers publish stories of vampires and werewolves, of women giving birth to rabbits, and houses rendered uninhabitable by ghosts. He has read of people possessed by spirits and living men whose own spirits have become trapped in horses, in furnishings, in articles of clothing. There are horrible transformations and mutilations. Things that should not be, if these stories are to be believed, have become not quite commonplace but hardly rare.

Thomas read it all with a fair amount of skepticism until the first leaf sprouted below his right nipple. He'd never heard of such a condition before, which suggests to him that while the newspapers' accounts may not be wholly accurate, they likely tell a distorted version of the truth. If violent fogs and men growing leaves are real, what else might the Peculiarities have wrought?

Who among his brother's guests, he wonders, craves the taste of blood or is possessed by a legion of murmuring voices or suffers from violent satyromania—something vaguely suggested by one of the papers? Which husbands and wives remain together, performing happiness, only because of the curses that befall contract-breakers?

He wonders how long these hidden victims of Peculiar transformation will be able to keep their secrets. How long will Thomas? What happens when the leaves begin to grow more rapidly or sprout from his forehead or hands or other places he cannot conceal? These feelings he has been struggling with, of the pointlessness of his existence—could that be an effect of whatever plagues him? Does his ennui come from the knowledge that he is turning into something vegetative, or is it a consequence of that transformation? Regardless of whether it is cause or effect, life has become a dull and bleak affair to Thomas. When he spent his days in drunken indolence, he never believed his life was without meaning, and surely then it was more meaningless than it is now.

Thomas feels a hand on his shoulder. He looks up to see Pearl, his brother's wife, smiling at him. She takes his necktie in her hands and begins to pull and stretch and adjust.

"Have you been sleeping in your clothes?" she scolds, but there is warmth in her voice. Her long nose wiggles above her smile. "How much have you had to drink?"

"Not nearly enough," he tells her.

"You might try to put on a good show." A quick jerk of her hands, and the necktie is now handsomely asphyxiating. "You know how Walter values appearances, and he does hold your fate in his hands."

"I think it's your hands I need to worry about at the moment," Thomas responds as he pretends to gasp for air like a newly caught fish.

"Little things matter," Pearl says as she continues to adjust. "You want to look your best for your bride-to-be." There is something in her voice that Thomas cannot quite interpret. Perhaps it is sympathy or perhaps she is merely playing the spy. Pearl is kind to Thomas, but she is married to Walter, and she would do whatever he asked of her. Thomas does not doubt it.

"He needn't have troubled himself to play matchmaker," Thomas gasps. "I am in no mind to marry."

Pearl finishes her fussing and releases her grip with a theatrical flaring of her fingers. She watches with mock disapproval as Thomas runs a finger inside his collar, pantomiming a desperate effort to preserve consciousness. "I understand drollery is fashionable, but I hope you will be pleasant with Miss—"and here she pauses as she prepares herself to form with her delicate mouth so odious a sound—"Feldstein." Pearl may be soft-hearted, but she is still an Englishwoman of her class, and she is in no hurry to claim a Jewess for an in-law.

Thomas, on the other hand, begins to wonder if the social awkwardness of marrying Miss Feldstein might be endurable if he can only continue to enjoy watching Walter's discomfort.

"When have you ever known me to be anything other than proper?"

She has heard stories, he is certain—late night debaucheries and whisky-soaked revels, brothels and brawls and mountains of money raked away at gaming tables. These stories have the ring of truth because they are, in the main, true, though generally money has been raked in his direction. He only played cards, and almost always walked away no worse for wear. He was always too prudent to remain at play at those times when luck was against him. Nevertheless, the flavor of these tales is accurate, which is why, he supposes, Pearl might, from time to time, think of him as a powder keg set to detonate with vulgar oaths and slurring, bawdy humor.

Pearl sighs. "You know, your life would be easier if you gave Walter what he wants. All of our lives would be easier."

The forced cheer drops from her face, and Thomas sees something like dread in her eyes. Has she, too, heard the whispers of Walter's mismanagement? Does she worry her home, her wealth, her standing might all be in jeopardy?

"Why did you marry my brother?" he asks.

Pearl shakes her head. "It is like every other marriage. Walter wanted a closer connection to my family. My father wanted to be rid of a daughter at the best possible price."

Thomas was at school at the time of his brother's wedding—to which he was not invited—and quite used to being outside the orbit of family matters. He hardly cared for any of the details then, but now he finds he would like to know. "There must be more."

"The truth about life is that there is nothing more, and revelations always disappoint. Now, please be good tonight."

Pearl squeezes his arm and turns from him to greet a new arrival. Thomas turns as well, and now sees his brother, not fifteen feet away, again in close conversation with Mr. Hawke. Walter reaches out to take a coupe of champagne from a silver tray, and there, visible for but an instant, is a flash of transgressive verdant between the bleached whiteness of the sleeve and sunless pink of Walter's skin. It is gone as soon as Thomas sees it, but there is no mistaking the emerald color and triangular shape. He has stared at such things for far too many hours. It is a leaf.

Whatever strange affliction ails Thomas ails Walter as well.

↦ THREE ↤

DISAPPOINTMENT

THE CLINKING OF silverware against china, the pouring of wine into glasses, the polite laughter at unamusing anecdotes, the relentless complaint of bows upon strings. These sounds wash over Thomas as he sits with Esther Feldstein on one side of him, Pearl on the other. Most likely she has been charged with reporting back to Walter on all she hears.

If she is a spy, she is an inattentive one, as she converses happily with the youngest son of a count, a handsome and square-jawed fellow not yet thirty, on her other side. Thomas tries not to look away as Pearl talks and her nose does its hanged man's spasm above her lips. He finds himself wishing his sister-in-law were paying more attention to his own troubles, for Esther Feldstein has not taken her eyes from her dinner. She puts tiny morsels on her fork which she deposits in her mouth and chews with narrow-eyed introspection.

They are currently on a fish course, so it is sherry in his glass. Thomas takes a long sip and is preparing himself to make a dull foray into conversation when he is derailed by the loud braying of Mr. Hershel Feldstein, Esther's father. He sits across the table and a few seats down, but the laughter is an icepick driven through Thomas's ear and straight to the core of his skull. Mr. Feldstein's daughter has clearly been isolated so that she might not retreat into a parental cocoon in order to avoid talking to Thomas. Or maybe not. Is she wincing every time the old fellow opens his mouth?

"Told me he'd take his business elsewhere," Feldstein barks. "Looked me in the eye and said he'd find another port for his money. 'Shove off,' I told him. I knew he'd be back in six months, his worth halved. Nothing but bluster, I needn't tell you."

Hershel Feldstein, though beardless and wearing a fine suit, is precisely what comes to most Englishmen's minds when they envision a Jew. He is balding and has an enormous ginger mustache. Thomas is also somewhat fascinated by his proportions, for he is barely five feet tall and narrow of shoulder, though the strength of his voice makes amends for his small stature. That he converted to the Church of England ten years past can make no difference. That there are other men of business around the table, all born Christian, who boast and shout and spew food while they talk with the same ill grace offers no covering fire. They are ill-mannered men of means, whereas Feldstein is a Jew. No conversion can erase that distinction in the eyes of Walter's guests.

Nevertheless, his behavior, so very much like what the other guests expect from one of one of his race, visibly mortifies his daughter. She appears to struggle with the urge to throw down her fork in disgust. Thomas thinks it only gentlemanly to distract her.

"You must tell me something of your interests, Miss Feldstein," Thomas attempts—lamely, by his own estimates.

The lady glances at Mr. Feldstein and then at Thomas. "Why? Do you fear that I shall be as fascinated by money and business as my father?"

"Nonsense," Thomas says, quite pleased with his ability to deflect. He remembers before becoming a bank clerk, before becoming so—literally and metaphorically—vegetative, he used to enjoy a bit of verbal sparring with ladies. "You and I are seated by one another, and dinner passes much more pleasantly with conversation."

She exhales a sigh and sets down her fork, though she does so gently. "Our families have thrown us together, but that does not mean that you and I must play the willing victims."

"It does not," he agrees, feeling himself puff up with conversational prowess. This, he recalls, is how it is done. The give-and-take. The playful exchange. Even in such awkward moments, there is joy. "Miss Feldstein, I like the idea of this union no more than you do."

"Oh?" Her eyes urge him, dare him, to say more.

Perhaps his optimism was unjustified. Is this lady rude, or has he forgotten how to spar? His confusion causes an unwanted eruption of consonant sounds from his throat before he can form actual words. "Well, I, you know. I was not, myself, seeking a wife, as it happens. I am not at a stage in which, I would wish, or rather—that is to say—"

She holds up a hand, and her face curiously rearranges. Her eyes narrow, her mouth purses into a rosebud, her skin flushes. The result is a placement of constituent parts that renders the whole entirely more pleasing. "Forgive me,

Mr. Thresher. You needn't justify why you have no wish to marry someone entirely unknown to you."

"I'm certain any gentleman who came to know you," Thomas attempts. "That is to say, one of the right sort of gentleman, would be most enchanted."

An overthick eyebrow forms an arch, and while her countenance has not returned to its former coldness, there is something unnervingly mischievous here. "The right sort of gentleman?"

Thomas feels like a fool, having let down his guard only to be lured into a snare. "You know what I mean. Let us not pretend there are not certain, shall we say, matters of . . . of background and of . . . of other things."

"Religion, perhaps?" And there is that eyebrow again. She seems damnably amused at Thomas's expense.

"Miss Feldstein," Thomas says, "I appear to have given offense, and for that I apologize. You and I do not know each other, and we do not like how our families attempt to arrange our lives without consulting our interests. If I step on something delicate, you may comfortably attribute it to ignorance, but I hope you will not think it malice."

She sighs. "Of course not. You were, in your own way, making an effort."

Thomas is suddenly struck by her youth. She cannot be more than nineteen or twenty. That makes her only a few years younger than himself, but they are crucial years, and women mature more slowly than men. He should treat her with care. "There is no harm in enjoying each other's company, though we must not enjoy it enough to give our families encouragement."

At last she smiles. "On that, I entirely agree, Mr. Thresher."

"Though I wonder if the food is not to your taste." He looks at her plate and notices that her fish is untouched. She has been eating only the carrots and cucumbers. "Is there some religious injunction against. . . ."

"Herring?" she asks, a twinkle in her eye. "Eating herring is very near to a Jewish commandment, Mr. Thresher. No, I abstain for personal reasons. I do not eat animals of any kind. I wanted to inform Mrs. Thresher so food would not be wasted, but my father forbade me. He did not want me, as he put it, making myself disagreeable."

"Not eating meat," Thomas repeats, trying to understand the concept. It is like someone deciding not to breathe air—or choosing only to breathe air at certain temperatures. How does one go through the world without eating animals? "Who put such a notion in your head?"

"Why would someone need provide me with ideas?" she asks. "And why is that the first thing you wish to know? When you express an opinion, are you accustomed to being asked to produce a history of how someone else's opinion came to be yours?"

"I merely meant that it is unusual," he attempts. He cannot figure out why this woman is being so difficult.

"I have read a great deal," she says, as though she were not irritated with him a moment before, "and I am convinced that the difference between humanity and animals, particularly higher animals, is one of degree, not of kind. Anyone who has ever owned a dog knows they have feelings, notions of their own, preferences. Among these, I am sure, is the preference not to be eaten or subjected to tortures in some horrible laboratory."

One of those anti-vivisection types, then. Thomas has heard of them, though with a certain amount of incredulity and distaste, much like one hears of cannibals, perhaps finding them interesting without ever wanting to meet one.

"I understand wanting to treat a beloved dog with tenderness," Thomas says, "but can we really extend these courtesies to a cow or a fish or a pig? Well, not a pig in your case, of course, but. . . ." Thomas lets himself trail off because Miss Feldstein is peering at him compassionately. Perhaps she has shifted her position from hostility to pity. After all, she indicated her sympathy for thoughtless creatures.

"We distinguish between dogs and cattle because we call one friend and the other food. It is a matter of our perception rather than the nature of these creatures."

"But there is a great gulf between man and beast, surely," Thomas says, struggling for some foothold onto this conversation.

"Less of a gulf than there used to be." Something lights up in her eyes, and she leans forward slightly, as though she is about to confide something confidential to a friend. "Have you heard of the rash of rabbit births?"

Is this what the world was coming to? Women talking of giving birth at dinner parties? Still, there is something rather thrilling about it, and Thomas cannot deny he is interested. "I have read about them, but these claims are rather extraordinary."

She arches an eyebrow. "You live in London. You have seen the fogs. How can you doubt the truth of the Peculiarities?"

Thomas fights the urge to shout *Doubt them? Why, I am afflicted by them!* Instead he takes a more skeptical footing. "Fog is one thing. Rabbit children are quite another."

"But they aren't rabbit children," Esther says. "The papers love illustrations of baby rabbits wearing bonnets and playing with rattles, but it's not at all like that. I've met women who have endured it. They delivered litters of live rabbits—rabbits that act and grow as ordinary rabbits do. There is nothing human about them that can be detected. The question of whether or not they possess souls is, of course, unknowable."

"You wish to argue that there is a link between people and animals, but then you bring in the Peculiarities. You cannot use unnatural occurrences as an argument for how we are to conduct ourselves ordinarily." Thomas grins, believing he has quite stumped the lady.

"If the Peculiarities are real," responds Miss Feldstein, "if they are a part of our world, then surely they are, by definition, natural."

His grin fades now that he has been defeated by axiom. Thomas considers how he might praise the lady for her successful argument without stepping into some trap or other, but Miss Feldstein has already launched a new line of attack.

"Of course," she says, "moving in such lofty circles, it may be that you have seen very little of the Peculiarities with your own eyes."

"Whatever can you mean?" Thomas feels insulted, though he does not know why.

"Only that the brunt of their effects are felt by the poor or those of the lower middling orders—not banking families. You've heard that contract- and oath-breakers suffer now. They are injured in accidents or lose their money. Some even suffer in a Peculiar way. The newspapers are full of such stories, but have you never noticed that the worst suffering is among the working poor?"

Now it is she who has shown her ignorance, Thomas thinks. "The fogs are everywhere, and, yes, the creatures called the Elegants are said to haunt East London, but surely you don't claim some sort of class bias to the phenomenon."

"I don't know why," she says, "but there is indeed a class bias. Yes, the fogs are ubiquitous, but rarely do they cause harm in the more affluent parts of London. You hear of no women of means delivering rabbit children. No men of wealth are transformed. No, it is the powerless and the voiceless who are being struck down, and I find that very curious indeed."

Thomas wants to tell her how wrong she is. Perhaps the poor are more visibly afflicted by the Peculiarities, but surely that is because they are less capable of concealing these manifestations. They can't afford to cover, to hide, to vanish from the public view. Thomas knows he is not immune. Walter is not immune. He could say something now that would utterly astonish her, perhaps even win her sympathy, but of course he will reveal no secrets. He believes it is better to say very little at all with this woman who thinks herself so wise.

"You have some very interesting notions, Miss Feldstein."

She smiles without humor and stabs at a piece of cucumber. Whatever else he might say about her, he would not call her an unintelligent woman. She knows when she has been dismissed.

FOUR

OPPRESSION

"PERHAPS WHEN YOU are no longer a junior clerk," explains Mr. Philpot, the senior clerk, "when you have benefited from some years of experience, you will find yourself in a better position to make pronouncements on what is, and what is not, irregular."

Thomas gazes upon Mr. Philpot, upon the aged and mostly hairless pate speckled with grape-sized liver spots. A cottony white fringe runs along the base of his skull, and the whole of the head puts Thomas in mind of a bird's egg, fallen from its nest, peeking up from pale tufts of grass. Thomas studies the senior clerk's hook-fingered and trembling hands—hands that have toiled at Thresher's Bank for decades, ceaselessly and without the unwelcome intrusion of variety or surprise.

Thomas finds Mr. Philpot fascinating in the way of an accident upon the road, with its dazed survivors and scattered detritus and screaming animals. Mr. Philpot, by contrast, hardly regards Thomas at all. From the very first he has dismissed the youngest Thresher as utterly inconsequential, the sort of dilettante who will learn nothing, achieve nothing, and one day slouch back to the bog of indolence from which he rose. Nevertheless, Thomas believes his point is worth pressing. At the very least, it is something Thomas finds interesting.

This is something new. Until today, his waking hours have been entirely dedicated to the duplication of letters, the reviewing of simple arithmetic, the delivering of stacks of ledgers to the documents room, where they will remain unmolested, gathering dust for all eternity. Pointless task piled upon pointless task, and these without end, and these performed in the company of dolts, overseen by a petty tyrant. From nine in the morning until eight at night, each day materially identical to the last and the next, this week the same as those that have come before and those that will follow. This is what Thomas's life has become.

Could the demons of hell devise a crueler torment? Thomas supposes they could. It would be worse to endure burning or flaying or dismemberment. If he were required to copy documents while nails were driven into his hands and his testicles flattened with a mallet, that would make him even less eager to enter the bank's lobby each morning. Nevertheless, his work, absent the physical agony, remains unpleasant.

He is therefore not entirely prepared to ignore something that stands out, something that adds a modicum of variety to his day. "Should I not bring something unusual to your attention?" he asks Mr. Philpot.

"If you find an error in numbers or transcription, you must certainly inform me," drones the senior clerk in the weary tone of a tutor reviewing for a particularly dim pupil what he has explained many times previously. "In this instance, however, you are commenting upon bank policy, and that is not a junior clerk's concern." Mr. Philpot's rather grayish lips gesture toward something not entirely unlike a smile, though not a human smile. Not even a mammalian smile. It is the smile of a lizard or shark or some other cold-blooded thing. If a worm wished to learn the art of smiling, it could do worse than study the Philpot method. "No, not for a junior clerk, however lofty his surname."

The other junior clerks—particularly those sycophants, Jenkins and Sullivan and Sherwin—shift in their seats just enough to let Thomas know that they have heard, that they are amused, but they shift no more than that. Only the serious Nicholas Roberts fails to take notice, as he is busy with his transcriptions. These other men, however, are of a species that delights in seeing Thomas run afoul of Mr. Philpot. They savor this moment of diversion before returning to the eternal contest—who can most anonymously and unremarkably complete the greatest number of nearly identical tasks. Mr. Philpot tallies the score, and someday, years hence, he will tap one of these junior clerks for elevation. Some will rise beyond even Mr. Philpot's exalted station. They will break free of a cocoon woven of drudgery and tedium and emerge as *bankers*. These exalted beings, once mere mortals, will stride into this very room and issue commands to this very senior clerk. Mr. Philpot shows no sign of resentment toward those whom he has lifted to a level of wealth and importance he can never know. A just and merciful God has given him the office of kingmaker, not king.

Hoping to look less like a whipped dog than he feels, Thomas walks hunch-shouldered back to his desk, to his pen and ink and ledger, to the strain in his eyes and the cramp in his hand. He cannot shut out the sounds of scratching all around him, the shifting of clerks' bottoms, and the scuffing of chairs on the wooden floor. Hardworking Nicholas Roberts offers him an understanding smile, to which Thomas replies with a discouraging nod. This fellow seems a little too eager to show sympathy to Thomas—and only to Thomas. Rather suspect, that, and Thomas does not encourage these little familiarities.

For want of alternatives, he turns to his work and tries to concentrate on numbers that have been stripped of all that make them interesting. Thomas has always loved numbers, loved probing their limits, manipulating them, coaxing them to reveal their hidden magic. Numbers at Trinity College were athletes and poets and warriors. At Thresher's Bank they are kitchen scullions and galley slaves. Still, he turns to them, trying to shut out the endless tick-tick-ticking of the wall clock that promises, but so rarely delivers, the movement of time.

Thomas looks up from the work that has been eluding his focus. His heart races as he thinks he smells something in the air, a hint of ozone and sulfur and something like freshly cut grass. Could it be another fog come to assault them? Then he hears the trumpet blast of Mr. Philpot's flatulence. Like the other junior clerks, Thomas pretends to have noticed nothing and returns to his ledger. There will be no respite from work, it seems.

The fogs had been growing worse over the past decade, though initially they did little more than blot out the sun for days at a time. They began assaulting people only this year, though they usually avoid more respectable locations. In this, though it pains him to admit it, Miss Feldstein was certainly correct, though Thomas had not considered the matter in terms of wealth and poverty. It had seemed to him to be about respectability and geography.

For a fog to battle its way into a Whitechapel chop house would surprise no one, but a bank is another matter. All was confusion when, two weeks previous, the dust-colored wisps began winding their way through Thresher's august lobby. The mist layered the floor like a carpet, cool and inviting, but it also reached out in tendrils, lashing and grabbing, knocking over ink pots and desk lamps. Then, and seemingly with the menace of a predator, it wrapped roping strands around one of the clerks.

Thomas was among those who ran to free their companion by swatting at the fog with canes, hastily shrugged-off coats, and accounting ledgers. He hadn't wanted to let another man perish because of his inaction, but Thomas wondered what would happen if he simply dropped to the floor and let the fog wash over him. Would he suffocate? Would he be robbed of his humanity all the sooner? Some of the more lurid newspapers claim the fogs are the source of the Peculiarities. Others maintain they are a symptom. Newspapers that seek the favor of the conservative prime minister, Lord Robert Cecil, insist that fog is fog, and the rest is nonsense. The Peculiarities, these papers say, do not exist.

Thomas did not give himself to the cool mist. Instead he swatted with an umbrella. The clerk had been saved and the fog withdrew, perhaps in search of a more appropriate hunting ground. For a moment Thomas felt a sense of accomplishment. He had done something tangible. He had helped save a man's life. Then the senior clerks and bank directors reminded the victorious junior clerks that this was not a holiday, so back to their desks they went, back to pens and ledgers and letters, and the less murmuring along the way, the better.

"Always growing!" one of the bankers called to them, as the late Samuel Thresher's motto had now become something of a rallying cry. The bank, it was understood, could never be large enough. There must always be more business, more clients, more loans, more money. Thomas understands that eternal growth is possible within the world of mathematics. The banking world, however, presents certain obstacles to so single-minded a goal.

Though he can recount each step of his descent into banking, Thomas remains unable to understand how he came to be in this place. He is like a man standing on the street, looking at the smoldering remains of his house, wondering what could have happened even while he recalls falling asleep with his pipe in his hand. Six months ago, Thomas would have thought it inconceivable that his waking hours would someday belong to his family's bank.

He was days away from departing with his friends, first to Paris, and then to wherever their desires should take them. They spoke of exotic destinations: Egypt, China, India. He planned not to return to England for months, possibly years. Only once his wanderlust had been fully sated would he consider what he wished to do with himself. A gentleman must occupy his time with something. He might have stood for Parliament. He had also given some thought to returning to Trinity College to further his knowledge of mathematics, should his father not object. Samuel Thresher had abruptly and inexplicably demanded Thomas leave early in his third year. There had been no monetary necessity to his departure, nor was Thomas required in London. He had simply spent enough time lounging about in Cambridge, his father said.

This had been a particularly crushing blow as Thomas had been preparing for Trinity College's celebrated examination, the Mathematical Tripos, and was considered likely to emerge as Senior Wrangler—the student who won first-class honors in mathematics. It was something of a public achievement, with the Senior Wrangler likely to appear in the newspapers and even have his face on cheap broadsides of the sort sold for cricket and boxing champions. He had savored the prospect of fame—up until the moment he received his father's curt commands.

This sudden expulsion was all the more unexpected because Thomas's father had been Senior Wrangler himself in his day. He had evidently—they never discussed such things—delighted in mathematics as a young man, but he saw no reason for his own son to be allowed to pursue the same interests. Thomas pled his case by letter but received only a curt denial.

Once in London, Thomas had settled into the sort of life one expects from a young man with ample money and no occupation. His friends soon joined him, and while his days—and more particularly his nights—had been full, he often thought about what sort of existence he might have led had only his father allowed him to live as he wished.

He'd been playing cards at his club when the word arrived. Samuel Thresher, who resided but a few miles from where he sat, whom he had not seen in the better part of a year, was dead. There followed a series of dreary proceedings—a funeral and gatherings and meetings with solicitors. That the bank directors chose Walter as the new governor surprised no one. He had been bred for it. He took to banking like a fish to water, the directors said. No one was in any way surprised by Walter's elevation. The surprise had been in Thomas's disposition.

After a lifetime of being told, all but promised, that he might—he *must!*—live the life of a leisured gentleman, Thomas was dragooned into the family concern from which he had been previously barred. It was no exaggeration. At twelve years old, flush with a newly discovered love of algebra, Thomas had imagined a future in which, after a schooling steeped in mathematics, he could use his knowledge to help the family enterprise. When he'd said as much, his father had laughed as though Thomas had claimed he would someday be a war chief among the moon men.

Yet, employment in the bank was precisely what his father's will required. Thomas was to receive no inheritance—not a cent—until he had worked at Thresher's Bank for a sufficient time and proved himself an asset to the institution. It was for Walter to say when this amorphous threshold had been crossed. This declaration had astonished Thomas, and seemingly enraged his brother, who had expected nothing of the sort and desired it not at all.

As was the tradition at Thresher's, Thomas would begin as a junior clerk, just as his father, just as Walter, had. He would rise in the ranks as his efforts merited. His initial salary, the same as any starting clerk's, would be but £140 per year, though it had just recently risen to £160, as Thomas has passed his six-month probationary period.

Now Thomas doubts he can endure another six months. Assuming he does not die of boredom or his own hand or from the manifestation of the Peculiarities that altered his body, Thomas fears the work itself will erase him from existence. He can distinguish himself by laboring with monotonous diligence, but not—as his conversation with Mr. Philpot made plain—by showing any inclination to advance. Ambition must be avoided by the ambitious. Interest must be shunned by the interested.

Nevertheless, as he gazes at the document that prompted him to ask Mr. Philpot his question, Thomas feels a flicker of what feels very much like interest. This mysterious letter, signed by his brother's hand, pertains to an effort to acquire just over thirty pounds of debt that a Mr. William Yeats owes to a tailor and a hatter. As near as Thomas can divine, Thresher's purchased the debt from these two tradesmen at a discount. The bank is now responsible for collecting the sums.

Why would Walter authorize this transaction? Debt collection is a vexing and uncertain business. Gentlemen view paying tradesmen not as an obliga- tion but, at best, as an act of charity to be performed annually, and only when the mood suits. Mr. Yeats might willingly present what he owes tomorrow, or perhaps, swayed by seasonal largess, at Christmas. However, he might just as well choose to ignore the debt until the following year, when, with the eternal optimism of men who live beyond their means, he expects to have more money in hand. It is also true that any element of benevolence that might prompt Mr. Yeats to pay for the services he contracted with a laboring man—presumably in possession of a family that requires food and clothing and shelter—would dissipate if an agent of the bank should come to collect. Thresher's, Mr. Yeats is likely to believe, will manage without his pittance.

Banking may have its arcane ways, but Thomas understands that its ultimate purpose is to turn money into more money and to do this on a large scale. For what possible reason would Thresher's look to lose money on a small scale?

Having completed the bundle of documents, Thomas receives permission from Mr. Philpot to leave the room and carry the papers to what will no doubt become their final resting place. This is a high-ceilinged chamber full of drawers and shelves dedicated to bank business. Thomas has heard other clerks speak of a new system of filing, invented in America, which allows for documents to be placed in vertical cabinets. Any letter or report can be located in a matter of minutes. Such a system would exponentially increase the efficiency of document filing and retrieval, and Thomas suspects that it will be decades before Thresher's turns to so distastefully novel a scheme.

The documents room feels to Thomas like a rarely visited shrine. A few tiny round windows permit only a few exploratory beams of light to probe the gloomy chamber where the gas lamps are lit only as necessity demands. Thomas's every footstep echoes like a heretical affront. The air twinkles with dust and fills his nostrils with the scent of long-forgotten tedium.

Perhaps because it is the only thing he has done as a junior clerk that ever sparked even a moment of curiosity, Thomas saves the Yeats letter for last. He approaches the designated shelves, on which are piled seemingly random bundles of papers. Are these in alphabetical order, chronological order, no order at all? He glances over his shoulder to make an inquiry of the head clerk, a gaunt fellow with a long beard and the wild-eyed expression of a medieval fanatic taking a brief respite from self-flagellation. Instead, Thomas grabs a bound folder and pulls out a handful of correspondence. Perhaps skimming the first few letters might provide some clues of the organizational scheme.

Hastily, he begins to thumb through the stack of pages, his gaze wandering over names, locations, amounts of debt—anything that might make a letter or series of letters stand out and announce a greater purpose. He is not searching for meaning, but a kind of coherence, a pattern. If this project has a purpose, it will show itself. Numbers are dependable in that way.

Reviewing the dates and signatures of the letters, Thomas sees this strange scheme was begun by Samuel Thresher and is continued by Walter. Could it be that his father stumbled upon something unknown to other bankers? The numbers say otherwise. All the debt contained in this folder amounts to little by the standards of the bank, so why pursue this project?

Encouraged by this question, Thomas tries to make sense not of the debt but of the debtors, a mixed and wholly unremarkable, lot. A coroner who owes for furnishings; a gentleman who owes for the renovation of a country estate; a chemist who owes for a pair of horses who died in a fire. There is no commonality but the pettiness of it all, the sheer absurdity, of a bank wanting to take command of trivial sums.

Thomas has all but given up, feeling the press of time more keenly than the lure of an equation that will not balance. Then something takes hold of his attention. He has barely glanced at a letter, but a string of words stays the movement of his fingers. A tremble radiates through his fingers before his reasoning mind comprehends what his soul has already absorbed.

The letter is addressed to a Mrs. Madeline Yardley, and it concerns her late husband. The amount is not great, and the letter pretends to no urgency. The lady has inherited of her husband a debt amounting to £73,12d, accrued over a period of three years from a variety of tradesmen and shopkeepers. The letter applies no pressure and suggests that, in light of Mr. Yardley's death, the bank little cares if she pays. Her choice, really. Those are not the precise words, but absent from this letter are the threatening tones that are the bread and butter of debt collection. No need, Thomas infers, for the widow to trouble herself and ask questions about how Thresher's Bank came to hold this debt. The numbers have made no sense because this equation is about people. Thomas sees that the bank sought some kind of leverage over the husband, Mr. Robert Catesby Yardley, and now that the man is dead, the debt serves no purpose.

Thomas supposed there must be several Robert Yardleys in the kingdom, but not with Catesby as a middle name. Bobby's father had been something of a wag and, in a state of annoyance with Parliament at the time of the son's birth, had named his boy after the leader of the Gunpower Plot. It put a distinctive, unmistakable stamp on the name.

Robert Catesby Yardley. Bobby Yardley to his friends. Thomas had been one of those friends. They had, in fact, been the best of friends at the age of twelve until a visit to his school by Thomas's brother. A week later, Bobby was packing his bags, expelled for no articulated reason, though it was hinted, quite explicitly hinted—hinted, in fact, in a way that suggested Walter wanted Thomas to know—that Bobby had been judged so pernicious an influence that the Thresher family applied money and influence to have the boy cast out.

Thomas wrote to Bobby several times but received no reply. He wondered, perhaps assumed, any letters addressed to him from that quarter were being cast into the fire. It infuriated and perplexed him, for there was nothing objectionable about Bobby Yardley other than the undistinguished blood and finances of his family. The boy was not a fighter or a gambler, such as Thomas was to become later. He was not profane and had not yet reached the age in which women became a source of temptation. Thomas would soon enough embrace profanity and vice, but these were yet dim shapes on the horizon. At the age of twelve, Bobby was a rather settling influence on Thomas. He had introduced Thomas to the world of mathematics. While other boys groaned, Thomas and Bobby had embraced the adventure of numbers. In short, Bobby had been precisely the sort of boy an older brother might hope would befriend a younger.

Thomas had been consumed with anger and confusion, but new friends took Bobby's place, and within two or three months—eons for a boy of twelve—the hurt had faded to a dull ache that was easily ignored.

Now here is Bobby, and here again is Walter's hand. Bobby is dead. That fact seems abstract, perhaps naturally so. Thomas hasn't seen the boy, the man, for half his life, and yet a distant grief tugs at him.

Thomas makes note of the widow's address and replaces the documents, approximating the original order as best he can. He leaves the newest letter, the one to Yeats, on top.

As he strides back to his chamber, Thomas feels something other than dread and tedium. He feels something more than the weight of meaningless weeks and months and years before him. For the first time since coming to Thresher's Bank, perhaps since leaving Trinity College, Thomas wants to *do* something.

The pentacle of the Sun, to be made on Sunday.

A Pentacle for Honor and Riches, to be made on Sunday, in the hour of the Sun.

1ˢᵗ Model.   2ⁿᵈ Model.

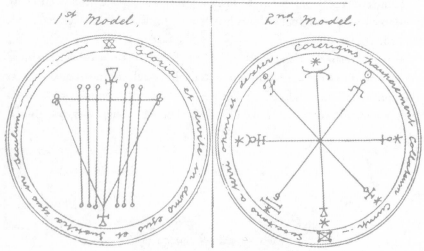

FIVE

CHANGE

O N SUNDAY, HIS only full day away from the bank, Thomas decides he will pay a call on Bobby Yardley's widow. He hadn't known if he could face the awkwardness of such a visit, but when the morning came, the need to escape from his brother's house drove him onto the streets.

The widow lives in the western suburbs, Chiswick to be precise, so Thomas takes a train and then walks the last half mile from the station. The September weather is not terribly cold, though the sky is domed with dark clouds streaked with silver, a sign that a fog may present itself in the next few days. The footpaths, at least, are quiet and empty, even compared to the streets of Belgravia, and Thomas allows himself to clear his mind, to enjoy, as much as he can, the simple act of walking on a brisk afternoon.

Thomas's school friends, if awake, are likely already drunk in some Paris café. No doubt they would mock him for spending his day in so dreary a fashion. Across the miles they whisper that he should be drinking, finding a juicy whore, enjoying himself while he can instead of squandering what little free time he has visiting some used-up widow.

These voices speak the sort of cosmic, immutable truths by which he has lived his life, but he chooses not to listen. Visiting Mrs. Yardley may be the best possible thing he can do with his Sunday. Thomas missed Bobby, quite painfully, after his departure from their school. Years later he was still thinking about Bobby, sometimes daily. The wound faded, yes, but now it is reopened. Thomas, until recently, enjoyed the company of his friends, but there has always been something superficial there, some chasm that could never be bridged by proximity and laughter and likeness in clothes and hair. Thomas realizes he desperately wants to know what happened to Bobby, where he went, how he lived, and how he died.

He steels himself as he approaches the house. It is red brick and conjoined to its neighbor on the left, though this unit is separated by a respectable gap from the other interchangeable pairs. A prim wooden fence, recently whitewashed, lines the footpath. It is all typical of these suburbs—unremarkable, each home much the same as another, but pleasant for all that. Quiet and peaceful and exact. The quintessentially chaotic elements of London are nowhere to be seen. The houses feature little lawns in front, no doubt a garden in the back. Thomas knows he would have sneered at such a place half a year ago. Now he looks upon it with naked envy.

At the door, Thomas announces himself to a young and thin servant as having come from the bank, a pronouncement that is met with horror usually reserved for confessed murderers. Nevertheless, the Thresher name proves sufficient to grant him admittance. The girl, too ignorant of money matters to wonder why a man from the bank would call on a Sunday, nervously directs Thomas to a pleasant, if small and unimaginative, parlor, the sort of room that feels more like the set of a stage play than a space anyone might actually use. The girl's skittish movements suggest that she is afraid Thomas will unleash upon her his terrible financial powers. She hurries out, without saying when he can expect her mistress, and so Thomas fidgets for perhaps ten minutes before Mrs. Yardley enters.

Discounting his early death, Bobby appears to have done quite well for himself. His widow is tall, almost as tall as Thomas, and with midnight black hair, pale skin, and large eyes of a dazzling green color. Her afternoon dress is a similar shade with a subtle paler pattern to break up the monotony. It is slightly, if not excessively, puffed at the shoulders, and cinched tight at the waist, giving her the slim but full-bosomed look of a woman in a newspaper advertisement. Her narrow eyebrows, dainty nose, and round face combine to make her a museum specimen of British beauty. Not a devastating beauty, to be certain, but she is certainly pretty, and those dazzling eyes make up for a great deal of otherwise lost ground.

Thomas notes that these are not mourning clothes. Bobby has been dead for more than a year.

Mrs. Yardley is clearly more perceptive than her help, for she begins by saying, "I am astonished to receive a visit from a gentleman of Thresher's, particularly on a Sunday." Thomas's anxiety about being exposed before the time of his own choosing is momentarily forgotten as she takes his gloved hand in hers.

"I have not come regarding the debt," Thomas assures her, doing his best to sound amiable. In fact, his heart is hammering, like he is a little boy about to demonstrate his ignorance to his Latin master. "I am employed by Thresher's, yes, but also I am *a* Thresher. Thomas Thresher at your service, and I call on you for personal reasons, not on behalf of the bank."

"Oh." Her expression is impenetrable. Is she surprised? Amused? Relieved? Mrs. Yardley, Thomas quickly concludes, is a woman he finds difficult to read.

The lady invites him to sit and calls for tea. She straightens her skirts as a signal that she is ready to proceed.

"I have learned but recently of the death of your husband," Thomas tells her.

Her lips perform something like a smile. "Thresher's is rather slow to circulate its information. I lost Bobby almost two years ago."

It is strange to hear that Thomas's childhood friend, only recently remembered, had been gone for so long. On the other hand, when he gazes upon the widow, Thomas wonders if he should not consider this good news. He is a rotten fellow for thinking of Mrs. Yardley in this way. He knows it to be so, but everyone is a rotten fellow these days. It is simply the new way of being. People have had their fill of religion and morality. There is nothing to do but enjoy one's self, as that fellow Oscar Wilde said in his pointedly shocking novel. Living for pleasure and all that.

Thomas and his friends never hesitated to open a bottle or deal the cards or seek out a whore. For what other reason had they been put on this earth? Now it seems as distant to Thomas as if those memories were but something read in a story. Even so, a man cannot change his nature. Perhaps he ought not to try.

"I have only recently begun working at the bank. When my father died, I was informed of a stipulation in his will that required I learn the family business."

"I am sorry for your loss, then." She inclines her head in a gesture of respect or sorrow.

Thomas thinks she is quite adept at this sympathy business. He must remember the head-inclining. Good stuff.

"I lost my own father not long after my husband," she continues. "Papa gave me a sense of purpose and direction, and I felt utterly lost without him. Yours was wise to make provisions that continue to guide you, even after he is gone."

A dozen memories materialize at once like competing spectacles in a fireworks display. Father pointing at him, when Thomas was still young enough to cling to his nurse's skirts, demanding to know who let that child in the room. Thomas attempting to make himself part of a conversation between Samuel and Walter and seeing the genuine anger on his father's face when he snaps that he must not be interrupted when speaking to his son. Thomas walking into a room while his father sat a writing desk, only to be ignored with taut hostility.

For all his father's cruelty, the most painful thing is to recall the times when he could not be bothered to dismiss Thomas personally. Most often he sent Walter to do the business. After the incident in which Thomas suggested that he would eventually become a banker, it was Walter who took Thomas aside. At twenty-seven, Walter was already growing plump, losing his hair—a distorted and smeared projection of how Thomas might someday look. He appeared utterly defeated by life, and yet Thomas had heard from his father, from the servants, from friends of the family, how well Walter did at Thresher's. He had sailed through his clerkship with astonishing ease and grace, and was now, for matters having nothing to do with his name, one of the most accomplished men in the bank. Walter brought in new business, unearthed and invigorated forgotten clients, invested and divested with the wisdom of a prophet. Thomas had not thought to compete with his brother, but only suggest that he might like someday to be of use.

"Whoever told you that you would work at Thresher's?" Walter had wanted to know. He was not angry but seemed puzzled, perhaps confused, as though something had broken down in the proper order of things.

"I merely presumed that when I was done with school—"

Walter did something with his lips. A smile? A smirk? Who could say? "Father has told me to say that you needn't trouble yourself."

When he returned to school the following week, Thomas found his allowance had doubled.

"Yes, fathers," Thomas now says, having no wish to disagree with Mrs. Yardley on any trivial particular. "Good chaps all around, but it was on the subject of husbands that I came to see you. Bobby and I were in school together when we were young. I last saw him when I was twelve years old, and, well, he and I were close."

Mrs. Yardley smiles indulgently. "So long ago, and yet you remember him. That is very touching, Mr. Thresher."

Thomas does not know for what he hopes. He does not want this lady to have spent years pondering the perfidy of the Thresher clan, and yet it is hurtful to think that Thomas was so easily forgotten.

"He never spoke of me?"

She wrinkles her nose and narrows her eyes in concentration. "I cannot recall that he did. Was there some adventure you two shared?"

Thomas never knew if Bobby had been told why he had to leave. Perhaps he hadn't understood that the Threshers were to blame. Perhaps warm memories fade more easily than bitter ones, and over the years Bobby forgot about Thomas's friendship. Bobby had been the target of malicious pranks from some of the others in their year who looked down on the charity boy. A few black eyes and bloodied noses clarified that Bobby was not to be mistreated without cost. That those very bullies later formed the core of Thomas's closest friends hardly mattered in the grand scheme of things, though in those first few months after Bobby's departure, associating with those boys had felt like a betrayal.

"It was Bobby who showed me that mathematics could be more than a task to be endured," Thomas explains. "He introduced me to one of the abiding interests of my life."

"Then I can see why you recall him so fondly," Mrs. Yardley replies with some warmth. Perhaps it gives her pleasure to hear of her husband recollected by people unknown to her. "His love of mathematics grew into a passion for engineering. He was working for the City and South London Railway when he died in an accident at a dig site."

The C&SLR is one of the underground train services. These, despite their tight spaces and stuffy air, have become a popular way to travel, particularly when fogs make street traffic difficult. Thomas experiences an unexpected churn of envy that his long-ago friend labored in an important and revolutionary enterprise while he was doing nothing more daring than testing the limits of what a shilling could buy him in a dark alley.

"I am glad to learn he did so well for himself." Thomas struggles with what to say next. It might be better to leave things as they are. He learned that his friend led a satisfying life and married well. His death was an accident, and there can be no mystery there. There is no need to press on, and yet Thomas presses on. "I came across a document at the bank. It concerned Thresher's buying up Bobby's debt."

Mrs. Yardley blushes. "Yes, I am aware of it."

"I do not mean to be indelicate. And, as I mentioned, I have no interest in collecting. The first letter I discovered involved someone entirely different, though he lives not far from here. I found the matter curious, so I glanced through the files to see if there were other such cases, which is where I found the bank's letter to you."

Mrs. Yardley shows every sign of finding this line of inquiry puzzling. What could this banker hope to learn from her? "I can only tell you that we first learned that Thresher's had become our creditor while Bobby was still alive, but the bank never pursued the matter. No one cared if we paid, and if you saw the letter I received, then you know that the level of indifference has only increased. I cannot see the sense of it, but I am not a banker like you."

"I am not much of a banker," Thomas tells her, deciding on candor. "It is merely my place of employment."

"Perhaps you should address your questions to the signatory on the letter."

Thomas would much prefer to avoid the abuse and contempt Walter would heap upon him if he dared to ask about bank business. He knows better than to pursue that course. "Men who could explain the matter are disinclined to indulge my questions."

Mrs. Yardley shifts in her seat and seems to rearrange herself. Not physically, but on some deeper level. There is a moment of fluctuation from which she emerges as a somewhat different person—warmer and less skeptical, perhaps even a little curious herself. "I'm afraid I don't understand what I can do for you."

Thomas leans forward and clasps his hands together. He is entirely sincere, but he is also uncomfortably aware of performing sincerity. He has no idea how he appears to this lady. "There are two reasons I have come here. First, having come across the name of someone I considered a friend, I wished to learn something of his life after we were separated. Though his life ended abruptly and too soon, it was, by all accounts, a happy one, and that gives me some comfort."

"And your other purpose?" Mrs. Yardley presses.

"I suppose to learn why the bank would seek to make ordinary people their debtors, and in such small amounts. As no one at the bank is likely to enlighten me, I thought you might have some insight. That is evidently not the case, and so I must thank you for your time."

He begins to rise, but Mrs. Yardley shakes her head and waves him down. "A moment, Mr. Thresher. May I ask what you do at the bank precisely?"

"I am a junior clerk." He attempts to speak without shame, but he feels his cheeks redden. "Everyone, even Threshers, begin at such a station."

"Starting from the bottom," she says. "A fine way to learn the business, provided someone will reveal its mysteries to you."

"Junior clerks are not encouraged to learn much or quickly," he explains.

Mrs. Yardley is quiet for a moment, appearing to consider if she should say more. "Once, when my husband received a bonus for his labors at the railway, he attempted to pay what he owed. The bank would not let him. They presented him with an astonishing number of forms to complete and locations to visit and people to interview. It was like dealing with Dickens's Circumlocution Office. He and I came away from the experience very much of the mind that the bank wished not for the money but to have him in its debt."

"I cannot imagine why the bank would want to put a railway engineer in such a position," Thomas says.

"Nor I," she agrees. "After his death, I was all but told that the bank would not be collecting, but they would not erase the debt either. Thresher's wishes to keep it in case—well, I don't know, but I now begin to suspect in case I ask too many questions about why they wanted it in the first place. The debt was to secure the loyalty of my husband, not me, and yet, why was Thresher's unwilling to let the matter be put to rest?"

"It is an intriguing question," Thomas says, "but sadly, I am in no position to answer."

"Certainly not at the bank," she says.

"I'm not sure I understand you."

"You are not at the bank right now, and you mentioned there was another debtor who lived not far from here. Perhaps he might be able to shed some light on these matters."

Thomas laughs. "It is one thing to speak to you, but to go about knocking on doors. It is not really something I do."

"But it is something *I* wish to do, Mr. Thresher." She leans in toward him and says in a near whisper. "I'm fearless."

I, however, am not sufficiently interested, are not the words Thomas wants to say to this lovely woman, though they are true. His curiosity was more about his late friend than the mysterious workings of the bank. That curiosity satisfied, he does not know that he needs to pursue this matter any further.

"Perhaps the bank that bears your name does not permit you to visit whom you like on a Sunday."

Mrs. Yardley is teasing him. More than that, she is challenging him, and a sense Thomas thought impossibly atrophied tells him that she has crossed the borderlands of uncertainty into the realm of flirtation. Thomas has no wish to talk to strangers about their debts. It is an awkward business. On the other hand, the idea of spending another hour or two in the company of Mrs. Yardley appeals to him mightily, and the alternative is to figure out how best to ride out the remainder of his friendless Sunday before he returns to Thresher's for another week of meaningless toil.

"Very well," he says. "Let's pay this Mr. Yeats a visit."

SIX

FUTILITY

YEATS'S HOUSE IN Beswick Park is but a short ride in a hansom cab from Mrs. Yardley's house off Chiswick High Road. Thomas considers it likely the man will be out on a Sunday afternoon, but in that he is disappointed.

William Yeats wears rounded spectacles and has parted his hair with the ferocious precision of a belligerent intellectual. When he joins Thomas and Mrs. Yardley in a small sitting room lined with bookshelves, he has the grim expression of a surgeon who has just stepped away from a disapointing operation.

"How can I be of service?" Yeats asks in his Irish accent. "A glass of brandy, perhaps?"

"That would be lovely," says Mrs. Yardley, to Thomas's delight. What is next? Will she accept a cigarette? This woman is full of surprises.

After the drinks are served by someone who was either an aging servant or the Irishman's mother, the poet settles into his chair as though he has no intention of rising any time soon.

"As I mentioned," Thomas begins, "my name is Thresher, and I am associated with Thresher's Bank. I came across a debt that you owe the bank, and I'm curious if you know any reason why Thresher's would wish to make certain you were its debtor."

"You are from the bank, you say," Yeats observes. "I dare say you ought to know more of the business than I."

"Indeed, I ought to," Thomas agrees.

"How odd," Yeats says. He then sips his brandy in silence.

"Has the bank ever asked you to do anything?" Mrs. Yardley attempts. "Suggested, in any way, that it wished to make some use out of your indebtedness."

"Never," the Irishman says, blinking owlishly. "I received a letter informing me that Thresher's had consolidated my debts, as they put it, and that I might pay at the time of my convenience. As no time has been convenient, I have not paid."

Thomas and Mrs. Yardley exchange a look. This is consistent with Bobby's experience, but it makes little sense.

"Do you know, or know of, this lady's late husband?" Thomas asks. "Mr. William Yardley?"

Yeats shakes his head. "I do not recall the name, but I am grieved to hear of your loss."

"You are kind," Mrs. Yardley says in a way that indicates she wishes to hear no more condolences. She looks about the room and something seems to catch her eye. Rising, she strides over to one of the bookshelves and lets her index finger rest gently—Thomas might say sensually—on one of the spines. She looks back at Mr. Yeats. "May I?"

"Of course," he says. "What have you there?"

She removes the slim volume and shows it to Yeats before handing it to Thomas. On the spine he reads *Key of Solomon the King (Clavicula Salomonis)* by S. L. MacGregor Mathers. It means nothing to him, and he hands it back.

"My husband possessed a copy," she says to Yeats as she returns it to the shelf.

"It is an important translation, but not widely read," Yeats says. "MacGregor Mathers will be pleased to hear of it circulating."

"You know the author," Thomas observes. "Perhaps Bobby did as well."

"I don't believe so," Mrs. Yardley says. "We did not move in such circles. Had he known an author, he would have thought it worth mentioning."

"A puzzle, then," Yeats agrees. "But I do not see how I can help you."

"We've taken enough of your time," says Mrs. Yardley. "Thank you so much for indulging us, Mr. Yeats."

"It has been no trouble," he tells her, but he speaks with the melancholy tone of a man lamenting the wasted moments of his life.

They walk the streets in silence, strolling in the direction of her home at a leisurely pace. Thomas is warm enough in his coat, and the widow shows no signs of discomfort. Perhaps they will walk all the way back to her house. Even if they do this in companionable silence, Thomas thinks it will be a pleasant way to pass the time.

Since the departure of his friends, Thomas increasingly finds his enjoyment of city life diminished. He no longer loves the crowds and the bustle and the thrum of life. He no longer finds the disruptive fogs amusing. A few months ago, he could never have imagined he would look upon a suburban life and see only its charm.

Even here, though, one cannot entirely escape London's poverty. Gypsies and East Indians and peddler Jews wander the streets. There are beggars of all stripes. A man sits with a tattered suit next to a sign that reads "I did not uphold the bargain." Thomas understands. He broke a contract, and now he suffers endless ill luck. Ten feet from this unfortunate sits a woman in front of a rusting metal basin full of trembling rabbits. Thomas thinks again of Miss Feldstein's suggestion that the Peculiarities are more common among the most desperate, but he is still uncertain if this is true or if the rich are simply more capable of concealing their afflictions. If the mother were a woman of means, she would display her monstrous offspring for all the world to see.

Mrs. Yardley drops a coin in the woman's hand as they pass. "Do you credit the claim?" she asks Thomas. "Do you believe the rabbits are her children?"

Thomas feels an itch, as though he has grown a leaf on his back at that very moment. He knows it might only be his imagination and struggles not to reach behind himself and scratch. "You evidently do."

"I believe that she is in need. As for the rabbits, I can hardly say. I have seen things, though, that make me think anything possible."

"What things?" Thomas asks.

"Surely you have not lived in London and witnessed nothing of the Peculiarities," Mrs. Yardley presses, somewhat playfully.

"I have seen things." Now the itching spreads to all the scars on his skin where leaves have grown. "There was a determined fog that forced its way into the bank recently."

"I've faced one of those!" Mrs. Yardley announces cheerfully, as though they are comparing holiday destinations. "A tendril of fog forced itself into my kitchen only last month. I heard the cook screaming, and when I ran in, I witnessed the thing on the countertop. It was like the tentacle of an octopus, knocking things over and making a terrible mess. I grabbed a knife and sliced at it. Even as I struck, I scolded myself for thinking a knife could hurt fog, and yet the tendril did come off. It flopped about for a few seconds like part of a living creature, and then it dissipated into mist."

Thomas studies her with a new appreciation. That was a rather bold thing to do. He has not known many ladies who would be inclined to slice at phantom appendages.

"If I see a fog with a stump," he tells her, "I shall know I am witnessing your handiwork."

"You tease me," she says, smiling broadly.

"Only to conceal my admiration," he counters. "You are very brave."

She shakes her head. "I acted out of impulse. It is another thing to act more deliberately." She looks at him knowingly. "Will you pursue this matter? With the debt?"

"I can't see that the bank means you any harm," he replies. "I have already come up against resistance from my brother, and it's clear after speaking with you and that Irish fellow that there is neither a danger nor any commonality in the cases. It gives me nothing to look for. This must be some abortive scheme by my brother, and he does not speak of it because he doesn't want a failure unearthed." Thomas had not thought of this explanation before he said it, but now that he's given voice to the notion, he rather likes it. He cannot help but enjoy the thought of the always certain Walter struggling with some failure or another.

"But there were commonalities," says Mrs. Yardley. "At least one. That book I showed you. My husband also owned it."

"Surely you do not suggest the bank is singling out people who own a particular book."

"Not that book," she explains hastily, as if rushing to get the idea out of her head. "My husband had an interest in . . . occult matters. Magic. And the Peculiarities. Mr. Yeats, in fact, had many of the same books as my husband. I would say we should start by looking at them, but I sold them all after he died. It must mean something."

"If the bank wishes to make debtors out of every Londoner curious about the occult and the Peculiarities, then they will have a great many from which to choose," Thomas says, not liking the dismissive tone in his voice, but using it all the same. "Half the newspapers churn out stories daily, and the other half seem to have no purpose but to deny the claims of the first."

"It is one thing to have an interest in such matters," Mrs. Yardley says. "It is another thing to be a scholar. Bobby had something of a passion for old books about the occult. He spent hours at the British Museum, reading anything he could find, searching for answers about the Peculiarities. He had theories about why it was happening now and contained in this country to London. You do know that other cities have their own manifestations, do you not?"

Thomas has read there were similar, though not identical, claims being made about Paris, Berlin, and New York. What is it about these places, and why do such strange events manifest only in cities? Superstition sprouts root more easily in the countryside, and yet no village or town in England, to Thomas's knowledge, has reported Peculiar happenings.

"But I'm not certain what I can do about it," Thomas says. "No one at the bank will tell me what I wish to know."

Mrs. Yardley turns her head slightly, and appears to peer at him, if just for a moment, as though he were a glass of milk turned sour. "What are your ambitions, Mr. Thresher?"

This question takes him by surprise, not because he hasn't considered the question, because he has, but because it is very forward. The answer is, of course, that he has none, but he doesn't wish to say that.

"At the moment," he tells her, "to be prove my worth at the bank so I will have the opportunity to perform more useful work."

"Bobby loved his work," the widow says in a wistful tone. "At times the labors or the people could frustrate, but he had a passion for what he did. It is clearly not the case with you."

Thomas is both ashamed and curiously pleased that she has seen the truth of it. Yes, he is an aimless wastrel forced into a position where he is expected to contribute to the family enterprise in the most minimal way, but he doesn't like for others to know that. On the other hand, to be observed so keenly by this woman makes him think she must find him of some interest.

"You have no wish to run the bank yourself?" she asks.

"Walter, my brother—" he begins.

Mrs. Yardley isn't having it, however. "Banks are not monarchies, Mr. Thresher. If you are a better man than your brother, then you will rise to the top. You must care about your family's business."

He has only just come to realize that this is true. He cares about Thresher's, its legacy, the goals established by his grandfather, that unknown man with the kindly eyes whom Thomas had imagined he loved as a child. Walter and his father were remote and unknowable, but the bank was always real, and it stood for something once. Even as he toils with the junior clerks under Mr.

Philpot's watchful eye, he sometimes wishes the bank could be more as its founder intended.

"Alternatively," she says, "perhaps your interests point in another direction— the loans or perhaps the Peculiarities. A person should pursue what interests him, I have always believed."

"Perhaps I shall," he says, though he doesn't know if it is true. It certainly might be, and acquiescing is certainly better than making a case that he is interested in nothing and cannot imagine his life ever improving. "I have no idea how I can squeeze the answers out of people determined to say nothing."

"Then you must ask elsewhere." This, no doubt, is the point to which she has been building. "You said you found my letter among many. You could look through them again. I wonder if you might look for one that is least like the others. Perhaps in the difference you will find what makes everything the same."

Mrs. Yardley squeezes his arm. It is a gentle touch and momentary, but Thomas imagines he could feel the heat of her flesh through her glove and his clothing.

"Oh, come on, Mr. Thresher. Where is your sense of adventure? This is a genuine mystery, and it involves a widow with nowhere else to turn." She bats her eyelashes comically, like a character on a music hall stage.

Thomas cannot help but laugh. "A charming widow, I would say."

"Then you must investigate," she says very primly, "so you can have an excuse to come visit me again and tell me of your findings."

Thomas has already considered this strategy. He has judged it a significant counterweight to the challenges posed by defying Walter and snooping around in bank business. He takes in a sidelong glance of Mrs. Yardley, of her pale skin and midnight hair and impossibly green eyes.

"I suppose I shall see what I discover, then."

"I cannot wait to hear all about it." She puts another hand on his arm, and this time it lingers just a little longer.

SEVEN
LUST

WHEN HE PROMISED the lovely widow, with whom he had at best a tenuous connection, to risk upturning his life that he might satisfy her curiosity, he surely spoke sincerely. Now, days later, he has begun to distance himself from that pledge. It is hard for Thomas to sleuth his way around the bank while under Mr. Philpot's watchful eye. An unauthorized departure from his desk cannot go without notice; the fifteen minutes allotted for his midday meal is enforced inflexibly; the length of his visits to the necessary are marked with contemptuous scrutiny. No junior clerk can claim to have witnessed Mr. Philpot make such a visit, leading to the speculation that he sits all day upon a pot and relieves himself behind his desk as needed.

Thomas does not want to lie to Mr. Philpot. He has signed a contract with the bank which includes, among other things, a promise to be forthright with his superiors regarding matters of work. He fears violating his agreement may render him vulnerable to some sort of Peculiar consequence. Do the leaves that grow on his body make him immune to further affliction—like a man under sentence of death who has nothing to lose by committing more crimes? Thomas would like to believe so, but of course he cannot know.

It is therefore some days before Thomas can get away to the records room. On Thursday of the week following his visit to Mrs. Yardley, a rare opportunity presents itself.

Nicholas Roberts, a fellow junior clerk, has made a considerable effort to befriend Thomas—almost certainly because Thomas is a Thresher. The interest cannot be genuine, as the two men hardly know each other. In fact, Thomas has performed a little experiment, rebuffing Roberts's offers to join him in food or drink not quite rudely, but certainly brusquely. Still, the fellow has persisted without indication of hurt feelings or diminished enthusiasm.

At times, Thomas worries he may have been needlessly unkind to the fellow. Roberts is not one of the clerks who titterers at every cross word Mr. Philpot casts in Thomas's direction. He is, in fact, an unremarkable man in all ways, well below average in height and weight, with the hollow-cheeked look of a consumptive. Despite his appearance, he writes, adds, and files more vigorously than any other clerk in the room, which contributes to his being generally disliked.

Even Mr. Philpot evidences an antipathy for Roberts, whom he chastises for getting ink on his sleeves, for having scratched spectacles, and once for needing a haircut, though Roberts hair has been remarkably consistent, suggesting a weekly trimming. Thomas believes Mr. Philpot, in his day, must have been the ringleaders of his own band of wicked clerks, and still finds himself in natural alignment with the most malevolent men in the room.

That Thursday, however, Roberts seems quite different. He squirms without cessation at his desk for the first few hours of the day, getting up to use the necessary twice. Thomas feels sorry for the fellow, clearly suffering from a stomach disorder, though Philpot berates him and makes accusations of malingering. By noon, Roberts's jittery movements intensify. He all but vibrates in his chair, and from time to time he snorts or hums or giggles. Several times he lashes an arm out into the air, as though raising a hand in a classroom, only to lower it after a moment, once with the assistance of his other hand.

"Have you gone mad, Roberts?" Philpot demands.

"Mad with desire to work," he responded with an unsettling titter. "Mad for Thresher's Bank, Mr. Philpot. That is all the madness I require."

It is nearly two o'clock when Roberts visits Thomas's desk. After receiving a pile of documents from Philpot, Roberts stops, at first saying nothing, merely looking at Thomas, turning his head this way and that, as though trying to determine what, precisely, he beholds.

"You have the look of a man who needs to do something." Roberts's face quivers, but then goes still except for the corners of his mouth. He is trying not to laugh.

"Are you quite well, Roberts?"

"Do you want my help or not?" It comes out as a hiss. Then Roberts slaps a hand over his mouth. An eye blink later, his other hand clasps over the first.

Thomas is not about to admit that he is looking for an excuse to visit the records room, but he feels like he must say something. Philpot, miraculously, has not looked up to observe this outrageous socializing, and this good fortune cannot last.

"I am only sick to death of being under Philpot's eye," Thomas says in a quiet voice.

Roberts lets go of his mouth. "I shall distract him. Await my signal." Then the hands go back to his mouth, and in that pose, elbows raised like wings, Roberts returns to his desk.

Thomas cannot imagine what such a signal would be. Will he know it when it comes? Roberts is behaving so strangely that anything might or might not be his secret sign.

When the signal comes, it is unmistakable. Thomas is following a maze of sums through a two-hundred-page ledger, searching out an error that one of the directors is certain must be hidden somewhere, when Roberts rises to his feet and stands like a soldier on a parade ground.

"What is it now?" Mr. Philpot barks.

Roberts does not answer. His eyes dart back and forth as though he is looking for something, and there is a strange smile on his face. No, not a smile, Thomas thinks. A leer. He looks like—it takes Thomas a moment to identify that expression, but then it comes to him—he looks like one of his old friends, well into his cups, when he sees a whore he must have. The realization is sudden and sure and strangely satisfying, as though Thomas has just remembered the name of a tune that he has been humming absently for hours.

"Back to work," Mr. Philpot snaps. He conducts himself as though he must chastise his workers constantly, but the truth is the clerks rarely require any correction, and now he seems at a loss as to how to manage this insurrection.

Then Roberts pounces. That is the only word for it. He leaps onto his desk, toppling a bottle of ink, which he steps in, proceeding to stamp his progress as he bounds from table to table. Only Thomas's own quick reflexes save his ledger from ruination. The clerk moves like a wolf on the hunt, loping across the room, all the more remarkable because during these gymnastics he manages to unbutton and lower his trousers, which, though bunched around his ankles, impede his progress not at all.

Even more extraordinary is Roberts's massive erection. At first Thomas thinks it significant for so small a man. Then he realizes it is significant, even grotesque, for any human male. Thomas is no expert on the subject, but he knows his own anatomy, and Roberts's member is easily twice as long and thick as his own. His testicles swing like a swollen, hairy pendulum, and the fellow's legs are covered in thick patches of curling hairs.

Roberts propels himself onto Philpot's desk and knocks the senior clerk facedown on the floor. He grabs at Philpot's trousers in bunches with both hands and rips them open as if they were been made of newspaper. He then places his hands upon the screaming man's hips.

Despite his days with his reckless school friends, many of whom regarded no iniquity too unthinkable to sample at least once, Thomas's tastes have always hewn close to the traditional, so he spends a moment genuinely confused before realizing Roberts means to violate Mr. Philpot.

"Someone help me!" cries the senior clerk. His wispy hair points in multiple directions, as if grasping for assistance. Mr. Philpot has never appeared disordered. He has never seemed afraid or uncertain. He has never asked for help. This, even more than Roberts's obscenely rigid penis, imbues the scene with the topsy-turvy unreality of a nightmare.

Several of Philpot's favorites shake off their surprise and spring into action, grabbing Roberts by the arm or collar or shoulder—anything above the waist. The little man thrashes and screams and, perhaps most terribly, tries to rub his enormous member against his assailants.

By this time a handful of porters in the bank's employ have heard the commotion and rush in. It takes them a moment, quite understandably, to recover from their surprise, but then they manage to overpower the wriggly Roberts and lock him in a storage closet until such time as he can be hauled away to an insane asylum. Thomas will later learn that when Roberts was removed, the walls were found to be entirely coated with semen.

But it is an indulgence to get ahead of ourselves, so back to the present moment. Philpot lies panting on the floor, his pale and puckered buttocks exposed, while Roberts is dragged to the closet. His voice suggests equal amounts of rage and delight as he promises that he will fuck them all in the arse. He will, he assures the men in the room, split them in two. The junior clerks look around, uncertain of what to do, what to say. No matter the extent to which each of them may have experimented with always available London debaucheries, nothing in their lives has quite prepared them for this moment. Thomas is—well, where is Thomas? Had his fellow junior clerks been less distracted, they might have noticed he has vanished. Is it possible that a man, especially one who finds his place of work so tedious, would wander away from so diverting a spectacle? Thomas has done so indeed because Roberts, perhaps mad, perhaps something else entirely, has created a distraction. He has given the sign, and Thomas has used the mayhem to slip unseen into the records room.

"Satyromania," Sherwin, one of the other junior clerks, confides to Thomas upon his return. He pronounces it *satire-mania*, as though it were a gathering of Rabelais fanatics.

Mr. Philpot is gone, and no one has said what is to become of him. It is a rare moment of camaraderie. The clerks are not ready to return to their routine, and there is no one to chastise them for their lack of diligence. They are like servants who have woken to find their masters vanished and the furnishings secreted away. The only thing that will answer is nervous chatter.

"Been on the rise, as they say, since the Peculiarities," Sherwin goes on, talking to Thomas only because he remains still and appears to listen. It is the talking that's the thing, not the act of communicating. "I've seen it before with my neighbor's daughter. Nymphomania, they call it, when it afflicts the female. She came over and did her business with every one of us in the boardinghouse. Didn't even have her titties yet. She went back home, where they say she died trying to please herself with a broom handle. Poor girl, not thirteen years old."

Mr. Hawke enters the room and tells them that Mr. Philpot is unharmed but understandably agitated. He will not return until the following week, and the clerks must show their devotion by continuing with their labors as though he were present. A week without Philpot seems like a fine thing, though it is small compensation to Thomas, who has just learned that he is working beside a man who feels no shame in taking a mad child to his bed.

On the other hand, Thomas has found what he has been looking for in the records room, and it has taken less time than he would have supposed.

Unfortunately, the debtor least like the others presents some challenges, and calling upon this person will require no small amount of courage.

After eleven hours of confinement, Thomas walks through the lobby, wanting nothing so much as to escape and breathe in the foul London air. His first disappointment comes when he hears the murmurings that the anticipated fog has rolled in during the waning hours of the afternoon. It's a bad one, they say. It has all the signs of a fog that means to plant itself and not move for some days.

The second disappointment is the hand on his shoulder.

"Going somewhere, young Mr. Thresher?" Mr. Hawke grins at him in that way that suggests he is looking down, even though Thomas is taller by several inches.

"I am done for the day," Thomas answers.

"Time to fly and be free," says Mr. Hawke, making an absurd wing-flapping gesture with his fingers, keeping the backs of his palms affixed to his waist.

"Yes." Thomas feels like this short conversation has gone on far too long and has run out of possible avenues of advancement.

Mr. Hawke continues with his openmouthed smile, like a dog in full pant, and while odd, it doesn't seem precisely false. His eyes crinkle with genuine amusement. "Rather exciting day, wasn't it? A bit more attempted sodomy than we're used to at Thresher's."

Always growing, Thomas thinks, but he does not say it. He wishes to say the thing that will allow him to leave as quickly as possible. "I always found Roberts a bit odd. I'm not saying I expected him to assault Philpot, but he always struck me as rather—"

"Solicitous," Mr. Hawke interrupts. "Quite so. Quite so. We had our eye on him for that very reason."

Solicitous is, indeed, the exact word, though solicitous toward Thomas and not anyone else.

"And yet, for all its disruption," Mr. Hawke continues, "I am made to understand that you spent some time among the records today."

The degree to which this man knows Thomas's business is less worrying than irritating. Thomas attempts to sound casual as he offers an explanation that is deceptive without quite rising to the level of an untruth. There is the contract to consider. "A junior clerk must perform his duties. Roberts had, by then, been subdued."

"And polluting himself quite aggressively in his confinement, I hear," Mr. Hawke says with his wide smile. "Assault most foul and all that unexpected nudity, yet you toil away. It is important to carry on the Thresher tradition. You never spent much time with the late Samuel Thresher, and you didn't know his father, but Walter revered both. By aiding Walter, you honor the family. Don't you agree?"

During his exuberant school days, when he ran with his friends who so lately left him on these shores for Paris, Thomas learned there were times when silence serves better than any answer. This has all the appearance of such a time. He meets Mr. Hawke's eye and waits.

"I see we understand one another," Mr. Hawke says. "A junior clerk should tend to his responsibilities and nothing more. That is how a junior clerk becomes a clerk, is it not?"

"I suppose it is." Thomas has no love of catechism, and he firmly believes that anyone who speaks to him in this way ought to be knocked down and perhaps kicked. Thomas has done some knocking down and kicking in his school days—less since leaving school, though he has not given the sport up entirely. There are times when it is required. Thomas prides himself on being both able with his fists and slow to use them. He wasn't the best fighter among his friends, but he was the most temperate of the skillful fighters. He has never sought a row and has only resorted to violence when there was no other way. Or if a fellow is begging for it.

Mr. Hawke, in his opinion, is begging for it. Still, thrashing one's superiors is not a sound path to promotion and would very likely violate the terms of his employment contract.

"I want only what is best for this bank." This, Thomas realizes, is entirely true, though his opinion of what is best may not be the same as his brother's.

"Like music to my ears," Mr. Hawke says.

Thomas watches him walk away and wonders, not for the first time, who Mr. Hawke is, what he does, and why in the name of God Walter tolerates him.

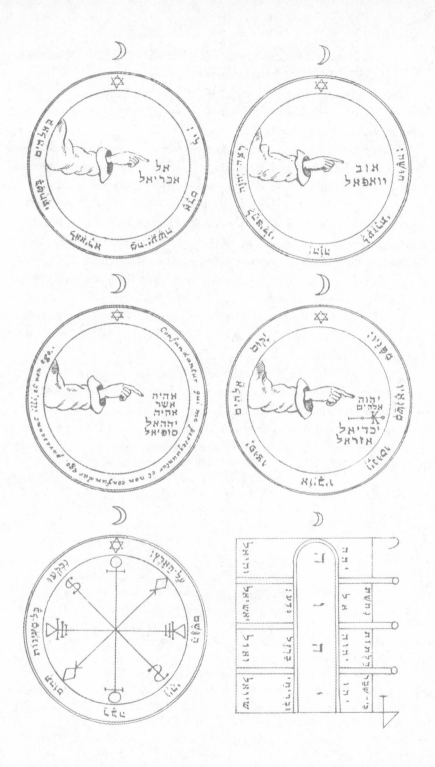

EIGHT

INTERFERENCE

I T IS DIFFICULT to see more than a few feet in any direction. The gray mist that settles over the city is denser and cooler than the fogs Thomas remembers from his childhood. It tastes less of soot. It promises hidden menace, and yet there is something comforting about it too, like a warm duvet on a cold night. The fog makes Thomas want to lie down and sleep. He has never spoken of this to anyone for fear of learning that the desire is not universal. What if other people—people whose bodies are free of foliage, for example—find these fogs unnerving?

Thomas knows that any sense of comfort is an illusion. Like sharks circling a whaling ship, thieves and pickpockets will be out to make best use of the obscured visibility. Does that make it a bad night to visit the woman whose name he uncovered in the archives? It is her location that has marked her out, that makes her, as Mrs. Yardley said, unlike the other debtors. All others live in quite respectable environs. This debtor makes her home in Bethnel Green, one of the most wretched neighborhoods of East London. Neighboring Whitechapel has become synonymous with the unfathomable depths of London crime and poverty, but Bethnel Green is little better. It has also been the site of some of the gruesome murders associated with the Peculiarities, beginning with Jack the Ripper. The Blind Headsman, Mister Fancy Pants, the Rabbit Hunter, and the Fool with a Hook all struck on those winding streets. These crimes are now believed to have been committed by the creatures known as the Elegants, though who or what they are remains unclear. Visiting Bethnel Green on such a night might be a very bad idea.

On the other hand, what conceals a hunter also conceals prey. Thomas will be hidden the same as any would-be assailant, and while he feels a bit of a coward for even thinking it, the truth is that the victims of those notorious East London murders are nearly always poor young women, and most of those prostitutes and, more recently, women with rabbit children. Thomas needn't fear having his head sawed from his neck or his legs hacked off at the knees or being run through with hooks. No one will be interested in harvesting *his* organs or devouring *his* rabbit babies. He needs to be concerned about the more typical assortment of London criminals: the desperately poor, the Irish, Gypsies, Asiatics with hatchets, Jews with knives, opium fiends, drunken whores (also with knives), and restless young men with great strength, no prospects, access to cheap liquor, and an abundance of time to stoke the fires of grievance.

These are real concerns, but ideal conditions for visiting a slum do not exist. Even on a bright and clear Sunday afternoon Thomas would be flirting with danger. Perhaps more so. His clothes and grime-free face would mark him as a target. He projects wealth and privilege in a thousand ways he knows are invisible to his own eyes.

There is also the fact that Mrs. Yardley—Madeline, as he dares to think of her in his private thoughts—sits in judgment. Not perhaps in her own mind, but he saw how she looked at him. Thomas Thresher, an outsider within Thresher's Bank. A person should pursue what interests him, she said, and was there not a hint of hope in that statement? Would Thomas, she no doubt wondered, be the sort of person who seeks out the mysteries of his own family's business?

Even now she awaits his report. "I am too frightened to investigate further, but I hope to find the courage soon," are not words to impress a charming young lady. Thomas prefers to regale her with tales of his striding into the fog manfully, knocking down brutes and assailants, disarming long-locked Chinese brigands.

Having stoked his courage, Thomas manages to flag down a hansom, one equipped with bright Peculiar lamps that cut through the fog sufficiently—if only just—to navigate the roads at a diminished pace. Before anything else, Thomas asks the driver's name, as is his custom. It can be useful information under certain circumstances. Drivers are always happy to comply, as the illusion of congeniality can lead to a larger tip.

That congeniality is short-lived. The driver sputters half-hearted objections when Thomas provides the address, and so the curtain rises on the tedious theater of negotiations in which Thomas must bribe the man into doing his job—on top of being overcharged, as he inevitably will be at the conclusion of the journey. He then sits back for what he supposes is going to be a nearly endless ride.

With the fog all around him, and the sounds of London's streets turning into a soothing drone, Thomas, hardly aware of what is happening, falls asleep. It is the coachman's voice awakens him. "As close as I dare get."

Thomas attempts to shake off the sleep. It does not dislodge easily. He realizes he has been dreaming. It is the face again. It always slips away when he wakes, but he thinks he can recall it better this time. It is long, with lank and disordered hair, thin lips, and a curiously small nose. The face is distorted, as though bent, perhaps hinged like an elbow. The expression was less terrible than he should have expected of such a face, however. Placid and patient, perhaps curious.

Thomas does not want to think of the face. It does not precisely frighten him, but he dislikes it all the same. He looks around, for all the good it does. He can see nothing but swirling mists all around them. "Where are we?"

"Columbia Road," the man says in a mournful tone, as if recollecting every poor decision that has led to him being in this sad place at this sad time. "You can hoof it from here, guv. I ain't crossing into Old Nichol."

"I bribed you to take me all the way."

"There's no bribe big enough for that," the man says. "Not on a Peculiar night."

"Then I shall have my bribe returned," Thomas announces.

We mustn't think Thomas cheap. Many a night he has bought drinks for his friends, and while he may have been aware that they returned the courtesy with some infrequency, he did not mind. Money is for spending, but there is a principle here. It is about ordering the universe, making the numbers balance.

"I insist you return my money," he says.

"I wish you much luck in that particular endeavor," the coachman says with an earnestness that borders on belligerence.

"I dare say I require no luck," Thomas tells him. "You entered into an agreement with me. A contract. Are you certain you wish to break it?"

The coachman looks at Thomas for some long seconds, blinking as he considers the implications of ignoring his bargain. He then drops the disputed coins into his passenger's hand.

This transaction resolved to his satisfaction, Thomas climbs out of the coach. The sleep is still on him, and the ghost of that face still hovers somewhere just out of sight, but the haze in his mind is nothing compared to the fog that surrounds him. The moment his shoes touch the street, his senses spring into full alert. He hears drunken laughter, the pots clanging, glass breaking, children crying, women calling out to strangers, street vendors shouting out oysters, pies, bread, soap, matches, hats, song sheets, penknives, old clothes. A riot of sound—cackling, screaming, weeping, shouting, hissing—pours from tavern doors. People pass him in the fog, and for the most part they mean him no harm. They are the struggling poor going from one dreary place to the next, to or from their labors, slouching toward or away from home, hauling their abused and malnourished bodies, immediately or with some diversion, toward their untimely deaths.

Thomas turns onto Fuller Street, which serves as something of a dividing line between the wretched and the middling. On one side stand decent homes that display an effort toward upkeep. On the other are tumbledown shacks and hodgepodge houses and twisting alleys, the gateway to the infamous rookery called Old Nichol, where the veil between poverty and death is particularly permeable. Thomas clings to the better side, though he knows the street itself holds no totemic powers to keep men or monsters from crossing.

In the fog dwell shapes highlighted by the sporadic cook fires and jouncing glow of handheld Peculiar lamps. There are the usual sort of East London sights that, under any conditions, would be concerning. A man in a bloody apron stumbles forward with a dripping knife in hand. He may be a butcher, perhaps traveling as he does to afford himself better protection. Thomas passes a shirtless behemoth of a man, mumbling and cursing, his tattooed skin stretched over a heaving mass of fat and muscle. He passes prostitutes who call out to him, who reach out to grab him. In their opium torpor, they undulate like lazy strands of seaweed beneath the waves. He passes children begging that they are starving. These he would aid, whether they tell the truth or not. They are children, and they doubtlessly need money, but Thomas has learned the hard way not to flash coin in this sort of place.

If this were the worst of it, he would have little noticed. Daily in London one witnesses scenes of wretched want and desperation. The sane mind dare not dwell upon them. There are things more terrible than poverty in the fog, however. He spies a dog that appears to be twice, possibly thrice, the length possible for its species and has an extra pair of legs. A little boy, not more than five years old, clings to the brick of a building near a second-story window. He hisses at Thomas and then crawls inside. A woman with pendulous ears like an elephant mutters to herself in the mouth of an alley.

All of this could be no more than the fog playing tricks with him. The dog might be two or three animals walking in single file. The woman might wear a hat. The boy could be a monkey fleeing its life of Italianate organ-grinding drudgery. Humdrum poverty can be as grotesque as any lurid newspaper account of the Peculiarities. Thomas knows it to be so, but when he walks through the thick of the fog, in this neighborhood, it is easy to believe anything is possible.

Ahead of him he sees a couple walking arm in arm, clearly from the better side of the street. But no, there is something odd about them, with their clothes from a decade or two past. The man wears a black cutaway, a high plug hat, and a silk puff necktie. Upon the woman is a tassel-skirted white gown that emerges from her too-short bell-shaped coat. They could be on their way to a formal occasion but surely not in this neighborhood.

Still, if they feel comfortable on these streets, then a strapping specimen of manhood like Thomas should be ashamed to cringe. As he passes the couple, Thomas touches his hat, and the gentleman turns to him. His face is gaunt, sunken-eyed, leathery, like something found beneath a mummy's wrappings. His nose is but two slits, his mouth a lipless grin.

Thomas staggers back, and the couple vanishes into the mist.

Has he seen truly, or have the fear and the fog created the illusion? Thomas is almost certain he has just passed the very likeness he has seen illustrated in the newspapers. He has come into contact with—and survived!—the creatures known as the Elegants.

A few minutes later he is knocking on a door and fully convinced he has witnessed nothing out of the ordinary. The fog merely unnerved him. He saw people. Only ordinary people. The house, in its simplicity, calms him. It is a modest structure on the better side of the street, and it appears to be solidly middle class. Gas lamps burn bright within, so Thomas knows someone is at home, and that means he will soon be off the street. It takes a long time for anyone to respond to his knocking, though, and he begins to fear he will have to go back along the street, back through the fog, having accomplished nothing.

Finally, the door creaks open and a broad-shouldered man forty or forty-five, heavily mustached, towers into the threshold. "What do you want?" he asks, perhaps as kindly as those words can be spoken. That is to say, not at all kindly, but neither as belligerently as may be imagined. His voice is a glottal expulsion of East London indifference.

"I am looking for a Mrs. Judith Topping," Thomas says. "Is she within?"

"Who's asking?"

Thomas offers his best smile. He is not a bill collector or a man with a grievance. He is a gentleman calling upon a lady, or at least a woman. He is an embodiment of respectable sociability, and he has nothing to hide. "My name is Thomas Thresher, and I beg a moment of Mrs. Topping's time upon a personal matter."

Thresher's is not one of the larger banks, and it is not universally known, but this man clearly knows of his wife's debt. He steps back, suddenly quite pale.

Thomas forces a smile. "My business is, perhaps, best discussed within doors, but I am not here to collect."

The man seems to recover a little. "No one enters the house until I'm satisfied he don't mean harm. And how do I know you are who you say?"

"Please let him in," Thomas hears a woman say, and there is something pleading, almost yearning, in her voice. "I told you he was coming. I *prepared* you."

"You didn't say it would be *this*," the man bellows into the house. "You said *someone*. And could be this one is up to no good. How would you know? You wouldn't, that's how."

"I didn't know," the voice replies, sounding on the brink of tears. "I didn't see it, but it was there. I missed it. Let him through."

The brute lets out a sigh and shakes his head like a bull preparing to charge, but he holds the door wider and retreats enough to let Thomas pass, though not enough to withdraw all sense of menace.

The interior has a musty smell and something of a musty look. The rugs are threadbare, the furnishings tattered, the wallpaper faded. Nevertheless, everything is clean and orderly, and there has been considerable effort made to keep up appearances.

There is also a hum in the house, a vibration, that Thomas recognizes as being the habitation of many more people than he can currently see or even hear.

The man turns to Thomas. "I'm John Topping," he says in a tone that suggests he is surrendering something he would much rather keep. "You'll be wanting my Judy."

John Topping leads Thomas into a sitting room, well lit, with a few chairs and a sofa surrounding a low table. A woman has already risen from the sofa to greet him. She wears a simple dress of a faded brown color, but with a cloak over it, hood up to cover her face, which is additionally concealed by a veil. Her hands are gloved, and it occurs to Thomas that he can see nothing of her at all. He thinks of the story of an invisible man of which he read a few installments in *Pearson's Weekly* a few years back.

"This is Mrs. Topping," John Topping says in a curiously formal manner. "This man *says* he's Thomas Thresher."

"I am so very pleased to meet you," the woman says in a voice much more refined than her husband's. She steps forward and takes both of Thomas's hands in her own, gripping his fingers with some strength. The gesture is strangely intimate. It is as though she is greeting a long-lost friend. Thomas does not pull away, as he has no wish to embarrass this woman or reject her before he has asked his questions. There is also something appealing about her. He has not seen her. He has only heard her voice, but he believes it is a good voice. It is the voice of the sort of woman he should trust.

"You are well?" she asks.

"Yes, thank you." He sounds uncertain, like a little boy, but he cannot quite shake the feeling that he does not know what is happening here. It is as though he has wandered into a foreign country and though he speaks the language, the customs confound him. This may be what visiting America is like.

"Please make yourself at home," says Mrs. Topping. "Do you mind?" she asks, gesturing toward her veil.

Thomas cannot imagine why he should mind or why it should be his decision if a woman wears a veil, and yet he finds he is uneasy. "Of course not," he says, though he does mind, even if he cannot say why. Perhaps it is because if a woman hides her face in her own home, there must be something about it best kept hidden.

Thomas soon sees his suspicions are correct. Mrs. Topping reaches up and removes her veil and then lifts her hood. Underneath she reveals a face snouted and fur-covered and most definitely not human.

The Mysterious characters of the Moon.

First, [symbols] ∪ 8 8 .

Second, [symbols] △ ⚸ N⁰ 7 N ♌ .

Third, X ◇ ꝺ ꝺ ⊔ ⅏ ꜱ .

The Pentacle of the Moon.

NINE

DEFEAT

THOMAS IS NOT certain what to say to a woman so very hairy. In school, he once went with friends to a traveling circus to see a dog-faced lady, but it turned out to be a rheumatic fat woman wearing a false beard. This is something else entirely.

Mrs. Topping is covered with a grayish brown coat, and her features are canine, or perhaps wolfen. Her ears grow to points and rotate like a dog's. She has a muzzle of a mouth, and her dark lips pull back to reveal sharp teeth.

"My appearance shocks you," says Mrs. Topping in a voice remarkable only for sounding kind and not something one expects to hear from her beastly muzzle. Indeed, her snout hardly seems capable of forming these words, though her lips twist as would a person's. Nevertheless, the product is astonishingly human. There is something most *peculiar* about it.

"I am not shocked," Thomas croaks. "That is to say, I am surprised—deeply surprised—and also unprepared, I should think. . . ." He finds himself trailing off.

"Seems to me," booms Mr. Topping in a voice full of unexpected good cheer, "that another word for all that might be 'shocked.'"

"I beg your pardon," Thomas says, recovering himself. He straightens his posture as a means of resetting his affect. "I am being rude. You are—you have been afflicted—I mean, perhaps, affected—by the Peculiarities?"

"Indeed, I have," she agrees. "If you are uncomfortable, I can cover myself once more."

"By no means," says Thomas, now fully on the road toward remembering his manners. "It is your home, after all, and a person cannot help their appearance. I cannot help mine. Ha ha."

"I reckon not," says Mr. Topping.

Thomas touches a finger to his face, wondering if there is something about his appearance of which he ought to be a bit more ashamed. It might explain a great deal. He decides the man is being droll. Enough women have told him he is handsome that he believes it must be at least somewhat true.

Thomas searches his mind for words he might utter if he were not speaking to a wolf matron. Finding them, he straightens his posture and decides it is time for him to tell her his business. "I am employed by Thresher's Bank, but I must begin by assuring you I have no interest in collection," he says. "I am here purely in an investigatory capacity, but I am trying to understand how it is that you have come to be indebted to Thresher's."

Something ripples across Mrs. Topping's face. Thomas cannot identify it. He has never been particularly skilled in the art of reading women, and the addition of hair and a snout does nothing to improve his skills. There is something here, though. Pain, perhaps? Regret. Thomas cannot begin to guess.

"You are employed by Thresher's?" she asks in a pointed way Thomas finds impossible to interpret. "And Thresher is your name. You are, perhaps, of the banking family."

"I am the son of the late governor," Thomas says, "and brother to the current governor."

The wolf-woman nods. "You are very well connected."

Thomas shrugs. "It is of no moment and certainly not why I am here. An old friend found himself with a similar debt. He has since died, and his widow asked me if I might learn more, find a pattern, if you will. My searches through the bank's records have led me to discover the bank has also purchased some debts of yours. I must again emphasize I have no interest in collecting. I merely wish to understand why the bank went to the trouble to acquire the debt."

"Really?" she asks, seeming surprised. "Thresher's has purchased some of my debt? What do we owe?"

"It was a very small sum. Just over twenty pounds."

"First I'm hearing of this," says Mr. Topping with a meaningful look.

Thomas tries to remember the letter. Specifically, he tries to recall the date. Perhaps it was so long ago that this couple has forgotten about a smallish sum that bank seemed to have no interest in collecting.

"You've stumbled upon quite the puzzle," Mrs. Topping says. She then invites Thomas to sit, and he takes an armchair with its back to the fire. She sits on the sofa across from him, where Mr. Topping joins her, taking her hand as though she were not a monstrosity. Thomas finds the bruiser's gentle affection unexpectedly touching.

"You know nothing of this debt, but you said you were expecting me," Thomas asks once they have begun to settle in.

"I read the tarot this morning," Mrs. Topping says, "and the results were most unambiguous. I was . . . surprised, of course. Very surprised. I did not think. Well, never mind. There will be time for that later. But as you see, the tarot can be quite specific for a receptive reader."

"That is a form of fortune-telling?" He speaks the words hoping they are stripped of all traces of skepticism, but he is uncertain of his success.

"I prefer the terms divination or cartomancy. Less of the carnival about them, but essentially, you are correct."

"May I presume, then, that you are interested in the occult?"

"I am," agrees Mrs. Topping. "Is that important?"

"It may be. You are the third person I have spoken to on the subject of these mysterious debts, and thus far an interest in the occult appears to be the single common factor." Thomas gives her the names of the other two, but they are not familiar to her.

"That means little, however," she explains. "I have been secluded here for three years, since the symptoms of my lycanthropy have become impossible to hide."

"Lycanthropy," Thomas repeats. "The newspapers have written of it, but their descriptions are unlike, that is, you are not. . . ." Again, circumstances leave him unable to articulate what no man should ever be forced to say.

"Transforming into a mindless beast when the moon is full," she says, lowering her gaze so that she might meet his eye directly. "A lot of nonsense. It is a physical change, yes, but a constant one, not coming and going with the lunar cycle. It is an affliction, if I may be so bold, much like your own."

Thomas experiences a shock of hot shame. It is like a dream in which he suddenly finds himself exposed in some public and mortifying manner. "How could you know?" He begins to grope about his exposed skin, fearing that a leaf has popped up somewhere visible.

Mrs. Topping opens her mouth in a canine smile and then sniffs audibly. "Heightened sense of smell. One of the compensations of my condition. The odor is all about you for those with a nose delicate enough to recognize it. I do not know that I can help you with your banking questions, but on this subject, I may be of some use."

✻

Sights, sounds, snippets of conversations—they all flicker in and out for a few minutes, such that Mrs. Topping inquires, more than once, if Thomas is quite well. Somehow a glass of brandy and soda appears in his hand, and he takes a series of hurried sips as though the drink were the only thing sustaining his life.

"I must apologize," Thomas says after he has begun to recover his senses. "I am—that is to say, this is not what I came here for. I wished to know about your debt."

"It is why you believe you came," says Mrs. Topping. "You are truly here for another reason. Something has led you to me."

Thomas does not believe in a world in which unknowable *somethings* maneuver people about their lives like invisible theater ushers showing patrons to their seats. He wants very much to tell her that he is not interested in any of that nonsense, but he cannot bring himself to do so. If she has information about his condition, he must hear it.

"Why am I truly here, then?" he asks.

Mrs. Topping stands. "Come with me."

Thomas follows her down a gloomy hallway and into what looks to be a dining room. There, three children sit at a table. Two of them are playing a game of draughts, while a third patiently awaits her turn. A young lady, sitting near the fire with a book in hand, nominally oversees this activity. Thomas can see the truth in an instant—that she hopes to ignore the children to the greatest extent possible, and her primary function is to smooth over any quarrels that may erupt. She will be happiest if she needn't speak to them until it is time to tell them they must go to bed.

Nothing could have been less remarkable except the young lady, like Mrs. Topping, is a wolf creature. Thomas is not even certain how he knows that she is young. He cannot see the smoothness of her skin, nor is the bloom of youth recognizable in any feature excepting a certain brightness in her eyes. Perhaps it is in her shape, the way she holds herself. Thomas wonders, in a most abstracted way, what thousand other codes and formulae he deciphers each day quite unknown to himself.

As fascinated as he is by the secret workings of his own mind, he realizes these questions are largely a way for him not to think much about the scene before him. One of the children—a boy, he thinks, but how can one truly know?—has the most nightmarish face Thomas has ever seen, ever imagined. It is a smooth egg of flesh, with no hair, ears, mouth, or nose. How does he breathe? How does he eat? Thomas cannot speculate, but the boy can clearly interact with the world in some way for as the adults observe, he raises a long and delicately fingered hand to manipulate a triple jump upon the game board.

His opponent is clearly a girl. Thomas can be certain of that much, and she might even be a pretty girl of about ten years except that she is black. Not black in the way of an African or East Indian. No, she is black like stone, though there are veins of pale gray that run though like—like marble, he thinks. Even her hair is a frozen in statuary stillness. After she moves her piece, her body moving quite fluidly, she sets her hand down upon the table with a weighty thud.

The third child, also a girl, is somewhat plump, but appears to be normal in all other regards. This, to Thomas, seems almost more terrible. What unspeakable secret is she hiding that brings her into such company?

Mrs. Topping opens her mouth, to make introductions no doubt, but the wolf nanny looks up from her book and sniffs loudly enough to interrupt. She stands at once and approaches Thomas with a menacing gait. He thinks she means to reach out with one of her hands and rip out his throat.

"This is my daughter, Miss Ruby Topping. Ruby, please meet Mr. Thomas Thresher."

The young wolf lady shifts her body language slightly and somehow seems less threatening, but there is a tilt to her head, a stillness to her posture, that continues to suggests a beast frozen in a wild landscape, ready to attack or flee at some unknowable cue.

"Thomas," she says in a slightly high, somewhat unexpectedly sweet voice. She leans in slightly and sniffs the air between his shoulder and chin. "Thomas. So very nice to meet you."

"Ruby." Mrs. Topping's voice is a low rumble of warning. "Remember your manners."

"Of course," says Ruby, even as she shockingly puts a hand on Thomas's shoulder. "I will remember. It is so very, very, very nice to meet you."

Mrs. Topping gently removes her daughter's hand, and the younger wolf-woman takes a step back, looking abashed. Dare we say sheepish? It is probably not the right word, and yet there is that look in her eye. Thomas fears there is something raw and carnal in it. This creature must live in a state of nature, he thinks, and were her mother not restraining her, she might pounce upon Thomas much as that deranged clerk pounced on Mr. Philpot.

"Is everyone here . . . a relation?" Thomas asks uncertainly. He cannot begin to guess why Mrs. Topping has asked him to view this scene.

"Only Ruby," says the matron. "It happens that when a person is affected by the Peculiarities, it can spread to their family. These things appear to be attracted to blood ties, particularly those between parent and child, but it can pass between other relations as well."

"Between siblings?" Thomas asks, thinking of the leaf that he observed growing under his brother's sleeve.

"I have heard of it happening," says Mrs. Topping.

A wave of guilt washes over Thomas. He has always hated the feeling of inadequacy, the sense that he does not quite belong in his family, but until recently it has been his lot to be a harmless appendage. The thought that he could somehow be responsible for spreading his affliction to the governor of Thresher's Bank, of risking his family enterprise, is proof of his worthlessness.

"These young ones have taken shelter with us," Mrs. Topping explains. "Children, wives, anyone who is cast out for being what they are may find a home here as long as there is room. The Peculiarities disproportionately afflict the poor, who are least prepared to endure the burdens of their affliction."

Thomas does not like to think that Miss Feldstein was correct in her assertions about poverty and the Peculiarities, so he chooses not to dwell on the subject. "It is surely a blessing for those who need help, but I do not understand why you wished for me to see this."

"We are merely passing through," says Mrs. Topping. "Come with me." She leads him into a corridor and then to the kitchen. There she strikes a match and illuminates a lantern.

"It is not so very cold tonight," she says. "I trust you can endure for a few minutes without your coat."

"I can," he says, though he does not know why he should want to do so. Nor does he know why Miss Ruby Topping has followed them and is standing directly behind him. As he turns, he sees she has raised a hand, as if to touch him, but having been observed, she quickly retracts her arm.

Outside it is quite cool, but Thomas thinks he can manage better than these women, though they have the advantage of fur. They take a few steps into the small garden and stand before a tree no taller than he is. It has but two branches, though there are twigs and sprouts emerging from its trunk.

Then the tree shifts toward them, and Thomas can see that it has a head, a neck, a face. The branches are arms, raised up, and they shift slightly.

"Mr. Osgood." Mrs. Topping's voice is gentle and coaxing. "I've brought a visitor."

The face, seemingly hewn from bark, creaks slowly into an unreadable change of expression. "Oh," says the slightly perturbed voice. "How pleasant."

The face seems to be that of a stout man of middle years. The nose is long, the lips full, the chin weak, the eyebrows, though now rendered in bark, look overly bushy. The wooden eyes blink with excruciating slowness and audible clicks. They shift back and forth, but do not fix upon anything.

This is my future, Thomas thinks. He no longer feels the cold. He can sense nothing but his own doom closing in upon him.

"Mr. Osgood, I present to you Mr. Thresher," says Mrs. Topping. "He has your condition."

"Like me," says Mr. Osgood. "That is good. I congratulate you, young fellow."

"You congratulate me." Thomas's repetition of the words is not a question. He is hardly aware that he has spoken.

"No need to be alarmed. I was, but no longer. And I travel. I visit so many wonderful places." With great slowness, and the alarming creak of a branch bending in a strong wind, Mr. Osgood raises his head toward the vault of heaven. "Do you see it? Saturn. The brightest star in the sky. Only it is not a star, is it? You already knew that. You know better than anyone, I think."

Thomas feels the breath catch in his lungs. It suddenly feels very cold outside indeed.

"I wished only to let him say hello," Mrs. Topping tells the tree. "I'll leave you alone now, which I know you prefer."

"It is best," answers Mr. Osgood in a distracted tone as he continues to gaze upward. "Alone is best."

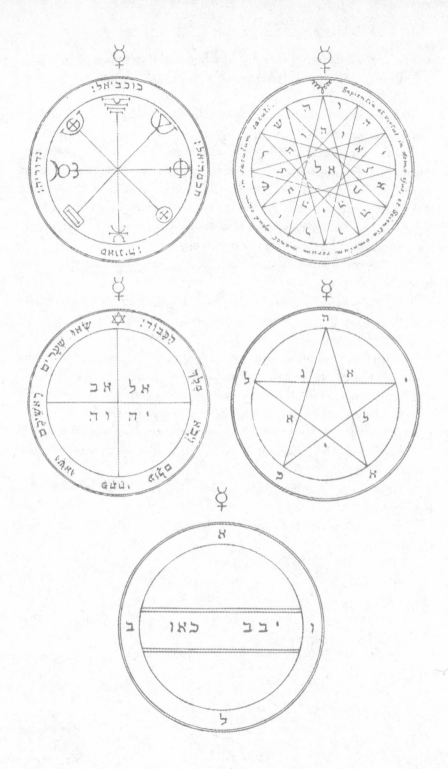

TEN

THE PRIESTESS

BACK IN THE parlor, Thomas sits near the fire that cannot warm him. He sips at his brandy and tries to form words that will not come. Ruby Topping had, at first, seated herself at his feet, letting her skirts pool around her, but her mother smiled and shook her head, and the young lady relocated to the sofa. Mr. Topping is there as well, looking as sympathetic as his hardened face will allow.

"Why did you show me that?" Thomas asks at last.

"You ought to understand what lies ahead," Mrs. Topping says. "It is called the arboreal plague, in as much as anything related to the Peculiarities has a name. There is no academic body deciding these things, so far as I am aware. There are rumors of a Special Branch of the government that is attempting to understand the Peculiarities, but that is another matter. As for this disease, you should be aware that it moves slowly, but it does progress. I suspect you have at least two years before the transformation begins to limit your ability to get about and care for yourself, though perhaps less time before you can no longer conceal its effects."

"Transformation." Thomas meant for it to be a question, but it comes out more like a dreamy statement. In response to his own dullness, he sips at his drink.

"You seem like an educated gentleman, so you might appreciate the Ovidian connotations." A weak, surprisingly human, smile shudders across her lupine mouth. The woman appears to have some trouble getting to the point. "You are becoming a tree, Mr. Thresher."

"He said he travels." Thomas is not quite sure why this seems important, but the idea nags at him.

"Not as you do," Miss Ruby Topping volunteers, sounding chipper for having something to add. "He is talking about his journeys along the astral plane, don't you know?"

"That's right, my dear," her mother says sweetly.

"Why do you wish to show me what doom awaits me?" Thomas asks. He does not want to hear any astral plane nonsense. "As you have transformed, do you take some pleasure in making others anticipate their own horrors?"

"I do believe there is hope," Mrs. Topping says, seeming not to notice Thomas's anger, "but you must take action. It can be tempting in the early days of a transformation to ignore the symptoms, to hope they will go away. It is what I did. I can offer you another option, however."

The most astonishing thing is that Thomas's glass is empty. How is he expected to listen to this babble with an empty glass? It is outrageous. Mr. Topping is no gentleman, but he evidently knows something of the terrors of an empty glass, and, with some effort, pries the vessel from Thomas's fingers. At a sideboard he refreshes the drink and returns it to its rightful owner, allowing matters to continue.

"I am turning into a tree," Thomas says. "And my brother!"

Mrs. Topping's face remains very still. At this moment she demonstrates no interest in discussing brothers. "I believe I mentioned these things often flourish in families. It is very painful to see someone struck by these alterations when they have not been exposed to the original contaminant."

"What contaminant?" Thomas demands in a tart voice. She makes it sound as though he works in a laboratory with chemicals.

"Now, that's something you don't know." Mr. Topping's sledgehammer-on-stone voice is modulated to tones of gentleness. He puts a hand on his wife's shoulder. "It's but a theory."

"I know it well enough." She turns to Thomas. "I should like to tell you some of my history, if that is agreeable to you, and then I will recommend a course of action. It is too late for me, but I believe there is still hope for you."

Thomas nods. He likes the idea of there being hope, of there being something he can do. He has been passive long enough. It's time to confront this leaf business head-on, even if it means listening to this wolf-woman talk and talk, which she appears to love doing. He will need another drink, however, and very soon. The only question remains is if he will be spared the indignity of asking for it.

Mrs. Topping recounts her story with the brevity and broad strokes of a woman who knows her audience wants only to hear what is vital. She was, along with so much of the country, caught up in the craze for mysticism that began decades back. First came spiritualism, which swept across class lines. She witnessed a few impressive things but far more dubious ones. The rare instances she believed genuine fascinated her in large part because the otherworldly voices with whom she heard mediums communicate seemed not to fit within the spiritualist's narrative. Mediums spoke of calling forth the departed, and yet the entities that communicated through the spiritualists' mouths denied being spirits of the dead. They made claims in twisted logic, referenced impossibilities, called upon alien and unknowable frames of reference. They said things that felt undeniably and obviously true yet could not be recalled moments later. Their words sounded like colors and felt like temperature or tasted of emotions.

The spiritualists, Mrs. Topping became convinced, were not speaking to the dead but rather with beings of other realms. The universe, she concluded, must be broad and deep in ways beyond ordinary human perception, and she was hungry to know more.

She began by reading the books of a Frenchman named Eliphas Levi, who had undertaken a project of compiling and organizing the hidden knowledge of the ancients in a manner accessible to ordinary readers. This was a new thing, for practitioners of the occult had always closely guarded their secrets. They transmitted their knowledge only to trusted apprentices, and what they wrote down they obscured or peppered liberally with intellectual labyrinths and blind alleys crafted to keep the uninitiated in a state of confusion. Levi, with both a keen mind and an appealing style, wanted to make knowledge of the occult available to all who had the interest and the capacity to understand.

Then came Helena Blavatsky and her Theosophy movement. Like Levi, Blavatsky claimed a desire to spread her discovery of secret knowledge to a wider world. Unlike Levi, who had written his books in the seclusion of his Paris apartment, Blavatsky enjoyed appearing before adoring crowds a little too much for Mrs. Topping's taste. There was some wisdom to be gained from her books, but it seemed as though her main interest was self-aggrandizement.

Learning what she could from these people, Mrs. Topping conducted her own researches in the reading room of the British Museum. It was there she met an enthusiast named Samuel MacGregor Mathers.

Thomas snaps to attention upon hearing the name. "I've encountered him already. Well, not him, but his name—that is, a book by him."

Mrs. Topping nods. "Yes, he was on the same quest that consumed me, though much farther along. His researches led him to a manuscript full of arcane rituals, which he found and decrypted. These formed the basis of the Hermetic Order of the Golden Dawn, which became more than a lodge for occult practices, but rather a system for acquiring scholarly and practical arcane knowledge."

Mrs. Topping joined the Golden Dawn and advanced through the ranks. There, she explains, she managed to catch glimpses of the wider universe. More than glimpses, really, for she touched other places and other beings. By means of astral projection, she separated her spiritual self from her body and visited inconceivable worlds, much as Mr. Osgood now does. She visited Venus and Mars and Saturn—though not the planets that can be seen in the night's sky. These are, she explains, realms associated with the astrological symbols of Venus and Mars and Saturn and have no connection with the planetary bodies of our physical reality.

"It was on one of these journeys that I believe I came into contact with something that caused me to change. Only years later did I understand this, did I realize that if I had—and I'm not sure how to say this—re-ordered things, I might have reversed the condition."

"What do you mean re-order?" Thomas demands.

"That I cannot tell you," she says. "Until you have gone where I have and seen what I have seen, the words do not exist. You must gain the knowledge and the frame of reference to understand. Then you must figure out from which astral realm your metamorphosis originates. Only then will you have a chance to halt, or even reverse, the transformation."

There is a great deal of information to process, presuming he can believe any of it. The words coming out of Mrs. Topping's mouth are nonsense. Occult orders and journeys to astral worlds that have the same names as planets but are not planets at all. Thomas should leave at once, but skepticism does nothing to solve the problem of the leaves growing from his body—and the knowledge of what he will become. He cannot dismiss what he has seen here tonight. The Peculiarities are far more pervasive, far more urgent, than he had previously understood.

The world itself is changing, and Thomas along with it. For once, he thinks, he is not outside of events. He is at the center of them.

"The connection of blood," Thomas repeats, his mind going to where it did so often. "You are certain I gave this condition to my brother?"

"Perhaps." Mrs. Topping looks away, as though this question causes her pain. She has passed her own lupine form on to her daughter. She turns back and takes a deep breath. "Thomas. I beg your pardon. I did not intend to address you so informally."

"It's fine, my dear," Mr. Topping tells her, taking her hand. "You can address him any way that suits you."

Thomas does not see that it is Topping's decision to make, but he is hardly about to object when this woman may possess information that could lead to his cure. Besides, what does it matter? People call each other anything they like these days—though generally not across the classes. That is a bit of a breach of decorum, but Thomas is determined not to care. He will indulge her by saying nothing, if not by granting permission. That is too much.

"No," says Mrs. Topping breathily. "No, forgive me, Mr. Thresher. Now, you must understand that some people, without knowledge or intent, travel the astral plane while they sleep. What they remember of it when they wake, they dismiss as dream. A dreamer may be exposed to the arboreal plague in this manner."

Thomas thinks of the bent, unblinking face he sees when he dreams. Does that indicate astral travel? He thinks it must. "Then that explains it. I have been having dreams, you know. I see a face. The same strange face, almost every night."

Mrs. Topping looks unconvinced. "That may be significant, but dreams in themselves do not necessarily indicate astral travel. If you were a frequent visitor of other realms, I would sense a—I'm not sure how to put this—astral residue, perhaps. To my mind, it is far more likely that you contracted the condition from this brother you mention. Either that or both of you contracted it from a parent."

Thomas shakes his head. "My mother has been dead since I was an infant, and my father half a year ago. I realize the time does not prove anything, but my father was a banker to his core. I promise you that he would have set himself aflame before taking the time to learn what you have outlined here tonight. Though I have no memory of doing any sort of astral journeying, I must conclude that I am somehow to blame."

"How curious," says Mrs. Topping, her voice heavy with melancholy. "Someone in your family is the source, and you conclude it must be you. I can only say that people are often other than how they present themselves. These relations of yours may have interests of which you are unaware."

To this, Thomas says nothing. His father was too driven by earthly concerns to consider astral travel, even in his dreams. *Where is the profit?* He could hear his father bellowing. *How does this make money?* Walter would not trouble himself to react so strongly. He would merely shake his head in disgust.

"You ain't here on a lark," pronounces Mr. Topping, brutalizing the words like they are sailors caught sleeping at their posts. "You're not wandering Bethnel Green in a fog to stretch your toddlers. You come for a reason, and that's the bank."

"John, as usual, is correct," Mrs. Topping says, squeezing her husband's hand. "Your father might have been a banker to his core, but the bank for which you work seems interested in owning the debt of practicing magicians."

Though the world is becoming an unrecognizable place, and werewolves and tree people are now real things, increasingly difficult for the public to deny, Thomas feels he must draw the line at the very notion of magic. He has seen wonderful stage performances in his time—ladies sawed in half and metal rings from which doves impossibly appear—but that is not what Mrs. Topping means. She is talking about—who knows what? Women flying upon broomsticks? Curses lobbed at a neighbor's cow? The Peculiarities, though they would have been impossible to imagine a decade earlier, are physical manifestations in the world. As the irritatingly clever Miss Feldstein observed, things that are in the natural world cannot be supernatural. Whatever the Peculiarities might be, they are nothing so absurd, so childish, as magic.

Yet, as John Topping has noted in his colorful language, it is not some random circumstance that brought Thomas to this house.

"This brother you mention," Mrs. Topping continues, her voice now as stern as a cross nanny's. "He may have some knowledge of whence your infection comes from. If that is true, it could save you weeks or months from your search."

It seems unlikely that any direct question on this subject will receive an answer. Thomas supposes there might come a time when it is worth his while to press his brother. For now, learning more about the bank's intentions could prove beneficial.

"If I join this Golden Dawn, I can be certain I will discover what I need to know?" Thomas asks.

"In the same way that if you study medicine you can be certain you will discover a cure for an illness," Mrs. Topping tells him. "There are no guarantees, but you require knowledge and tools if you are going to track your condition to its source. My astral travel theory might very well prove wrong, but the Peculiarities are magical—and I use the word as magicians use it, not as laypeople who understand nothing of magic do. If you wish to push back against what afflicts you, it stands to reason that you must know magic as it is understood by those who practice it. I do not believe, in all of human history, there has ever been a better, faster, or more efficient way to gain this knowledge than through the teachings of the Golden Dawn."

"Surely every school of occult teaching thinks it's the best," Thomas says.

"It is not as though London is bursting with occult lodges," Mrs. Topping says.

Thomas feels foolish, but how should he know if there is one or a hundred?

"There are some Masonic organizations with occult leanings," she continues—despite Thomas's demonstrable lack of interest, "and a sprinkling of Rosicrucian lodges, but the Golden Dawn is far more sophisticated. And unlike Madam Blavatsky, it claims no messianic interpreters. The Golden Dawn does not purport to offer anything new. Rather, its founders have organized compatible systems of ancient knowledge and devised a pedagogy that allows people to gain this knowledge more methodically than has been done before. Think of it as a novel method of teaching old material. If you like, I can write a letter of introduction for you."

"I am sorry," Thomas says. "The idea of magic is simply too much for me. I cannot accept such a thing is real."

"It is only because you have no idea what magic is," Mrs. Topping says. "Forget the notions from nursery stories. Magic is merely an understanding of certain aspects of the natural world that are generally unknown because they are difficult to perceive."

Thomas, who spent his time at Trinity College studying the aspects of the natural world that are difficult to perceive—that is to say, mathematics—does not much like to picture himself peering into a crystal ball while wearing a star-covered robe and pointed hat. This Golden Dawn, no matter how systematized, can hardly be for him. Whatever secrets the universe holds can be found in the movement of numbers, not in the dusty old scrolls of pagan priests or medieval alchemists. This is the modern world, and surely there are no more hidden truths but those being uncovered by science.

On the other hand, he faces the prospect of turning into a tree. He supposes being a plant would not be significantly different to being a junior clerk at Thresher's. It could hardly be more tedious, and the absence of pressure might be restful. In a way, he is sort of a vegetable already. Why should he fight it?

Nevertheless, Thomas is not quite ready to surrender to an arboreal future. He supposes it could do no harm to at least meet these Golden Dawn chaps.

He finishes his brandy and soda—his third or fourth, and so his limbs feel a little undependable—and rises to his feet almost steadily. "I must thank you, but I fear I have taken up enough of your time."

The one bright spot in his life has been Madeline Yardley. He has so looked forward to returning to her and telling her that her idea has borne fruit. Yet now that prospect makes his mouth feel dry and dusty. He hardly wishes to tell her that his next step is to join an academy for wizards. Even less, he does not wish to tell her that the only organization he can join in the future will be a grove.

Ruby is now standing in front of him, smiling slyly. The way she holds her hands, he can see she is struggling not to touch him. "I'm very strong," she says.

Thomas, for reasons he does not quite understand, blushes. "I am certain you are."

"If you go after this evil bank, and they push back," she says, "if they send toughs after you, I can help. I will fight for you, Thomas. This is our cause too."

"I shall keep that in mind," Thomas tells her, making every effort to hide his discomfort.

Ruby grabs his hand in both of hers and pulls him in so that she may press her snout to his ear. He is overwhelmed by her loamy scent, which is alarmingly unfamiliar, though not at all unpleasant.

"I can do anything you like," she says. "Anything."

Thomas backs away and forces a smile. "You are very kind."

"Mr. Thresher appreciates the offer, dear," Mrs. Topping says. "Bid him good night."

"Good night, Thomas," she says, and walks out of the room, casting one sly look over her shoulder before vanishing.

"Forgive her," Mrs. Topping explains. "She is eager to be of use, and it is hard for a young lady to be confined to a house."

"I am certain it is so." In fact, Thomas is not certain of anything at this point.

Mrs. Topping leans forward and unexpectedly presses a maternal kiss to Thomas's cheek. She smells very much like her daughter. "Ruby is quite right, you know. You're one of us now. A Bethnel Green Peculiar. We must all hang together."

"Thank you, Mrs. Topping," Thomas says, surprised that her declaration has touched him. For all his friendships and debauches, he cannot remember an instance of anyone ever being this kind to him. Not polite, but kind, radiating a concern unscripted by manners or propriety or obligation. When he was a child, his nannies would be sacked if they demonstrated too much affection.

"Mr. Topping will see you out," Mrs. Topping says. "I do not like to be too near the open door where I can be observed."

Thomas walks to the door with John Topping, who hands Thomas his coat. "I reckon you're wondering what so educated a lady sees in a moucher like myself."

Thomas, shrugging into his outerwear, has actually been wondering why a strapping cove like Mr. Topping remains devoted to a woman who looks like a beast. "I am no expert on matters of the heart," is as much as he can politely offer.

"Or maybe you wonder why I stuck around when she got all wolf-like," Mr. Topping proposes.

"Again," Thomas says, "it is not my place to ponder such things. That there is affection between you is evident. I require no explanation."

Mr. Topping nods. "Best woman I ever knowed. Didn't bother me she came with a child when I married her. Wouldn't leave her on account of the change. Truth be told, I've taken a shine to the fur. Something to hold on to. You know what I'm getting at there?" This he says with a leering grin and a few light punches to Thomas's arm.

"I celebrate your domestic happiness," Thomas offers.

"Though a tree," Mr. Topping says with a shake of his head while handing Thomas his hat. "Don't know if I could abide that."

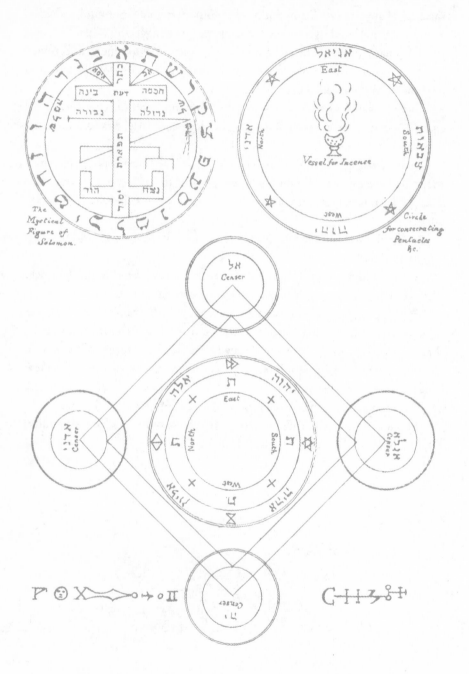

The
Mystical
Figure of
Solomon.

Circle
for consecrating
Pentacles
&c.

ELEVEN

THE MAGUS

WHEN THOMAS IMAGINES meeting the founder of the Golden Dawn, he braces himself for an effete conversation over tea regarding the astral plane and lost manuscripts of Atlantis. These magical types might be of some use to him, but he dislikes all of them before meeting any, and he has no desire to converse with a self-proclaimed wizard.

It is therefore with some relief that Thomas receives a note the following day from Judith Topping. It explains that, to accommodate the growing interest in the occult as a result of the Peculiarities, the Golden Dawn now holds open houses once a month. If Thomas will attend the one the following Sunday, he will find Mr. MacGregor Mathers expecting to exchange a few words with him.

Thomas writes at once to Mrs. Yardley to let her know that he believes he may have found some sort of connection between the bank and people interested in the occult. He hopes to learn more the following weekend. The note is brief and solicitous, very respectful, he thinks. He in no way embellishes it with flattery of her appearance or her intellect, nor does he say how much he looks forward to reporting more to her in person. She is, after all, the widow of a friend from many years previous, and he does not think it entirely proper to have amorous feelings for her. At least, he does not think it proper to demonstrate amorous feelings for her until she indicates that they are welcome.

Why a woman of a solidly genteel standing, who has sufficient means to maintain a lovely home in a respectable neighborhood, would welcome attention from a junior bank clerk is difficult to say precisely. Perhaps Mrs. Yardley believes that Thomas is an heir to an incalculable banking fortune, the sort of wealth that would lift her from respectability to opulence. It might even be that he is. Thomas has no idea what he can expect from his labors at Thresher's. He cannot guess when or if his brother will promote him or cut him off without a penny or cast him back to his life of indolence. He feels a slight twinge when he considers this last option—not of longing but of something like regret. This puzzles Thomas, as he takes no pleasure in his life as a junior clerk, and he has no realistic expectation of evolving, like some Darwinian creature, into a being akin to his brother. He is in limbo, and that is never desirable, but he sees that he was in limbo in his old life as well.

He can say nothing of his uncertain future to Mrs. Yardley. He has made no effort to deceive her about his prospects. He told her quite plainly that he was a mere drudge at Thresher's. He will have to keep an eye upon things, however. It would be exceedingly painful to have to explain that he has no money, and he would rather avoid this conversation.

Still, a meeting to report his discoveries, if not precisely recounting his visit to Mrs. Topping's house of malformations or his forthcoming exposure to the Golden Dawn, is something to which he might look forward. It makes the following week all the more bearable. Every morning Thomas awakens at six to check himself for leaves (which, more often than not, manifest while he sleeps), wash, dress, and eat a large breakfast. This, at least, his brother provides, though it is done without any hint of good humor. Thomas pours himself coffee and then visits the sideboard to take his fill of eggs, bacon, sausage, grilled tomatoes, deviled kidneys, and bread still warm from the oven. Usually Walter, already finished eating, remains at the table, reading his newspaper with great seriousness. Occasionally he will glance up, distressed by the thunderous collision of Thomas's knife and fork or the jarring din of a coffee cup crashing home to its saucer. On those occasions when Walter departs the table first, he does so without a word. He takes his newspapers with him, lest Thomas be tempted to linger or enjoy what has been paid for with another man's coin.

A coachman takes Walter to the bank every morning. Upon beginning his employment, Thomas assumed he would ride with his brother, but in that he was mistaken. "It would be improper for you to be seen riding with the bank's governor," Walter explained.

Thomas takes an omnibus to the city. He squeezes into the gloomy box, stinking of the proximate bodies, and jounces unhappily for the near hour it takes him to reach his destination.

These morning rituals Thomas usually endures with all the optimism of a prisoner awaiting execution, but now there is something to which he might look with some anticipation. It makes the copying, the adding, the filing feel like something he might somehow survive.

When he reaches his desk, he finds that there is a new junior clerk, hired evidently to replace Roberts. "Thresher!" says the new fellow, a genial, brown-haired man in his early thirties with a neatly trimmed mustache. He is named Bradford Drummond. "Thresher and Drummond! I say, we make a capital pair! Shall we get a drink after the day is through?"

Thomas smiles and says he has an engagement, which is certainly not the case. He does wonder, however, that the only other junior clerk who'd made an effort to befriend him should be replaced by a fellow with the same inclination. The universe was once a place where such things could be dismissed as meaningless coincidence, but that may no longer be the case.

On Sunday afternoon, Thomas dons a jauntily cut brown woolen suit and vest and steps away from his brother's house to enjoy a surprisingly pleasant autumn afternoon. The streets are less crowded on Sundays, and Thomas speculates it will only take him an hour or so to reach Hammersmith.

Realizing he is making good time, perhaps too good, he stops at a Crowley's Ale House—an eatery with branches scattered about London—for a ham sandwich and a beer. Perhaps he is merely delaying. It is a strange thing for him to go, alone as he is, into the unknown. He has never been bold in that way, yet he knows he will not turn around.

He finds that the counterman has overcharged him by ten pence, an insignificant sum, perhaps, but one that must add up over time. It seems unlikely the man could make an error about an accounting he must do hundreds of times per day, and when Thomas notes the mistake, the fellow has the good grace to blush and produce the correct change with an apology.

As Thomas finishes his sandwich, he decides that visiting the Golden Dawn alone will not be so bad. He went to Mrs. Yardley's alone. Even more impressive, he thinks, was his visit to Mrs. Topping's house in fog-laden Bethnel Green. Sharing a glass of punch with a pack of crystal-gazers should be nothing by comparison.

When he reaches his destination, Thomas is surprised to see what appears to be an ordinary-looking brick building of some four or five stories upon a suburban market street. There are no statues of ancient gods framing the door nor mystic runes upon the outer walls. Thomas is ushered within by a polite and inconspicuously dressed doorman who inquires if he is there for the open house. He is then directed up a flight of stairs.

What Thomas finds seems more like a club than a magical society. Men and women mill about with drinks in their hands. Some sit on chairs or sofas in deep conversations. Some stand and laugh and gossip. No one is chanting in ancient tongues or attempting to levitate tables.

Thomas searches the room trying to find someone who might give him either introductions or a drink. When he turns around, he finds both. A rugged-looking mustachioed fellow, perhaps forty years old, thrusts a glass of champagne into his hand.

"You must be Thresher," he says.

Thomas's eyes go wide. Surely this is no more than a clever trick. "How did you know?"

"Lucky guess, let's say. Ha ha! I'm Samuel MacGregor Mathers." He offers his hand like the thrust of a bayonet.

"The very fellow Mrs. Topping wanted me to meet." Once released of the man's iron grip, Thomas sips at his champagne, grateful to have met his contact so soon. He can be gone from this place all the quicker.

"I am he," says MacGregor Mathers. "How's the old girl doing? Shaggy as ever?"

"I dare say rather shaggy," Thomas agrees. "The daughter too."

"Shame when it affects the children. Still so much we don't know. Judy tells me you are considering initiation into the order?"

"I have questions, personal questions, and Mrs. Topping seems to think that the Golden Dawn can help me find answers."

"We all have questions, Mr. Thresher," MacGregor Mathers announces in the good-natured bluster of a colonial viceroy surveying his domain. "What is the soul? Can I meet God—or the gods? Can I become a god? It's the nature of mankind to question, and in these times, when the very fabric of the universe appears to be undergoing a transformation, well, let's just say our membership applications have swollen. You needn't fear, of course. A recommendation from Judy is all I want. We've opened new temples across the city and we're still turning people away, but the cream of the crop land here at Isis-Urania. Shall I introduce you around?"

MacGregor Mathers begins to move about the room, not so much introducing Thomas as casting names at him. Florence Farr, Maud Gonne, Arthur Machen—Thomas can hardly keep up. He hurriedly shakes hands with an Irish writer named Bram Stoker, and across the room Thomas spots another

Irishman, William Yeats, but decides not to mention that they have met.

"A poet," MacGregor Mathers explains.

"You seem to have quite a few literary men among your numbers," Thomas observes.

"The excess of imagination," MacGregor Mathers says like an entomologist showing off a strangely adaptive limb on a specimen. "The same fanciful mind that can spin words into substance can coax meaning out of the hidden mysteries of the cosmos. You recognize that fellow over there? Artie Doyle. He writes the Sherlock Holmes stories. Joined almost a year ago. Ah, and speaking of scribblers, here's a fellow I'd like you to meet. Come say hello, Crowley."

MacGregor Mathers waves over a tall, wild-haired man of about Thomas's age, dressed rather artily, Thomas thinks, in a thick sweater rather than a coat. He grins at MacGregor Mathers and steps forward.

"This is *Frater Perdurabo*—his magical name, you know. Thomas Thresher, meet Aleister Crowley. He's a crack poet and something of my apprentice, if I may so flatter myself."

"I should hope so," Crowley says with apparent cheer, though it's unclear if he is confirming the apprenticeship or the flattery.

"He's the most dedicated young man we've got," MacGregor Mathers says, "and he can answer any questions you might have. Thought you'd rather hear it from a chap of your own age than the old man. Ha ha!"

MacGregor Mathers walks off, and Thomas immediately looks over to Crowley for signs he resented being saddled with a stranger, but the young magician seems perfectly amiable.

"Thresher," Crowley says with a grin. "I've cashed checks from the bank."

"I ate at a Crowley's this very afternoon," Thomas says somewhat defensively, though he chooses not to mention the incident with incorrect change.

Crowley laughs, apparently unaware of having given or received insult. "My uncle's business, as it happens. Well, what's your interest in the Golden Dawn? This is serious stuff—not for the casual seeker or for the fellow looking to put a spell on his girl to get her to spread her legs. It requires real effort, Thresher, but if you put the time in, you'll be astonished what you get out of it."

Thomas has been exposed to the word magic from the cradle. The stories his nannies read to him were laced with the stuff, and then there were the wonder workers who could be seen at carnivals and taverns and occasionally a friend's birthday party—certainly not his own. In recent years, with the rise of the Peculiarities, talk of magic has been everywhere, but Thomas realizes he hasn't the vaguest notion of what magic actually is. He is a man of logic, a man who wants to know how things work and why. The idea of speaking a few words and waving a wand in such a way that the laws of reality are suspended, it hardly rings true for him.

Now here is this sturdy young man, bluff and dominating, who asserts that magic is a real thing and he knows precisely what it is. Thomas is intrigued.

"And what would I get out of it?"

"True knowledge," Crowley says. "And true power."

Thomas makes every effort not to show any sign of skepticism, but he imagines a berobed actor on a stage, hands outstretched, calling out laughable incantations in execrable Latin. "What sort of power?"

"To transform frogs into mighty warriors who will fight to the death for you," Crowley says with a laugh. "I can see what you're thinking, but it is nothing like that. I speak of power to take command of your life. Power to make the world bow before you. I go where I want and do what I please, and no one bars my way. If I want a thing, it's mine. If I desire a woman, she gives herself to me. Money? I have all I could wish for. Influence? I am already on my way to being regarded as the greatest poet, the greatest mountaineer, and the greatest occultist of this age. *That* is power."

Thomas isn't certain what to make of all this. This fellow with his uncombed hair suffers from no lack of confidence, but does he truly stride upon the earth like a colossus, crooking his finger at any woman who catches his fancy?

"And could you make yourself king if you chose?" Thomas asks somewhat cheekily.

Crowley takes the question seriously. "Likely not. You cannot use magic to do things that cannot be done. There's no transforming frogs into warriors because frogs don't turn into warriors. I have no connection to the royal family, so magic alone would not allow me to become king. Can I use it to become the most consequential man of our time? Yes, but only because I am inclined to be consequential. An ordinary man could not hope for so much."

Thomas ought to find this sort of boasting distasteful or tedious, but there is something amiable in Crowley's confidence. "What if I am looking for answers to specific questions? Let us say I want to discover someone's motivation for a particular act or a—an original cause of a chain of events? Could magic help with such things?"

"Nothing is hidden from the universe," Crowley assures him. "Any truth can be learned."

"And the other people in this group?" Thomas asks. "What are they like?"

"As you'd expect," Crowley says, with some disappointment. "MacGregor Mather's a capital chap, and a crack scholar of magic. The rest are mostly an earnest lot. Some are mere tourists, here for the thrill of touching the unknown, but without the will or the intellect to become true magicians. I don't think I have much of a problem with anyone here except maybe him." With a flick of his finger, Crowley gestures toward the Irishman, Yeats.

"I met him briefly," Thomas says. "A little serious, but otherwise I took no objection."

"*Frater Demon est Deus Inversus.*" Crowley smirks. "A third-rate poet. I find his jealousy of my work trying. It saps the energy out of a fellow. You're not a poet, are you?"

"No, I am much better with numbers than with words."

"Splendid," Crowley says, perhaps not sensing, or perhaps sensing very well, that Thomas hadn't quite finished. "We want no more poets here. What we want are dedicated chaps and perhaps a few more good-looking women. I'd not complain if that one chose to join."

Thomas follows another flick of the hand and finds himself quickly sputtering on a mouthful of champagne. The woman Crowley has gestured toward is Esther Feldstein.

⊷⇒ TWELVE ⇐⊷
THE ROOT OF THE POWERS OF EARTH

"**H**ER?" THOMAS NEARLY chokes on his drink.

"I haven't spoken to her yet," Crowley says. "But these gatherings are a jolly good way to meet women. There's a type, you know. She's looking for something, and it's easy to entice her into a different sort of novel experience than the one she thinks she's seeking."

"But surely not her!" Thomas sputters.

Crowley is clearly amused. "Do you have a connection with that creature?"

"I have met her," he offers, but that sounds rather vague. "My brother does business with her father."

"Ah," says Crowley. "You won't mind if I fuck her, will you?"

Crowley evidently believes he can have Miss Feldstein in the same way an ordinary man believes he can have a pint of lager when he calls for one. Should Thomas be disgusted? Impressed? Skeptical? He compromises by feeling all three at once.

"I can't imagine it's my concern," Thomas finally tells Crowley.

The big man laughs and claps Thomas on the shoulder. "I like the exotic ones—the Jews and Orientals and Africans. There's a bit of spice in a dark nipple."

Thomas blinks rapidly, feeling like the flutter of his eyelids represents a question unasked or a comment unspoken. He finally settles on something like what he wishes to ask. "This ability with women? Does it come from what you've learned at the Golden Dawn?"

"Yes and no," Crowley says with the philosophical air of a man who has given the subject much thought. "I was fending off pretty servants by the time I was thirteen. It's my will, you see. It has an effect on other people, but will is also what allows a man to rise above the common sort in magic. Most people here make the mistake of thinking it's intellect, which is necessary, but not sufficient. The number of things you must learn, the complex principles to be understood, eliminate the common sort of thinkers, but even the cleverest initiate fails if he lacks the will to break through the barriers of perception. That's why most of our members never do more than learn the basic concepts of magic."

Thomas wonders if he has the stuff to succeed in the Golden Dawn. He knows himself to be intellectually capable when it comes to mathematics, but perhaps it was a lack of will that left him a mere component part in a group of friends. With a stronger will, he might have been more than a forgotten appendage in his family. He might have shouldered his way into a consequential position in the bank.

Yet there was another time, was there not? Back in the Bobby Yardley days, when he'd been a leader of other boys and a champion for the downtrodden. That was a long time ago, and it feels like another life, but he *had* been assertive. He had forged his own path, and other boys followed. It was his life, he tells himself, and there is no reason it cannot be again. The appearance of Mrs. Yardley might be a sort of sign, one pointing to his better self.

Esther Feldstein appears to have caught sight of Thomas. He would have expected her to turn sharply, pretending not to see him, and vanish into the crowd, but instead she offers a crooked smile and makes her way toward him.

"Good afternoon." Thomas decides he wants to play the gentleman. "Miss Esther Feldstein, may I present Mr. Aleister Crowley."

The two shake hands, and Crowley meets Miss Feldstein's eyes for a long and, Thomas thinks, incendiary moment. Then he glances away, and it is like a candle has been snuffed. "Always a pleasure to meet a beautiful woman with an interest in secret knowledge."

Miss Feldstein smiles mechanically, suggesting that she is not instantly charmed by Crowley. Thomas finds he likes her very much for that.

He expects the magician to press his case with Miss Feldstein, but Crowley takes notice of some older gentlemen beckoning him from across the room. "A pleasure to meet you, Miss Feldstein," he says, lured perhaps by magical goals that supersede his amorous ones. Perhaps he does not feel he has to stay when he can summon Esther Feldstein any time he likes with a wave of his wand. "And Thresher, if I can be of any service, do let me know."

He then walks off, leaving Thomas with Miss Feldstein, entirely uncertain how to feel about being alone with one another.

"Well," Thomas says after a moment, "you did indicate an interest in the Peculiarities."

She raises her eyebrows lightly. "And you, pointedly, did not."

"Are you demanding an explanation?" Thomas asks.

Miss Feldstein looks rather taken aback, as though Thomas has insulted her. "You owe me nothing of the kind. As someone long fascinated by the changes happening in the city, I was merely curious what changed your mind."

Thomas feels his face redden with shame. He has insulted this woman and for no good reason. "I beg your pardon. I was rude. I suppose I am somewhat ambivalent about being here."

She smiles quite openly at this. "Believe me, Mr. Thresher, I know what it is to have interests the world says you should not. You needn't explain anything to me."

Thomas is not prepared to speak to her about the inner workings of Thresher's Bank. Her father has something Walter wants, and who knows what could give that old fellow some secret advantage. He does not want to trip up his brother, but more importantly, he would not want to do anything that might harm the bank. It is better to remain vague.

"I witnessed some things for which there can be no rational explanation," Thomas offers. "There was an incident at the bank." He reddens again. The attack upon Mr. Philpot is not something he can speak of to a lady. "Well, several things, really. After making inquiries, a person of admittedly little acquaintance offered to introduce me to MacGregor Mathers. Once I agreed to that, and received the invitation to this function, I could hardly refuse."

Miss Feldstein is polite enough to step gingerly around the elisions in his story. "Do you think you will join?"

"I'm not sure I believe all of this is right for me," he says. "And yet, what they offer is tempting."

"Power?" she asks, arching one of her impossibly thick eyebrows.

"Knowledge. It is hard to enumerate all the ways in which the world is changing. Science has discovered and created so much. And now here are the Peculiarities, which suggest there is so much more to the universe that science can't explain. If these Golden Dawn chaps could put me in a position to better understand this new landscape, to help me make sense of all the things I see and read of—well, that would be something."

Miss Feldstein smiles. "That is how I feel precisely. My father rails against me for my interests, but all he cares about is what is directly in front of his face. I want to understand what is happening all around us, and I don't see how that is wrong."

She grows rather passionate as she speaks. Her harsh features soften, and she comes into her stubbornly un-English face. Thomas feels as though he is witnessing an entirely new kind of beauty, and it is for him alone to appreciate. He knows that's nonsense, as Crowley was admiring her only moments before, but it is that the sensation is novel for him he finds exciting. This, it seems to him, is what the Golden Dawn has to offer—a fresh perspective, a new light upon what is hidden but simultaneously right in front of him. In that moment he knows he will apply to become an initiate of the Golden Dawn.

It is also the moment the screaming begins.

Women shriek in terror. Men also shriek. People attempt to move one way and then the other, shifting back and forth like automata caught in a stuttering loop. Champagne bottles crash to the floor and glasses crunch under the press of feet. A fat woman shoves Esther Feldstein out of the way, and Thomas watches in horror as she falls beneath the fast-moving current of legs.

Things seem to slow down as Esther raises her arms to protect her face while more people trample past the young lady, hardly caring if they stomp on her along the way.

Seeing a man about to plant a foot on her torso, Thomas casts him hard to one side. It causes a domino effect, and three or four other people go down, no doubt to be trampled on themselves. That is not Thomas's problem, however. He doesn't know them, and they are behaving like beasts.

He takes Miss Feldstein by the elbow, enduring a few glancing blows in the process, and hauls her to her feet. She looks pale, and her limbs tremble, but she shows no sign of injury.

It is time to find a way out. This is not an insightful conclusion, but it's the best Thomas can do. Unfortunately, he can discern no means of escape. A terrified crowd is attempting to push its way up the stairs, colliding with an equally determined group who want to descend. Thomas and Miss Feldstein are certainly trapped and have no choice but to face whatever may be causing this panic.

The lady clings to his arm in a way he finds distinctly gratifying, even under these harrowing circumstances. It is a pleasure to be depended upon for something other than scribbling down numbers or, in his previous life, a willingness to pay the bill in an alehouse. Miss Feldstein's hair has become disordered, but the effect is more determination than fear. She grips his elbow as if to say that it is the two of them against the world. There is something wild and feverish there, and some distant part of his mind, the part not actively thinking about escape, stamps this notion into his memory.

Thomas sees the writer, Arthur Conan Doyle, crouching between a tall case clock and a statue of the god Pan. He gives every appearance of a man trying to make himself small.

"Doyle!" Thomas snaps, as though he has known the man for years and has become accustomed to treating him as a subordinate. "What the devil is going on?"

Thomas's tone of voice has the desired effect. Doyle doesn't notice that he is being addressed by a much younger man he's never previously set eyes on. "The Elegants," he says, his voice little better than a whimper. "They're here."

"Nonsense." From what Thomas has read in the papers, the Elegants have never been seen outside of East London, and there only at night and when a Peculiar fog engulfs the streets. That they would be in Hammersmith in broad daylight is impossible. Doyle might as well have said a unicorn is below gouging people with its horn.

"We know nothing about them," observes Miss Feldstein, whose mind has been racing along similar lines. "We can't assume we know the rules. We only know what we've observed."

It's true enough, and certainly less important than getting away. Surveying the room, Thomas looks for an unconventional exit. There are windows, but this gathering is two flights up, and it seems unlikely he could jump to his safety, let alone bring Miss Feldstein along.

Thomas thinks back to the invasion of fog at the bank. It was a supernatural force, but working with the other clerks, they managed to send it packing. If the Elegants truly are here, there are only two of them. Surely dozens of people are enough to keep them from doing harm.

"Listen to me," Thomas shouts, waving the arm unencumbered by Miss Feldstein. "We must work together. If we do so, we can beat back whatever it is that assails us."

"And who the devil are you?" demands the crouching Arthur Conan Doyle.

"I have some experience," he says. "I have faced Peculiar incursions at Thresher's Bank."

"A banker," scoffs the great writer. "I'll not put my life in a banker's hands."

"Thresher's right," shouts MacGregor Mathers, who has emerged from somewhere, with Crowley at his side. "Working together is the answer." MacGregor Mathers is now, for some reason, wearing kilt and a fur cloak and a ridiculous form-fitting cap. He looks like a Scottish highlander prepared for battle. Indeed, he cradles a large collection of swords in his arms.

"Are those the ceremonial swords?" someone demands.

Crowley nods. "Most of them are dull, but they're the only weapons we could find."

"They'll need to be re-consecrated!" Arthur Conan Doyle objects from his crouch.

No one replies to this. Crowley begins taking swords from MacGregor Mathers and handing them to any able-bodied men who appear willing to wield one. Thomas steps forward and grabs a sword by the hilt. It is heavy, and if it has no edge to it, as they say, then at least it will make an effective club.

"What exactly is happening down there?" he asks.

"Hell is happening," Crowley says, his face shining with wonder.

Thomas wonders if, like MacGregor Mathers and his ridiculous change of costume, Crowley sees himself as the hero on a great adventure.

There is a sound that comes from downstairs, a hiss that makes Thomas's molars vibrate. At once, all the men brazenly holding dull swords take a step back. Everyone moves away from the staircase when two figures appear at the top. They have not climbed the steps. They are simply there. It is a kind of shifting, much like a magic lantern show in which the images progress and a group of picnickers flicker from standing to sitting to holding chicken pieces in their hands. A space is empty, and then two well-dressed figures stand, surveying the room.

Thomas knows them. He passed them in fog-shrouded Bethnel Green, but in this well-lit room, they still bring a haze with them. Even so, he thinks he can see them better. They are gaunt and pale, their features suggesting the skeletal, though they have atrophied noses and lips and there are eyes, however sunken. The skin is stretched impossibly tight over their features and looks ready to snap, to let something spring free. Indeed, something seems to press beneath the skin, like fingers clawing at an imprisoning membrane. It is terrifying and nauseating, and Thomas looks away to keep himself from vomiting.

There is something familiar about them too, though Thomas cannot at first put his finger on it. Perhaps it is that he has seen them before, read descriptions, looked at illustrations based on the accounts of eyewitnesses. But no, that it is not it. There is something about them that reminds him of the face in his dreams. That face does not look like these faces, and they lack the same crooked, jointed quality, but even so. It is like meeting someone related to a person whose face he knows intimately.

The Elegants wear the finest of clothes, but they are years out of date—from the '80s or even '70s. There is something comical about this, Thomas thinks rather hysterically. If they were dressed as Restoration courtiers it would somehow make more sense than their being twenty years behind the times, as though they were hard up for money.

The creatures make a show of looking about, their heads turning slowly one way and then the other, not quite in sync, not quite independently of one another. Then there is another blink of the slide show and they are farther inside the room. Their gazes wander until they fix, at the same precise moment, at someone in particular.

They are looking at Thomas. They peer at him as though they find him both wondrous and alien. It is how a scientist might peer at a curious sample in a microscope. The Elegants are intrigued.

To his shame, Thomas takes a step back, but then steadies himself. He raises his sword, clutched in both hands. As it happens, Thomas has absolutely no idea how to use a sword, but he stands ready to swing and bash as best he can. He believes brute force will do the job as well—or as poorly—as finesse.

Meanwhile, MacGregor Mathers and some of the other Golden Dawn members, women and men, are standing with books open. Looking like a choir with their hymnals, the magicians chant something that sounds suspiciously like Hebrew. Thomas risks a glance at Miss Feldstein who raises a heavy eyebrow to suggest she has no idea what they are doing, either.

The creatures take note. There is another incongruous slide-show shift, and they are now facing the chanting occultists. Arthur Conan Doyle, perhaps the only person in the room not utterly entranced by these events, sees his opportunity and dashes for the exit. There are some fifteen feet between the writer and the top of the staircase, and he plunges forward as best he can, shoving aside the horrified and the shocked and the stupefied obstacles in his way. He keeps his head down and one arm forward, like a rugby player, and it seems to Thomas that he is going to make a path for himself.

Thomas considers his options. Is it possible he could grab Miss Feldstein by the hand and follow the writer? For reasons he cannot explain, he doesn't wish to leave. He wants to see what will happen, but he does not trust these feelings. Is it like drawn to like? Does he, a creature of the Peculiarities, share an affinity with other beings of his kind? He remembers seeing these monstrosities—or, he supposes, others very much like them—on the street, and, now that he considers it, there was something knowing about the way they gazed upon him.

He must do what will best protect Miss Feldstein. He never asked for a connection to her, but his brother has caused there to be one, and he will not consider leaving her behind. Life so infrequently hands him a right thing to do, and he doesn't wish to make a hash of it now that there's one directly before him.

He turns toward her, hand out, ready to make his move without taking the time to explain it, when the slide changes again, and the Elegants are now directly in front of Doyle. The female's arm is back, and then her hand slashes forward like a blade. Her long fingernails glide effortlessly through the flesh of Doyle's throat. There is a flash of red mist in the air. Blood spatters the banister, the wallpaper, the bystanders, but somehow entirely misses the two monsters directly in front of the victim. The writer collapses in a convulsing, frothing tumble.

Dead. Or perhaps irreversibly dying. Thomas realizes that his mind is not processing this properly. These creatures have just killed the most famous person in the room. Surely none of them are safe. It is even more urgent that he get Miss Feldstein out of there, and yet he cannot imagine how he could do so without subjecting the both of them to a horrible end. Also, he is now gripping the sword in one hand and holding hers with the other. This accomplishes nothing now that he is no longer planning on fleeing, but there is no polite way to disengage.

He lets go of her when there is another change of slides, and the Elegants are now standing in front of him. The male leans forward gently and gives Thomas a tentative sniff as though checking for freshness. Its lipless mouth pulls back in a horrible grin showing black gums full of tiny white worms that wriggle and crawl. On his cheek, Thomas sees the clear imprint of a tiny hand—all five fingers and the palm—pressing out against the flesh.

With a sudden realization, like dark curtains being torn open, Thomas thinks all of this has been for him. They are not here for the Golden Dawn magicians or the celebrated writer. They have come for their fellow Peculiar.

The male Elegant raises his arm, and Thomas understands that it is time for his own throat to be opened. A kind of calm comes over him. If this is his end, then so be it.

But no, they are not looking at him, but at Esther Feldstein. He sees it in her eyes. She knows it too. They mean to strike out at her. To kill her. In his surrender, Thomas's sword had already begun to slip from his hand. Now he tightens his grip around the falling weapon and grabs the blade, not the handle. It is dull, though not as dull as advertised, and he feels the bloom of pain as it slices into his palm, yet he manages to take hold of the hilt. It is slick with his blood, but he has it firmly in hand.

The Elegants stumble as though they missed a step in the darkness. The female staggers backward. The male stutters in and out of existence. Then he is solid once more and raising an arm. They are looking at him, now. Miss Feldstein has been forgotten. The Elegants are like dogs, provoked by an injury to forget who is an enemy and who is a friend.

There is a flash of light and pain, and Thomas is several feet away from the Elegants. He is slumping down, and he somehow knows one of the creatures has struck him with astonishing strength. His face is numb, but there is a vague prickling that portends pain. The back of the head feels dull and wet. Miss Feldstein stands nearby, her hand over her mouth. Thomas suspects she has let out a little scream, though he can't recall hearing it. It's only a feeling. Much like his legs giving out under him are just a feeling.

With the Elegants well away from the staircase, people are now beginning to flee. The monsters ignore them. Miss Feldstein has been forgotten, and they hover over Thomas tentatively, like they have encountered something entirely outside their experience.

There is a break in continuity. Not like a change of the slides, Thomas thinks, but more like he blacked out for a bit. It could be no more than a few seconds, because very little has changed. The major addition to the scene is Aleister Crowley, wearing a black robe with silver trim that can only be described as ceremonial. He is also holding a cup in one hand, a dagger in the other. Both appear to be made of silver.

Crowley holds the dagger sideways, at about chest height, while the cup is thrust forward, as though that's the thing the Elegants ought to fear. He is chanting something, and this also sounds like Hebrew. Is this a magical lodge or a synagogue?

The words command the Elegants's attention, however. They turn away from Thomas and toward Crowley. He continues to chant and wave the cup at them, and the Elegants step back. Thomas thinks maybe he will be all right. Maybe he is strong enough to help Crowley. Then he loses consciousness.

THIRTEEN
TRUCE

WHEN THOMAS WAKES, he concludes he has not died of his injuries, and he finds he is relieved. It was not so long ago that he considered—no, let us say "toyed with"—the idea of ending his own life. Since that time, life has become much too eventful for him to consider bringing it to a close.

He reaches up and touches his head, finding it encased in a bandage. There is no bandage on his hand, though there is a thick scab. Clearly the cut on his palm was not as bad as he feared.

Next, he quickly runs his hands along his arms and torso, his legs and his back as best he can, looking for leaves that may have sprouted up while he has been unconscious. He sees no sign of new growths, which suggests he has not been insensible for so very long.

Time has a stretched-out feeling, though. Thomas feels like he has been dreaming endlessly, exhaustively, though he cannot remember any details. Except, of course, the face. There is always the face, peering at him, tilting this way and that, much like the Elegants at the Golden Dawn temple. It seemed to find him somehow inexplicable. Thomas feels the same way.

He rings the bell on his bed table, and a moment later one of Pearl's maids appears. He does not recall the girl's name—not because he cannot be bothered to learn the names of servants, but because he has never before interacted with her. This may be for the best, as the woman peers at Thomas with a mixture of shyness and revulsion.

"That bad?" he asks her.

"No, Mr. Thresher," she says, glancing away. "Only a bit of bruising. And the bandage." She makes a wrapping gesture around her own head should Thomas have no idea what the word bandage means and where it might have been applied.

"How long have I been here?" he asks.

"Since yesterday afternoon," she says. Thomas looks for his watch but does not see it. Still, he can tell from the light peering in through the curtains that it is morning, probably late morning. He has already missed a day of work, a realization that fills him with childish glee.

Then he remembers that poor fellow Doyle, cut down by the Elegants. Was anyone else hurt? Killed? He thinks of Miss Feldstein with considerable alarm. He had appointed himself her protector, and the thought that his injuries may have endangered her is a difficult one to endure.

He cannot ask this servant. Instead, he says, "I presume my brother brought in a doctor."

She nods. "Mr. Thresher asked me to convey, should you wake, that waking is a good sign. It means the injury likely won't kill you."

"You are certainly full of encouraging news," he tells her. "Any other medical pronouncements?"

She has shifted from one foot to the other long enough, and now busies herself with some needless straightening of picture frames. "Rest. Broth if you've a mind to eat."

"Food would be most welcome." He is suddenly aware that he is rather hungry. "Is my brother in? Please send him up."

The girl looks at him as though he's mad for suggesting she tell Mr. Thresher to do anything. "He is not at home." She is already hurrying out of the room. By the time she returns with a silver tray, on which sits a hearty bowl of beef broth, Thomas has used the necessary and dressed. He does not like the idea of lying about all day in his nightshirt. He has gazed at himself in the mirror, and he is not a pretty slight. The left side of his face is purpled with bruises, and the bandage around his head is stained brown with dried blood. Inside his skull, a regular beat pounds incessantly, but all things considered, he doesn't feel entirely wretched.

Despite being dressed, Thomas dozes off again soon after eating. He awakens in the dark to a loud banging sound. The origin of the noise is Walter storming into his room, very possibly after hurling the entirety of his weight against the door.

"Awake, are you?" he asks, and it sounds like an accusation. A servant scurries ahead of him, lighting the lamps so that Thomas can see that his brother's face is florid with anger.

"I was," Thomas says. "And now I am again."

"I hope you're pleased with yourself." He tosses a newspaper onto the bed.

It is folded open to the interior, and it takes Thomas's eyes a moment to register the words and the images, but at last he can see the cause of his brother's anger. There is a picture of him, of Thomas, right there on the page. He is lying on the floor in the Golden Dawn temple, and his head lying in a dark pool of what is certainly his own blood. A quick scan of the article mentions only his injury and Arthur Conan Doyle's death. He hopes he can conclude from this that neither Crowley nor Miss Feldstein were harmed.

"For the whole world to see," cries Walter. "This notorious writer murdered, you knocked senseless, fortune-tellers and make-believe conjurers. This is an embarrassment to the bank."

Knowing he is unlikely to succeed at containing his sarcasm, Thomas opts not to make the attempt. "In the future, I shall make every effort to limit my exposure to murder."

"Don't play the fool with me." Walter is not shouting, but it is a near thing. His face purples considerably as he paces alongside Thomas's bed. He gazes at the windows, the walls, the floor—at anything other than the injured man before him. "I've given you every opportunity, and you've squandered them all. I reach out a helping hand, and you slap it away."

Thomas can recall no opportunities squandered nor hands slapped. Since accepting his change of life, he has arrived at his desk early, remained until the appointed time, and in between labored at his work as diligently as he has been able. He has considered it all wasted time, but he has done it. He has heard the whispers of Walter ruining the bank, and he has held his tongue. Thomas thinks he has been rather cooperative under the circumstances.

He takes a deep breath. "If you want to know the truth, when I lived a life of leisure, I always felt like I was cheating. You may recall that there was a time I thought to study mathematics, but Father never encouraged that, and I ended up associating with some unambitious sorts. I—I don't even know how, precisely, but I always had the odd feeling that Father wanted it that way. My point is that though I cannot say I enjoy the work of a junior clerk, I take pride that I am contributing to Thresher's. I feel that there's more I could be doing to help the bank, but I hope you can see that I am trying my best."

"Hang your best," snaps Walter. "No one cares to hear about the years you wasted in drunken degeneracy. And spare me your boasts. I dare say a monkey could be trained to handily complete the tasks that tax you. I am talking about what matters. You are to marry Esther Feldstein."

"Then you know she is unharmed?" Thomas asks eagerly.

"I don't expect you to marry a corpse," Walter spits out. "Of course she's unharmed."

That is a great relief, at least. Thomas is pleased to learn she emerged from the Golden Dawn temple in better shape than he. That does not, however, mean he wishes to make her his wife. "Honestly, I cannot see why whom I marry is of such import to you."

"I don't require you to see!" shouts Walter with the fury of a man whose patience has been tested beyond endurance. "I require you to obey!"

Something hangs in the air. Perhaps it is the absence of Walter's bellowing. Thomas struggles for something to say, and he considers that, after the events at the Golden Dawn temple, he imagines Esther Feldstein very differently. It is still impossible to consider life married to a Jewess or to accept an arrangement that links him to that horrid father, but the woman herself intrigues him. On the other hand, Aleister Crowley also intrigues him, and Thomas is as likely to marry the one as the other.

To refuse directly will only further sour things with his brother. Perhaps that doesn't matter, but something else does. Thomas has been picking at Mrs. Yardley's words, her articulation of the very thing that most troubles him, that he has no purpose. He would very much like one, and if Walter will not hand it to him, he must attempt to take it for himself.

There is no reason Walter would hand him the opportunity he seeks since what Thomas wants, he realizes, is to learn whether or not the bank is in good hands. He realizes that it is precisely what he most desires. This is an institution founded by his grandfather. It blossomed under his father. Now, in Walter's hands, it shows every sign of faltering. Thomas knows numbers, but he does not know banking. He has no idea if Walter is mishandling things, but he has wondered if his steady, competent, efficient brother is behaving irrationally.

Family is what matters. Thomas has always thought this to be true, even if he was made to feel that he didn't precisely matter to his family. When he thinks of the importance of family, he does not mean one's warmth toward one's brother and father, but family in the larger sense, the continuity of it all, the line that reaches down from a benevolent grandfather. When one faces life as a tree, it puts things in perspective, and Thomas sees that Thresher's Bank *is* his family. It is, at least, the embodiment of it, a symbol of health and success and, yes, growth. Thomas must know for certain that Thresher's is in good hands.

If it is not, he must do something about it. Doing so shall be his purpose.

That and finding a way not to become a tree.

Thomas turns to his brother and offers his most ingratiating smile. In the past it has melted the hearts of simple country girls, convinced policemen not to trouble themselves with the antics of young men, reminded innkeepers that there may, indeed, be one more room available, even for a group of disruptive young men. He knows it will do no good with Walter but hope springs eternal.

With his smile shining more radiantly than the sun, he begins to articulate his proposition. "I shall be happy to meet Miss Feldstein again and get to know her better."

Walter snorts to convey that this is too little too late, and yet he will accept it. In this little thing, Thomas has some power. "You will stay away from those Golden Dawn charlatans. You've always been a poor sort of Thresher, but your actions nevertheless reflect upon me."

"I shall be happy to get to know Miss Feldstein better," Thomas continues, thinking it best to ignore Walter's interruption, "but I want something in return."

Walter stares at him. "You dare make demands?"

Thomas decides this is the time to hold his ground. And, yes. He will dare. Why should he not? It is his family's bank. In a larger sense, it is *his* bank—at least in part. "I have made every effort to endure this absurd arrangement, but I shall do it no more."

Walter chews upon his lip as he considers this. "What is it you want?"

"I want to be freed of the junior clerk's office," Thomas tells him. "I wish to learn banking. Proper banking. And yes, I know it is not done thus, but I believe I have learned all that letter copying and ledger proofing can teach me. I wish to understand how Thresher's operates."

"You think to extort an unearned promotion from me?" Walter asks with a sneer.

Thomas shrugs. He has considered that he might need to drive a difficult bargain in order to move his brother. "If I cannot learn banking at Thresher's, then I shall learn it elsewhere. I am willing to wager that my name will win me, at the very least, a comparable position with any of Thresher's competitors."

Walter expectorates a derisive laugh. "Do you think I would permit such a thing? Do you imagine my name has no force behind it? No one will trust you if I denounce you, which you may be certain I will do. I have no doubt that you can find work as a clerk in some other industry, but a junior clerk is all you will ever be. You will be cut off from this family and its wealth forever. If that is what you wish, you need but speak."

"You would cast me out because I won't marry a stranger?" Thomas's head has begun to throb like tribal drums, but he cannot let go of his anger.

"If you will not set aside your own petty preferences to help this family, then you deserve nothing from it," Walter tells him.

They stare at one another, neither speaking. Thomas believes his brother means what he says. If Thomas does not comply, Walter will cut him off. Thomas would be a Thresher in name only, a man without a family. This frightens him in ways he does not fully understand. It is more than simply the money. It is also the family name, the bank, the responsibility he feels toward the institution founded by his grandfather.

For all that, he cannot bring himself to surrender. "What I propose is this," Thomas says. "I shall get acquainted with Miss Feldstein, and you shall advance my position at the bank. If things do not proceed as you would like, you may always cast me out and pauperize me at a time of your convenience."

Thomas knows he takes a risk. Walter would certainly destroy his brother if he felt the need, but Walter wants Thomas to marry Miss Feldstein. It is important to him for whatever reason, and Thomas has gambled that Walter will give a little, will swallow some measure of pride, to get what he desires.

Walter glowers at Thomas, his eyes wide, his lips bloodless. It is as though he cannot fathom that his brother still resists him. He then opens his mouth to speak, though it is all wrong. His upper lip curls upward, revealing his teeth. He tries again and forms his mouth into a less monstrous shape.

"You will court the girl?" he asks.

"I shall get to know the girl," Thomas counters. "I shall see if we are suitable for one another."

Walter reddens once more. He balls his fists. He snarls. "Then I shall attempt to determine if you are ready for advancement," he says at last.

"No." Thomas is still smiling. Still calm. Still sitting while Walter is standing. "Forgive me if vague promises do not serve. I wish to advance, or I shall have nothing to do with Esther Feldstein. Those are my terms, Walter. They seem rather easy to me, but you may refuse if you like. You, after all, are governor."

Walter turns away, muttering, swearing under his breath. It occurs to Thomas, with a kind of adolescent glee, that Walter cannot make this decision without his constant companion. Can it be that he *needs* Mr. Hawke? He was there for their father as well. Is he the genius behind Thresher's growth? Is he the cause of its current troubles?

Thomas usually won at cards because, among other, more numerical skills, he knew the right moment to bet everything. This is such a moment. He puts all he has in the pot. "If you wish to ask Mr. Hawke for his approval, I can wait upon his decision."

I've killed him, Thomas thinks. *I've killed my own brother.* He is certain that his little irritant, piled atop too much rich food, too little sleep, and ceaseless toil, has pushed Walter into an apoplexy. His skin turns pink and then red and then purple. His jaw clenches so that it must soon snap, and his mouth forms an impossibly stretched-out line.

Walter opens his mouth—to shout, to wail in pain?—Thomas cannot even guess. No sound comes out, which is even more terrible.

Then Walter's color becomes something more commonly found in human creatures. His muscles relax. Like a steam engine, he lets out a hissing blast of air through his nostrils.

"Mr. Hawke serves in an advisory capacity," he says in a voice so calm, so unseasoned with irritation and grievance that Thomas hardly recognizes it as Walter's. "Banking decisions, both large and small, are made by the governor."

Thomas cares to show none of his relief that he has not irritated a man to death. "Then I await the governor's decision."

"You will seek to win Miss Feldstein's affections?" Walter asks. "An agreement will have the force of a contract."

Thomas doesn't know if that's true. By giving his word, will he enter a binding deal, one with all the consequences implied in this Peculiar era? Will he bring misfortune upon himself if he does not do what he says? It may be, but he tells himself that there are many kinds of affections. The hearts of women swell with a wide variety of species of love. Thomas finds he rather likes the idea of being held in high esteem by Miss Feldstein, of having her count him among her friends. He believes he can agree to these terms without dissembling. "I shall make every effort to see if we can come to like one another. I give you my word."

"Then I shall find a way for you to advance." Walter's voice and expression are curiously blank, as though he were reading meaningless words from a book.

"Splendid," Thomas says in a cheerful tone. "How wonderful when brothers can agree to advance the interests of their family."

Walter loses his faraway expression and, once more, shows every sign of permanent irritation and impatience. "There is nothing splendid about it. You must always insert yourself where you are not wanted. And know that if you have deceived me, if I find you are merely delaying, I will consider you to be in violation of the terms in my father's will. I will owe you nothing more. You will be like a thousand other talentless men in this city, left to swim, or more likely sink, by your own merits—meager as they are."

Thomas sighs. He begins to shake his head, but there is too much pain involved, so he settles for looking unhappy. An image appears before him— Walter at the dinner party, the emerald flash inside his sleeve. This arboreal plague afflicts him as well. They are linked not only by blood, but also by the Peculiarities. Why can they not speak of it?

"Do you never wonder about the changes happening around us?" Thomas asks, his voice soft. Perhaps over this, if not the bank, they might, at long last, forge a bond. Thomas has tried so many times before, but the differences in their age and dispositions have always proved too great. In this, however, they are the same. "I mean the Peculiarities. Do you not wish to better understand?"

"I understand what is important to the bank," Walter says as he leaves the room. He closes the door harder than necessary, but not as hard as he might have. Perhaps this is his nod to brotherly affection.

FOURTEEN

WORKS

B
Y WEDNESDAY, THE bandage has come off and the bruising has begun to
fade to a sickly greenish yellow. He has, in this time, sent a brief note to
Miss Feldstein inquiring after her health and has received a surprisingly
solicitous response. She both assured him she suffered no harm and wrote some
surprisingly warm lines on the subject of Thomas's courage. He did not feel
particularly brave having his head knocked about, but he is glad of her generous interpretation of events.

Returning to Thresher's gives him considerably less joy. Perhaps everyone at
the bank has been told to say nothing to him, for no one speaks of the incident
with the Golden Dawn or the dead writer. He expected the other junior clerks
to mock him, but most make no eye contact with him. Perhaps, he thinks, they
fear exposure to the Peculiarities is contagious. Only the new fellow, Bradford
Drummond, shows any interest in Thomas's injuries. He makes several sympathetic comments, offers to shoulder the burden of some of Thomas's work, but
curiously makes no inquiries into how Thomas has come to be in such a state.

Perhaps none of them know the true story. For nothing Thomas has
seen in the newspapers is accurate. Arthur Conan Doyle suffered death by
misadventure, not murder, according to the police, and they have made it clear
that no one will be charged. "A tragic accident," according to a Scotland Yard
spokesman, "involving ceremonial swords used by the writer during a ritual.
He appears to have mishandled the blade, and a stumble upon an unseen stair
led to a fatal mishap." Despite Doyle's most famous creation being a tenacious
investigator, the case is soon discarded.

As for the injured banker whose picture appeared in the *Times*, Scotland
Yard takes no position. Thomas never filed a complaint, and no one has been
demanding justice. For all the police know, the picture is an artful arrangement
or shows the aftermath of yet another accident. Newspapers favor the lurid over

the truthful. It was a stroke of luck that the Thresher name did not appear with the picture. That helped to mollify Walter's rage, and he thanked his good fortune that so few people of consequence knew Thomas's face. It might well be that this Drummond fellow recognized Thomas in the picture. Perhaps he says nothing to be polite, but there is a kind of cunning quality to the silence that makes Thomas uneasy.

During his midmorning break, Thomas seeks out Walter to remind him of their bargain. Walter sits at his desk surrounded by ledgers, letters, files, and tomes. Above him hangs a painting of their father, looking grim, and their grandfather, looking benevolent. Inexplicably there is also a painting of Cronos devouring his children, which as far as Thomas is concerned, is a bit too appropriate for this family.

"I haven't forgotten," Walter tells Thomas as though speaking to a particularly dimwitted child. "These things cannot happen at the snap of a finger."

"We entered into a binding agreement," Thomas reminds him.

"You think I don't know about binding agreements?" he roars. He is on his feet, staring at Thomas as though they are but moments away from a brawl.

"I should think a man in your position understands very well," Thomas says quite calmly. "I merely wished to remind you for your own sake. And I certainly hope that there are tangible signs of your making good on your promise before my next meeting with Miss Feldstein."

He does not stay to hear Walter's response. He doubts it would be of much value.

Thomas has no desire to pay a visit to Mrs. Yardley until his injuries are no longer visible. He has manly evidence that he has pursued his interests, as she advised, but it is unattractive evidence to be sure. While still in his sickbed, he composed a letter that provided a vague and sanitized version of what transpired. He explained that he was unhurt in the main, and that he may be closer to understanding the bank's interests in her late husband's affairs. He promised to call on her soon.

Instead, after his day at the bank is completed, Thomas takes a cab to the Golden Dawn temple, where he is pleased to find both Aleister Crowley and Samuel MacGregor Mathers on hand. They bring him upstairs, which has been cleaned of blood and damage. One would hardly know that a pair of well-dressed monsters had attacked the place mere days before.

"Things rather calmed down once you were unconscious," MacGregor Mathers explains, as though the appearance of the Elegants had been something of a routine bother. "After you cut yourself on that blade, the creatures' attention seemed to wander."

"I'd have thought blood would encourage them," Thomas says. "They are killers."

"Evidently they like it when *they* draw blood," Crowley observes. "There may have been something of an element of unintentional sacrifice when you cut yourself. It could be a weakness. There's no knowing, as we have no idea what these things are. Not demons."

"Certainly not," MacGregor Mathers says. "No, something new."

"New to us," offers Crowley.

MacGregor Mathers gives Crowley something of a side glance. "Quite. Though, I must say that while I think your cutting yourself upon that sword sent them packing faster than they would have liked, I had the strangest feeling they would not have done much harm to you."

"Seems like they were testing you," Crowley adds.

"Whatever for?" Thomas demands.

Crowley laughs. "You mustn't read too much into it. Beings of that sort can find people, animals, even inanimate objects fascinating. I once observed an ectoplasmic manifestation toy with a mouse for hours. There were other mice in the room, but it didn't notice them. Just that one. You can drive yourself mad looking for meaning in the behavior of entities from worlds built upon alien logic."

Other gentlemen lounge about, drinking and smoking, deep in conversation or study. Ladies are among the company as well. Thomas is briefly introduced to MacGregor Mathers's wife, Moina, a wild-haired beauty at least ten years younger than her husband.

"Another Hebrew delight," Crowley whispers into Thomas's ear.

After the woman leaves, and a waiter delivers the three men brandies, it feels to Thomas that a page of some sort has turned.

"I am glad you've chosen to return," MacGregor Mathers says. "After the unpleasantness, I think we might have lost a number of prospective members. Quite a few good ones, too."

"Does that sort of thing happen often?" Thomas inquires.

"Magical attack?" MacGregor asks with a guffaw. "From time to time, but nothing so overt. Usually attacks will take the form of mishaps and unfortunate coincidences that can be explained away by the unsuspecting. Lost keys or a late omnibus. That sort of thing. An incursion of the sort you witnessed is something we have never seen."

"Never does indeed sound correct," Crowley agrees.

"I cannot understand what those beings were doing in Hammersmith, in broad daylight," continues MacGregor Mathers. "And how to explain their animosity toward Doyle? They have only been known to go after prostitutes. Quite the mystery."

"A mystery that, perhaps, Doyle's mind might have unraveled?" Thomas proposes.

"I say!" MacGregor Mathers looks quite impressed. "That is a rather interesting theory. Of course, it leads us to a bit of circular reasoning. They killed Doyle to prevent anyone discovering the mystery of why they killed Doyle."

"Unless Thresher's inadvertent sacrifice prevented them from carrying out their real business," Crowley proposes.

MacGregor Mathers shakes his head. "We'll likely never know. Those things won't get back inside here. We have redoubled our magical defenses and performed several protective rituals. There is no place in London better defended than this very building, but you could not have been aware of that before returning. Very admirable, sir—your thirst for knowledge."

Thomas never even considered the danger of returning, perhaps because he knows there is no running from the Peculiarities—not for a man with leaves growing upon his back. He nevertheless prefers for these men to believe that he is forging ahead out of courage, a determination to learn great truths. Thus Thomas agrees that he will become an initiate of the Golden Dawn.

The ceremony is held a week later, and Thomas seriously doubts he has done the right thing. He stands in the cavernous and torch-lit chamber in the Isis-Urania Temple that is now redolent with the scent of burning incense. Thomas wears an unadorned white robe, and he is surrounded by men and women wearing robes of various colors, some with metal masks that glisten in the firelight. They hold cups and wands and swords. Different members of the order adopt roles and recite lines as if it were all a stage play. And the dialogue is atrocious. *Child of Earth, unpurified and unconsecrated, thou canst not enter the path of the West.* They shift their positions on cues. Thomas stifles the urge to laugh.

When they address him in the ceremony, they do so by his Golden Dawn name. This required a bit of thought on his part. Crowley's is *Perdurabo*—Latin: I will endure forever. MacGregor Mathers has favored something in Gaelic: *'S Rioghail Mo Dhream*, Royal is my Race. Thomas is now *Frater Ostium Et Speculum*—Brother Door and Mirror. He was told to meditate upon the name, and this is the nonsense he has come up with. Thomas feels it is entirely absent of meaning, but the other members show every sign of being impressed by his choice. They coo over it as though it were a rare gem.

He supposes he would feel some sense of wonder if all these rituals were actually doing something. Gods and spirits are invoked, but no gods or spirits reveal themselves. Dressed in elaborate costume, MacGregor Mathers plays the role of the Hierophant, the high priest, and calls upon elements and cosmic powers, but Thomas feels no change in temperature, no surge of wind nor splash of rain. Nothing crackles in the air. There are real things out there. Thomas has seen them, felt them, lived them, been knocked insensible by them. They grow upon his flesh, and yet as he stands in that gloomy space, torches flickering on the wall, people—mostly old, mostly men, mostly fat, truth be told—chant in ancient tongues and say very flattering things to entities in whom no one has believed for millennia.

When it is all over, and he has removed his robe, MacGregor Mathers puts in his hands a privately published book with leather binding and gold leaf.

"You are now a novice of the Golden Dawn, *Frater Ostium Et Speculum*," he says. "You have taken a first step into unlocking the mysteries of the universe, but it is only a step. Perhaps you are disappointed that you haven't been dazzled with stunning displays of sorcery."

"A bit," Thomas agrees.

MacGregor Mathers laughs. "We all feel that way, and such manifestations could be in your future, but magic—real magic—is not a showy thing. Learn what is in that book, and then you will become a novice and join the first order of the Hermetic Order of the Golden Dawn. That will be your first step."

"I thought the initiation was my first step."

"Your first real step," MacGregor Mathers clarifies.

Thomas opens the book and flips through its pages. It contains information about the letters of the Hebrew alphabet, astrological symbols, tarot iconography, and so on. It is like a basic vocabulary. He would rather be learning spells that allow him to shoot lightning from his fingertips, but he supposes he must begin somewhere.

"Don't lose it," MacGregor Mathers tells him.

"Is this dangerous?" he asks somewhat dubiously.

"No," MacGregor Mathers says. "But if it's misplaced, you'll have to pay for a new copy."

Later in the week, he feels sufficiently healed to visit with Madeline Yardley, and they agree to meet at a tea shop near her house. Thomas makes his way through the city streets after he finishes his work at the bank. He considers taking the underground railway, but his previous experimentation with that mode of travel has not left him with much enthusiasm. It is dark, dank, hot from the compressed bodies.

However, Thomas's limited funds compel him to avoid unnecessary spending, and he enjoys walking. On a brisk autumn evening, with the whole of the city making its way to and fro, London feels like a living, breathing, pulsating thing. Were other places so alive? Paris has a beating heart. He has been there and felt its vibrancy. Perhaps New York and Berlin were much the same. Was that what attracted the Peculiarities? Was there something in these quickened cities that drew unnatural forces? Thomas thinks of his Golden Dawn book, hidden under his bed in his room at his brother's house. Perhaps once he has mastered its contents, he will know the answer.

He is well on his way there. In truth, there is not so very much to learn. He now knows the Hebrew letters and the sounds they make. He quizzes himself on astrological symbols. The tarot iconography is taking more time, but he believes he will have mastered it by end of the week. With any luck, he will be able to advance to novice this weekend.

Thomas has the long-forgotten sensation of accomplishing things. Things like Madeline Yardley? It is a question he cannot answer. He finds himself bristle with excitement as he anticipates sitting with her for an hour, sipping tea or chocolate, perhaps indulging in a piece of cake. His senses come alive as he imagines gazing upon her lovely face. And yet, what does he expect will come of this flirtation? What can he offer Madeline Yardley? Does he have a future at Thresher's? Only if he marries Esther Feldstein, and that would present some obstacles to a relationship with Mrs. Yardley. If he refuses to indulge his brother's plans, he can expect Walter to carry out his threat of disinheritance. Thomas cannot ask a woman like Madeline Yardley to shackle herself to a man without money or standing.

Considerations of marriage, he knows, are premature. He has spent so little time with Mrs. Yardley, but he cannot think of her without his mind taking flights of fancy. How good it would be to reorder his life, to become her husband and move into her house. He imagines sitting at her breakfast table, reading a newspaper, sipping coffee, laughing at her clever observations. He could become a different person entirely, though he does not see how a wife, no matter how delightful, would resolve the difficulties posed by his Peculiar condition. A tree, he suspects, would make for a poor spouse.

But the evening air is something to be enjoyed, and the cool on his face is invigorating. He listens to the cries of the peddlers and cacophony of wheels rolling and hooves clopping. Life is not so very bad so long as you restrict your thoughts to the proper things.

Thomas has become very good at estimating how long it will take him to travel from one place to another by foot, and he is pleased to arrive at the tea room ten minutes early. He is even more delighted to peer through the window and see Mrs. Yardley already seated at a table.

An obsequious little Italian is upon him the moment he steps through the door, snatching away Thomas's coat and hat and then showing him to Mrs. Yardley. He is very happy to see *signore*, he says, as though Thomas has been there before and seeing him today was just what he had most hoped for. It is the sort of fawning that foreigners think will make customers return, but it is more likely to keep Thomas away in the future.

Unless, of course, Mrs. Yardley likes it, and then he will return every day if he must. When she stands to greet him, it is as though clouds have parted to reveal the moon, bright and swollen. Her beauty is that brilliant. He thinks this even while he understands that it really is not. Mrs. Yardley is undeniably pretty, but not out of the usual way. There is, in fact, something rather ordinary about her prettiness. It is a kind of generic English attractiveness to be found in the ranks of housemaids and farmer's wives. Put her in a crowd of ladies her own age and she would vanish like one sugar cube in a bowl. At least most people would think so, but Thomas would find her out. Thomas would never lose sight of her. It is this knowledge that he sees the exceptional beauty behind the ordinary beauty that makes her even more appealing to him. She is his special, secret treasure.

"Oh, my dear Mr. Thresher." She gently skims the surface of his cheek—now only mildly blotched—with her gloved finger. "You have been hurt indeed."

"It is nothing." He hopes not to show how much he relishes this touch. It is brief, and the leather barely brushes his skin, but Thomas cannot but think she would not have made the gesture if she did not care for him. "At least now it is nothing. You should have seen me the day after. I was a fright."

"I feel responsible," she says as they sit. "You would not have been there if I had not sent you on that ridiculous quest." She now reaches across the table and takes her gloved hand in his gloved hand. It is a fleeting moment before she lets go, but in that moment, Thomas imagines he can feel the warmth of her flesh through all that leather. He can feel their pulses thrum together as one. What would it be like, he wonders, to touch her hand, skin to skin?

"That is absurd," Thomas says once his hand is free. He can still feel a ghostly tingle where her fingers pressed against his. "You will recall that I am the one who came to you asking about this business."

"But it was my suggestion that put you in that place during the attack. Oh, it must have been so terrible."

It was indeed terrible, and it occurs to Thomas that he has not spent very much time thinking about facing the Elegants, those frantic moments of absolute madness. Has he somehow set these thoughts aside to preserve his sanity, or is he truly untroubled by all he witnessed? Perhaps he is made of stout stuff, and the sort of incident that would ruin another man's quiet merely rolls off his back. Or, he thinks more worriedly, could this be a part of the arboreal plague? Perhaps he is losing his ability to feel as his brain turns to bark and leaf. What is next? His appreciation of beauty? He could not bear it.

"Tell me everything that happened," Mrs. Yardley says.

Thomas tells his story, but not quite everything. He leaves out Miss Feldstein because she is not relevant, and he has no wish to explain how he knows her. He also doesn't wish to discuss her remarkable composure under difficult circumstances. It might be unpleasant to have to praise another woman to Mrs. Yardley.

He also isn't entirely certain he wants to tell her about joining the Golden Dawn. He fears that all the robes and chanting and ritualistic wand-waving might make him appear foolish.

"You have seen the Elegants," she says in a quiet voice. "And was Mr. Doyle truly killed by them?"

"There is no doubt." His voice is grave, for these are serious matters.

She takes a moment to consider all of this. "I think you must set this investigation aside. It is one thing to try to uncover secrets when you are merely curious. It is another if you put yourself in danger."

"I cannot say that the danger has anything to do with my inquiry," he assures her. "It might be related only to the Golden Dawn." This is where not telling her about his continued involvement in this organization has come in very handy.

She reaches out once more and squeezes his fingers before withdrawing. "Whatever the great secret your bank is keeping, it cannot do me any harm, and it is certainly not worth risking your own safety. I think I wanted to pretend this was a story, and that we are great adventurers, but we are not. It was wrong of me to use you to add some color to my life. It's been so lonely since Bobby died, and when you appeared on my doorstep, this mysterious figure from the past, well, I suppose I become caught up in the moment. Now I see what my fantasy has cost. I cannot endure that I would put a bank clerk in danger to relieve my boredom."

Thomas sips his tea to hide his shame. Is this truly what she thinks of him—that he is nothing but an insignificant bank clerk? Well, he supposes that's true. It is precisely what he is. He is the son and grandson and brother of banking giants, and he is a drudge who lives under another man's roof. She doesn't even fully understand the extent of his humiliation, but she reads it plainly enough upon his face.

And yet, is he not something more? He has wrestled with a mighty fog and has done battle with the Elegants. He has met werewolves and tree people, he has entered a magical order, and faced monsters while holding a magic—or at least ceremonial—sword. If you look at it from the proper angle, he is a hero on a great adventure.

"You have been a great help to me, Mrs. Yardley," he tells her. "You have given me wonderful notions of what to do next, but I hope you will forgive me if I say I have not done these things *for* you. That is to say, I would gladly have done so, but I was upon this path when I met you. I appreciate your concern for my well-being, but I cannot stop what I have begun."

"But why ever not?" she demands, her face a mask of puzzlement.

The question is reasonable. Why would an ordinary man, burdened with a long workday, who was not—let us say, just as an example, metamorphosing into a plant—trouble himself to expose secrets inside the very institution for which he works? There is no sound reason for an ordinary bank clerk, but Thomas is a Thresher, and this gives him the very excuse he needs.

"Because the bank bears my name," he pronounces. "It was founded by my grandfather. I have a responsibility to learn what I am not being told."

"Well, then," she says with a pert little smile. She shifts ever so slightly in her seat, like a theater goer settling in for exciting happenings upon the stage. "If I cannot stop you, then you must continue to tell me everything. Absolutely everything."

Thomas feels himself swell with pride. He has somehow, with all his dissimulation and half-truths, managed to give this lady precisely what she hoped for.

FIFTEEN

GAIN

M R. HAWKE AWAITS near the entrance of the bank. Thomas is not ready for the factotum's jack-o'-lantern grin this morning. He's had a restless night of vivid dreams. He would nod off only to be jolted awake by visions of the terrible, hinged face. Over and over again. Now he stands in the lobby with Mr. Hawke leaning forward in a way that suggests a bow without quite being one. "Mister Thomas Thresher," he proclaims, as though trying out an elevated nobleman's title for the first time. "Our newest banker. Would you care to set your eyes upon your office, or should you prefer to spend a few more days sharpening your skills amongst the junior clerks?"

So, it is finally happening. Perhaps Walter has received some sort of assurance from Mr. Feldstein on the disposition of his daughter or whatever business arrangement props up the intended marriage. Perhaps he has merely found a moment to see done what he promised to do. There is no telling. Thomas does not feel excitement so much as a deep sense of bewilderment.

This feeling is by no means lessened when Mr. Hawke leads him not toward the stairs that will take him to the second floor, the location of the bankers' offices. Instead they make their way through the lobby, past the tellers' desk, to a door that Thomas never previously noticed. This leads to an equally obscure stairwell, narrow, dusty with disuse. They climb past the second floor, which is blocked off, as is the third. They emerge in an attic with a sloping roof and rounded windows, more like portholes, glazed with smoky glass. The room is dark and cold, but it contains a large desk as well as a smaller companion, and it has been recently swept. Thomas notes that in most of the chamber, he should be able to stand without stooping.

"It is somewhat isolated," he observes.

Mr. Hawke looks about, as if trying to understand what Thomas could mean. "Your elevation came upon us suddenly. Like a refreshing breeze on a

119

summer's day. Consequently, we had nothing for you in the building's more populated regions. On the bright side, you shall be able to get much done without fear of constant interruption."

"But what if I need to speak to others or consult records?"

Mr. Hawke smiles as though indulging a child. "It is not so very far a walk for a vigorous young man." He rubs his hands together with enthusiasm or perhaps for warmth, for the room is quite chilly. "I shall leave you to it."

"To what?" Thomas asks. "I'm not entirely certain what I should be doing."

"You are to make money," Mr. Hawke says. "As to the how of it all, it is the sort of thing your time as a junior clerk ought to have taught you. Your worth as a banker is tied to how much business you bring into Thresher's, and bankers who do not prove their worth do not last long. If you are uncertain how to proceed, you might wish to extend your apprenticeship."

"There is no need," Thomas tells him. "I am quite prepared."

He is not, and they both know it.

Mr. Hawke closes the door behind him, leaving Thomas in the gloom. There is no fireplace to increase warmth, but there are gas lamps. They are inadequate for comfort but sufficient for muddling along.

Thomas then sits at his desk, taking in a feel for the place. His office. He has achieved something, hasn't he? *Here I am*, he thinks as he runs his hand along his desk, feeling dust coat his fingers. *I am banking.*

He knows, of course, he is doing nothing of the sort. He places his hands under his arms to generate warmth while he considers that his brother has merely shifted him from one harmless, irrelevant position to another. Thomas wonders if he has made his life more difficult. He has moved from being an adequate junior clerk to exposing himself as a failure of a banker. How, he wonders, will his sitting uselessly in this cold office help to protect his grandfather's legacy? Meanwhile Madeline Yardley will become more unattainable, and Thomas will sprout more leaves.

It will not do. No, Thomas Thresher is not to be so easily thwarted. He has decided that he will make certain that Thresher's is in good hands, and that is precisely what he means to do.

Thomas sits up straighter in his chair. Yes, he decides. That is what I shall do. *Here I am*, he says to himself, except this time he means it. *I am banking.*

Thomas begins by writing out notes. He needs to formulate his ideas, clarify his questions. He wants to proceed systematically, but to do so he will need a better understanding of what he wishes to know. He wears gloves while he writes, which slows him down, but his fingers quickly grow numb without them.

His work, slow and sporadic, is interrupted by a knock at the door. Bradford Drummond, the solicitous junior clerk, enters with an enthusiastic good morning, and proceeds immediately to the smaller of the two desks in the room. He sits down, rubs his hands together, and looks about him as if expecting something to happen.

"Quite cold up here," he says.

"Something I can do for you?" Thomas asks, affecting the air of a man with pressing matters.

"Did they not tell you? I'm to be your assistant."

Thomas isn't certain how he feels about this. There is something about Drummond's friendliness that Thomas cannot quite trust. On the other hand, he cannot think of a junior clerk he would trust more. And having an assistant is a sign of something, surely. Thomas does not know what to do with his own time, let alone how to apportion another's. Even so, the development makes him feel a little less like an imposter.

"What shall you have me do?" Drummond asks.

"I'm not entirely certain," Thomas says. "I am still formulating ideas."

"Regarding what, sir?"

Is there something challenging in Drummond's gaze? Does he mean to suggest that Thomas is not up to the task—that he, Drummond, would have a sound notion of how to proceed?

"My first task," Thomas says, "is to familiarize myself with Thresher's soundness. I mean to review streams of income and liabilities. I must know where the bank stands if I am to know what action is required."

"Perhaps a review of current outstanding loans would be the best place to begin," Drummond suggests. "Shall I visit the records room and collect that information for you?"

Thomas presumed he would have to go groveling for the information himself. He rather likes having an assistant. "Yes, that would be most helpful. And see what you can find about a fellow named Hershel Feldstein. Why should the bank wish to forge a closer connection to him? Any information you can unearth would be of great help."

"Right away, sir," Drummond says, moving toward the door.

"Oh, and Drummond."

The solicitous fellow turns around.

"While you're there, see what you can learn about Mr. Hawke. Where does he come from? What does he do? Where does he live? Anything at all."

"Perhaps we may even discover if he has a Christian name," Mr. Drummond says with a smirk. He is out the door and heading down the stairs before Thomas can respond.

Something else happens that day.

It has taken all of the morning and a good part of the afternoon for Thomas to realize he may take breaks when he wishes. His time is his own. He might, if he so desires, smoke in his own office, but he has grown used to taking a cigar outside, and he feels that being out of doors may inspire some new ideas. He is crossing the lobby when he sees someone familiar, a man of middle years with thinning hair and a gray beard. It takes a moment for Thomas to place the name, but then it comes to him: *Frater Quaero Aeternum* of the Golden Dawn.

Thomas turns aside, lest he be seen, though he does not immediately know why he has done so. Only when he hides himself behind one of the bank's massive Corinthian columns does he begin to realize why he does not wish to be seen.

Once he is certain *Quaero Aeternum* is out of view, Thomas relinquishes his hiding spot and heads not for the street—his cigar is now forgotten—but to the records room. Drummond has harassed the clerk on Thomas's behalf several times already that day. Piles of records tower on his desk, but now there is more information to be gleaned.

Thomas glances at the records clerk, who appears very much put upon by the sight of an intruder in his realm.

"Good afternoon, Mister. . . ." He allows himself to trail off.

"Handleworth," the clerk says, as though he has surrendered something. "Have we not entrusted enough documents to your new endeavors already, Mr. Thresher?"

"I've much to learn," Thomas says cheerfully. "But have no fear. I shan't trouble you. I know where to find what I seek." If nothing else, his time as a junior clerk has prepared him to navigate the labyrinth of data as well as anyone save Mr. Handleworth himself. He locates the shelf where his quest began, and he searches through the letters detailing the acquired debt. He sees once more the communications with Mrs. Yardley and Mrs. Topping. There is the letter to Mr. Yeats. And there at last he finds precisely what he thought he would find, a letter to a Mr. Isaiah Ruddington. Thomas only met him once, and they did no more than shake hands and exchange words, but this is *Frater Quaero Aeternum*'s true name. Thresher's has acquired more than three hundred pounds' worth of the fellow's debt, and now, here he is, visiting the bank.

It could be nothing more than what Thomas sees on the surface. The fellow owes money, and he wishes to pay it off. It is possible, certainly, but the letter appears to make no demands of repayment. Perhaps there are other letters, not preserved here. Perhaps Ruddington wishes to clear his account or has found an error in the bank's reckoning.

Such things are certainly possible, but Thomas reaches a much more logical conclusion.

Thresher's Bank wants to make use of magicians.

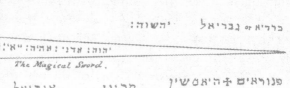

The Magical Sword.

כרריא or גבריאל   יהשוה:

יהוה: אדני: אהיה: יא':

פנוראים + ה'יאטשין   סריון   רגיון

נמורין + דבלין   ד'יאל or רפאל   יטטון   למדין + עירדים

 אוריאל

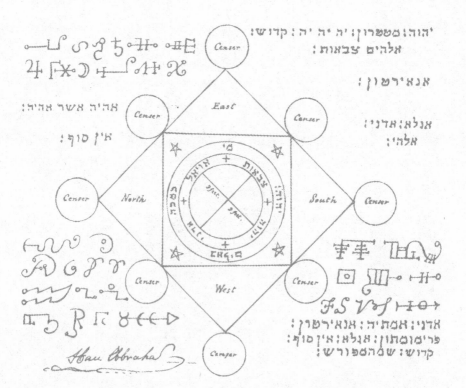

The Burin.

יהוה: מטטרון: יה: יה: יה: קדוש:
אלהים צבאות:

אנא'ירטון:

אנלא: אדני:
אלהי:

אהיה אשר אהיה:

אין סוף:

Censer   East   Censer   Censer   North   South   Censer   West   Censer   Censer

אדני: אמתיה: אנא'ירטון:
פרימומתון: אנלא: אין סוף:
קדוש: שמהמפורש:

⤙⤚ SIXTEEN ⤙⤚
PRINCESS

INCE THE INCIDENT at the Golden Dawn temple, Thomas has begun to entertain the strange notion that perhaps Miss Feldstein has more to recommend her than he initially imagined. He has taken the time to consider—as a mere exercise in thought, nothing more—what it might be like to marry her. He has no desire to do so, but he supposes it is inevitable that he consider the possibility, much like a soldier might wonder what his life would be like if he returned from war missing a limb.

A deal has been struck, and the junior clerk has been elevated, so it comes as no surprise when Walter announces that Thomas will be picnicking with Miss Feldstein that Sunday afternoon. There is a meeting of the Golden Dawn that evening, however, but he does not imagine that he will have any difficulty getting to Hammersmith on time. He has kept himself awake late every night studying his book, and he believes he will be quite ready by Sunday to advance to the level of novice. It will mean another absurd ceremony, but he will endure the discomfort in order to gain more knowledge. Thomas longs to learn what secrets are hidden in the next volume of the Golden Dawn instruction. He is rising at the bank and he will rise within the order.

On Sunday morning, Thomas enters Walter's coach. Pearl, dressed in an elegant coral gown, joins them, her face an unreadable mask. Also present is Mr. Hawke, whose reasons for attending are incomprehensible. Thomas presumes they are going to Hyde Park or some other equally innocuous location, but it seems that Walter is a bit of a sentimentalist and wants to picnic at the family mausoleum in Highgate Cemetery.

"Is that not a little gloomy?" Thomas inquires.

"I know you did not care to spend time with my father during his life," Walter replies. "Now will you object to spending time with him in death?"

"It is a beautiful spot," Mr. Hawke adds with his typical cheer. "Quite suitable for an amorous afternoon."

Thomas looks at his brother's factotum, sitting happily in his seat, hands in his lap, smiling like a simpleton. Once again, Thomas wonders what the point of this man is. Most people don't require a point. They simply are. Mr. Hawke, he thinks, should have a purpose or he should not be. At the very least, he should be somewhere else.

"We will be certain you have an opportunity to speak to Miss Feldstein alone," Pearl says. Her voice is flat, as though she is reading a line she has rehearsed.

"I've spoken with her alone before," Thomas points out.

"To ask for her hand, you imbecile," Walter growls. "Must I explain everything you?"

Thomas thinks not changing his facial expression is very important, and he works hard to make this happen. Now that he has risen out of the clerk's room, however feebly, Thomas does not wish to anger his brother. On the other hand, he has learned things. He has seen records, and he knows what perhaps Walter did not wish him to know.

As the rumors have suggested, Thresher's finances are not upon the best footing. That may be putting things rather optimistically. Thomas has begun his review of the loans, and while he has quite a lot of material yet to read, he has seen loans that ought never to have been granted. Some of these date back to Samuel Thresher's tenure, but most have been issued under Walter. Thomas has seen loans to men who are likely never to repay. Thomas knows many of the names he sees on these documents. They are politicians and gamblers from otherwise respectable families and proprietors of failing businesses. Interestingly, the father of one of his old friends, Mawson, is there, having been refused by a half dozen other banks. The worthy men favored by the bank's founder, those struggling to pull themselves up by industry and diligence, have been neglected. Instead Thresher's favors men who bluster and strut around town in fine clothes for which they cannot pay. Thresher's favors image over substance, and Thomas fears the bank may stumble, perhaps even fall, if the course is not corrected. Only a few days ago he feared that he might be cut off from the bank's fortunes, but now he fears that there may soon be no fortune from which to be separated.

He has said nothing to Walter. How can he? He has more to read, more to learn before he even considers it, but the knowledge of Walter's mismanagement frequently bubbles to the surface of his thoughts.

For now, he must appear to move things along with Miss Feldstein, but Walter will not be satisfied with mere scraps. "I hardly think she's inclined to marry me at this moment," Thomas says, though he knows this objection will not get him very much.

"You hardly think at all," Walter returns. "That is why I am doing the thinking for you."

"Your brother is attempting to help you make your way in the world," Pearl notes in her most soothing voice. She puts a gentle hand on Walter's arm, but he shakes it off.

Pearl's face often has something of the quality of a trapped mouse, but there is something else today. It is as though she is desperate for Thomas to move things forward with this proposed marriage, as though she will be blamed for any lack of progress.

"I will not propose to her when I know she will reject the offer," he says softly. "But I shall do my best to get to charm the lady."

"Miss Feldstein's father is very well off," Mr. Hawke offers. "When you marry his daughter, I suspect he will be inclined to set you up nicely. It could be your making, young Mr. Thresher."

Thomas believes that as one of Samuel Thresher's two sons, he doesn't require making. He ought already to be made.

"And I have it on good authority she will be more receptive than you suppose," Mr. Hawke continues, favoring Thomas with a wink. "In any case, her father will accept on her behalf. Oh, how I envy young love."

The carriage stops near the family mausoleum, a rather garish structure, gothic and gloomy with its cyclopean stones. It is the very sort of thing from which one can imagine a vampire emerging. Walter leads the procession up the hill with all the cheer of actual funeral-goers. Meanwhile the servants scurry about, arranging braziers, which they light to beat back the cold. It occurs to Thomas that picnicking in October is not the best idea, and there is an enormous amount of fuss to avoid the disagreeable conditions that arise from eating al fresco so close to winter. He knows, however, that expressing his opinion will prove to be, at best, a pointless exercise.

With his hands shoved in his pants pockets, his belly thrust outward, Walter looks around testily, pivoting on his heels, while his footman sets out blankets and arranges folding chairs. "I chose to arrive late so we would not be waiting upon their pleasure, but that self-important Jew still isn't here."

Thomas sits in one of the chairs and raises his face toward the sun. It is a nearly cloudless day at least, and the warmth of the sun on his face is a pleasing counterpoint to the chill in the air. There is a curious sensation of the light coursing through his veins, and he wonders if that is a function of his vegetative metamorphosis or the more animalistic pleasure of being warm while the world around him is cold.

A few minutes later a coach lurches into view. The driver, Walter opines, is moving with provoking slowness, though it seems to Thomas the proper speed. At great length, the conveyance comes to a halt and out comes old Mr. Feldstein and his daughter. Under her unbuttoned coat she wears a plain ivory dress with a blue floral pattern and a matching white broad-brimmed hat. Her expression is not precisely amused though certainly something in the irony family.

The father studies the scene with some distaste, and then takes the daughter's arm, as though she were a prisoner rather than a beloved child, and leads her up the hill. Thomas is struck by how much taller she is than her father. When they reach the top, Mr. Feldstein is wheezing and red in the face. His eyes are moist and foamy saliva has gathered at the corners of his mouth.

"Ah, Mr. Thresher," he says, looking at Walter. He takes no notice of either Pearl or Mr. Hawke, as though they are but mere servants. He also ignores Thomas, whom he allegedly wishes to draw into the bosom of his family. Mr. Feldstein grins as he pumps Walter's hand with both of his until Walter snatches his appendage away.

"Enough of that. We all know why we're here."

Everyone takes their seats, and the maid begins to assemble plates for the silent guests.

"Eeeehhhh," Mr. Feldstein shrieks in the manner of terrified tropical birds and delighted East Londoners, "I see you've brought some of that sausage I favored at your little soiree. Very good, very good. The finest pork is what I like."

Miss Feldstein slumps in her seat, and Thomas glances over at her, his heart full of sympathy. In being brought together by their relations, whose behaviors are different but equally mortifying, they are, at least, alike.

A moment later, the maid places a plate of food in Miss Feldstein's hands. It contains an indecently swollen sausage, as well as a substantial hillock of salt beef, and a chicken leg island rising from a sea of jellied fat. It seems no one has troubled to learn, or to remember, that Miss Feldstein does not choose to eat meat. Without speaking a word, Thomas takes the bread and cheese off his own plate and sets it on hers.

She glances at him and smiles. "You are very kind."

"No need for you to be cold, bored, *and* hungry," he says. He glances over at the three other gentlemen, whose chairs are clustered away from them. They have been given the privacy to talk as they like, provided they keep their voices low.

"I hope not to be bored," she tells him. "The last time I spent with you was many things, but not boring." Something must have crossed Thomas's face, for she suddenly looked pale. "I am sorry, Mr. Thresher. I did not mean to make light of your injuries or what happened to Mr. Doyle. It's just that. . . ."

"We cannot stop living our lives?" he suggests.

"That's it precisely." Her too-big mouth turns up slightly at the corners. "It was terrible of course, but also astonishing. Those things we saw—I don't know what to make of them, but they were real. They were as real as anything or anyone else. The world is changing or revealing things about itself that have previously been hidden. So many refuse to accept it or try to hide it, but you and I can no longer pretend."

You and I. Miss Feldstein wishes to bind them together. Thomas is not naïve enough that he doesn't recognize a deliberate strategy when he sees one, but he does not think Miss Feldstein is flirting with him. She has something else in mind, and he decides he will let her explain it to him in her own time.

"You were very good to write to me," she says.

"I was relieved to hear you emerged unharmed," he tells her. "And I apologize that I was unable to see to your safety."

"You did well enough," she says earnestly. "And Mr. Crowley was good enough to put me in a cab when it was all over."

Thomas does not like to hear this. He asks himself if he is jealous of Crowley and concludes that he is not. It is more the feeling of resentment one feels when the world moves on in one's absence—not unlike what he experienced when he learned that his friends set sail for Paris while he would be chained to his desk at Thresher's.

"Will you join the Golden Dawn?" she asks.

"I already have." He is surprised he tells her the truth. He does not hesitate. He supposes it is because, unlike with Mrs. Yardley, he is not trying to impress her. He is not afraid she will think spending hours studying astrological symbols, let alone Hebrew letters, is frivolous. She knows what is out there, almost as intimately as he does. If becoming a Golden Dawn acolyte is not an effective way to face it, she will not blame him for making the attempt.

"Will you?" he asks, hoping she will say she will not.

"I don't believe so," she says, "and I can see it relieves you. Oh, come now. Don't try to pretend. You don't want to see me everywhere you go. I understand entirely."

Thomas feels somewhat mortified that he is so transparent. For a moment, he considers with some warmth the notion of having someone he knows by his side at the Golden Dawn, learning the same things he learns. It would be as though Miss Feldstein were a school chum. However, he would not like to see her exposed to the same dangers to which he might have to expose himself. There is also the matter of Mr. Crowley's clearly amorous interest in her. He cannot allow her to be exposed to so dangerous a predator.

"You misunderstand me," he tells her. "I simply think a place that has been assaulted by malevolent forces once might be subject again."

They sit in silence. Miss Feldstein puts some cheese on a piece of bread and nibbles at it. Thomas eats a bit of his sausage and worries that he might be offending Miss Feldstein. He looks over at his brother, who continues to speak quietly, but with a great deal of hand-waving, to Mr. Hawke and Mr. Feldstein. Pearl sits with her plate on her lap, but she eats nothing.

"Mr. Thresher, shall we take a walk?" Miss Feldstein says. "If we show a little interest in each other, it may placate our families. Besides, there is something I would discuss with you."

Thomas nods, more than happy to move away from the rest of their party. Miss Feldstein is the one to tell them of their plans, and her father nods very solemnly.

"That's right, my dear," he drawls. "You are Mr. Thresher have a nice little stroll. No need to hurry back."

Thomas believes that this girl's father is encouraging him to take liberties. Does he think these two will lie down on the cold ground of the cemetery to consummate their mutual lust amid the departed?

They wander for a while through the tombstones, moving over a hill and then down into the valley of mausoleums. Thomas has the very distinct idea that Miss Feldstein is trying to move them away from their party's view. Does she want him to kiss her? He cannot think that is it. Nevertheless, she takes his arm as they walk, and he finds the experience pleasant enough.

"I've learned a thing or two about our family's interests," Thomas says after a several minutes of silence.

Something twinkles in her eye. "Indeed. As have I. Your brother wishes to buy my father's brokerage house."

"That's the very thing I learned!" Thomas announces. It is what Drummond, his assistant, found in the records room.

"I'm sorry to have stolen your thunder," she tells him.

"Not at all," he answers. "It is good to have a confederate in these matters."

"Are we confederates then?" she asks.

"I hope we are." Thomas stops and looks at her. "Miss Feldstein, I do not wish to marry you, and you do not wish to marry me. I do not believe either of us has any mixed opinions on the subject, and so neither of us can hurt the other's feelings on that score. That said, we have interests in common, and we are natural allies in the cause of not becoming husband and wife. I would think that, under the circumstances, we must depend upon one another."

There is a blankness to Miss Feldstein's face, and Thomas fears he may have offended her, but then she breaks out into a smile that lights up her eyes. "Mr. Thresher, you have surprised me in the best possible way. I could not agree more."

"Then let us get down to business. Your father wishes for this marriage because he thinks allying himself with my family will improve his social standing. Is that not right?"

Miss Feldstein nods. "As nearly as I can understand it."

"But if he sells his business, what good is an alliance with the Threshers?" Thomas asks. "He'll no longer control the very thing he wishes to make more powerful."

"The money," Miss Feldstein proposes. "Perhaps he will start a new venture once he is connected with an Anglican family of consequence."

"It cannot be enough money for that," Thomas counters. "And a banking family's name is not worth much in this kingdom. A connection to the Threshers is unlikely to open many doors currently barred to him. And your father has worked his whole life to build his business. Without it, if you will excuse me for saying so, he is but another brash, moneyed man."

She shakes her head. "Honestly, I don't pretend to know much about my father's motivation, but your logic is sound."

"My brother's motivation is also puzzling," Thomas says. "I have only been involved with the bank for a few months, but I can see that acquiring Feldstein's is not so great a prize. Your father's business has tended to be among his fellow Jews. They have continued to do business with him since his conversion, but it is unlikely many will remain once Thresher's acquires the concern. What can my brother hope to gain, and why is it so important to him?"

"On that score, I think I may know something," she says, and Thomas understands they have come to the heart of the matter.

"Before he died," Miss Feldstein says, "your father tried to acquire not my father's business, but the building from which it operates, Westerly House. He made an offer on it perhaps a year ago. A very generous offer—far more than the building itself could be worth."

"Your father chose not to sell?" Thomas asks. The question is implied: if he cares only for money, then why not?

"It may be he sensed your father's desperation, and so he held out for a better offer. He suggested a face-to-face meeting with your father, who declined. I suppose he had become ill at that point, and he did not want a man with whom he negotiated to see his weakness."

"Are you saying my brother doesn't want your father's business, he wants the building from which it is run?" Thomas asks.

"I don't understand it," she says, "but that is how it appears."

"And how does this explain why they want us to marry?"

She smiles. "That I do not know. However, I did learn that my father grew curious during the initial negotiations about the building. If your father was willing to pay nearly twice what it was worth, there must be some advantage, and he wanted to know what it was so he could exploit it—either for himself or in negotiations. He did not find it, but he did manage to find out something else. Your father, and now your brother, is in the process of buying other buildings, spread all over the center of London. I know of six of them, but there may be more."

"What sort of buildings?" Thomas asks.

She shrugs. "Well, I can make nothing of them. Most appear to be of an ordinary variety of London properties. Several private homes, one with a shop at the street level. Another is a warehouse. If there is a pattern, I cannot discern it."

"And your father told you all this?" Thomas asks.

She laughs. "I am only a daughter, and that means I have to eavesdrop and sneak into his office and read his correspondence if I wish to know these things."

Thomas grins. "I say, is there any chance you'd be willing to give me a list of these buildings? Perhaps I could find some reason they are of value. If not, I might go and have a peek."

"I shall make a bargain with you," she says. "I'll give you that list if you promise to take me with you when you go for that peek."

"Miss Feldstein, have you not had enough of adventures?"

"Mr. Thresher," she counters, "what I've had enough of is being told what to do and where to go. I suppose there might be some danger, but I cannot think it likely. This is London, and one takes a risk when one steps foot out of doors. It does not keep me from doing so."

"Very well," Thomas says. "I accept your terms."

When they return to the mausoleum, they are walking arm in arm, and Miss Feldstein is grinning broadly. Thomas sees his brother and Mr. Feldstein exchange glances.

In the coach on the way back, Walter studies Thomas as though he were a dog expected to perform a trick. Mr. Hawke smiles and hums to himself ever so quietly. Pearl pushes herself backward as though she wants to vanish into the upholstery.

Thomas, for his part, has been thinking about his conversation with Miss Feldstein. He has taken such delight from their newly established partnership that he has entirely forgotten that his brother expected him to force a partnership of an entirely different sort.

It is Pearl who breaks the silence. "You mustn't keep us in suspense, Thomas. Did you ask her?"

Thomas is thinking about bank properties and secret dealings. He is taken aback. "Ask her what?" He knows he sounds like a servant who is being asked about missing silverware while the silver bulges in his pockets.

"Did you ask her to marry you, you dunce?" Walter booms.

"Oh, that." Thomas decides that being easy on the matter is his best approach. He shall no longer push back or question or demand explanations. He shall simply delay in the best-natured manner he can manage. "You know, Miss Feldstein and I never cared much for one another, but I feel that today all of that changed. I have come to see her in a new light, and I believe the feeling is mutual. Had I proposed to her under such conditions, she would have thought my new regard a pretense in the service of family business. It simply was not the time."

"Not the time!" Walter bellows.

Pearl places a gloved hand on his sleeve. She gently makes contact with the wool, but is careful to apply no pressure, lest the fabric brush up against her husband's skin. He does not try to escape her touch, which makes this the most affectionate display Thomas can recall seeing between husband and wife. Thomas looks away, embarrassed by this intimacy, as Pearl whispers something into her husband's ear.

"Damn it," Walter growls. "But if you've landed on the beachhead, you'd better damn well conquer. Unless you want to find yourself out on the streets looking for work as a porter."

Thomas knows his brother is speaking to him because he could be addressing these words to no one else, but Walter does not look at him or use his name. Thomas thinks back to try to recall Walter ever using his name, and he can recall nothing. Never in conversation. Letters, rare as they were, always began with whatever urgent news prompted their writing.

"Thank you for your advice, Walter," Thomas says, as if to prove a point. He is not entirely sure what that point is, and he knows with absolute certainty that it is lost on his brother.

SEVENTEEN

DEBAUCH

THOMAS SITS IN a remarkably comfortable chair on the second floor of the Golden Dawn headquarters. The evening rituals have been completed, and Thomas looks inward to poke at a strangely empty feeling. There was more theatrical gesturing and chanting in foreign tongues and waving of implements, but nothing happened that he, that any ordinary person, would call magical. He now understands that these people define magic as something that comes from within, stemming from his consciousness and his understanding of the universe. He understands that the common definition of magic, as held by people who in no way believe in it, is something less subtle and intellectual and contemplative. Nevertheless, a few lights or sparks or summoned spirits would go a long way to soothing the growing concern that he may be wasting time that a man in his condition cannot spare.

He is also attempting to conceal his disappointment. He spoke to MacGregor Mathers about moving up a grade shortly before the ceremony began, but the old fellow only laughed good-naturedly at his ambitions.

"Promotion to novice after only a week?" he blustered. "It cannot be done."

"I've learned the material," Thomas protested.

"But have you *learned* it, *Frater Ostium Et Speculum*?" MacGregor Mathers asked, clapping him on the shoulder. "Have you truly come to understand it? It's not simply a matter of memorization. It has to become part of you, lad."

"Wouldn't it become part of me better if I could do something with this knowledge?" Thomas pressed.

"Read it," MacGregor Mathers insisted. "Every day. Make it part of your life. It's not time wasted. It's part of the process, and you can't rush these things. There's no point in advancing when the learning is on your skin rather than in your blood."

Now, as he sips a brandy and water, Aleister Crowley comes and sits next to him. "They don't like it when initiates move too quickly."

"I don't see what is gained by continuing to study material I have already mastered."

"They're used to lesser men moving at a snail's pace," Crowley says. "They don't know what to do when they find fellows hungry to learn. The damnable thing is that it means they're likely to lose men like you if you're made to sit on your hands for two months."

Two months is not an insignificant span to a man turning into a tree. If he has two years of animate functioning left to him, this represents a little more than eight percent of his remaining time. There is no way to calculate it more precisely—not without knowing exactly when he will become incapacitated, or if there could ever be a clear moment, a specific day, when a neutral observer could say empirically that a new phase had begun. Even without precision, however, he can say that he has little time and he does not wish to squander his small portion. Would telling MacGregor Mathers about his condition make a difference? Thomas will never find out. It would be too painful, too humiliating, to confess his affliction.

"You seem like a game chap," Crowley says in a quiet voice. "Come visit my flat. I'll give you private lessons. No one has to know."

"You would do that?" Thomas suddenly feels a wave of affection for this brash fellow.

The magician grins like a circus ringmaster. "Why ever not? I also learned the initiate material in the first week—knew most of it before that really—and they made me wait until they were ready to wave me forward. Now I know enough that I can learn what I wish without the order's permission, but you've still got to get the basic building blocks."

After making plans to further his education secretly, he is about to take his leave, when he sees Isaiah Ruddington across the room, speaking to a few other fraters. "What do you think of that fellow?" Thomas asks Crowley.

"Ruddington? He's not impressed me with his learning, though I hear he's quite skilled at cartomancy and clairvoyance. Not seen any evidence of it myself. Why do you ask?"

Thomas isn't sure how much to reveal, but he doesn't want to lie. "I saw him at the bank the other day. I was wondering what he was about."

"Why not ask him?" When Crowley sees Thomas's expression, however, he raises his eyebrows. "You are an interesting fellow, Thresher."

✳

The following night, Thomas knocks on the door to Crowley's flat several times before the magician finally answers, wearing a robe loosely tied to reveal much of his expansive chest and, inexplicably, an ornate Egyptian headdress. Thomas has to take a step back to let a woman who smells of sweat and wine squeeze past him. She is attractive in a jarringly common way.

"Pardon me, lovie," she says, brushing her shoulder against him.

"Found her on the street," Crowley explains once Thomas is inside. He putters about in his slippers as he mixes a drink and then, remembering he has a guest, mixes another one. He then removes his headdress and places it on a wig stand. "A prostitute, I suppose, though she didn't ask for payment. So, a whore. I think we can agree to that term. Game, but not as game as she imagined. I may have been more than she bargained on."

Thomas is convinced that coming here was a bad idea. He was never overly prudish with his school friends, but he hardly knows Crowley, and he doesn't much want to hear about his minutes-old conquests when the man hasn't even put on clothes. He is in no way comforted when Crowley lights a pipe that is clearly not tobacco and offers it to Thomas.

"What is it?"

"Opium." Crowley grins lecherously. "Have you never tried it?"

"No, I'm afraid not," he answers, hating to feel like the fuddy-duddy. This must be how Walter feels all the time. Still, Thomas makes no move to take the pipe.

"You mustn't resist new experiences." Crowley take another puff. "Opium can expand your perception. The conservatives at Isis-Urania gasp if I mention it, but there are those of us who know that certain substances enhance the magical process. Summonings, meditation, astral travel—all of these things are more powerful with opium. Sex is also a powerful magical tool, but predictably the old fellows at the temple don't want to hear about that, either. I've been experimenting with sex magic quite a bit lately. Fucking works upon the consciousness differently than opium, of course."

Is Thomas supposed to say *of course* in response, as though he could possibly have an opinion upon the subject? He is in no way ready to weigh in on the subject of sex magic. He cannot yet speak to chaste magic with any authority.

"But that's all a little advanced for you," Crowley says with a smile that Thomas wishes he could believe was not condescending. What is he doing here, he wonders, with this new man, this aesthete? In the old days, Thomas and his friends might have regarded a fellow like Crowley as good for a laugh, someone to be mocked. And yet, Thomas makes no move to leave, because whatever else Crowley might be, he is a magician.

The walls are lined with bookshelves, stuffed with newly printed volumes and old folios, bound manuscripts, and, yes, actual scrolls, sheets of parchment rolled into tight little tubes and tied with ribbons. A crumbling cuneiform tablet leans against the wall. There are swords and spears and wands, some displayed as though museum pieces, others simply lying about as though Crowley might have need to grab a spear at any moment and—who can say?—hurl it at an astral antelope. Anything is possible. There are stacks of tarot cards, a human skull, a jar full of desiccated lizards, and even a crystal ball, though Thomas notices with inexplicable relief that it is sprinkled with a fine covering of dust.

None of these physical things prove Crowley is a magician, and yet Thomas somehow *knows* him to be one. It is not merely his audacious confidence, which Thomas finds simultaneously infuriating and magnetic. No, it is a sense. Maybe it is his connection with the Peculiarities that gives him this intuition. Maybe it is Crowley's mystical energy, whatever that might be.

After taking a few more lusty puffs of the opium, Crowley sets down the pipe and heaves himself to his feet. He takes a moment to orient himself and then begins to rummage languidly through his bookshelves. He has the air of an old man who has forgotten what he is about but soldiers on all the same. At last he finds what he is looking for: a slim, privately printed volume very similar to his Neophyte's manual. He sets it in Thomas's hands.

"This will be presented to you when they deign to raise you to the Zelator, which I have no doubt they should do at once." He smiles lazily. "I am not supposed to have this, so by all means don't lose it. You'd not believe who I had to fuck to get my hands on it."

Thomas wonders if Crowley is trying to shock him, but he thinks they may be beyond that now. Crowley is merely being Crowley. "I shall be very circumspect."

The magician makes his way back to his seat, using his hands as though the room were shrouded in darkness. "I hope you don't mind the invasion of privacy, but I did a bit of checking up on you?"

Thomas feels a lurch in his stomach. What precisely does this mean?

"A tarot reading. And I consulted the *I Ching*." Having dropped to the edge of his chair, he now wags his finger mockingly at Thomas. "You're far more interesting than you let on."

"What precisely have you learned?"

"Oh, you don't get an itemized list, you know." Crowley leans back, letting out a sigh of contentment, like a laborer who had finally taken a rest after a day of exertions. His legs are spread out appallingly. "It's not like hiring one of these private detectives the newspapers are always on about. It's more of a general feeling, a shove in the right direction. You have a significant secret. Oh, I know that is standard fortune-telling rubbish, but in your case it's true. A bigger secret than most. So big, I'm not entirely certain if you know much about it yourself. And you're on a bit of quest, aren't you? That's what your interest in the Golden Dawn is all about. It's not mere intellectual hunger or a desire to master the new way of things. You have something you want urgently to get done." He opens his mouth and unleashes a protracted, feline yawn. "Some connection to your family, I believe."

Thomas makes an effort not to change his facial expression. "You don't want me to say if you're right or wrong."

"Good God, no." Crowley snorts dismissively and, by the somewhat surprised expression that crosses his face, unexpectedly. "I either get a clear reading or I don't, but I'm never uncertain about which it is. But I am curious about your dreams."

Thomas perks up. "My dreams."

"I feel like someone is watching you. Maybe some*thing*." He yawns once more. "Or studying you, perhaps. It's so deuced difficult to be certain."

Thomas feels horrified at the prospect that his dreams are more than his own twisted imagination. At the same time, it is a relief to know that his mind has not been in some way disordered. "What can I do about it?"

Crowley shrugs. "You are doing it. Golden Dawn study is what you want. I don't get the sense that this observer means you harm just now, but best to be cautious. That should suffice."

Thomas thinks that someday it would be nice to feel so certain about his magical abilities. Or anything, really. Once he felt that way about mathematics— or nearly so. Thomas knows he was never destined to be one of the greats, but he was good. Being good is something. He likes to tell himself it is.

With his host apparently moments away from nodding off, it is time to take his leave. "You have been very kind."

"Nonsense," Crowley tells him. "I simply hope to see the cause of magic, of powerful magicians, furthered. It is our time, you know. This century, the century of steam, draws to a close, and it saw the world transformed. A man from 1799 would not recognize the world in which we live, and now, just as we are getting used to what we have wrought, the world changes again. The twentieth century will be unrecognizable to us—an age of magic. Just as there has been an industrial revolution, there will now be a magical revolution."

"You truly believe that?"

"If you deny it, you are like a bewigged eighteenth-century gentleman who thinks factories are but a momentary folly. The Peculiarities have changed everything by bringing magic out into the open, and men are too greedy not to profit from these changes. Men like your brother, who live to line their pockets, will become obsolete if they do not adapt."

"And you will rise in such a new society," Thomas prompts.

"To the very top," Crowley assures him. He then snaps to his feet. The opium torpor appears to have vanished. "It is still early. I could use a few drinks, and there's something I'd like to show you."

"Perhaps another time," Thomas tells him. "I must work in the morning."

"Then you will go to work with little sleep and a head full of drink," Crowley announces. "Let me dress, and we shall be on our way."

Crowley vanishes into his bedroom, and Thomas now feels that he has no choice but to go along with whatever the magician decides to do.

Crowley brings a flask of whisky for their journey, and during the cab ride he insistently passes it to Thomas after taking long sips. For his part, Thomas is no longer used to such strong drink consumed in such quantities and so quickly, and by the time they tumble out of the carriage in who knows what part of town, he is unsteady on his feet.

They are on a crowded street in a part of town Thomas doesn't recognize. There are gentlemen and working men and whores. Peddlers and shopkeepers cry out their wares. One man plays a fiddle, another an accordion, and both musicians duel for attention. A sawhorse coffee vendor pours out steaming mugs.

"What are we doing here?" Thomas asks for perhaps the first time, perhaps the sixth or seventh. He is not entirely sure.

"We're having an adventure," Crowley tells him. The people around them—high and low, fashionable and desperate—cannot be said to belong to any sort of group, but even so, Crowley does not belong. In his striped trousers and matching vest, and his overcoat so light brown it is almost tan, he looks a bit too effete for this rough-and-tumble world. Not that it matters to him. Crowley seems to believe he belongs no matter where he goes.

They make their way through the crowd until they reach a building guarded by a burly looking fellow with a massive and ridiculously styled mustache. He wears livery, and he stares straight ahead like a beefeater. Crowley whispers something in the man's ear, and the guardian immediately pulls the door open for the two of them.

A feeling of dread washes over Thomas as he comes to understand that Crowley has taken him to a whorehouse. Is that really the best the great magician has to offer? It is impressive in its own way. He has just finished with one woman and is already eager for the next. Thomas admires stamina, but, all in all, he would prefer to crawl under the duvet in his cold room.

He has been to many whorehouses, of course, and he has sometimes enjoyed himself. More often, he has pretended to do so. It is difficult to suspend judgment concerning the implausibility that some poor woman, desperate for food and shelter and clothes on her back, could be brought to moaning, writhing pinnacles of ecstasy by the likes of Thomas or—even more improbably—Thomas's friends.

He never shared his misgivings with those friends. No doubt they would have laughed and mocked, and so he'd gone along and felt uneasy about himself. Sometimes he overpaid, not when given a particularly gratifying experience, but usually when the woman proved too hungry or drugged or miserable to rise to the expected levels of performance. The money was less charity than a means of appeasing his conscience.

Does he now have the courage to tell Crowley that he will not pay for intimacies with one of these women? Will he say that he's had enough? Thank you very much for the loan of your illicit book, but I shall not partake of these whores. He needs Crowley. His time is short, and if magic is to save him, he must learn to be a magician. Crowley seems to be his best bet, and he cannot risk alienating the fellow.

But Thomas has had enough of accepting scraps from other men. He has had enough of powerlessness. He has lived this way since his father's death. No, longer than that. He has lived this way his whole life, and if he is to be a tree in a few years, he will be a man until such time as his roots pierce the ground.

"All very amusing," he tells Crowley, "but I am in no humor for this place."

"If you are ever in the humor for a place such as this," Crowley replies, his face suddenly quite serious, "then I have quite misjudged you. We're not here to indulge, Thresher."

"Then why are we here?"

Crowley smirks. "I think you should tell me."

Thomas has no idea what to say to this.

Crowley barks out a laugh. "It was in the tarot. I am supposed to take you here."

"The cards told you to take me to this whorehouse in particular?" Thomas asks.

"Oh, yes," Crowley assures him. "After a fashion. There's a lot of complex symbolism involved in reading the tarot on an advanced level. And sometimes the symbols do more than sit there. They, I don't know, get up and walk about. They say more than they say. When I was looking into your life with the cards, I had the most distinct impression that I should take you here, so here we are." He waves he arm about the room like this is all a dazzling show for Thomas's benefit. "I am eager to learn what this is all about."

Thomas looks out, following the arc of Crowley's hand, and that is when he sees that these are no ordinary whores. They are dressed in the usual tight and revealing gowns, running their hands down men's chests and cupping their chins, sashaying away while taking a man by the hand. That much is all standard, but here, in this particular brothel, there is something more.

These women are all Peculiar.

There are wolf-women, like Mrs. Topping and her daughter. There are women with wings and no feathers, feathers and no wings. There are women with scales and tentacles. In a massive glass container, two naked women with the fishy lower bodies of mermaids swim about and beckon to any man who comes close. Thomas witnesses with horror a woman with an elongated neck, with leaves sprouting from her shoulders, with skin hardened into bark, turgidly leading a man upstairs. With perhaps only a few months of human existence left, she is reduced to this.

There is more. A ring is set up in one portion of the house where boys, no more than eight or nine years old, fight like boxers. Instead of hands they have lobster claws. One of the boys is bleeding from a gash on his forehead, and his eye is swollen shut. In a pit, customers throw garbage and unwanted food and the dregs of drinks on a turtle with a human head that seems utterly insensible to its plight. A man walks about offering skewers of meat he claims to be rabbit born of human woman.

Thomas feels light-headed at the unexpected grotesquery of his surroundings. He takes hold of a chair to steady himself. Then he rounds on Crowley. "Is this your idea of amusement? Can you imagine I believe your nonsense about the cards?"

"If you doubt I can do as I say," Crowley asks, "then why have you put your trust in me?"

To this, Thomas has no answer.

"It is hard, I know, to commit fully to accepting a world that is beyond what we perceive." The magician's voice is soft, understanding, almost fatherly, Thomas supposes. It is what he imagines other people's fathers might have sounded like. "You have seen a thing or two, but you will need to see more before you accept the truth of how small a part of the universe our senses reveal. I can only say that somehow your being here is right, Thresher. I don't know why. Perhaps you are meant to see all this, to experience the revulsion you rightly feel. This is what the world is becoming. The government denies that the Peculiarities exist, but they can hardly continue to do so for long. In the meantime, these unfortunates are being exploited, turned into commodities to be bought and sold. I sense that you want to do something about the problem, but in order to do that something, you must understand the nature of the problem."

Thomas nods. "Very well. The cards said to bring me here, and you've done so. Now I've seen it, and I am ready to leave."

"I would hope so," Crowley says, but he makes no move to leave. "You are an interesting fellow. You are clever and inquisitive but also, if I may say so, timid. That suggests to me that you are driven by something. I should like to know what it is."

How much of his life does he keep secret from everyone? Thomas wonders. He shares so little, and yet, here is this strange and infuriating man who seems willing to help him. It occurs to him that having someone like Crowley, an athletic fellow intimidated by no one and nothing, would aid his cause. Could he confide in this man? Not everything, of course, but he cannot hide his needs if he is to expect help.

"My family's bank is acquiring properties throughout London," Thomas explains, surrendering to what he knows might be a foolish impulse. "I have no idea why, but I believe it has something to do with the Peculiarities. The bank is also collecting debts owed by magicians, some associated with the Golden Dawn, though I have not yet determined to what end."

Crowley narrows his eyes in concentration, attempting, no doubt, to piece together the unconnected and seemingly unconnectable elements. "Is that why you asked about Ruddington?"

Thomas nods. "I saw him at the bank, and then did a bit of research. He owes over three hundred pounds. I understand none of it. Perhaps you would care to help us investigate?"

"Us?" Crowley grins, like he knows Thomas has revealed something delicate.

He supposes he has. Still, there was no recruiting Crowley without revealing some basic facts. "Miss Feldstein is aiding me."

Crowley arches his eyebrows. "Is she now?"

"Look here, Crowley. I need your word that you won't make any attempt on her."

"Afraid I'll steal her from you?"

"Egad, man, I don't want her, but I need to know I am not delivering her into the hands of a wolf. You must agree to my terms."

Crowley waves his hands dismissively. "I shouldn't object to having a taste of her, but there is no shortage of willing women about. You needn't fear, Thresher. You have my word."

Having resolved that, Thomas is ready to move on. He is about to say as much when he hears a laugh cut through the crowd with the force of a swinging ax. It is a staccato business, like a woodpecker choking. Thomas turns to see his friend Reggie Willingham sitting at a table.

The faces of the men with him are obscured, but when Thomas steps forward, he sees George Leggett, Doug Fisher, and Ollie Mawson. These are his school chums, the very fellows he was supposed to be with in France. What are they doing in London?

Crowley forgotten, Thomas steps forward to the table. The four of them look up, and there is a general dampening of mood. Fisher, in the process of lifting a glass of champagne to his lips, sees Thomas and sets it back down with the look of a man who has learned of a sudden and unexpected death. Willingham's laughter cuts off with the suddenness of a guillotine dropping. Leggett and Mawson develop a sudden fascination with the tabletop.

"I thought you were in Paris," Thomas says.

Willingham recovers himself, takes a sip of his drink, and offers a grin in Thomas's direction. "Thresher, old boy! Here you are, and in such a game spot! And at this hour! Don't you bankers have to be up with the sun?"

"When did you return?" There is no warmth in his voice. "And why?"

"I say, I don't like that tone," Fisher says with a guffaw. He looks about the table, his eyes prompting encouragement. "You'd think I was being interrogated by my old grandma."

Mawson, who is quite drunk, puts a hand over his mouth to stifle a giggle. He was always fat, and he has gained weight since Thomas last saw him. "Stop it," he says to Fisher, swatting at him as though he were a fly. "My father will have me trampled to death if we anger the Threshers."

Fisher gives Mawson an unkind shove, and the drunk fellow leans significantly toward the other side of his chair. He then looks up at Thomas. "Still here, Thresher?"

"I'm confused," Thomas says. "Did something happen in France?"

"Just a matter of money," Mawson volunteers before Fisher can say more. His voice is a drunken approximation of solicitousness. "Nothing more than that. Funds were a bit thin on the ground, and we decided we'd be better off at home."

"For all of you?"

"If one of us is having difficulties," Leggett says, "the rest cannot go on without him."

"Evidently they can." This observation is met with silence and shifty eyes, and so Thomas forges ahead. "Why did you not inform me you were back in town?"

"Well, you know how it is." Willingham has what appears to be a lady's ribbon in his hands, and he fidgets with it as he speaks, rolling and unrolling it over his fingers. "Been a lot to do. Things to settle. And we presumed your toils in the old family mill would make it a bit of a moot point. You're a working gent now. You haven't time for larks with lads like us."

This conversation is like a deep, throbbing, itchy wound, under a bandage. Thomas does not want to see it, but he must unravel everything and gaze at the damage. "There's something you're not telling me."

Fisher, the largest of the lot, gets to his feet and turns to Thomas. Mawson objects and tries to yank at his clothes, but Fisher is having none of it. He pulls roughly away from Mawson and turns on Thomas. "I don't know what you're getting at, old boy, but I don't much care to be interrogated. Perhaps you've had too much to drink, or you are distracted by one of these Peculiar girls, but whatever the reason, you're being tiresome."

Thomas has never shied away from a brawl, but he doesn't think he is a match for Fisher, who is bigger than he is and far heavier, though not all of that weight is muscle. Fisher is also a brute. Thomas fought when circumstances required it. Fisher was the sort of chap who looked for fights and who kept punching when his foe was in retreat, kicking when his enemy was on the ground and helpless.

"There's no call to get angry," Thomas tells him, trying to keep his voice reasonable, though not friendly. He does not wish to be friendly. "I merely wish to understand why you didn't tell me you've returned."

"A misunderstanding," Mawson slurs. "Nothing to trouble yourself about."

"The poor fellow's feelings are hurt," says Leggett, who Thomas has come to see is nearly as drunk as Mawson. "He always was a whiner. No wonder we had to be paid to—"

Fisher turns around and snaps, "Shut it, you drunk fool." When he turns back around, his face is red with anger. "I'll not ask you to leave again."

"I should think not," says Crowley, who appears at Thomas's side. "What seems to be the trouble here, gents?"

"Who's the dandy?" Fisher demands.

Thomas is not entirely unhappy about having some assistance but doesn't want to seem like a man who can't handle his own affairs. "I'm quite capable of dealing with this."

"I don't doubt it," Crowley says. "If this buffoon takes a swing at you, I know you'll lay him out. What I doubt is that you have the resolve to get to the heart of the matter."

"What do you mean?" Thomas demands.

"These men are lying to you," Crowley says. "You can see it in their eyes."

"There's still only two of you," Fisher says.

Then he begins shrieking because Crowley takes hold of his wrist, which he bends back with an audible snap. In an instant, the hand is off the elbow and over Fisher's mouth, reducing his screams to muffled grunts.

"It hurts, I know," says Crowley sweetly, like a nursemaid to a sickly child, "maybe worse than anything you've ever experienced, but you cannot possibly prepare yourself for what will happen if I bend it further, so speak up, and do it quickly."

"It was his brother," Fisher gasps when Crowley moves his hand to let his victim speak. "He paid us to take Thresher to France. He paid for all of us. But when the father died, the money dried up. Most of it."

On the fringes of his vision, Thomas sees Mawson put his face in his cupped hands.

"Except for what he was paying you to keep quiet?" Crowley asks.

Fisher nods quickly, like he can get this over with all the soon.

"And how long was this going on?" Crowley demands. "How long were you in the brother's employ?"

Fisher doesn't want to speak, but the most gentle of movements on Crowley's part makes him grit his teeth and blow out his air. "Years," he says. "Since we were boys. From the beginning."

"My brother paid you to be my friend?" Thomas asks. It is as though a spirit has entered his body and is making his lips move. Thomas, the real Thomas, is floating far away somewhere.

"It wasn't a hardship," Mawson volunteers, quite forthcoming now that the cat is out of the bag. "You weren't difficult to be around. Might have been friends with you for nothing at all. And we didn't know it was all of us. It was only once we were away that we realized we were all in the same boat."

Thomas wants something, but he can't think of what. He has this terrible feeling that this situation calls for him to do something very particular, to make a certain kind of statement or gesture, but he cannot conceive of what it might be. He doesn't think it will come to him for hours or maybe days, and he doesn't want to stand here impotently while these dimwits, men with whom he spent nearly all of his free time for the past decade, prattle on. He should strike one of them, all of them, but it doesn't feel quite right. He should speak the words that will put them in their place, but such words don't exist. The world has turned askew. He feels more estranged from his life than when he learned he was turning into a tree.

"Let's go," he says to Crowley.

The two of them step out into the street. They have not been in the brothel terribly long, but Thomas expects to find a blasted landscape free of people, dotted with blackened buildings and skeletal trees, devoid of sound save a reedy wind. He is momentarily confounded to see a world entirely unchanged. The fiddler and the accordionist still vie for attention. The street vendors still cry their goods.

Crowley claps him on the back. "Whatever you need, Thresher, just speak the word. I'll be there for you."

Thresher blinks at his new friend, trying to comprehend unasked for loyalty coming hard on the heels of such devastating betrayal. "Why?"

"Your brother is plotting a secret real estate venture having to do with the Peculiarities. He is attempting to infiltrate the Golden Dawn to bend magicians to his will. Now we learn that he has been paying louts to befriend you for half your life. By God, this is damned interesting stuff! I'm all in."

EIGHTEEN
PRUDENCE

I T IS AFTER midnight when Thomas returns to his brother's house. He hasn't had so late a night since moving in, and he is not entirely certain how he will gain entrance. Presumably the servants will be aware that he has not yet returned, and one of their number will have remained awake to admit him. He certainly hopes so, though he supposes sleeping on the porch would be a fitting end to his adventures.

To his relief, the door opens soon after he rings the bell. He expects to find the house dark and cold, but the downstairs gas lamps glow brightly, and Thomas wonders if he somehow confused the time.

"Mr. Thresher is waiting for you in the parlor," the servant says.

Thomas's stomach twists in anticipation of trouble. He then blinks several times, dispelling the sensation. What sort of trouble could he face? Who has the power here? Walter desperately wants something from Thomas, who is now in possession of secrets. It is Walter who should fear Thomas. That is what he tells himself, but he cannot make himself believe it.

He finds his brother sitting in a stiff-backed chair, smoking cigars with Mr. Hawke, who is standing. The two of them look up as though they have been most unaccountably disturbed. Walter scowls and chews at his cigar.

"Have you any notion of the time?" Walter asks him.

"Late enough that I would rather be getting to bed than standing here discussing the hour," Thomas responds. "Was there something you required?"

"I require to know what you think you're doing." Walter's voice is harder if not louder. "This is how you behave after I give into your extortion and promote you?"

"To an isolated office," Thomas observes, "seemingly designed to make certain I accomplish nothing."

Walter's laughter is false and staccato. "You expect to be given authority after this? You are determined to squander your every opportunity by resuming old habits."

Thomas takes pleasure in the calmness of his tone. "I should hope that my efforts will be judged by my work at the bank, not how I occupy my time away from it."

"Keep your voice down!" Walter cries, his volume significantly louder than Thomas's near-whisper. "My wife is asleep, and I'd like at least one member of my household to be undisturbed by your gallivanting."

"Really, Walter, you needn't concern yourself," Thomas says with forced cheer. "I am quite my own master. If my work at the bank suffers, I would welcome your counsel, but as things stand, I do all that is required of me and more."

"I *require* you marry the Feldstein woman." Walter's voice is dangerously low. "No one cares what you are about in that garret."

Thomas has had quite enough of his insignificance being rubbed in his face by the man who may very well be destroying their family's source of wealth. "You seem awfully dismissive of my efforts, when it is your own that ought to concern you."

Something crosses Walter's face. At first Thomas thinks he has pushed his brother too far, but it is not rage that emerges in those lines around Walter's eyes, in that curious twitch along his mouth. It is something almost like a smile. "On some other occasion, I should love to hear a critique of my governorship by a man who knows nothing. At the moment, however, we are here to talk about you. Where were you tonight?"

Thomas opens his mouth to lie—to say something blandly innocuous—but he won't do it. Why should he not tell the truth? What could Walter possibly do to him to that he has not already done? He conspired to separate Thomas from a true friend years ago, and then set about putting him in the company of a group of blockheads whose only mission, as near as Thomas can tell, was to keep him busy with frivolous nonsense. There is nothing to be gained from asking why or even revealing that he knows. He does not see, however, why he must not speak the truth about his interests.

"I attended a meeting at the Hermetic Order of the Golden Dawn," he says, "and after I went to a curious establishment, one featuring Peculiars, with an accomplished magician."

Had he said he'd gone out to kill prostitutes and box up their organs he could not have shocked Walter more. "You say these words to me?" he thunders. "In my own house?"

"Why should I not?" Thomas keeps all heat from his voice. "Why should I not have my interests and pursue them at my leisure?"

Walter's face reddens. His teeth grind, and the severed butt of his cigar tumbles out of his mouth, dropping like a bird felled in flight. "I told you to stay away from those people!"

"And I chose not to obey." Thomas meets Walter's gaze. "You are my brother and my employer and my landlord. It is a curious arrangement, but one not of my choosing. If you wish an alteration, I am ready to discuss terms. I am not, however, your servant or your child, and you have no authority to order me about. I believe we are quite finished for the evening."

"Do not tell me what I am!" Walter booms. He is on his feet now. All concerns about Pearl's sleep have been relegated to their proper place. "You have no inkling of what I am to you, and I will say when we're finished!"

"Perhaps I might have a word alone with young Mister Thresher," volunteers Mr. Hawke in his most unctuous voice. This is the first he's spoken since Thomas entered the room.

Walter's color begins to fade to its normal pallor. His breathing slows. His fists unclench. His jaw is locked with rage and he cannot speak, so he merely nods his head.

"Come, sir, let us go to your room," says Mr. Hawke.

With a marked feeling of unreality, Thomas walks upstairs, Mr. Hawke in tow. This strange man's footsteps make no sound, and the most sensitive floorboards fail to creak or yelp under his slight weight. Thomas looks behind a few times to make sure the man is still there, and also because he can't quite understand why he is being followed.

Mr. Hawke turns up the low gas lamp and closes the door. He gestures for Thomas to have a seat on his bed. Feeling as though he is in a dream, Thomas does so.

"You must know that the elder Mr. Thresher only wishes what is best for you," says Mr. Hawke with his queer smile. A few years ago, Thomas might have called it peculiar, but he can no longer use that word for quotidian matters.

"I don't know that at all," Thomas responds. "Nor do I care. I do my work and stay out of his way. That ought to be enough for him."

"But it is not," says Mr. Hawke. "It cannot be. You are his nearest relation. He has no heir, which means if something were to happen to him. . . ." Mr. Hawke allows the terrible thought to drift away, but then he rallies. "If he were to be cut down, taken from us in his prime, then you would need to carry on the Thresher tradition."

Thomas feels absurd, sitting on his bed while Mr. Hawke stands before him. They are shut alone in his bedroom. How did he come to be in this unaccountable situation?

"You and I are not so different," Mr. Hawke continues. "I was quite interested in mathematics in my own university days. Oh, such happy times and so long ago."

"Yes, well that is—quite interesting," Thomas manages. Why does this preposterous man not leave?

Mr. Hawke gracefully drops to his knees and begins to remove Thomas's shoes. He smiles as though this is the most delightful thing he has ever done. His slender fingers deftly undo the buckles. He hums ever so softly. "So thorough you are. Diligently looking into the bank's business. Why, you have even shown some interest in my own insignificant history with the bank. It is all so flattering."

Thomas has had enough. There is simply too much disruption in a life that previously indulged none at all. This very moment is the breaking point. He tenses his leg, fully prepared to yank it away, to kick Mr. Hawke in the face if need be.

Mr. Hawke will not have it. He holds Thomas's foot still with one very strong hand while the other nimbly works at the buckle.

"Let me do this little thing for you," Mr. Hawke says. "Let me show I am not angry, that I have no fear of anything you might uncover. Strip me bare. I have no secrets. None whatsoever. Can you say the same, my dear Mr. Thresher?"

Thomas tries to pull free his foot again, but Mr. Hawke is too strong. "Damn you, let me go. I don't want you meddling with my feet."

The smile does not quiver, but Mr. Hawke shakes his head. He then lets out a sigh and stands once more. "Beat a dog often enough, and it knows not a kindness."

Thomas rises. "If that is how you choose to see it, I shall not argue." He opens the door and gestures for Mr. Hawke to leave.

"It was the late Samuel Thresher's wish that his bank be always growing," Mr. Hawke says in his gentle, lecturing tone. "Our founder dreamt of a small bank to serve small men, but we have moved beyond such things. That is why the late Samuel Thresher sought my services, and it is why I continue to serve his son. I know he can at times appear hard and uncaring, but he is doing all he can for you, while you look for faults and number his imagined errors. You seek out nasty widows when a pristine bride is offered."

Mr. Hawke knows of Mrs. Yardley. Thomas feels like a schoolboy caught at some naughty adventure. He reminds himself that he is a grown man and may choose his company. "I'll thank you to mind your business, sir."

"Oh, I always do. Why do you suppose you are under this roof? Why do you work at Thresher's? Samuel Thresher had great things in mind for you."

"Great things in mind for me?" Thomas feels his face grow hot. After what he has learned tonight, this is really too much. "Then why the devil could I not stay at Cambridge? He studied mathematics at Trinity, but he made me give it up. Why did he seem to engineer for me a life of insignificance?"

Mr. Hawke looks as though this question causes him genuine grief. "A man such as Mr. Samuel Thresher must balance many forces pulling him this way and that. . . ." He shakes his head at the wonder of it. "Do not nurse your wounds, youngest Mr. Thresher. Do not trouble yourself with how you came to be here, only marvel that you are on the right path."

"I have no idea what you mean," Thomas says. "My family has worked against me my entire life. I shall not sacrifice myself for some hidden goal."

"At most any sacrifice would be temporary," Mr. Hawke says. "I beg you give the elder Mr. Thresher six months. Do the simple and easy things he asks of you, and if you are not satisfied at the end of that time, come see me and all shall be as you desire. If you wish to be free of the bank, you shall be. If it is money you want, then you shall have what you need. If you wish a position at one of the universities teaching mathematics, that too can be arranged. I think, however, when you see what Mr. Thresher does, when the fullness of his schemes begins to bear fruit, you shall not ask for anything of the kind. The bank will grow, and you will grow with it." Mr. Hawke widens his eyes and blinks languidly. "Will you do this for me?"

"Doing as my brother wishes includes marrying against my wishes," Thomas notes.

Mr. Hawke puts a hand on Thomas's shoulder. "He is asking for you to marry in the best interests of the family. Is this something new or unheard of? Have there never been any such arrangements? Really, sir, you are being childish. If you are unhappy with Miss Feldstein, seek comfort elsewhere. I do not doubt you know how." Mr. Hawke licks his lips and grins. "In his youth,

Mr. Walter Thresher—oh, the stories I could tell you. Suffice to say they would surprise you. It is only marriage we are talking about. Nothing more. Can wrecking your family's plans really mean nothing to you? I don't believe you are so cruel."

So saying, he gives Thomas's shoulder a little squeeze and he exits the room.

·➤ NINETEEN ◄·
POWER

I T IS A Sunday afternoon, one week later, and the weather has become significantly colder. Flurries of snow drift down, and the ground is slippery
with ice. The wind, at least, is no more than a gentle breeze.

It is Thomas's one day off, and he thinks back on the previous week of labors,
having little to show for his time. He and Mr. Drummond have continued to
review documents. They have continued to find evidence of misguided loans
to men whose circumstances make clear they can never repay. Thomas has seen
ledgers that suggest the bank's finances may begin to stumble by the middle
of next year. The bank might fall before the beginning of the next. There is
some internal documentation that suggests concern on the part of some of the
older directors, but for the most part there is silence. The ship that is Thresher's
glides uncaringly toward the cliffs, and no one seems willing to right it.

It has been a week of questions. Now, perhaps, Thomas shall find an answer.

He stands in front of a house on a quiet stretch off Cannon Street. It is a
residential neighborhood, with few shops or eateries nearby. Inside most of these
houses, people are huddled around their fires, reading books or playing cards or
listening to a child awkwardly coax a tune from a piano. There are plush rugs
and steaming cups of cider and perhaps a sleepy cat curled upon someone's lap.

The things Thomas longs for have changed in recent weeks. He cannot
imagine having before felt envious of such a domestic scene. On the other
hand, he could not have imagined breaking into a house with a self-proclaimed
magician and a Jewess, but here he is.

Perhaps oddest of all, he is beginning to feel almost like a banker. Thomas
was intrigued enough by drunk Mawson's words at the Peculiar brothel that he
did a bit of digging. Mawson's father's name had drawn his attention before, but
he had not yet sought more information. Now he has learned that Mawson's
father owes a great deal of money to other banks—a crippling amount that, if

called in, would quite ruin him. The family has long since held a substantial amount of Indian property, and his income has depended in great part upon the rents, but this money has been in short supply owing to recent Indian crop failures. Now that crops on the subcontinent appear to be on the mend, Mawson has sought additional funds to restore his properties to their former glory and reestablish a steady flow of income, with which he will repay old debts and new. A few candid conversations with some of the bankers led Thomas to conclude that Mawson had been turned away elsewhere, and rightly so. A new loan, whatever grand plans Mawson might pronounce, would mostly go to pay off Thresher's competitors. For all that, the notes in the file suggest Walter has all but decided to approve these new funds. Learning more, Thomas has decided, will be the first order of business for the new week.

For now, it is housebreaking.

"It's not really burglary," Crowley said as they prepared for the adventure at his flat. "You own the place, after all."

"The bank owns it," Thomas corrected.

"You're a Thresher," Crowley said. "There's not a bobby in the city who would dare to arrest you for making your way into a building owned by your family's bank."

Thomas is not so certain, though he supposes it is a fair bet. As for how they will actually get inside, Crowley says they are to leave it to him.

Miss Feldstein is another matter. It is she who knew the location of the building in question, she who did the hard work of sneaking into her father's office and reading through what was surely fiendishly dull correspondence. She certainly has the right to insist on being present during the actual felony, though Thomas cannot guess why she should want to be.

Of course, that's not true. He can guess. He supposes she must be very bored in her life. She is an intelligent woman, and as she speaks little of her acquaintances or social circles, she must be lonely. Her father is not the sort of man to let his daughter indulge in the freedoms enjoyed by so many other young ladies these days. When they communicated to arrange for this excursion, it required the exchange of several notes in which Miss Feldstein dithered quite irritatingly as to whether or not she could get free and, if so, at what time.

But she has managed it, and Thomas is pleased by her attitude which is, for want of a better word, manly. She is not fidgety or chatty or playing her part like an actress. Her greeting to both Thomas and Crowley was businesslike—efficient without being rude. She is not here to be a lady among men. She is one of a trio.

Thomas's concerns about Crowley appear to be unfounded. The magician treats Miss Feldstein with entirely appropriate warmth. He behaves as though she has every right to be among them, but he does not flirt with her. Thomas finds Crowley to be deeply flawed and somewhat insufferable, but now he feels a rush of affection for this man who has, when he considers it, proved himself to be a good friend. He may not be precisely the sort of person Thomas might have chosen to spend his time with, but Thomas's tastes have proved to be poor indicators of worthiness.

In the weeks since Thomas's initiation into the Golden Dawn, Crowley has thrown himself into the role of magical tutor. He has given Thomas further materials to study, covering the essential Golden Dawn subjects of alchemy (magical, not chemical), the branch of Jewish mysticism called Kabbalah, the uses of the tarot, and in-depth detailing of the realms and beings associated with the astrological symbols. They have studied herbology and magical squares and summoning circles. They have practiced the core magical rituals: the Lesser Banishing Ritual of the Pentagram, the Rose Cross, the Middle Pillar, the Adorations of the Sun.

These rituals make Thomas feel rather silly, and Crowley has seemed troubled when they practice, but he has said nothing more than that it is a learning process. This suggests to Thomas that he may be missing some essential elements in these procedures. It is all about will, says Crowley. It is about seeing what one says in one's mind. Thomas, however, struggles to see gods and energy and his will made manifest. He struggles to invest the power of his imagination into the words he speaks. In this aspect of magic, he believes himself terribly maladroit. As for the scholarly aspects, Crowley seems quite pleased with his progress.

Thomas is certain he is making much greater progress with Crowley than he is in the Golden Dawn. Thomas is turning into a tree, and nothing he is doing at the Iris Urania Temple or at Crowley's apartment seems to offer any hope of slowing the progress. Perhaps that is why he has agreed to this plan. Breaking into a house may be mad, but at least he is doing something.

Despite the cold, they walk around the block as they discuss their options. Thomas and Miss Feldstein both propose various ridiculous notions—crawling in through a window, attempting to gain access to the roof—but Crowley dismisses these. He is undoubtedly the person in their group with the most experience with all things frowned upon by society. He certainly presents himself as someone who has much housebreaking experience upon which to call, and so it is easy to let him take the lead.

"We simply go up the steps and make our way inside," Crowley says. "No one will trouble themselves to take note of two respectable gentleman with a lady. The more we circle the block while shifting our glances back and forth, the more conspicuous we become."

"And how do we get past the locked door?" Miss Feldstein asks.

"Leave that to me," the magician tells her breezily.

When they round the corner and make their way back to the house, however, they see that there is a figure lurking on the porch.

Thomas's first impulse is to run, which he soon realizes makes him the most cowardly member of his group since Crowley and Miss Feldstein march purposefully forward. *How dare you step onto our porch*, their posture seems to say. Thomas hurries along behind them.

As they get closer, they see it is a woman, slender and unthreatening in her posture, though her back is toward them. At the sound of their footsteps, she turns, but they cannot make out anything of her face, which is covered with a hood.

It is all too familiar, and Thomas stiffens with alarm before he even realizes he knows this person.

"Hello again, Thomas," says Ruby Topping. She has a hand on Thomas's arm before he can retreat, and she sniffs generally in the direction of his armpit.

Thomas frees himself and takes a step back. "Miss Topping. What are you doing here?"

"Mama said I should keep an eye on you." Her answer is clipped and slightly impatient, as though Thomas has asked an unforgivable, stupid question.

"But how did you know I would be *here*?" Thomas insists.

"Oh, that's easy," she explains. "I followed you from your home."

"And how did you know to do so today?" Thomas presses.

"I've been doing it every day, haven't I?"

Thomas can no longer avoid introductions, and he makes them reluctantly. Miss Topping hasn't precisely removed her hood, but it has shifted farther back, and Thomas has no doubt that his companions must see her wolfish features as she leans in and gives both Miss Feldstein and Crowley very thorough sniffs. They are polite enough not to demonstrate their alarm.

"You may thank your mother for her kind concern," Thomas says evenly, "but I don't require a young lady to follow me about the city, and this is certainly no time for you to be lurking about."

"I'm to keep you safe," Ruby insists. "Mama says so."

"I'm sure if she understood—"

"I'm to keep you safe," she says again, as though Thomas has wasted quite enough of her time.

"How exactly do you know the young lady's mother?" Crowley asks in the breezy tone one hears in pre-prandial conversation. Nothing alarming to Crowley—just a wolf-woman sniffing at him before they commence committing crimes.

Thomas provides a very brief explanation of his connection with the Toppings, and it is enough to intrigue Crowley.

"Then she's a magician," he says, "and one clever enough to point you toward the Golden Dawn. She sent her daughter to watch over you. Perhaps this Mrs. Topping has seen something that suggests we need her daughter with us."

"She does go on about the future," Ruby says, by way of offering up more evidence.

Miss Feldstein turns to Ruby, her expression showing a kind of sisterly concern. "We may be facing genuine danger, and certainly the possibility of legal trouble."

"That don't bother me," Ruby insists. "I can handle danger, and no nabber'll catch me. I'm too quick by half."

"Do you trust these people, Thresher?" Crowley asks.

"I have no reason not to," he begins, though he gets no further.

"Well, if the young lady wants to help, and her magician mother thinks it wise, we ought to be grateful rather than resistant," Crowley concludes. "As it happens, I saw something in the *I Ching* this morning about receiving help. I thought it meant the two of you, but here's this young lady."

But she is always sniffing at me is not the sort of objection Thomas wishes to lodge. He can see Miss Feldstein nodding at Crowley's words, and Thomas understands that he has been outvoted in the investigation of his own family's bank.

"Very well," Thomas says in defeat, "but don't do anything untoward."

"Never," Ruby assures him, "though I don't know what that means."

Evidently satisfied by how these events have played out, Crowley ascends the steps and then takes from his pocket a slim bar of metal with a handle made of wrapped leather. He inserts this into lock and from his other pocket he takes a stone. He smashes the bar with the stone. The sound, which seems to Thomas like a shotgun blast, echoes along the deserted street, but no windows fly open, no slobbering guard dogs bark, and no policeman blows his whistle. Meanwhile, the door swings open.

Crowley grins at them and pushes wide the door for Miss Feldstein to enter. Thomas is more concerned for safety than theater, however, and he insists on going first.

"Good thinking," Crowley said. "For a moment I forgot this was more than a routine bit of housebreaking."

Miss Feldstein casts him a look, but she chooses to say nothing. Thomas is convinced this is the wisest course.

Once they are inside, with the door closed—which it remains only because Crowley has used his stone to keep it that way—they are unsure what to do. It is, in most ways, an ordinary house. There are empty, unfurnished rooms. It is as cold inside as out, perhaps colder, but that is no surprise.

The smell is another matter. It is musty, like a wet dog, but also full of decay. Urine and feces hang heavily in the air. Miss Feldstein heroically tries to appear unperturbed, but Thomas isn't fooled. No one would be, because there is no pretending that this is something mildly unpleasant. It is vile beyond anything Thomas has ever encountered.

Now that they are off the street, Ruby removes her hood and takes an undisguised sniff around. She partly closes her eyes and shakes her head a little. "That's right nasty."

Thomas, with his less keen sense of smell, agrees.

"Also, it's rabbits," Ruby says.

"Rabbits?"

"A lot of them."

There is something else, something beyond temperature and stench, he supposes. There is a feeling, Thomas would call it, but that's not quite right. It is as though Thomas is using a sense for the first time—like a man raised in absolute quiet who hears his first sound. He would know, Thomas supposes, if it were good or bad—a pleasing melody or a shriek of terror—but he would not know what it was. That is how Thomas feels, and whatever he is sensing, it is something he does not like.

"Any ideas?" he asks Crowley.

The magician shakes his head. "Nothing good."

"I don't think we should be here," Thomas says.

Miss Feldstein looks around uneasily. "That's rather the point."

Thomas supposes it is.

All four of them look at the staircase. There is no doubt that what they smell, what they feel, comes from above. Perhaps there is a particular way to approach this unknown. Thomas has no idea what that might be.

"Anything we need to do to prepare ourselves?" Thomas asks.

Crowley shrugs. "There is something at work here. I can feel it, but I cannot guess what that might be. That means I don't know how we can make ourselves ready."

"Then I suppose we'd better go up the stairs," Miss Feldstein says.

She is as scared as Thomas is. He can see it in her eyes, but he appreciates that she is putting on a brave face. Thomas doesn't quite see the point in doing so, but perhaps that is the privilege of being a man.

The debate seems to have reached its end, so he begins to climb the stairs, though Ruby deftly moves in front of him, holding him back with one hand as she advances. "I'll go first."

Thomas opens his mouth to object. He cannot let a young lady, no matter how odd, face danger before he does, but Crowley shakes his head. "Think like a magician," he says.

Thomas doesn't know what that means, but he supposes Crowley does, and he falls into line behind the wolf-girl. Miss Feldstein follows, and Crowley takes up the rear in case they are attacked from behind by demons or vampires or bad-smell creatures. The thought of it makes Thomas want to giggle, but he supposes the notion of beings made from foul scents is no more absurd than many of the other things he's witnessed.

They reach the second floor, passing by regularly mounted wall sconces. They are either empty or contain the remnants of candles. These, however, are not dry and dusty. They appear to have been recently lit.

The various unpleasant sensations grow stronger, but they encounter nothing else but empty, dusty rooms. On the third floor they begin to hear the sounds. There is scratching, like an animal digging in the dirt, and a faint vibrating hum. Ruby sniffs at the air and grimaces. Thomas and Miss Feldstein look at Crowley, but he merely shakes his head. All three of them seem to have come to the conclusion that talking is ill-advised.

They ascend the final staircase to the fourth floor, and Thomas is completely unprepared for what they find. This is, in part, because he expected to find either nothing out of the ordinary or, alternatively, something so strange it would be beyond the ability of his mind to comprehend. The reality is a little of both, but mostly it is disturbing.

The top floor is a garret, and—at least from an architectural perspective—a nicer one than that which serves as Thomas's office at Thresher's. It has large windows letting in the gray light of the day. In the center of the large space is a wooden frame, perhaps three feet in diameter. It is of a circular shape, fashioned intricately out of polished oak. It stands on legs that prop it up, and around the doorway a circle has been drawn in chalk onto the floor. Within it are smaller circles, many of which are broken up into squares. Each of these squares contain writing—Hebrew and Greek letters are common, but so are words in Latin and even what seem to be Chinese characters.

The frame itself opens into blackness. It is, Thomas concludes, a gateway of some kind.

TWENTY

RUIN

A T FIRST IT seems as though the frame is linked to another world that is currently night or, perhaps more nightmarishly, always dark. Thomas decides it is something else. It is more that light does not penetrate the doorway. It opens to something, but he cannot see what. That he can see nothing in no way suggests there isn't a place or beings or monsters just on the other side of the door, ready to squeeze through. It does not suggest that they cannot themselves crawl in, though Thomas believes doing so would be a very bad idea.

He wants to shift around, to see if the portal looks the same from the other side, but he is disinclined to move. He thinks the chalk of the circle surrounding the portal has been set down so as not to be easily smudged, but he would have to step on some of the writing to maneuver around the room, and he isn't sure such an act would be without consequences.

Uncertainty about whether to move allows him to consider the more mundane horrors in the room. The rabbits.

There are cages full of them. Dozens and dozens of rabbits. They hop lethargically, perhaps because of the cold, perhaps for want of food or water. There are dried scraps of vegetable matter, but the bottoms of the cages are now carpeted with droppings. That, Thomas thinks, is bad news. Some rabbit-minder could arrive at any moment to tend to the animals. Alternatively, they might be left for days more. The rabbits appear to have no purpose except to die under miserable conditions.

There is a table directly across from the wooden doorway, and it is covered with blood and bits of fur. A dagger, the blade stained with blood, lies upon it. It has an ornate and ceremonial handle, also shaped like a rabbit.

"It smells of soil," Ruby pronounces. "Behind everything else—the rot and the nasty business—there's soil."

163

Thomas has already been pondering the symbols for Taurus, Virgo, and Capricorn—all earth signs. And there is the symbol for Saturn, which rules Capricorn.

"Rabbits are associated with earth, are they not?" Thomas asks Crowley.

"In Chinese astrology," Crowley says with a nod.

"Rabbit children," Thomas says out loud. He had no intention of doing so. He wasn't even aware that his mind was racing, but it seems to have been processing things quite on its own.

"Yes," Crowley agrees. "This is the point at which it reaches through."

"What are you saying?" Miss Feldstein asks. "That this . . . this whatever it is causes the rabbit births."

Crowley rubs his chin. "What do you know of astral travel?" he asks them.

"Mama does it," Ruby says, "but she won't teach me."

"I know it's part of the Golden Dawn system," Miss Feldstein answers. "The ability to send one's soul to another place—a place of spirit."

"Not quite," says Crowley. "The spirit does travel, but not to realms of other spirits—merely to other realms. It is why it is often difficult to communicate during these travels. If a being of flesh were to send his spirit to our world, only one in a million, one in ten million—a person such as myself—would be able to sense such a being. Often during astral travel, one wanders through a strange landscape, and the experience is wondrous, but also lonely."

"You've done this?" Thomas asks.

"Many times," he says. "It is one of the first truly magical things you will learn to do. That is, one of the first things that you will see as being something other than ordinary."

"What's it got to do with this nastiness?" Ruby asks.

"I think this is a stable portal to another realm," Crowley says. "What is the nature of the path by which my spirit visits another plane of existence? No one knows. I think that unknown means has been recreated here in this gate. It allows some of that world's nature or essence or the rules by which it is governed—whatever you wish to call it—to bleed through to ours. The doorway requires magic to stay open, and likely to close, and that magic, I imagine, in turn requires blood sacrifice."

"Are you suggesting some sort of land of the rabbits?" Miss Feldstein asks incredulously.

"Possibly," Crowley says as if he finds this notion much less absurd than Miss

Feldstein does. "Or there may be some inherent leporidan nature to it. Or rabbits here correspond to something entirely different there, but the link, of some astrological or Kabbalistic or spiritual association, is an exact one. Or it may be that the rabbits used for sacrifice causes a bleed effect into our world, which causes the rabbit births. Perhaps the connection between rabbits in this world and their correspondent in the other is so true and pure that even the act of understanding it would destroy our minds. It could be any or all or none of these things."

"That's a door?" asks Ruby, pointing at the portal. "If I were to go through, I'd pop out in some other place?"

Crowley shrugs. "Likely, but it might well be a world of fire or one in which the gravity will crush you the instant you pass through. I would not suggest trying the experiment."

Thomas feels like he is not quite understanding all of this. "Each of the Peculiarities have their own portal? There is a room like this for . . . for the Elegants or wolf-people or, or people turning into trees." He tries to keep his voice neutral on this last, and thinks he has, in the main, been successful.

"Who can say?" Crowley appears genuinely puzzled. "A portal like this might account for two or a dozen different Peculiar manifestations. It is also possible that these portals magnify a natural bleeding effect caused by ordinary astral travel. Perhaps I, myself, when I visit other realms somehow cause unintended consequences in this one. However, I suspect that with some of the more common Peculiarities, there must be a corresponding portal of this sort."

"Then we must close it down," proclaims Miss Feldstein.

"Is that right?" Ruby sounds like she is using her nanny voice. Her hands are on her hips. "We don't know what we're doing, so we just want to smash it all to bits? And something don't sit right to me. Someone went to a lot of trouble to put all this together, right? They got all these poor creatures and did up all this magic hoopla, and then what? They put a lock on the door and forget it? Never occurred to them that someone might wander in here and do some damage?"

Crowley rubs his chin. "The young lady has a point. There weren't even spells to make uninvited guests disinclined to enter the house. Those would be easy enough to set up. I have them in my flat, and they are remarkably effective."

"Then we leave it as it is?" Miss Feldstein asked. "We walk away and leave women to suffer rabbit births? I cannot do that."

Thomas feels inclined to take her part in this conflict. "We came here to learn. Perhaps we ought to learn what happens if we destroy this portal."

Crowley appears intrigued by this line of reasoning. "Unfortunately, it is not exactly clear how to do that. It could be nothing more complicated than smashing that wooden frame. Problem solved. It could also be that the frame is there not to permit the flow of energy or power or what have you, but to contain it, and smashing it might unleash an even more destructive force, perhaps turning every birth into a rabbit birth."

"Aren't you supposed to be some sort of master magician?" Miss Feldstein asks challengingly. "Surely you have some ideas."

"I *am* a master magician," he tells her with casual sincerity. "I have no doubt I shall become the greatest magician of this age, but that doesn't mean I know everything—merely more than everyone else. I'd also point out that we are dealing with something entirely new. Still, if you give me a moment, I may come up with something."

While Crowley moves around the chalk circle, studying the writings, Thomas—with much less real or affected confidence—also tries to make sense of what he is looking at. Some of the writings are mysterious beyond his ability to understand, but what captures his attention is something that looks strangely familiar. It is not that he recognizes the meaning itself, for he is looking at a hodgepodge of Roman, Greek, and Hebrew letters, but it is more the organization. Some letters are oversized, whereas others are small and elevated. There are lines that seem to suggest division and parentheses implying function.

Thomas realizes he is looking at a complicated set of mathematical functions.

It is its own notation, and there are no numbers present, but something catches his eye.

"Miss Feldstein," Thomas says, "do you know Hebrew?"

"Not well," she answers. "My father did not wish us exposed to our culture, but I have learned a little on my own. Why?"

"Because I don't think those can be words," he says, gesturing at the section that interests him. "My Golden Dawn studies require a rudimentary understanding of the language, but I've never seen a word with three letter alefs written consecutively."

She nods. "Alef is usually a neutral letter, carrying a vowel sound, so it wouldn't be repeated in that way. I know the writing in Yiddish is different. Could it be that?"

Thomas doesn't think so. He supposes it is possible to have two neutral letters back to back, but three seems unlikely. Besides, this is high magic, and the writing will be in one of the languages of high magic. That means Hebrew. Yiddish, as he understands it, is the tongue of peddlers and pawnshop keepers.

"Those are numbers," Thomas says as the reality grasps him. From his study materials he has learned that the Hebrews used letters for numbers, much as the Romans did, and he has memorized their values. But this isn't some simple tally. It is a process of some kind—a problem being worked out, and a complicated one at that. "That's why it looks familiar. Some of these Greek and Roman letters are replacements for more traditional symbols, but there can be no denying that these are formulae we are looking at."

He knows that it is so. He can begin to see it now. At the center of everything is a value, indicated by a Greek omega and a Hebrew alef, the last and first letters of their alphabets, respectively. Is there meaning in that? The beginning of the end? The end of the beginning? Thomas cannot speak to such things, but what he is looking at is astonishing, complex and tantalizing. He wishes he could write it down, that he had the leisure to toy with it at length. "It is solving for omega-alef," he says. "Look, I think that section there is describing an area. And I think that could be calculating a vector quantity. It is hard to know for certain, because the symbols are unique, but the syntax makes sense. This is—this is an algorithm."

"What's that?" Ruby asks as though it may be dangerous.

"It's a set of directions for performing a task," he explains. "In this case, the task is solving for the value of omega-alef, which is something always changing. Observe this section." He steps closer.

"No one is doing maths." Crowley sounds like a schoolmaster, frustrated that his pupils have missed a lesson's point. "This is magic. Imagination and will are what matter here, not logic. And I believe I have figured out what sort of ritual we are looking at. Very dark stuff, I assure you. Do you see that?" He points at a section of the writings. "Straight out of Agrippa. Well, not quite straight, is it? That looks like a bit of an Enochian twist on the 75original design, but I think I see what they're getting at."

"Sounds like a lot of mumbo jumbo," Ruby says. "We smash it, or we don't."

"Tinker with a circle and you could free a demon or spirit or astral creature of terrible power," Crowley says. "Not the best way to go unless you are very certain you know your business."

"I know mathematics," Thomas assures him. "And this part here quite looks like calculus, but there's also some complicated geometry. I think it may be directing a flow of energy or power or what have you based on this symbol, this omega-alef, which describes a polynomial function."

As often happens when a man discusses mathematics, the room remains silent.

"We must do *something*, surely," Miss Feldstein says after a moment, absently hugging herself. She is eager to get out of this house, and Thomas cannot blame her.

Crowley's face suddenly appears quite wicked as he smiles at Miss Feldstein. "Are you so certain? Would you kill these defenseless creatures?"

At this Miss Feldstein blushes, and Thomas thinks rightly so. He tears himself away from the symbols on the floor. "See here, Crowley, there's no need to be a bully."

"I am merely pointing out that these things have a cost. Magic is a kind of energy. It does not come from nowhere. Just as you must burn gas or a candle to have light, you cannot effect magic without a source of power, and in this case that source may be rather bloody." He gestures with his head toward the rabbits.

"There must be another way," Miss Feldstein says.

"Rabbit death or rabbit births?" he says to her. "That is the choice. Which do you want?"

Ruby steps forward, placing herself between Crowley and Miss Feldstein. "I don't care for your tone, Mister Magician."

Thomas agrees, and he's somewhat mortified that Ruby spoke up before he did. It must be her animal reflexes, he decides.

Crowley is unperturbed by all this. He walks over to a rabbit cage and grabs one of the pathetic creatures. It squeals as he pulls it by the scruff of its neck and slaps it down upon the stained table where it squirms. Its eyes are wide, and its mouth opens soundlessly.

"Hold on one moment," Thomas says, looking at the symbols again. He can do this, given enough time. He is sure of it. "Give me an hour and I can do something with this."

"An hour is nothing," Crowley says. "The magician must take his time learning, but he must also be resolute." Having declared his intent, Crowley lifts the dagger and drives it into the creature's neck, separating head from body. It is a sudden and swift blow, and the animal is dead before it even knows what is happening.

Ruby snarls quietly. Miss Feldstein has let out a little shriek. Her gloved fingers are pressed to her mouth, and her eyes are wide with fright and disgust, but there is something else there too. Thomas wonders if she is perhaps a little bit impressed with Crowley's manful display.

"Don't be so squeamish," Crowley tells her. "Have you never wondered how your meat makes its way to your table."

"Miss Feldstein does not eat meat," Thomas offers lamely.

Crowley holds out both hands, like a stage magician—as opposed to the sort he actually is—preparing to dazzle the audience. He then grabs hold of the headless rabbit and thrusts it in front of him like a shield. He approaches the portal and begins let the rabbit's blood drip onto the wood. He then tosses the carcass into the portal. To Thomas's surprise, it lands with a wet slap on the other side. He supposes he expected it to vanish into nothingness. That it didn't is a bit of a letdown. On the other hand, the portal is no longer black. It is merely a hole in a wooden frame. Thomas did not see it fade out of ripple or anything else to suggest magic. It was one way and then it was another.

Miss Feldstein seems to be recovering herself nicely. "What did you do, and how did you know that would work?"

Crowley grins with the satisfaction of a soldier who has survived a dicey charge. "I didn't *know* precisely. It simply seemed to be set up that way, much like finding a machine with a single lever. You would conclude that it turns the thing on and off. In this case, it seemed likely the magicians who designed the portal needed a way to shut it down. It's how I would have ordered things."

Crowley now removes a new weapon from his coat pocket—a ceremonial dagger. Within the confines of the magic circle, allowing it to conscribe his motions, he begins to move. Thomas recognizes what he is doing before he hears the ritualistic words.

"The Greater Banishing Ritual of the Pentagram," he explains to the ladies.

"The greater ritual of hooey, is more like it," Ruby says.

A moment later, as soon as he is finished, Crowley steps out of the circle. "It is done," he pronounces. He turns to the portal and raises his foot. He clearly means to kick it over. Perhaps this will destroy the thing utterly. Perhaps this is merely a bit of theater.

Two things happen almost simultaneously. First, just before Crowley's foot can make contact, the portal, once again, turns black.

Second, the floor vanishes underneath Thomas's feet, and he plummets to his death.

Crowley once told him that magic cannot be used to accomplish that which cannot be done without magic. Once again, the great magician appears to be wrong, because floors cannot vanish, and people cannot be cast from a garret into the abyss. Yet, that is happening.

With his eyes squeezed shut he falls and falls and falls, waiting for the sudden jolt of firm ground and death. After endless seconds, when he is not broken against the earth, he forces open his eyes to see he is not falling at all. He is merely lying on the floor, his mouth open, drool pooling near his face. He sees Ruby Topping also on the floor, her snout open and her tongue lolling. She tries to push herself up and falls back down again after gaining only a few inches.

Thomas lifts his head and he is stuck by an explosion of nausea and vertigo. He squeezes his eyes shut, waiting for it to pass, but it does not. Closing his eyes eases the sensation, if only a little, but he cannot lie here. He must do something.

His eyelids flutter open once more, and he forces himself to lift his head. Crowley and Miss Feldstein are also in the process of trying to rise. Thomas tells himself that what he is feeling is not real. He is not falling; the room is not moving. The portal is having some effect on him, on his sense of balance.

It is not real. He chants this quietly while he pushes himself upright, first sitting and then managing to get on his feet. Sort of, in any case. He is crouched down low, trying to minimize his center of mass.

He moves first to Ruby, who is closest, and gives her his hand. "It's not real."

"I bloody well know that," she gasps. "But it feels real."

Crowley is helping Miss Feldstein rise. She appears greener in complexion than any of the rest of the group, though Thomas cannot vouch for his own appearance. He imagines it must be awful. He keeps closing his eyes, trying to steady himself, and nearly toppling over.

"We have to get out of here," he says.

"We haven't closed the portal," Crowley counters.

"Obviously, but if we can't stand and move around, we're not going to figure out how to close it. Let's get to the wall. We can use it for support."

Waddling like ducks, they make their way to the wall and then inch toward the stairs. Ruby takes the lead, and Thomas hangs back to make certain Miss Feldstein is managing. Of course, Ruby is no less female and equally deserving of his attention, but she seems more self-sufficient, hardier. Thomas doesn't know if this is true or simply a prejudice he has formed because of her accent. Nevertheless, he feels he must see to Miss Feldstein.

She looks horrible, drawn and sunken-eyed and as though struggling not to vomit.

"Take my hand," he tells her.

She nods, but she cannot summon sufficient energy to speak.

They reach the stairs and, gripping the banister, begin to make their uncertain descent. Moving down is harder than walking on the floor. Each step Thomas feels like he is tumbling in an abyss, like each footfall misses its target even when he can see it pressed against the wood of the stair. It seems to take them an eternity to descend to the third floor.

Thomas hopes that the falling sensation will diminish as they descend, but as he rounds the staircase and heads down another flight, he feels no different. There is no relief, and a terrible thought occurs to him. What if the sensation comes from within themselves, not from the house? What if they carry this horrible feeling with them wherever they go, for the rest of their lives?

He tells himself he is being absurd, but he cannot know that. He is, after all, metamorphosing into a tree. Ruby has turned into a wolf creature. This could be another manifestation of the Peculiarities. That he has not heard of it before means nothing.

He can only hope. He moves forward, and he hopes.

It is impossible to say how long it takes. Time is distorted and twisted and seems to slow and accelerate and double back on itself. He forgets himself for long periods of time, but then he feels horribly, painfully present, unable to think of anything but this current moment.

At last, however, he descends the final staircase. He tries to increase his pace, but he cannot, not without falling, and he fears if he falls, he may not be able to rise. He proceeds at his tortoise pace, one step following the other.

Ahead of him, Ruby reaches the landing and then, palms pressed to the wall, makes her way to the front door. It requires only a little effort to make it swing open, and she is out.

It swings closed again, so Thomas doesn't know if she is free from the sensation of falling. Is she standing upright, or is she gripping the stoop's banister in horror?

Thomas reaches the door and manages to lean against it. He emerges into the cold, foul, sooty, beautiful London air. It is beautiful because it is as though he has stepped through a portal into paradise. He is himself again. He can stand and move and swivel his head without ill effect. It is almost like waking from a dream, for while he remembers feeling horribly inside the house, he cannot quite recall what the horrible feeling was like. All he knows is that it is over.

He turns and takes Miss Feldstein's hand as she comes out. "It passes," he tells her. "You are fine."

She looks at him and grins, spreading her arms wide as if to embrace the world. Thomas turns back to see if Crowley needs any aid, but the magician comes out of the door, straightens up, and then nods at the universe. All is as it should be, his expression seems to say.

"What was that?" Thomas demands of Crowley.

He shakes his head. "Nothing I've ever felt before. The portal must be under some protection, perhaps from an entity in another realm. I hardly know. This is all new to me. It seems, however, that shutting the thing down may be trickier than I supposed."

Thomas bites back a sarcastic reply. If only Crowley had let him study the formula longer. Of course, he knows perfectly well he may not have discovered anything useful or beneficial. Had he tinkered with the formula, things might have gone just as badly or even worse, but even so. He ought to have been allowed to try before all the rabbit butchering began.

"I think we've done all we can do for one day," Crowley says. "I will need to consider what we've seen, consult the tarot, and ponder our next steps."

Thomas is about to reply, but then, before he knows how it has happened, he is holding Miss Feldstein in his arms. She has stumbled, perhaps some residual effect from the house, and he grabs her lest she slip on the steps. For a moment he assumes she lost her footing, though there is no ice. Then he sees it is something else. Her eyes are half closed, showing only whites, and he braces himself for her to turn to dead weight.

Her eyes shoot open and she gasps as though startled. She is under her own steam once more, alert and independent, pushing herself away from Thomas.

His first response is that he must apologize for touching her, but she shows no sign of having taken offense. Her hands clutch the guardrail as she leans over and vomits onto the footpath.

A policeman walks by at just that moment. His mouth twists under a bushy mustache. "Does the lady require assistance?"

Ruby has turned away to be certain her condition is unseen. Crowley, on the other hand, meets the policeman's eye. "We have the matter in hand."

The policeman continues. He does not notice that behind Crowley the door with the broken lock does not close.

Miss Feldstein vomits again, and then merely hovers over the railing breathing heavily. The others wait, not sure how to help her.

At last she straightens up and forces a smile. "I thought it was all over, but then I felt something—something different, but still quite powerful."

Ruby, for all her crudeness, knows what to do and rushes over to help steady Miss Feldstein. Her hood is back up, concealing her face, but Thomas can hear her exaggerated sniffing. Perhaps the scent of vomit conveys more intelligence to her nose than it does to Thomas, who has carefully shifted himself to an upwind position on the stairs.

The sniffing continues, and Thomas fears he may have overestimated Ruby's ability to rise to the occasion. The wolf-girl sniffs at Miss Feldstein's face, her neck, and then, quite scandalously, her torso.

"What are you doing, Ruby?" Thomas demands, believing he must act *in loco parentis* for this relative stranger to the group.

Ruby shakes her head but continues to sniff. The head-shaking was meant to silence them. She looks like a dog tracking a scent trail, and it is almost comic, but there is unmistakable alarm in her eyes. Her nose points at Miss Feldstein and she takes a step forward, gasps, and then steps back, though she keeps a hand on Miss Feldstein's arm for support.

"It's changed." Ruby wrings her hands and looks down at the ground. "It wasn't like that before. I'd have noticed. I can always tell, and right away. Someone walks through the front door, I'll get the scent if I'm upstairs, even in the garden. I'd have smelled it on you before, but I wouldn't have said nothing because it ain't my business, but now—now it may be. I don't know."

Miss Feldstein taps the hand on her arms. "What is it, my dear? You must tell me."

"You wasn't before, but now you are," Ruby says. "You're expecting."

"Expecting what?" Miss Feldstein asks. But then she knows. Thomas can see it in her eyes. She didn't understand and then, like a slap across the face, she does.

Something happened in that room, and now Miss Feldstein is with child, and there can be no expectation that her offspring will be human. Miss Feldstein is pregnant with rabbit children.

TWENTY-ONE
SORROW

T HOMAS CANNOT BELIEVE it is because he is uncomfortable—human reproduction hardly seems like the sort of thing to render Crowley ill at ease—but the magician soon excuses himself, saying he has other matters to which he must attend. Apparently being bested by a portal to another world and witnessing parthenogenesis are but elements of his busy day.

Thomas, however, cannot simply walk away from Miss Feldstein. He knows too well the shock of discovering one's body has been overtaken by inexplicable forces. Unfortunately, he has no notion of precisely what he can do with her. Taking her for a cup of coffee or a slice of cake seems a bit callous.

It occurs to Thomas that if he delays his brother by but a few months, he will be able to put all wedding plans to rest. Walter would not insist he marry a visibly pregnant woman. Even as he thinks this, he chastises himself for his selfishness. He also understands he is being naïve for imagining that an inconvenience like pregnancy would stand in the way of Walter's plans—whatever they might be.

"Let's take her to Mama," Ruby suggests. "She'll know what to do."

Of course. Mrs. Topping. Who better to talk to about one's body being taken over by a mysterious force from the astral world? Thomas almost lets out a bitter laugh, but he controls himself. It might be misconstrued—or worse, properly construed. Thomas believes he has done a fine job of remaining sane the past weeks, but it has been a taxing day, and surely no one would blame him if he simply went mad.

Lamentably, going mad will have to wait. Thomas has things to do, and most pressing among these is seeing to Miss Feldstein. He and Ruby help her into a cab, where she sits dazedly as they roll toward Bethnel Green. Miss Feldstein hardly seems aware of her surroundings as she wanders out of the hansom and up the stairs toward Ruby's house. Thomas prays there are no monstrosities in plain sight when they enter.

On this score he is relieved. Mr. Topping meets them at the door, and after glancing at his daughter and then the pale face of the stranger with her, he knows it is his wife that is wanted.

Thomas and Ruby lead Miss Feldstein to the sitting room, and Mrs. Topping appears a moment later in a gown of heavy gray felt. Her face is entirely uncovered, and she looks to Thomas like an illustration of the wolf in the tale of Little Red Riding Hood.

Ruby whispers a few words into her mother's not inconsiderable ears, and Mrs. Topping nods. She then turns to Thomas. "If you would be so good as to step away for a moment."

Torn between the awkwardness of refusing to leave while delicate female matters are explored and spending time alone with Mr. Topping, Thomas briefly hesitates, but Miss Feldstein nods, so he removes himself from the room.

As he fears, Mr. Topping awaits him in the hall. "What have you been getting up to with Ruby, then?"

Thomas sighs. "Mr. Topping, if you imagine that I have designs on your daughter—"

"Designs!" The word comes out in a choking laugh. "Designs he says! I was talking about what dangers you're leading her into, but you say designs. On *you*, of all people?"

That he should be considered beneath the dignity of this working man's beast-child is a bit of a blow. Yes, he is becoming a plant, but he comes from an excellent family, and he doesn't think the outside world would consider him so bad a prospect. Still, he has more important matters than Mr. Topping's opinion with which to concern himself.

"The girl simply showed up," Thomas explains. "We didn't ask her to join us."

"Didn't ask, he says," Mr. Topping mocks. "If she's there, her safety is your responsibility, Thresher. Yours. Don't matter who asked for what."

Thomas begins to feel indignant. Who does this man think he is, ordering him about because a willful girl goes where she chooses? "I can hardly be responsible for—"

"You *are* responsible," Mr. Topping says, jabbing Thomas in the chest with an un-gentle finger.

Thomas is about to say something moderately belligerent, but it is at that moment he recalls the formula written in the circle at the house on Cannon

Street. Crowley thought it was nothing, but Thomas is not convinced. "Mr. Topping, have you a piece of paper and something to write with?"

Mr. Topping shakes his head and walks off, but he returns in a moment with a blank sheet and a dull pencil. Thomas takes them with a rushed thanks and begins writing down as much as he can recall of what he saw chalked on the floor. He is sure he is getting most of it, but he knows he is missing a great deal. It was simply too much to comprehend, and yet it left an impression, almost like a wound or a scar. In mathematics, one always searches for immutable truths, and he is sure that is what he has found here.

He has only finished jotting down his notes and folding up his paper when he is invited to join the ladies. There is something heavy in the air, and Thomas has the uncomfortable feeling that some sort of examination may have transpired. He feels his face growing hot.

After Mrs. Topping invites him to sit, Thomas gazes about the glum faces in the room.

"I shall leave it to Miss Feldstein to decide how much she wishes to reveal to you," Mrs. Topping begins.

It seems likely she had more to say, but Miss Feldstein is not one to hesitate. "Mrs. Topping has confirmed Ruby's suspicions. It seems—it seems that *something* happened to me in that house, and I have some sort of life growing inside me."

"But surely it cannot be." Thomas's face burns. How can he be expected to discuss these things? "A woman cannot—it does not happen like that. I was there. I saw nothing—unusual."

"I'm afraid we may be bumping up against the limits of your personal experience," says Mrs. Topping.

"Surely there must be another explanation," Thomas insists. "There is only one known instance of such an event, and that is our Lord, Jesus Christ." Thomas hates how this situation is turning him into a prig, but he can't sit silent while Christianity is cheapened.

"Don't be such an old man," Mrs. Topping tells him with entirely inappropriate familiarity. "There are many examples and from all over the world. Tales of parthenogenesis are quite common in mythology and folklore. In China, the Yellow Emperor's mother conceived him when she was struck by lightning."

Honor demands Thomas push back. "This isn't some oriental myth. This is Miss Feldstein we are talking about."

"My point is that this sort of thing need not be understood as a purely Christian manifestation," Mrs. Topping says with strained patience. "Frankly, I've seen it often enough."

"Parthenogenesis? That is what you have seen often enough?"

"More since the Peculiarities," Mrs. Topping says. "And before you say anything about women lying, there are ways to investigate such claims."

"But if such things were common, then would we not know about them?"

"They happen to *women*," Miss Feldstein says wearily. "And as we have just witnessed, when a woman makes a claim about her own body, men may find it convenient to disbelieve her."

To this Thomas has no reply. The mysteries of the world, it seems, are bottomless.

"Rabbit births happen mostly to poor women," Mrs. Topping continues, "perhaps precisely because such women will be disbelieved. I can only suspect that what happened to Miss Feldstein was owing to her proximity to the portal."

"What can she do now?" Thomas demands.

Mrs. Topping shakes her head. "I have not been able to discover any remedy. There are means to ending pregnancies—"

At this Thomas winces and turns away.

"Don't be stupid," says Ruby, who has been rather contained until now. "If you want to help your friend, then you can't be squirming every time someone mentions lady things."

Thomas supposes they are right and steels himself for more discomfort.

"Those methods," continues Mrs. Topping, "are not effective with rabbit pregnancies."

"There is nothing to be done?" Thomas asks.

"There must be something," says Mrs. Topping, "we simply don't know what it is. Magical problems will have magical solutions. Unfortunately, it remains for us to discover what they might be."

In the cab on the way to Miss Feldstein's house, Thomas finds himself struggling for words. He knows he cannot remain silent, and yet speaking is so damnably awkward.

"Miss Feldstein, whatever I can do—"

"The bank is the key to all this," she says coldly. "I hope you can do a great deal."

Thomas tries to adopt a helpful and solicitous tone. "I shall certainly make every effort."

"I do not care for platitudes." She turns away as she speaks, and he struggles to hear her over the noise of the street. "Your family has done this to me. They bought that house, presumably for the purpose of creating that portal—and the portal has left me in this state. Your family has raped me."

"Good God!" Thomas cries. He has an image of himself putting his hands over his ears, but, fortunately, he is able to restrain himself.

"Does the truth offend you?" she asks. "It may not be the sort of brutal rape that men carry out every day, but it is a rape all the same. I have something growing inside me, taking command of my body. How would you feel?"

Thomas dislikes this accusation of rape set at his family's doorstep. He also has the perfect defense to the charge of insensitivity. How would he feel? He can answer that from experience. There is nothing quite so—even in his own mind he struggles for the right way to phrase this—so delicate about what is happening to him, but it is nevertheless happening.

He will not speak of it, however. It is a private matter, and while Miss Feldstein appears to have no limits on what she will say, Thomas is made of different, more English, stuff. As for her rage, he supposes he cannot blame her.

"I will not abandon you," he says quietly. "If a solution may be found, a means of exorcising this thing from you, I will find it. You have my word."

Miss Feldstein meets his gaze. "You mustn't exclude me from anything. No matter the danger. This isn't about your curiosity anymore or your concerns for the bank. This is now my fight more than ever, and I don't want to hear that I am too delicate to participate."

Thomas merely nods. He has already concluded that Miss Feldstein is made of sterner stuff than he.

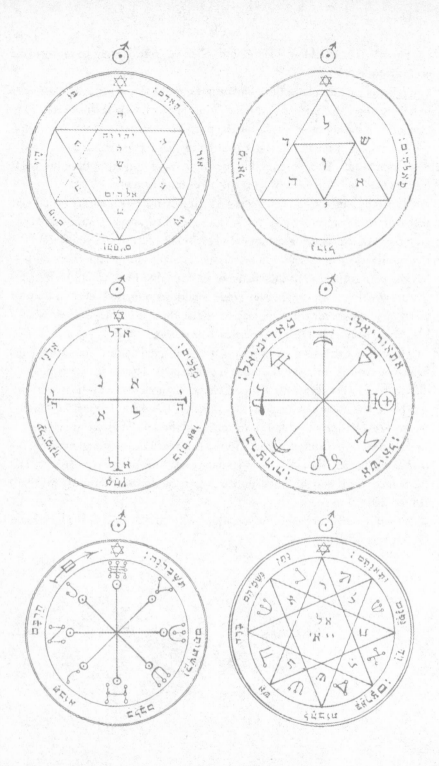

TWENTY-TWO
WORRY

THOMAS SUFFERS FROM disturbing dreams that night, most of which he cannot remember, though there are rabbits hopping everywhere. Once, he supposes, a dream full of rabbits would not have seemed so menacing, but now—now he can hardly endure the thought of it. And there is also the face. Always that face, bent and impossible, peering at him as though Thomas does not quite belong in his own dream.

There was something else as well.

He takes out the piece of paper on which he tried to copy the formula from the house on Cannon Street. He is not certain if he remembered more of it in his sleep, or if he is now inventing something new, but he makes a few more notations. It would take hours, maybe days to work through this, and he hasn't the time, but he feels certain it could be important. This value, this omega-alef, is surely important. He cannot rush it, however. He sets it aside and knows that the answer may come to him, when he least expects it, in a moment of inspiration.

It is time to take more decisive action. Thomas would not like to become a tree, but not becoming a tree is hardly a point of honor. What has happened to Miss Feldstein, however, makes him angry. He cannot say it is guilt or regret, precisely. She chose to join their group—rather forcefully—and Thomas can think of no mistakes he made that resulted in her current condition. Nevertheless, he was there when a woman became pregnant, and if history is any guide, that makes her welfare his responsibility.

Walter is not at table when Thomas sits down to his breakfast. It is something of a relief, and he piles his plate with eggs and sausage, more than he would eat if he were under his brother's parsimonious gaze. Perhaps parsimony isn't the issue, as Walter would certainly rejoice to see the food be tossed into the rubbish rather than go to his own brother.

Thomas has only been enjoying the meal and the quiet for a few minutes when Pearl steps into the room. She wears a pale green dress, and her hair is compressed into a savagely tight bun. Everything is crisp and neat, but there is something disordered in her eyes, as though she has just woken from an unplanned nap.

"Thomas, good morning." She tries on a smile and finds it does not suit. She has never joined him for breakfast before, and neither of them will be able to pretend this is a chance encounter between two people who shelter under the same roof.

Pearl sits in a chair next to Thomas, and after a few seconds of experimenting with how best to place her hands, she thrusts them in her lap and grimaces. She is not happy with their final disposition, but she will soldier on.

"You must stop doing whatever you are doing," she tells him.

"Eating breakfast?"

"Don't be cheeky. Whatever you are doing to upset Walter, you must stop. You simply must."

Does she mean what he and Drummond are doing at Thresher's? The failed expedition to Cannon Street? "Has Walter asked you to speak to me?"

"Certainly not!" She laughs as though the notion is absurd. "But I've seen him, I've overheard him talking to Mr. Hawke. No more than a word or two, but he is quite wroth. I don't know what you are doing, but you are making him very angry."

Thomas fears Walter is taking this anger out on Pearl. Not with his hands. Walter is not physical like that, but there are other ways to be cruel. "What has he done?"

She shakes her head. "He is as he has always been, but it is you I worry about. He holds your future in his hands. You mustn't toy with him."

"I'm not toying with him," Thomas says. "I am trying to find out the truth."

"I can think of nothing more foolish," she tells him, and folds her hands, as if to indicate that there is nothing more to say.

Arriving in his garret that morning, Thomas has some very clear ideas how to proceed. He finds Drummond already at his desk, reading through what appears to be a pile of letters.

"I'm beginning to put together a timeline," he says as if in answer to a question. His eyes are red-rimmed, but they show flashes of excitement. "I should have more for you in a day or two, but I have a very curious notion. It seems that these disastrous loans of which your brother seems so fond began during your father's time. They have increased markedly since his death, but I speculate—speculate, mind you—that a line can be drawn directly. The emergence of a policy, if you will."

"Can you make any sense of it?"

Drummond shakes his head. "Certainly not, especially in light of the way contracts seem to work in the Peculiar era."

"You're thinking of the charter," Thomas proposes.

"Precisely. Your grandfather founded this bank to help small men who would face difficulties at other houses. Your father wanted to make the bank something else."

"It may be that these are not bad loans, but they are failing because the violate the charter," Thomas says.

"Exactly," Drummond agrees. "And I'll tell you one thing more. The shift in policy away from the original intent appears to begin around the time Mr. Hawke emerges on the scene, some three years prior to your father's death."

"So, long after the first manifestations of the Peculiarities?"

Drummond blinks rapidly, like a confused bird. "Yes. Why should you ask that?"

Thomas lets himself fall into his chair. "Because nothing would make more sense to me than that all of this, everything that is happening to London, is my father's fault."

"I've seen no evidence for that, though I've often blamed my own father—" Drummond is smiling, looking like a man about to make a quip with which he is rather pleased, but then his expression changes. "Do you know, you may be on to something."

Thomas leans forward. "Tell me."

"It may be that certain aspects of the Peculiarities—well, I would be guessing at this point. I will need to learn a few more things, so do not press me. Maybe tomorrow. Certainly by the end of the week."

Thomas nods. "I'll not pressure you. I must say, Drummond, you've been a huge help."

"Uncovering hidden secrets," he says. "That is my specialty."

Feeling that Drummond has things in hand, Thomas decides to take a trip to the Foreign and India Offices. He is shuttled about the massive and ornate building, passed from one beleaguered official to another, until he ends up with a junior clerk, a fellow whose responsibilities are not much different from a junior clerk at Thresher's. Still, Thomas is not one to dismiss out of hand the expertise of a minor functionary, and this fellow, whose employment calls upon him to copy a great number of documents concerning agriculture and climate conditions, turns out to be precisely whom Thomas needs.

They speak for only a few minutes, but Thomas learns what he wishes to know. Indian crops failed quite badly a few years before, and indeed they did seem to be rebounding heartily in the early part of the year, but the monsoon season again was a failure over the summer. India, it appears, is destined to suffer another year of famine.

Armed with this information, Thomas walks to the Mawson house, which sits near St. James's Square. The home is a gorgeous property of the previous century, a neoclassical monument to wealth and imperial aspiration, but there are signs of decay. The masonry needs work, and, once Thomas is admitted, he sees neither carpeting, furnishings, nor wallpaper have been refreshed in the past half century. The Mawsons are certainly a family whose best days are behind them.

The elder Mr. Mawson looks very much like his son. He is fat and florid, and his breath smells strongly of sherry. His clothes hang loose upon him, as though made in anticipation of weight not yet gained. Thomas has met the man many times before, but he never paid him much mind for he had only been a friend's parent.

"Always a pleasure to have a visitor from the Thresher family," Mr. Mawson says after inviting Thomas to sit. "And one of my son's school friends as well! It is a fine thing to see someone I once knew as a boy come to me now upon a man's business."

It would be polite to ask about Mr. Mawson's son, but Thomas finds he does not want to hear any news of his former friend. The less he considers him, the happier Thomas will be. He wants only to talk bank business, and to do that as efficiently as possible.

"I understand," he begins, "that you have requested a substantial loan from Thresher's. You already owe one of our competitors in excess of ten thousand pounds. The additional moneys are to manage your Indian properties ravaged by years of famine. Is that correct?"

"It has been a hard few years for the colonials," Mr. Mawson agrees, "but we now find ourselves upon a better footing."

"The India Office tells me there are concerns for another crop failure this year," Thomas says. "Would this not affect your ability to repay what you already owe?"

"Such predictions are made every year," Mawson says airily. "It is the difficulty of managing land so far away. One is always subject to rumor, and it is my experience that such rumors are inevitably pessimistic. My people in India tell me another story entirely."

"But should the predictions of another famine be accurate," Thomas presses, "how will you manage the new debts?"

Mr. Mawson suddenly looks very grave. "Mr. Thresher, I can certainly appreciate your enthusiasm for your work, but you must know that your brother, with whom I have spoken, has not put me to the question in this way."

"Begging your pardon, sir," Thomas says, "but he ought to have done so."

Mr. Mawson appears to rearrange his expression. He lets out a little cough that no one could believe involuntary. "Surely this will not be your decision."

"As I said, I am here discover why it is—"

"Yes, yes," Mawson says hurriedly. "Do you know that another appointment of mine has quite slipped my mind? I was so delighted to receive a visit from you that it quite escaped me." Mr. Mawson continues for perhaps thirty seconds upon this theme, and he then excuses himself, leaving Thomas alone in the parlor.

Thomas collects his coat and hat and steps out the door. He has not yet reached the street when he hears the door open again and a different Mawson—the son this time—comes running after him.

"Thresher, old boy, wait a moment." He is panting from his efforts. He stands outside hatless, his coat hastily thrown on. His breath fogs the air between them. "A bit winded from all the rushing. I heard you were in the house. I thought I'd see if you wanted to get a drink."

Thomas gazes upon the red and puffing cheeks of his former associate. He cannot bring himself to call him *friend* any longer. Thomas simply cannot comprehend the enormity—the absurdity—of Mawson's betrayal. It is an equation that will not balance. Why? For what reason? What could be the goal? There is no answer. It is a question shouted into the void. One might as well ask the meaning of existence or what is the weight of the soul.

"I'm afraid I'm rather busy." Thomas keeps his voice deliberately cool.

"Bank business, eh?" Mawson says and then laughs as though he has said something funny.

"Always growing," Thomas says, as though brushing off an underling.

"You mustn't take the other night too seriously," Mawson says. "We'd been drinking, and I feel you may have misinterpreted. But that place! It was really quite something! Did you taste the rabbit? Exquisite!"

It is hard to imagine anything Mawson might have said to appeal less to Thomas. He was already inclined to sympathize with the poor women and children, cast out from society, forced to debase themselves in that place, but now to think of Miss Feldstein's condition, the life that grows within her—and this puffed-up fool who sees it all as literal fodder for his pleasure.

Thomas isn't entirely sure what he is feeling. Anger. Irritation. Sadness. Disgust. It is a rich and hearty stew, and he has no wish to stir the pot. That part of his life is behind him.

"We all always liked you," Mawson says, something like genuine emotion rippling to the surface of his heavy cheeks. "We would have been your friend without the money. And I wanted to tell you. Many times I wanted to, but I couldn't. I don't mean I didn't have the backbone. It was like the words would not rise to the surface. It was as though something was choking them down. I spoke of it once with Willingham, and he said it was the same for him. It was—well, once we'd have called it peculiar, but that means something else these days."

Mawson smiles at his own witty observation.

Thomas turns away.

"The thing of it is," Mawson continues, still puffing, still red, though now more likely from the cold rather than the exercise of rushing out the door, "my father needs that loan. He must have it. I don't know what you fellows do over there at Thresher's, but that's what he needs. That always-growing business. He must have it. If you—if you have any fond memories of our friendship at all, then you will put in a word for him, won't you?"

Thomas feels he ought to say something, ought to dig deeper, ask more questions, but he will not do it. He has the strangest feeling—it is so alien that he pulls at it and turns it over and takes it apart before he recognizes it for what it is. Thomas has learned more than he has revealed. He has taken more than he has given. Thomas, in this little exchange, has all the power. Ollie Mawson has none.

"Good day, Mawson," Thomas says, turning away, allowing himself the indulgence of a pitying shake of the head.

✳

The garret is empty when Thomas returns to his office. This is no surprise. Drummond spends a great deal of his time in the records room and away from the premises entirely. Thomas isn't certain where the fellow goes to get his information, but he is getting it.

Thomas glances over at Drummond's work table, however, and is somewhat alarmed to see that the usual mess is absent. Gone are the piles of ledgers and documents.

Something is not right. Thomas is preparing to perform a more thorough examination when there is a gentle knock upon the door. It opens before Thomas can respond.

It is utterly unsurprising to find Mr. Hawke, his mouth open in a canine grin. "I thought I'd clear up any possible confusion. Confusion does not aid productivity, I think you will agree. And we do prize productivity here at Thresher's."

"What do you need?" Thomas is never certain what tone to strike with Mr. Hawke. It may be a function of not knowing who he is or what his responsibilities might be.

"Only to inform you that there has been something of a change of personnel. Mr. Drummond, your assistant, is no longer with us. I'm afraid he could not remain. Did you know about him, I wonder?" Mr. Hawke looks at Thomas, shifting his head back and forth as though searching for a clue. "No, I don't think you did. He had you fooled. But I can say no more about that."

"Then who can?"

"Perhaps Mr. Drummond," Mr. Hawke says with a shrill laugh.

Thomas feels himself seething. Drummond was close to something, and evidently Mr. Hawke got wind of it. "I shall have to speak to him about some unfinished business. May I have an address where he can be reached?"

"That, I'm afraid, is part of the trouble," says Mr. Hawke. "A bit of routine business required that a Thresher's employee visit Mr. Drummond at his home. The address he provided was not an accurate one. Now we have no way to reach him. It is for the best."

There is nothing to be done about that now. If Drummond has something to say, if he has learned anything of important about Mr. Hawke, he will find a way to contact Thomas. In the meantime, the work must go on.

"May I hire a new assistant?"

"I hardly think it necessary," says Mr. Hawke. "When you bring in the sort of revenue that requires an assistant, we can revisit the discussion. In the meantime, carry on, Mr. Thresher. I have no doubt you can continue to do great things quite by yourself."

TWENTY-THREE
KNIGHT

T HOMAS HEARS ONCE again from Mr. Drummond, much sooner than he would have imagined. It is only two days later, and Thomas has only just returned home from work. Walter and Pearl seem not to be at home, and Thomas sits alone in the parlor, sipping a glass of sherry. It is not the sort of behavior in which he indulges often, as Walter has made it clear he is not to treat the house as though it were his own, but Thomas feels he could use something tonight to help him to sleep. Perhaps with a drink or two he will not dream so vividly.

He sits in the dimly lit room, enjoying the drink, enjoying the fire, considering the strangeness of his life. He thinks of Madeline Yardley. What would happen if he were to tell her of his adventures? Would she think him mad? How could she not? On the other hand, she has fought a fog tendril in her own home. She knows the world is not what everyone once believed. To tell her all, however, would require that he explain his motivation, and he does not want her to know about his arboreal condition. He cannot endure that she might look at him with pity.

Distantly he is aware of the bell and muffled voices. He ignores it, comfortably certain it can have nothing to do with him. Then one of the servants enters and tells him that two gentlemen are here to see him. They are from the Home Office.

Thomas cannot imagine why anyone from the Home Office would want him. Could this be related to the incident at the Golden Dawn temple? Or have they learned about the break-in on Cannon Street? That would be a concern for the police, not the Crown. Still, he worries.

Thomas says that they should be shown in, and in a moment two men in tasteful suits enter the room. They are both tall, with brown hair and brown eyes, and are clean-shaven except for their tastefully subdued identical mustaches. The men look nothing alike.

One, however, is known to him—not as a government man, but as a Thresher's employee—Bradford Drummond. Thomas is fatigued, and the sherry has begun to work upon him, but he can deduce a few things without much effort. Bradford Drummond was an employee of the Home Office all along. All the efforts to befriend Thomas now make great sense, as does his sudden departure. Mr. Hawke clearly discovered the secret.

The man beside Drummond looks as though he is made of rising dough. He has a swollen and tilted nose, flattened lips, and misshapen ears of a perpetual brawler.

"It is good to see you once more, Mr. Thresher," says Drummond. "I apologize that I was less than forthright in the past, though I did give you my correct name. I am indeed Bradford Drummond, and I am with the Special Branch of the Home Office. This is Mr. Hhhh." He pronounces the name as though its sounds don't quite belong in the English language. It is as though he is choking and exhaling at the same time.

"You were spying on Thresher's," Thomas says.

"Gathering information," Drummond says with a grin. "Attempting to, I should say. I learned very little before I was dismissed without cause."

"It is fortunate, then, that you had other employment," Thomas says.

"Very droll, sir. But, as you might have surmised, the Home Office is most interested in Thresher's. I was able to learn a great deal, and I am certainly grateful I was spared my predecessor's fate."

"Your predecessor." Thomas is thinking aloud. "Nicholas Roberts."

"Precisely. He was discovered by the bank and dealt with by some sort of Peculiar means. He still isn't quite himself. I think a sacking was rather merciful in my case, and I shall not complain. But my work is incomplete, and I hope you might answer a few of my questions."

Thomas moves to the sideboard. Should he be angered by Drummond's deceit? Probably, but Thomas cannot quite summon any true indignation. He wants too much to know what Walter is up to at Thresher's, and Drummond may have the answers. "Can I offer you gentlemen a sherry?"

"I do not drink alcohol," says Mr. Drummond. "Mr. Hhhh does not drink anything."

"Ah," says Thomas, sneaking another glance at the misshapen Mr. Hhhh. He can think of nothing clever to say, so he pours himself a generous amount of sherry and then invites the men to sit. "Providing Mr. Hhhh sits," he says with a smile.

"He does not," says Mr. Drummond, who does sit. Mr. Hhhh stands silently beside him, his face strange and unreadable.

"That must make traveling by coach a challenge," Thomas says with forced laugh.

Mr. Drummond ignores the quip.

"I'll cut to the heart of the matter. We have come not about Thresher's but rather some other people who've caught our interest."

"Caught your interest in what way?"

"I am afraid that is something I cannot tell you," says Mr. Drummond.

"And this Special Branch of yours," says Thomas. "It is concerned with the Peculiarities?"

"I cannot comment on that, sir."

"And the research you were doing for me—did you learn anything that you did not have a chance to report before you were cast out?"

Mr. Drummond smiles. "Mr. Thresher. I'm afraid that in this conversation the flow of information must be in one direction."

"Did you not suggest to me that you were on the cusp of some interesting discoveries?" Thomas asks. "You had notions you were going to share."

"Those notions now belong to the Crown," he says. "I may not share them."

"Ah." Thomas takes a long sip of his sherry. "And what is it you would like to know?"

"About your associations with Mrs. Judith Topping, Mr. Aleister Crowley, Mr. Samuel MacGregor Mathers, Miss Esther Feldstein, a Jewess, and Mr. Arthur Conan Doyle." At this final name, Mr. Hhhh shakes his head vigorously. "We can omit that one," Mr. Drummond amends.

"As he is dead?" inquires Thomas.

"Precisely," says Mr. Drummond.

"And the people you name other than Miss Feldstein—have they religions?"

Mr. Drummond exchanges a look with Mr. Hhhh. "I fail to understand the relevance."

"I only inquire because you mention Miss Feldstein's religion," says Thomas. He cannot imagine why he is making this point, but Miss Feldstein has enough with which to contend. A woman who has been made magically pregnant need not endure this masquerader's scorn.

"Mr. Thresher," says Mr. Drummond with the tone of a man who cannot believe that he is being subjected to an indignity. He is a man who has had quite enough. "Shall we focus on the matter at hand?"

"I don't believe I understand the matter at hand," Thomas says. "I know the people you mention, but I cannot imagine what, precisely, you are asking me. We were looking into my family's bank and their mismanagement. We were looking into Mr. Hawke. You say nothing about these things, and you wish to know of my associates? Why?"

"The why of it needn't be your concern. We are asking the nature of your acquaintance with these people."

"I presume if you are here you already know that my reason for associating with these people is a shared interest in occult matters. You seem quite adept at finding ways to observe people. However, my association with Miss Feldstein is social."

"Social," repeats Mr. Drummond. He glances at Mr. Hhhh, whose lumpy face shifts and bends and folds itself into a smirk.

Thomas does not love being smirked at by a man who does not sit or ingest liquids. "Gentlemen, I am certain there is nothing illegal about studying the occult."

"Not at this time," concedes Mr. Drummond. "I shan't speculate on what the future holds."

"Then I cannot see why these associations are of any consequence to you."

"To your knowledge," asks Mr. Drummond, "have any of these people plans to harm the Queen?"

Thomas nearly spits out a sip of sherry. He has expected all sorts of probing questions, but not this one. "Harm the Queen? Of England?"

"Is there some other queen you had in mind?" Mr. Drummond asks archly.

"For all I know, you come about some danger to the queen of fairyland."

Mr. Drummond again glances at Mr. Hhhh, and he again is rewarded with a brief shake of the head.

"The Queen of England," pronounces Mr. Drummond with some authority. "Victoria," he adds after a brief pause.

Thomas is not entirely certain these men are not having fun at his expense. "Is this a serious question?"

"I promise you that it is very serious."

Seeing nothing to be gained from resisting this inquiry, no matter how absurd, Thomas decides it is time to give them the very easy answers they desire. "No one with whom I associate plots against the Queen. Crowley is a bit of a free thinker, but he has expressed no political beliefs. As for the rest, I cannot imagine anything more absurd than to imagine that these people are spies or anarchists or whatever it is you suspect."

"You would tell us?"

"I suppose I would," says Thomas. "Though it is also certainly true that if these people advocated such views, I would not associate with them and we would likely not be having this conversation."

Mr. Drummond stands and hands Thomas a card. "We shall accept that for now. I must ask you to report to me anything suspicious you hear from the people I mentioned, or indeed anyone else who happens to move in these circles. These are dangerous times, Mr. Thresher, though I am certain you already know this."

Thomas stands and takes the card. "I promise you our concerns are scholarly, not political, and certainly not violent or anti-social."

"So you said." Mr. Drummond studies Thomas for a moment.

The two men show themselves out.

It is only a few minutes after Thomas has decided he needs at least one more sherry when Mr. Hawke steps into the room. His movements are as smooth and undulating as a snake's. He smiles cheerfully before fixing himself a drink and sitting across from Thomas.

Does this man never go home? Does he sleep somewhere in the house? Perhaps he lies down like a dog on an old piece of carpeting somewhere. Thomas has never seen him take meals with the family except at dinner parties, but he is present while Walter and Pearl are out. There is no explanation that can suffice.

"You were entertaining some very exceptional guests," Mr. Hawke begins.

"Yes," Thomas answer, deciding to act as though there had been nothing remarkable about the visit. "Home Office."

"I am familiar with Mr. Drummond," says Mr. Hawke. "I find it the height of cheek that he would come here. We discovered his deception, which is why we removed him with all due haste. You see, you think yourself a banker already, but there are things you cannot perceive. A spy in your own house, and you did not see it."

"I did not choose Mr. Drummond as my assistant," Thomas points out.

"He took the initiative and appointed himself," Mr. Hawke explains. "Philpot hasn't been himself since the incident, or he would have noticed his underling's absence sooner. But we mustn't just blame an old fellow with spots on his head. You were fooled too, young Mr. Thresher. You must be cannier if you are to be a banker."

"I am canny enough to see that Thresher's is bleeding money," he offers, thinking to change the subject. "I've reviewed loan after loan that looks like a bad prospect. Just recently I spoke with Mr. Mawson, and though there is not a chance he would be able to repay what he has requested, he feels certain Thresher's will provide him the money. There is much I do not understand about banking, it is true, but I know we are meant to make money, not lose it."

"Mr. Mawson," repeats Mr. Hawke. "Harvests. India. Were we speaking of that? I do not believe so. Your concern on that subject only proves how little you understand of our business. Even in banking, sometimes sacrifices must be made."

"Surely not a sacrifice of profits."

Mr. Hawke shrugs. "The road to profits may be indirect. But now I wish to hear what the men of the Home Office wanted with you."

Thomas decides there is no reason not to tell the truth. "They were interested in the people I know with occult interests"

"The elder Mr. Thresher will not care for that," Mr. Hawke observes.

"I expect not," Thomas agrees. "On the other hand, I will not concern myself with his cryptic demands and concerns. He may go to the devil."

"Oh, come now, young Mr. Thresher," says Mr. Hawke with what he surely imagines to be his most ingratiating grin. "Surely you don't mean that. You would not have strife in the household. You would go to any lengths to keep the elder Mr. Thresher from learning of this visit. Is it not so?"

It is not so, but clearly Mr. Hawke wishes to make certain Walter doesn't learn of the Home Office's visit. Curious to see where things will go, Thomas says nothing.

"I would be willing to keep the matter hidden from Mr. Walter Thresher," says Mr. Hawke. "I do not like to keep secrets. It is not my way, but in the interest of family concord, in the interest of the bank, yes, in this case I could do so, though I would require something of you in exchange, sir. A token of your sincerity, of your interest to put the bank above all."

"And what token is that?" Thomas asks, though the thinks he already knows.

"A promise to marry Miss Feldstein. A commitment to a date. It is all I ask."

Thomas thinks to press what little advantage he has, to demand Mr. Hawke explain why the marriage so important, but he is tired, and he is under no illusion that this time, at long last, he will get answers, so he sets down his glass and stands. "I am done with games. Tell Walter what you like. I hardly care. I have no reason to be ashamed. Perhaps I shall tell him myself."

Mr. Hawke moves like a pouncing cat. He is across the room faster than Thomas's eyes can track. His hands are on Thomas's shoulders. "You mustn't." His voice full of breathy desperation. "Say nothing. Nothing at all."

Thomas takes a step back. Mr. Hawke's fingers cling to the fabric of his jacket and he is forced to raise a hand to the fellow's chest to separate himself. "You thought to extort concessions out of me so that you would do what you wanted done all along?"

Mr. Hawke lowers his head, shakes it while he grins in the manner of a boy caught being a scamp. "I am a banker, and if I can get something for nothing, I have only done what I ought. But you cannot know how this visit will upset the elder Mr. Thresher. It was a great blessing he was out tonight, so do not squander that good fortune. Say nothing of this visit. I beg of you."

Thomas yanks his wrist free. "Enough, sir. I shall not tell him." He makes this promise mostly because he wishes to leave the room and be as far from Mr. Hawke as he can. This inept attempt at bribery is mortifying, but Thomas fears it is but a first step, and something tells him that he will not like what comes after.

"Thank you, young Mr. Thresher," says Mr. Hawke, clasping his hands together like a grateful orphan in a music hall production. "Thank you, most wise and kind sir."

Thomas hurries out of the room, feeling as though he has just escaped from a dog trying to mate with his leg. As he climbs the stairs, he wonders what it can mean. Can it be that Mr. Hawke hired Drummond in the first place and now wishes to conceal his mistake? It is possible, but Thomas has never seen Mr. Hawke put his concerns before Walter's. It is more likely that Mr. Hawke fears Walter will be angry, that he will follow through with his threat to cast Thomas out, and the factotum seems desperate to prevent such an outcome. As to why, it is a mystery on the order of the marriage with Miss Feldstein.

Thomas wonders if he should go down that path, explore the possibility of riling his brother. Walter has been manipulating him for much of his life, and perhaps by making him angry Thomas can finally be free of that manipulation.

Whatever discomfort he endures as a result, whatever hardship, surely it would be worth it. He wants to defy Walter, defy Mr. Hawke. He wants to swing a club and smash their plans into bits, to see their secret designs broken into nothing. He imagines his satisfaction, but that pleasure is tinged with fear. He is afraid of being cast out, of being on his own, and he does not know why. It is not the poverty or the obscurity, it is something else, something he cannot identify. He will stay where he is for now, he decides.

It feels like a decision, but he is not sure that is the right word. It is simply what he will do. It is, he thinks, almost as though he never really had a choice.

TWENTY-FOUR
FAILURE

A T THE GOLDEN Dawn's Isis-Urania Temple, the fraters and sorors sip whisky and make conversation. They have finished their ceremonies, hung up their robes, locked away their daggers, and now they are again but a club of gentlemen—and some ladies—gossiping, talking politics, acting like their communion with other worlds and strange gods is of no immediate importance. They are like millenarians who plant their crops even while they expect the world will end before the harvest.

Thomas and Crowley have spoken in hushed tones about the incident at the rabbit house and Miss Feldstein's fate. Crowley says he is investigating matters further, but Thomas hears the lack of confidence in his voice. The great magician is out of his depth.

Thomas increasingly suspects that time spent at the Golden Dawn gets him nothing. His head is full of information, but he hasn't the first notion of its use. It could be years before he learns how to do anything that will help him. It is *meant* to be years. Every time he presses any of the advanced members of the temple to move faster, he is told that it is simply not possible, not safe, not practical. Being a magician, they say, is as much about coming to accept new realities as anything else. That process cannot be rushed.

And yet Thomas must rush. If he does not do so now, then he will run out of time. Crowley seems very eager to teach him more, to let him read material that is supposed to be forbidden to neophytes, but reading isn't enough for him. He is becoming a tree. Miss Feldstein is pregnant with rabbits. Thomas can no longer be idle. He needs to act.

He considers confessing all to MacGregor Mathers. He is supposed to be the most accomplished magician in the country, perhaps in Europe. Even Crowley speaks of him with respect. Why can he not tell MacGregor Mathers what he faces? He has been too ashamed in the past to even consider such a confession, but Thomas realizes he has nothing to lose.

He is preparing to make his way across the room when a little man steps in front of him. He is small and noticeably stooped, breathing with much labor. He is perhaps a little older than forty, but the years weigh heavily upon him. He has the bushy dark hair of a much younger man and a matching bushy mustache.

It is the eyes, however, that concern Thomas. He has seen this man, *Frater Iehi Aour*, around the temple, and Thomas has always felt the revulsion one experiences around the chronically ill or deformed. Thomas knows he should be more generous, for he will be both of those things in the not-very-distant future. Also, he cannot see precisely what is so terribly wrong with this fellow other than he has poor posture and some disruptive respiratory difficulties.

"Little brother," he rasps at Thomas, "you have been meddling with the Goetia."

Thomas stares at him. "I have no idea what you mean. What the devil is a Goetia?"

The man fixes him with his foggy dark eyes. "Hmm. Perhaps it is the Goetia that has been meddling with you." He nods to himself as though he's said something very wise.

Thomas has no idea how to respond. He looks around, hoping for someone to rescue him, but Crowley is talking quite intimately with MacGregor Mather's wife. Standing just beyond Crowley is another man, so Thomas's eyes meet those of Isaiah Ruddington, *Frater Quaero Aeternum*, the very magician Thomas spied lurking the halls of Thresher's Bank. Now he is staring at Thomas from across the room. Ruddington's face grows pale and his lips quiver. At once he makes for the stairs.

"Excuse me," Thomas says to the wheezing *Frater Iehi Aour* and sets off after Ruddington.

It will be a task to catch him up, but Crowley, who appears to have missed nothing, has already broken away from the lovely Moina Mathers and approached Ruddington on the stairs. He has a hand on the man's shoulder and is smiling as he speaks, but Thomas does not miss the elements of menace.

"What is this about?" Ruddington asks.

"You tell me." Thomas, having closed the distance, walks toward him, feeling the menace radiating from him. He has had quite enough, and Ruddington seems just the person upon whom he can vent his frustrations. "Explain your business at Thresher's."

"A man can b-bank where he likes." This comes out in a wholly unconvincing stammer.

"He can," Thomas agrees, "but I see no evidence of you doing business at Thresher's. I see only that you are in its debt."

Ruddington looks up quite helplessly but says nothing.

"Let's discuss this elsewhere," Crowley says amiably. "There's a public house down the street that will do nicely."

"I don't choose to go," Ruddington says.

"You will endure," Crowley says with a smile.

They sit at a table in the back, each holding a mug of ale that Crowley has purchased. Ruddington clutches his for comfort but does not drink.

"Come on, then," Crowley says. "Speak up."

"I have nothing to say." Ruddington's gaze shifts nervously around the room, as though looking for someone to come to his rescue.

"In that case," Crowley says, "we're going to have to hurt you."

"What, really?" Thomas asks.

"I broke your friend's finger with less provocation," Crowley recollects.

"I suppose that's true."

"All right!" Ruddington says. He raises his hands and pushes himself back in his chair. "This is more than I signed on for. Yes, I owe the bank money, and they have asked me to do some things for them—things I would rather not have done, but I was in a bind, so I did them. I had no choice."

"What sort of things?" Thomas presses.

"Magical things," Ruddington says. "I'm not the only one, you know. There are quite a few of us that Thresher's has the squeeze on. Mostly it's been harmless. I don't even understand half of it. Once they blindfolded me and brought me somewhere, had me perform rituals. I don't even know what it was about. But this latest thing. Damn it, I don't feel good about what I've done. Maybe it's best you've found me out."

"What have you done?" Crowley demands.

"It was just a small curse. Upon Mr. Thresher here. Something to make things not go his way. Lost keys here. A missed omnibus there. Nothing too serious."

"The Goetia?" Thomas proposes.

Ruddington's eyes widen. "How did you know?"

"Thresher doesn't muck about," Crowley says harshly. "As you can tell."

Thomas, who still doesn't know what the devil the Goetia is, asks, "Who has been giving you your orders at the bank?"

"An odd fellow named Hawke."

"And he told you to curse me?" Thomas presses. "When?"

"Only a few weeks ago. He asked me to do something very small," Ruddington assures him. "He wanted to make sure that you were not killed or disfigured. He only wanted you inconvenienced."

Thomas thinks back over the past few weeks. What minor incidents have gone against him? The uncomfortable conversations at the Topping house? Discovering that his friends were but paid stooges? Certainly the events at the rabbit house, though that ended up being far worse for Miss Feldstein than himself.

"I'll remove it, of course," Ruddington volunteers.

"And you'll say nothing of this to Mr. Hawke," Thomas presses.

"Of course not. I wouldn't want him to know I've told you."

"Who else in the temple is in league with Thresher's?" Thomas asks.

He provides a list of eleven names. Thomas knows Yeats and a few others, but the rest are unknown to him, though Crowley snorts at each one. He says they're a pack of second-raters.

"I believe we're done here," Crowley announces. He rises and Thomas follows him out to the street. The cold air feels good after the heat of the enclosed space.

"What do you know about this Goetia?" Thomas asks him.

"It's serious stuff," Crowley says. "MacGregor Mathers translated it from a medieval text. It's not the sort of thing to tinker with if you don't know what you're doing. No matter what Ruddington says about making things right, we'll have to get you cleansed."

"You seem awfully familiar with what you are not supposed to meddle with."

"Bit of a lark," Crowley says with a grin. "I once summoned a creature and instructed it to kill the Queen. Didn't work."

Thomas thinks about his encounter with the men from the Home Office. He decides he will pretend he never heard this.

"I think I've had enough of the Golden Dawn," Thomas announces. "I can't trust the fraters, and I'm learning nothing. All it's gotten me is cursed."

"The curse is easily remedied. Don't trouble yourself. I understand your concerns about the fellows in league with your brother, but the Golden Dawn is still your best bet for learning."

"Learning what?" Thomas demands. He cannot sit still any longer. He cannot stand by while he becomes a plant and Miss Feldstein delivers her rabbit brood. "I've studied their books, and I've memorized their mumbo jumbo, but what has it gotten me? I want to *do* something."

"Such as?"

"I'd like to know what to do about the rabbit house," he says. "I want to be able to help Miss Feldstein."

Crowley shakes his head. "You will have to aim a bit lower for now. That is beyond anything I've ever seen."

Thomas gives it some thought. Maybe he can achieve the same goal through less direct means. He became involved in the Golden Dawn at Mrs. Topping's suggestion, and she believed the answer to his predicament could be found in astral realms.

"Astral travel," he proposes.

Crowley grins. "Then let's see to it." He begins to walk to the stairwell.

"Where are we going?" Thomas sets down his glass and follows after him.

Crowley grins. "We are going get your curse cleaned up, and then we are going to another world."

In Crowley's apartment, Crowley performs some cleansing rituals that involve a lot of dagger-waving. Once he sets the ceremonial weapon down, he squints at Thomas and proclaims his aura is clean.

"Now," Crowley says, "let's smoke opium."

Thomas holds up his hand in protest. "I don't know that opium is for me."

"You seem like a man in a hurry." He lights a pipe, takes a puff, and hands it to Thomas. "You can learn how to travel on the astral plane through meditation, but it can take months. Years. Opium is a shortcut. Don't take too much. A man who is unused to it will feel the effects strongly. You must aim to open your mind, not fall asleep."

Thomas had hoped to be the sort of person who lived his entire life without smoking opium, but he does not have months or years to learn astral travel. He takes the pipe and allows the bitter, oily smoke into his lungs. After a moment, Thomas does feel sleepy. Perhaps that's not it. He feels dreamy and unmoored from the movement of time. It is as though he has just woken up and there is a memory of a dream clinging to him. He can almost grasp it, almost fit the pieces together, but not quite.

Crowley has dimmed the lights in his flat. He has lighted candles. Incense burns. He has convinced Thomas to strip off most of his clothes and he sits in a thin dressing gown, his legs twisted into a position that Crowley says is most conducive to the sort of trance that facilities astral travel. He has learned to breathe precisely as Crowley has instructed, in through his nostrils, out his mouth.

There is less overtly magical activity involved than Thomas would have imagined. No magical circles or talismans or charms. Prior to attempting the astral travel, they perform the Lesser Banishing Ritual of the Pentagram, but that is to clear the room of harmful energy and to shed any remaining debris from Ruddington's curse, not to facilitate the process by which his soul shall take a holiday from his body.

Crowley has taken a white card on thick stock, a black symbol of Venus—a circle from which a cross extends at the bottom and another half circle, like a crown, from the top—and propped it up on the coffee table in front of them. Venus, Crowley explains, is among the easiest places to travel for a beginner. There are far more distant worlds that require focusing on specific tarot cards, but Thomas is not ready for such journeys. For now, he is to focus on the symbol and banish all other thoughts. He is to internalize it and to see it with what Crowley calls his third eye. "The most important element in performing magic is will," Crowley tells him. "You must want it and know you will make it happen. When you begin, when you leave your body for the first time, you may feel exhilaration and freedom. It is certainly what I felt. Some people, however, feel terror. It can seem less like flying and more like tumbling through an abyss, such as what we felt at the rabbit house. If you panic, you will be drawn back to your body like a stone dropping to the ground, and we will not be able to continue today. It is very common, and it means that you will be better prepared for the next time we try. If you keep calm, however, and go with the sensations, you will see things that right now, at this moment, you cannot begin to imagine."

"But how will I know where to go?" Thomas asks. "Does that question even make sense?"

"Yes and no," Crowley says with much seriousness. "Right now, there is no common frame of reference, so it is hard to tell you what you should expect. You should know, however, that no matter how you wander, you will always be able to find your way back. There is no chance of getting lost. You are particularly fortunate, however. Most of us must work all this out on our own, but I will be waiting for you when you leave your body. I will show you some wondrous places. Astral travel is thrilling, and the delights of the first time are an experience without equal."

Thomas would certainly welcome an experience without equal. He sits and breathes and visualizes precisely as he has been told. He imagines the symbol as a place, and he imagines moving toward it. He tells himself he is drifting upward, away from his body. The opium does make him feel somewhat floaty, but he knows that is not his soul taking flight. He is looking for something else, something actual and concrete, a change of being.

He waits. He breathes, he visualizes. His feet begin to feel leaden, and he shifts his position. He expects Crowley to chastise him, but when Thomas peers through mostly-closed eyes, he sees that Crowley is still, hands on his knees, palms facing upward. He has the slow and shallow breathing of a man in deep slumber.

Thomas closes his eyes and tries again. He goes through the list of things he is supposed to remember, but it feels harder this time, more forced. He wonders if the opium is wearing off. Should he smoke more? Should he have smoked less? He remembers he must assert his will, but he isn't quite sure what that means. He suddenly realizes that his thoughts have been drifting. He's been thinking about the symbol itself, how the semicircle is a bit smaller than the circle, so that if it were completed, it would fit inside the larger. How much smaller is it? Thomas catches himself beginning to do the calculations in his mind.

He reaches a point where he realizes he is never going to astral travel. He is going to continue to try, certainly, but he knows in his heart it is never going to work.

At long last Crowley opens his eyes and peers at him. "Where were you?"

"I appear to be unable to leave my body?" Thomas answers sheepishly.

Crowley unfolds himself with elastic ease and rises to his feet. Thomas does the same with considerably more difficulty.

"Did you try?" Crowley asked.

"Of course I tried!" Thomas snaps.

"If you had failed," Crowley says, "that is, if you had left your body and become frightened and returned, I would have seen you at least for a few seconds. Time can feel different there, so I don't think I'd have missed you, but did you have that sensation?"

"No," Thomas admits. "I did all you said, but then I began to grow uncomfortable and I became aware of how odd my position was. I was unable to concentrate."

A rare look of worry crosses Crowley's face. "That certainly should not be happening to you at your current level of study. I wonder if that curse goes deeper than I thought."

"Is there anything to be done about that?" Thomas asks.

"No doubt," Crowley says. "We need only know what we're dealing with. Let's have a look, shall we?"

What Thomas wishes most of all is to change back into his clothes. He has no desire to spend his time with Crowley while the two of them are nearly naked. Crowley's dressing gown has come partially undone, and Thomas finds himself exposed to large swathes of muscular and hairy chest. It is unpleasant and intimidating. In the aftermath of the opium, his head is pounding.

Crowley, showing no modesty or aftereffects of the drug, sits down and takes out a deck of tarot cards.

"Do you honestly think that can provide real answers?" Thomas asks.

Crowley cocks an eyebrow. "I don't know how to respond to that question. Either you believe that the process we call 'magic' is real or you don't. Skepticism is your worst enemy."

Thomas retreats to the bedroom to dress. When he returns, the magician is still laying out cards in a circular pattern. He nods or widens his eyes or grunts with the revelation of each new card, as though listening to someone tell a story.

Finally, Crowley looks at the cards and then back to Thomas. He reverses the process, and then starts over again. He then collects the cards into a stack, wraps them in a silk handkerchief, and sets them aside.

"Well," he says, "as a magician, I'm afraid you're shite."

Thomas stares at him. "What do you mean?"

"I mean, you're shite. Some people, such as I, are naturally gifted like athletes. Others have potential but must work hard to develop strength and skills and whatever they need to compete. And then there are the weaklings and cripples, the fellows who can work as hard as they like and still accomplish nothing. For such men, making the attempt is not merely a waste of time, it is a humiliation."

"And that's me?" Thomas asks. "I'm a magical cripple?"

"That, it seems, is you." Crowley looks very solemn.

"And you saw this in the cards?"

"The cards showed me, yes."

"What if the cards are wrong?"

"That question is part of the problem." Crowley shakes his head with evident disappointment. "You see the tarot as a fairground trick. You are thinking of astral travel as though it's calling a hansom. I'm afraid you simply don't perceive the world like a magician. I don't know if this is something inborn or acquired. Perhaps if you'd had a different type of upbringing, associated with different sorts of people, you might have the necessary insight, but there's no turning back the clock. Magic requires creativity and imagination, the ability to reach for the sensations our bodies hide from us. You may be too much of a literalist to be a magician."

"All this time I've spent studying is for nothing?" Thomas can see the time he's dedicated to studying magic like sand pouring through an hourglass. That part of his remaining life has been squandered on foolish hopes and chicanery.

"Is the acquisition of knowledge ever really pointless?" Crowley asks, oblivious to Thomas's mask of horrified shame. "The truth is, you are no different than most of the fellows in the order. I doubt one tenth of them have the perception or the will to be real magicians, and the majority of those are ladies for some reason. Haven't sorted that one out yet."

Thomas shakes his head. "I was a fool to bother with any of this."

"You are thinking too much like a banker," Crowley tells him. "Is reading a poem a waste of time when it gets you nothing but itself? Is looking at a painting or fucking a woman? Not everything must be productive. If a thing satisfies you, if it give you pleasure, or fills you with wonder, then it is enough."

Thomas is on his feet. "I'm not looking for wonder, you self-important dolt! I'm trying to—oh, never mind."

With his days numbered, he embarked on a study of magic—of *magic*—because he was advised to do so by a dog-faced woman. He feels like he has been taken in by a confidence artist. That something undeniably magical is happening to his body is, in his passion, forgotten. The manifestation of leaves must be regarded as a disease, like consumption or a cancer, and he has been hoodwinked into buying worthless potions.

Crowley leans back, his robe yet further open, smoking on the refreshed opium pipe. "I don't care to be called a dolt," he says languidly.

"Then don't be one." Thomas hurries toward the door. Is it wise to insult this bull of a man? Likely not, but Thomas is beyond caring.

Crowley rises, and though he moves in slow and undulating ripples, like a man under water, he somehow beats Thomas to the door and bars his path.

"I suppose your manhood demands you strike me for insulting you," Thomas says. "I think you'll find I don't go down so easily."

"Your lack of magical talent isn't the only thing I saw in the tarot," Crowley says gently. "Perhaps you should sit down."

Thomas shoves the man out of the way. He is clearly not so immovable as he imagines himself. Thomas is down the hall and descending the stairs before he can consider that Crowley is trying to be a friend. Thomas, however, wants no friends. He wants nothing. He wants void and emptiness and silence, and he supposes he is a lucky man, because he is, not so far in the future, going to get precisely that.

⟶ TWENTY-FIVE ⟵
COMPLETION

IT SEEMS INEVITABLE that Walter is waiting for Thomas when he arrives home. He believes if he refuses to show his face in the parlor it will become an ordeal, so Thomas decides to appear himself only to say he is too ill to talk. He has smoked opium and confronted the inevitability of his demise. He presumes his appearance will sell the argument.

Walter is, of course, sitting with Mr. Hawke. It is he who greets Thomas. "Young Mr. Thresher, please do have a seat."

"I am afraid I am not well," Thomas says. "Another time."

"No one is making a request," Walter tells him. "Sit down."

Thomas meets Walter's eye. "I am in no mind for more pointless arguments."

"I do not engage in pointless arguments," Walter says, "and if you don't wish to sit, you may stand, and I will address you as though you were a servant. Your wedding date has been set. Two weeks from Sunday. Mr. Feldstein and I have grown weary of waiting for consent from a pair of feckless ingrates who will never agree to anything but what indulges their own appetites."

Mr. Hawke spreads his arms to suggest the breadth of Walter's goodness. "We have relieved you of the burden of deliberation."

Thomas opens his mouth to speak. Another deflection, a wry comment, a pronouncement that he will not discuss the subject further. Delay, delay, delay, but how can he play for time when he is a man with so little time to spare?

Is this, as Crowley said, evidence of his failed imagination and will? Imagination, perhaps. Thomas is a logical thinker, not a dreamer. He will accept that. And it is true that he has been passive in recent years, but that does not mean he lacks will. It would be a mistake, he decides, for Walter to make that assumption.

Now, at this moment, Thomas has had enough. He is turning into a tree, and any illusions that he could reverse this process have been cast aside. He is a dying man. He can no longer hope for a miracle, and he will not allow his last days to be spent in a loveless marriage or in endless conflict with his brother. He will play this game no more.

"I shall not marry her." Thomas's voice is so forceful he half expects the curtain to rustle and the lights to flicker, but the material world is indifferent to his resolve. "If you wish to sever ties with me, to cast me out of this house and from the bank, then do so. You allow me to do no good at Thresher's—I can only look on while you ruin what our grandfather made. What I will not do is marry Miss Feldstein. Not in two weeks and not ever."

"I beg you to think of what you are saying, young sir." Mr. Hawke's voice is shrill with alarm.

"Does he never shut up?" asks Thomas. "I am sick of hearing this simpering man. What is he to you, Walter? Your master? Your lover? I cannot determine why he is always by your side."

Walter has the color and expression of a man trying not to vomit. "I shall make you a director," he says, his voice hardly more than a whisper.

This offer seems to have taken something from Walter, who may very possibly be on the brink of tears.

Mr. Hawke, however, is grinning like a child who sees the pile of presents on his birthday. "Your insightful comments upon the bank's current debt load has proved your merit," Mr. Hawke volunteers. "Come and be part of the governing board. Let us benefit from your wisdom. Do you see what we offer you? It is everything you have ever wanted."

What can this mean? All Thomas's life, Walter has worked against him and now, to make this marriage happen, he will elevate him to the governing board? It makes no sense. Thomas cannot ask why. He knows he will receive no answer. He needs a different approach.

"Will you excuse us?" Thomas says to Mr. Hawke. "I would speak to my brother alone."

"There is nothing you have to say to me that Mr. Hawke cannot hear," Walter protests.

"That is for me to decide," Thomas tells him, "as they are my things to say."

Mr. Hawke continues to grin as he rises out of his chair. "A little time with one's family. Of course. There is nothing more natural." He steps outside, closing the door. He never stops grinning, never stops looking directly into Thomas's eyes until he vanishes from view.

Thomas decides he needs no invitation and sits.

"How long will you continue to defy me?" Walter asks.

"Walter, you cannot ask me to marry a woman I hardly know for reasons you refuse to tell me."

"It is for the good of the bank. I have said as much."

"But you haven't told me why."

"You have been at the bank half a year. You cannot understand my plans."

"And yet you will make me a director."

"Because you are being so unreasonable!" He slams his hand down on the table. Glasses rattle, but nothing tumbles or breaks.

It is time to stop holding back. There must be reasons Walter has always been cold to him. Thomas doesn't know what they are, but surely they exist. He is not an excessively sentimental man, and perhaps Thomas has taken personally what was never personal. Perhaps Walter has resented how Thomas wants Walter to be someone other than who he is. Perhaps, in the end, Thomas is to blame.

"Why did you pay those fellows to befriend me?" His tone is free of anger. It is almost gentle. "For all those years, you contrived for me to associate with them. Why?"

"Who told you such a thing?" Walter demands.

"They did," Thomas said.

"You cannot trust such men," Walter says. "They are drunks and wastrels. They would not know the truth from a lie if their lives depended on it."

"And yet you do not deny it."

"Must we dig up old business?" Walter throws his hands in the air. "Will you pummel me with grudges decades old?"

"I only want to understand," Thomas says wearily.

"There is nothing to understand. You must do what I tell you. Our family depends on it. The bank depends on it."

"But you will not tell me why."

"I should not have to!" Walter again slams the table. This time a glass falls to the floor and shatters. Walter looks at Thomas with an accusing glare.

Thomas prepares himself to say something he has never spoken aloud. "I cannot marry Miss Feldstein. I cannot marry anyone. I am—I am unwell, Walter. I believe I am dying."

Thomas takes hold of his jacket. He is going to strip down, to show Walter the scars from where leaves have grown. Walter will finally see that there are more important things than his secret plans for the bank. He will understand that Thomas, though he is much younger, and has always been so very different, is his family. Perhaps it will make Walter confront the growths he's found upon his own body.

Thomas barely gets as far as shrugging his shoulders before Walter stops him. "How can that make a difference? If you are ill, a wife will be of service to you. If you die, it little matters whom you marry."

Thomas finds himself frozen, his hands upon his lapels, his eyes incapable of blinking. Walter stares back, a *get on with it already* expression upon his face.

"That is all you have to say to me?" Thomas asks. "You do not wish to know the manner of illness or what kinds of hardships I face?"

"Let us not pretend we have ever been close," Walter counters. "You have been estranged from me since the moment of your birth. You live here and work at my bank because it is what Father commanded of me, and though I cannot understand his reasons, I have obeyed. Your condition is—lamentable. I should prefer you were not unwell, but I can do nothing about it. I could offer words of comfort, but you would not believe them, and they would mean nothing."

"You don't know that," Thomas says. "Yes, things have always been strained between us, but I'll be damned if I know why. It's not too late to start again."

"If you wish for a new start, find it with a wife. You will marry Miss Feldstein."

If there is more to say, Thomas cannot think of it. He has laid himself bare to his brother, and his brother was unmoved. Can it be that there is nothing more to him than the bank, this desire to toil at the family business even as he destroys it? Perhaps Walter has never cared for Thomas because he has never cared for anyone, because he is fundamentally broken, a clockwork mechanism that is wound up for the purpose of meaningless toil and nothing else.

"Walter, are you a magician?" Thomas asks.

"Good God, no!" Walter's face twists in disgust. "I have no time for magic and mathematics and all the frivolities that so fascinate you. You want to know why I paid those fellows? It was to keep you from that path, for all the good it did you, for here you are, a nothing, just as I feared."

"You feared I would become a mathematician or a magician? Which is it?" Thomas keeps his voice calm, almost indifferent. He dare not show just how desperate he is to learn the answer. Magic and mathematics, as he has learned, could not be less related, so what precisely did Walter fear? And if he did fear for Thomas's future, does that mean, in his gruff way, Walter has cared about him all along?

"What I have done, I have done for the bank," Walter answers, as if to make certain Thomas does not entertain any notions of familial affection. "You were becoming someone who would have harmed Thresher's, and I took steps and did so with my father's blessings. I will say no more than that."

"How could my friendship with Bobby Yardley have mattered to the bank?" Thomas demands.

"Are you deaf as well as stupid?" Walter snaps. "I said I would speak no more of it."

And ugly silence hangs in the air. Walter picks up a pen and begins to look through some papers on his desk. He seems to want to pretend he can no longer see Thomas sitting before him.

"Do you know what I think?" Thomas asks.

"No, I haven't any notion of your thoughts," Walter answers wearily. He would stand up and leave the room before hearing more if he could, yet Thomas holds the key to what Walter wants. He therefore settles in to endure another barrage of intolerable emotion.

"All my life I have sought your approval," Thomas says. "If I could not have that, I tried for your attention. I believed you ignored me because I was unworthy, but now I realize that it was because you were determined never to notice me. You cared nothing for what I did or didn't do. If I excelled or blundered in my studies, it made no difference. I drank and whored and spent as much of the family money as I could, and you never turned your head. It seems I have wanted something that did not exist."

"If you want my approval, you know what you must do," says Walter, clearly wearied by having to make the same argument yet again.

"What will that get you?" Thomas's voice has something pleading in it. He hates how it sounds, but he hates not understanding even more. "Tell me. Tell me what that gets you!"

"Everything." Walter's voice is empty, as though he has said *nothing important*. "All will be different. And the marriage is of no significance. Leave her later if you wish."

"Marriages are not easy to dissolve," Thomas observes, "and now there are added obstacles. I do not wish to be a contract-breaker and suffer Peculiar consequences. Have you not considered that, in light of the bank's charter and its current clientele, the reason Thresher's is experiencing difficulties—"

"Rubbish," Walter says with a wave of his hand. "There are no difficulties. Only a strategy. All contracts can be broken. They *will* be broken. The only thing that matters is growth. Thresher's must be always growing." The last he says as if by rote, as if it were a prayer.

Thomas sits quietly. He has come to his part of the play, and he knows his lines, but does he have the courage to speak them? If he does, everything will change. His life, what there is of it, will never be the same. That, however, cannot be a bad thing to a man who has wished for his life to cease. He tells himself it is better for his life to change, for him to live in chaos and discord, than to fade into nothing.

"Very well," Thomas says. "How you get her to the altar is your affair, but I will do it."

Walter blinks several times and then nods. This is as much emotion as he will allow himself. "Then you have come to your senses. Please close the door on your way out."

Thomas rises, and leaves the room, closing the door behind him. He then leans against it, trying to order his thoughts. What has he done? Is he mad? Has he lost the will to fight? No. None of these things. Thomas has never felt more like a brawler than he does at this moment.

He has two weeks—two weeks in which something drastic must happen, because Thomas is never going to marry Miss Feldstein. In those two weeks, he must learn the purpose of the marriage, and he must hope that he can use that knowledge to take control of the bank for himself. Or simply take it away from Walter. That's all that is required.

By the time he reaches his room, however, he is full of doubt. Is two weeks enough time? What can he do if, at the end of that time, he is no closer to discovering his brother's secrets than he is now? Then there is Miss Feldstein to consider. She has troubles enough, but when she hears of Thomas's acquiescence, she will view it as a betrayal. He will have to speak to her tomorrow, make certain she understands, but with each passing moment he understands his own motivation even less. In a pique of anger, he made a decision that seemed sly and strategic, but now perhaps he wonders if he merely blundered into his brother's trap.

With the gas lamps burning low, he readies himself for bed. Not for sleep. He doubts it will come, and perhaps he does not want it to. He does not want to see that terrible face leering at him as though it cannot quite figure out what Thomas is. Not in his waking life, not in his dreams, can Thomas hope to escape.

Then he sees the silver tray upon his writing desk. Someone has delivered a letter. From nearly across the room he recognizes Mrs. Yardley's hand, and he rushes forward as if this is the thing that will save him. The letter must surely contain some good news, a counterbalance for all that has gone wrong in his life. The universe owes him some small thing—a suggestion that they take tea or stroll through the park. Thomas does not require anything grand. A little thing will mean so much.

Once again, he is disappointed. Then he is horrified. The letter is short, and the hand loose, as though written in a great rush. The sentences are disordered, but the core of it is impossible to dismiss. *I cannot see you again. You are in great danger. Please take care and know you are in my thoughts.*

He almost laughs aloud. He is in danger? Of course he is bloody well in danger, but the question is how she could know such a thing. There is only one possible answer. Someone has threatened her. Someone has dared to menace this generous, caring woman whose only crime was to show kindness to a man scorned by his own family.

This will not stand. The determination he felt when he agreed to marry Miss Feldstein has returned, and this time he will cling to it. This time he will not let it go. He has endured enough outrage in injustice from his brother to last a thousand lifetimes. It must end.

He stands in the gloom, clutching Mrs. Yardley's letter, teeth grinding with rage. All his life, Walter has conspired against him. Now it is time to push back, to protect the people and the things for which he cares. Thomas knows what he wants in the little time remaining to him. He wants to save his grandfather's bank. He wants to set it on a proper course to avoid ruin. Most of all, he wants revenge, and one way or another, he will have it.

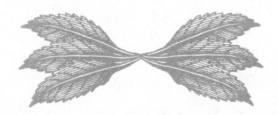

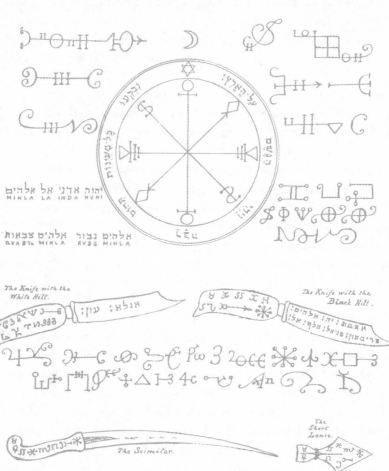

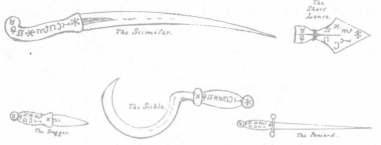

The Knife with the White Hilt.

The Knife with the Black Hilt.

The Scimitar.

The Short Lance.

The Dagger.

The Sickle.

The Poniard.

The Staff.

The Wand.

TWENTY-SIX

STRENGTH

THE IRONY APPEALS to Thomas. Walter has taken steps to utterly control Thomas's life, and yet, in accepting the command to marry Miss Feldstein, Thomas is freer than he has been since before his father's death. He has chosen not to go to the bank this morning. Perhaps he will choose not to go tomorrow. Why should he bother? No one cares about what he does in his garret.

It has taken some negotiation, some back and forth, to get Mrs. Yardley to agree to see him. Was not the point of her letter that she did not wish to do so? He insisted, however, and won the day by making her understand that he must know what prompted her to write. She would not meet him in a private setting, however, and at last they agreed upon the tea shop they visited before. Thomas would have preferred to see her at her home given the many personal things he wishes to discuss, but he did not feel the need to force the issue. He can speak with a quiet voice. The world, as he well knows, does not always order itself to his pleasure.

He would also prefer if he could not feel a leaf emerging just below his collarbone. It began itching as he rode on the train. Now the worst of it is over, but he can feel it there, a little distraction. It is a reminder, he supposes, of the urgency of his mission. He has little time left, and he must live all he can in his remaining months. He must stop his brother from ruining his family's bank, he must uncover the secrets of the bank's relationship with the Peculiarities, and he must, yes, secure some measure of happiness for himself. Whatever has been said to Mrs. Yardley must be answered with determination and force.

Thomas is a few minutes early, but Madeline Yardley is already seated when he walks through the door. The obsequious Italian is all upon him, taking his coat, and Thomas is careful not to let the leaf snap as he moves his arm. Lately they have had more sap, and he doesn't wish to have a stain appear on his shirt.

As he approaches the table, Mrs. Yardley seems to smile despite herself, and for a moment Thomas forgets all his troubles. Her dress, a cheerful blue in color, heightens her complexion and suggests a certain vibrancy that Thomas finds as heady as a glass of brandy. A flickering candle at the center of the table only heightens the effect. There is something different about her, too, about a perfume she wears—it is more urgent and vital. When she takes his hand in greeting, Thomas feels a quickening of his heart and slightly dizzying tightening of his stomach. It is the same thing he used to feel upon sitting down with a whore he had chosen. Intimacy feels near, like a cloud of smoke surrounding him, but he does not know if he senses his desire or hers.

"I wish you had not troubled yourself," she begins. "I only wanted you to understand and to—to be careful. Now you are neglecting your work at the bank."

Thomas ignores her protests. "You must tell me everything. Surely you can see that. If someone has threatened you, I must know."

She shakes her head. "I have overreacted. The letter I wrote you was more strongly worded than was required, I now think. I only want that you should succeed, and that your friendship with me not cause you grief."

"I can do nothing of the kind," he tells her. He wants to ask her what it was that caused her to write, to hear everything at once, but he knows he cannot force her to speak. Women must be coaxed, not commanded, or they become timid and cowering things like Pearl.

She blushes ever so slightly, as though she can read his thoughts. "I ought never have encouraged you to pursue matters at Thresher's. It was selfish of me. It was an indulgence that has gained me nothing and may have cost you much."

"You mustn't think it a waste of time," he says. "I have learned that the bank was deliberately seeking to put magicians in their debt in order to force them to perform certain tasks. I suspect the men behind this scheme would have made use of your husband had he lived, though what task they might have assigned him we shall never know."

"I am no expert on banking, but these activities seem unusual." The fear seems, at least for the moment, to have vanished. She seems more like a student at a lecture now.

"They are, but I have some theories. I think my brother is losing money, that his loans are failing, and that this may be happening because of the Peculiarities. You see, the bank had a charter, a sort of statement of purpose.

This charter outlined that the bank's purpose is to help small men who have no other recourse. My father began to change all that, and now my brother continues that work."

Mrs. Yardley raises her lovely eyebrows. "And in the era of the Peculiarities, the binding nature of that charter has caused these loans to fail?"

"It is what I suspect. Walter may be turning to magicians to find a way to reverse all that."

The waiter interrupts them to take their order. Thomas is happy for the dramatic pause. When the fellow is gone, Thomas looks back to Mrs. Yardley, who has been unable to maintain her brave countenance. Now, Thomas thinks, is the time to press.

"Mrs. Yardley. Madeline. You must tell me what has happened."

"No." She shakes her head. "Yes. Oh, I don't know what to do. I was warned not to tell you, that it would go badly for you if I did, but I cannot let you stumble in the dark. I must say it all for your sake, not for mine."

Thomas's heart is pounding. He feels ready for something, but he does not know what it is. "What are you telling me?"

She turns pale and looks away. "I received a visit from a horrible, horrible little man. He would not stop grinning at me."

Thomas feels that he has always known it must be him. "Mr. Hawke."

"Yes, that's what he called himself. He said I mustn't see you again, that it would be your ruin if I did. That harm would come to you. He said I mustn't tell you about the visit. That he would know if I did. He told me—" Here she stops and takes a breath in order to summon her courage. "He told me that I must break things off with you, as though you and I—as though I were a—it was mortifying."

Thomas is filled with rage and humiliation. How dare Mr. Hawke speak to her in that manner? But also, would it be so terrible if there was something between them to break off? Of course she does not mean it that way, he tells himself. At least she does not necessarily mean it that way. There is hope yet.

"Did he threaten you?" Thomas asks. It is a challenge to keep his voice from trembling.

"No," she says. "Only you. I did not want to see you because of it, but I thought it unfair not to tell you why I would not see you."

"I cannot imagine not seeing me could be so very great an inconvenience," Thomas says.

She gasps and takes hold of his arm. "You must know that isn't true."

Everything has changed. Thomas feels that it is so. Madeline has all but confessed her feelings for him. It is as much as he could have hoped for. And as for Mr. Hawke—let him issue his threats. He can do nothing to Thomas, whom they need to marry Miss Feldstein.

Once Madeline takes her hand away, Thomas feels his voice return. "Mr. Hawke will not dare harm me. I'm glad you've told all of this to me." He feels the itch of the leaf along his collarbone again, and he longs to scratch at it, but doing so would ruin the moment. "My investigations of the bank may be cutting a little close to the bone."

"In what way?" Madeline asks breathlessly. "Supposing your brother knows what you've learned about his efforts to break away from the bank's charter. Would that truly trouble him?

"I think that is only part of what my brother has in mind. You see, Thresher's has been acquiring buildings around the city. I do not know why the bank needs these specific buildings, but they are being used to create—portals, if you will. I know this sounds mad, but they are portals to other realms, to places in the astral worlds, I suppose. I don't know the correct terminology. There may be none, but it is my belief that the establishment of these portals has some relationship to the Peculiarities. It may be meant to free Thresher's from the constraints of its charter. Regardless, these portals are clearly harming others, no matter how beneficial to my brother's schemes, I am determined to do something about them."

"Do you mean to say that Thresher's Bank is responsible for the Peculiarities?"

"I doubt the bank is the sole source of these events," he says. "I do think some of the more persistent manifestations, such as rabbit births, may be linked to these open portals. I have seen it with my own eyes. My associates and I attempted to disable it, but we were not effective. Still, I have a notion that it can be done. I mean to make another attempt."

Mrs. Yardley's eyes are wide with wonder. "Where is this portal? And are there others that you know of?"

"I may be able to find them," he says, ignoring the first part of her question. He cannot take the risk that she will visit the house on Cannon Street. She might think it nothing more than satisfying her curiosity, a bit of Peculiar tourism, but he knows too well the dangers.

"What can you think you can do to stop them?"

Thomas feels himself to be on the spot here. He does not want to start talking about maths, however. There is nothing that makes a man sound less heroic. "I will not trouble you with the details, but I have a notion, and I have no choice but to try. To be honest, Mrs. Yardley, there are things about myself I haven't told you. One of the purposes of my quest is rather personal."

"Oh, Mr. Thresher," she says, "you needn't tell me anything."

"I do wish to, but I fear it will make you uneasy. And yet, I would rather there were no secrets between us."

She nods eagerly. She too, it seems, would prefer to hear everything.

"The Peculiarities are not merely an abstract interest for me. You see, I am afflicted." And so he tells her. Mrs. Yardley listens, riveted by his words. Tears of sympathy make her eyes glisten. His description of finding leaves on his torso leads her to blush. When he is done, Mrs. Yardley appears as though she is the one with a terrible condition.

"Oh, Mr. Thresher," she says, taking his hand. "Thomas. I am so sorry to learn of this. It must be—well, I cannot know how it must be. I will not insult you by guessing. But you cannot give up. If there is a portal for this condition, you must find a way to destroy it."

"In the next few weeks, I plan to throw myself into this project," he says, "to do all I can to discover if there is a means of preserving myself. But I will be defying the interests of my family's bank. You must understand that I care about Thresher's, about what my grandfather wanted to create when he founded it, but my father and brother have led it astray. While what I intend to do is surely in the best interests of the bank, Walter may not see it that way. Even if I succeed and force the bank to return to its intended, and profitable, original purpose, he may retaliate by rendering me a pauper."

"And this distresses you?"

"No," he said. "But I am afraid it may distress you."

"Oh," she says. Then her eyes go wide. "Oh! Thomas, are you asking me— do you mean to say—" She cannot finish.

"I mean nothing so direct," he said. "I cannot know your feelings. In truth, I hardly know my own. I cannot know how I feel about my life, about my future, until I learn if I shall have a life and a future. But I felt that that there is a connection between us, and I wished to discuss my plans with someone who I believe has only my own interests at heart."

"I must tell you that I have never thought of marrying again," she says.

"You need not explain yourself," he says. "I don't wish to make you uncomfortable."

"You did not. You merely surprised me. And flattered me too. But I was once very much in love with a wonderful man, and then I was a widow. I would give anything to have Bobby back, but I have learned that I do not mind living alone, being mistress of my own affairs. I have enough money to live comfortably, and I find that is all I need."

"I understand." Thomas keeps his voice steady and dignified, though he feels a powerful admixture of shame and regret and sadness coursing through his veins.

"I hope you do," she tells him. "What I mean is that should I ever decide to marry again, a fortune would make little difference to me. The lack of a fortune would also matter little."

Thomas takes her hand. He knows now that he has something for which he wants to fight. He wants to find the right words to say to her, to convince her they have a future, but he does not know that he would believe them himself. That they have a present, however, seems to him something remarkable, and it will have to be enough.

Madeline Yardley has gone pale while he has deliberated these matters. She pushes her chair back and stands, but having done so, she seems frozen in terror.

It is the Elegants, here in the restaurant. They are near the front, leaning forward and rhythmically tilting their heads upward, as if sniffing the air. The Italian waiter drops a plate, and it shatters loudly. A woman screams and others soon join in.

Thomas feels that this is all strangely familiar. *What, the Elegants again? Ho hum.* He almost laughs madly, but he controls himself. He has survived before, and perhaps he will survive again, but survival is surely not enough. He must protect Madeline. He must protect these other people. The Elegants are here because of him. It may be, as Crowley and MacGregor Mathers suggested, that they do not wish to harm him, but that does not mean they will not harm others. The death of Arthur Doyle proved that.

Protecting the people near him is easier said than effected, of course. All he did to stop them before was allow them to knock him unconscious.

Except that isn't true. He cut himself. MacGregor Mathers seems to think that made a difference. Thomas looks around. There is a butter knife on his table, but he could saw at his flesh for minutes and not break his skin. Surely there must be a sharp edge somewhere in this place, but he if goes in search of it, he will have to leave Madeline behind or drag her with him—making her a target.

The Elegants have advanced into the room, flashing from one position to the next in their jittery way. People scream and beg for mercy and flee. They knock one another down in their desperation to reach the door.

The lights in the tea shop seem to dim or change or become fundamentally different. It is as though, for a brief second, the world is illuminated by an alien sun. Things appear too dark, too bright, colors have inexplicable saturations that hurt his eyes. There is a strange feeling of being weightless—not the vertigo of the rabbit house, but more like floating. Except it doesn't feel real. It is merely the effect of that inexplicable, disorienting, confounding shade of blue.

Then color and light are as they should be, but the Elegants are still there. They have moved, shifted, blinked in and out, and they stand before a man and a couple in their fifties. They seem like unremarkable middling sort of people, he in his suit, she in her pleasant yellow and green gown. They are nothing. They are like a thousand couples in London. The Elegants lean in to sniff the woman. From where he sits, Thomas can see the imprint of a tiny foot, like that of an infant, press out from the male's cheek.

Madeline gasps, and the Elegants snap their heads in her direction. It is as though they are forest predators who have heard their prey rustle the leaves. Seeing Madeline, their lipless mouths broaden in cruel and abhorrent smiles. The female raises her hand and points a boney finger. It is not Thomas they want. It is Madeline.

Of course it is. They are somehow in league with Thresher's or Walter or Mr. Hawke. They cannot harm Thomas because they need him for their absurd marriage. Their appearance at the Golden Dawn temple was meant as a warning. Mr. Hawke visiting Madeline, likewise, was a warning. He told her it was Thomas who would suffer, not her, because Mr. Hawke gambled upon her goodness. Thomas did not heed the warning, and now there must be consequences.

Whatever there is to be done must be done immediately. The Elegants are fast. They can move from one place to another in an instant. They can slice a throat in the blink of an eye. At least he believes they can do all these things. He has seen it, but he does not know if they can always behave thus. He must assume they can. He must prevent them from harming Madeline Yardley the woman he—*loves*? He is not certain. He knows he cares for her. Admires her. He would risk all to protect her. That may or may not be love, but it is unquestionably something good.

He risks a glance at Madeline and sees her terror. Thomas can no longer delay acting. He looks at the candle in the middle of the table. Would fire harm them? Perhaps, but he cannot imagine himself chasing after them with a little wax taper no longer than his thumb. Perhaps he could burn his own flesh instead of cutting himself. Would that be enough?

Then it comes to him. He quickly unbuttons his shirt. His fingers tremble, but he forces them to obey his commands. Madeline stares in horror and puzzlement as he reaches in and grabs the leaf that has been growing all morning. He hears the snap as it comes off. He then holds it by the stem— upon which a little droplet, half of blood, half of sap, glistens—and places the leaf above the flame.

The Elegants study Madeline—both of them tilting their heads this way and that, moving in eerie coordination. The male hisses. Things writhe beneath the taut skin of their faces.

And then they are gone. They don't vanish in any sort of theatrical fashion. There is no smoke or flash of light or clang of cymbals. They are simply no longer there, replaced by a disorienting emptiness and silence.

Throughout the restaurant, people glance about, uncertain what to make of this strange event. Some weep. Some hug. Some flee. The Italian calls after those who have not paid their reckoning.

Thomas looks at Madeline, and she throws herself in his arms. At first he thinks she means to kiss him, but she hugs him like a child, clinging to him with relief. For Thomas it is enough. He has saved her. He has done something that matters. He has faced a magical enemy of unknown origin and enormous power, and he has banished it.

A shite magician indeed.

TWENTY-SEVEN

ART

Now it is time to act. Thomas does not know who was behind the attack. Was it Mr. Hawke, Walter himself, some other collection of unseen men he hardly knows? Thomas need not understand everything in order to strike back.

Madeline was shaken after the encounter with the Elegants, and he saw her home, where he proposed staying with her. What if they make another attempt upon her? He didn't ask the question aloud, but he didn't have to.

"I don't claim to understand what is happening," she told him, "but it seems they came after me because I was with you."

Thomas had not been willing to say this to himself, but he cannot deny it. The Elegants are somehow doing the bank's bidding. Now that he considers it, he wonders if they would have actually harmed Madeline. Frightening her is one thing, but could Walter expect Thomas to cooperate if Madeline were killed? There may be no profit in speculating about what Walter thinks, however, and it may also be that he has limited control over these beings with which he has allied himself.

"I will put an end to this," Thomas tells her.

She takes his hand once again. "I have no wish to send you away." It sounded like the opening of a longer speech, but after a moment, Thomas understood that it was the totality of her statement.

"Can you forgive me for putting you in danger?" he asks her.

"You did nothing of the sort," she tells him. "You couldn't have known."

After he left her house, Thomas's misery sits like a shard of glass in his throat. While standing in the entryway, he considered declaring his love for her, but he did not do so because it felt unfair, perhaps even manipulative. They had only just survived a terrible ordeal, and how could they truly know what was in their hearts? That was not the only reason, however. Thomas could not stop grappling with the fact that he did not know for certain that love was what he felt. How could he, who had never been loved, know such a thing? He admires her. He finds her lovely, and when he is with her, he wants to be better than he is.

"I will be safe here," she told him, and he had the unmistakable feeling that she was ushering him out the door. And so he left, but not before she kissed him. It was a quick peck upon the cheek, notable in its absence of passion. On the train he considers whether it was sisterly and decides he would have no way of knowing. He has never had a sister.

Thomas returns to the house on Cannon Street. It is late in the day and will begin to grow dark soon, but there is time enough for what he wishes to attempt. He has a piece of chalk wrapped in a handkerchief in his pocket. It is the only magical device he requires.

What will Crowley say when he learns what Thomas has in mind? Thomas declares to himself he does not care, but he knows this is a lie. He wishes to make Crowley eat his words. He wishes to make Crowley see that Thomas is a great magician. He knows that is vain and foolish, but it is human nature, and Thomas will enjoy being human for such time as is left to him.

As for Ruby and Miss Feldstein, they will be angry he did not ask for their assistance. Both have made clear that they wish to help, but they shall have to be disappointed. Neither can help him with what he means to do.

When he approaches the door to the house on Cannon Street he finds the lock is still broken. The door is closed, but it swings open with hardly any resistance.

He knows his adventure may end here. It is possible that the moment he steps through the threshold he will be overcome by vertigo. He has wondered if he could force his way through it, manage to make his way upstairs despite the horror and disorientation. He knows he cannot. Yet Thomas does not believe he will be afflicted. The house must be tended, after all, the rabbits fed. The curse or spell or whatever it is must have a temporary duration. It may happen again while he is there, but he hopes it will not be until after he has done his work. It may be that his work will prevent the attack entirely.

He takes a tentative step forward but feels no vertigo. Thomas sighs with relief, though he is not foolish enough to believe there will be no danger. The air in the house is heavy with a musty odor. The smell is not quite the same as the last time he was here. The foul stench of waste and urine has lessened, and there is something sharp and fresh, almost like the wind after a storm, only somehow more alarming. There is the faintest hint of rot, like a decaying corpse. It is colder inside the house than out, and there is a hum in the air. It is not precisely a sound, but a sense of vibration.

Thomas slowly moves his way up the stairs, fearing with each step that the vertigo will return, but it does not happen. He is attacked by nothing physical or magical. It seems, to all appearances, nothing but an abandoned house.

He reaches the top floor and examines the scene before him in the dying light of the day. The portal stands, opened to blackness, but otherwise much is different. The cages that once contained rabbits are still there, but they appear to have been cleaned out. They contain no creatures or food or droppings.

The rabbits have moved, but they have not gone far. When Thomas looks at the floor, he sees it is a field of gently undulating fur. There are rabbits, countless rabbits, sleeping in a huddled mass. They keep their distance from the portal, however, huddled as though afraid to get too close. This is good news, as the chalk circle surrounding the portal is uncovered by animals. Each rabbit, Thomas notices, is white with gray splotches. It takes him an instant to realize that they all have identical splotches—a vaguely hourglass-like shape on one side, a near perfect circle and an undefined mass on the other. There is another large circle of gray over the left eye, a tiny one above the right. Each rabbit is a precise copy of the others.

But this is not the biggest surprise that awaits him. In the center of this field that must contain hundreds of creatures lies Mr. Hawke. He is fully clothed, curled up on his side, sleeping, as the rabbits press up against him. They breathe in and out, their little bodies contracting and expanding, all at the same time, in perfect harmony with Mr. Hawke's breaths. If he concentrates, just over the sound of the wind against the windows, Thomas can hear their uniform respiration.

It is an odd time of day to be sleeping, Thomas thinks madly. Mr. Hawke does often stay up late, however. Thomas tries to push away these foolish ideas. There is no normal for Mr. Hawke. He is what he is. That he should lie sleeping amid rabbits is no more inexplicable than a thousand other things that could be said of the man.

His presence, however, presents certain problems. Thomas has anticipated he might be interrupted by the vertigo curse. That a person might be present never occurred to him.

Thomas glances at Mr. Hawke in an effort to determine how deeply he sleeps, and he notices something about the man's position. His neck is craned upwards, and his cheeks contract rhythmically. Then Thomas sees one of the rabbits move near Mr. Hawke's face. It hops into the sea of its identical confederates, and another rabbit moves forward to take its place. The new arrival lies on its side, and Mr. Hawke's lips protrude. It takes Thomas a moment to realize what he is seeing. In his sleep, Mr. Hawke suckles upon the rabbit's teat.

Thomas closes his eyes, trying to accept a world of madness and dream logic. He did not expect matters to go entirely smoothly, and here is a difficulty that has taken him by surprise. So be it. If Mr. Hawke awakens, then Thomas will deal with him. In the meantime, he knows how to be as quiet as the next fellow.

He steps into the mass of rabbits, placing each foot carefully so as not to harm any of the animals. He does not know if rabbits cry out in pain, but he doesn't want to panic the creatures. He manages to move forward without causing more than a minor ripple in the field of fur, and so he takes another step, and then a third. Slowly, careful to maintain his balance, he proceeds. Only when fully stopped, arms out like he is a circus performer balancing upon a tightrope, does he care to glance back at the sleeping Mr. Hawke. Other than the twitching motions required to suckle, he does not move at all.

Each step seems to drag on endlessly, but at last he reaches the circle surrounding the portal. The light is fading, and so he knows he will have to act quickly. There is the formula, or what he believes to be the formula, but it is not the same as what he wrote down in his notebook. Did he get it wrong? It is possible that, in his haste, he forgot or misremembered details, but what he wrote down worked, and he doubts he could have accidentally produced something that balances. And yet this is new, more complicated, more refined. He can see that. And in the center of it all remains the mysterious omega-alef, the value that the equations that power the algorithm must try to soothe and assuage and satisfy. The omega-alef, that unknowable polynumeral, increases, and yet Thomas believes that if he can render it zero, the portal will shut down.

But now there are more equations than he remembers, more factors that add to its value like the ever-turning gears of a machine. Still, he must try. He squats down and examines what he sees, all the ways in which the core value fends off diversions and distractions, increasing its value.

The omega-alef, it occurs to Thomas, is always growing.

He begins to make some notations in chalk. At first, he is tentative, but then he begins to see how he can invert the equations, render the omega-alef nothing at all. He writes and he writes and he writes, trying to fit everything into the cramped space of the circle. There have been times when he has been lost in mathematics, fully caught up in the beauty and creativity of the pure truth found only in numbers. He has imagined a writer or a musician or sculptor must feel this way when he can see his craft and creation as vividly as if it were already complete. It is how he feels now as he turns this formidable symbol, this abstract and dynamic notion with the power to join worlds, into nothing at all.

When Thomas is finished his hand is cramped, and all his ideas begin to slip away like water from an overturned glass, but he feels sure that, in the moment, he understood it all and everything has balanced.

When he looks up at the portal, it is no longer black. It is entirely empty.

Of course, Crowley's rabbit sacrifice had the same effect, and mere seconds later came the vertigo. Thomas hopes the difference is the that he has properly turned all the levers to shut down the machine whereas Crowley, the master magician, merely kicked it over and smashed it. Thomas begins to make his way to the stairs. He wants to be away from the rabbits, as close to escape as possible, should the vertigo come upon him again.

When he reaches the stairs, he looks back. The portal is still dead, a mere circle of wood. The rabbits, however, are stirring. Not one or a few. All of them, and at once.

Their eyes flutter and then open in a single, coordinated instant. They each, at the same time, raise their heads. Their ears spasm in unison. Then every rabbit in the room turns to look at Thomas. Their pink noses twitch as if searching something out.

And then they find it.

Moving as though they were the single appendage of an unknown beast, the rabbits surge forward. Thomas cannot say why he is afraid. Is it their great number? The simultaneity of their movement? Rabbits are harmless creatures, sweet and nervous and easily startled, but these beasts display no fear or hesitation. They move with a ferocious intent, lunging like panthers.

Without pausing to consider his options, Thomas runs.

Grabbing the bannister, he leaps halfway down the first flight of stairs. He reaches the third-floor landing and then hurls himself in an arc so he can bound over the first five or six stairs of the next flight. He hears the rumble of little feet behind him. He can smell them. The heat of so many bodies strikes his back like a wave.

If they catch him, he will die. He knows it. He can see himself being swallowed, not by mouths, but by numbers. He knows somehow what it will be like, falling to the ground, as the rabbits swarm over him, burying him in their bodies as his nostrils and mouth are clogged with fur. In his mind, he can see it as they try to force their little bodies into his mouth, as they smother him with deliberate and mindless intent.

Thomas trips toward the end of the flight and falls forward onto the second floor. His palms strike the ground hard, and the pain vibrates through his wrists, but he is not seriously hurt. He feels almost certain of it, but there is numbness where there might be pain, if he should ever have the leisure to stand still. He is on his feet and running again, some primitive part of his brain having taken command of his body. The part of him that he thinks of as Thomas has become a mere spectator.

Then he is heading down the final flight of stairs, and he is driving his body again. The animal panic has eased, replaced by a more intellectual and manageable terror. Behind him, growing closer, is the soft thunder of so many padded feet striking the stairs. He hears the hissing scrape of countless thousands of rabbit nails tapping upon wood.

Thomas hurls himself from the staircase, leaping over the last half-dozen steps, and swings open the door. He throws himself outside and pulls the door shut. A heartbeat later he feels the reverberation of bodies slamming against the barrier. There must be hundreds throwing themselves forward at once, for the blow ripples up to his shoulders. *Thud thud thud.* Over and over again. He hears what sounds like a wet slap and then another. He hears bones cracking. Blood begins to leak from under the door as the rabbits break their bodies, shatter their skulls, in an effort to destroy the barrier that stands between them and the thing they must kill.

Does he need to be pulling the handle toward his body? Thomas reminds himself that rabbits don't have hands. They cannot open a door. Yet, when he slackens his grip, he can feel something trying to open the door from the other side. He pulls harder, but his hands are growing both cold and numb. His shoulders have begun to ache. He does not know how long he can hold the door this way. Another hour? Almost certainly. Two? Four? And then what?

Will he be drowned in a tide of identical lactating rabbits? Will London be overwhelmed?

The blood continues to flow under the door, pooling around his feet, making the ground slick. The rabbits still hurl themselves. *Thud thud thud.* He hears the fainter sound of lifeless rabbit bodies falling upon the pile of those already dead.

Then, at once, the noise stops. The blood trickles, but at a slower pace. On the other side of the door all is quiet. Can Thomas let go? Perhaps it is a trick. Can rabbits engage in deception? It would once have been an absurd question, but the world is no longer a place for such distinctions.

He dares not let go. Not now at least. He must see if he can outlast whatever it is the creatures plan.

Then he hears a voice behind him. "They were merely frightened, but I have calmed them. They shall trouble you no longer."

Thomas is so startled that he lets go of the door and turns around without realizing what he has done. He gasps at the realization of his foolishness and because of the man he sees standing there and facing him.

It is Mr. Hawke.

"They meant no harm," Mr. Hawke says with his casual smile. "Such excitable creatures." He conducts himself as though this were the middle, not the beginning, of the conversation, and as though there were nothing unusual about their circumstances. He is dressed in a brown suit but wears no coat or gloves. He shows no sign of being cold. Unlike Thomas, his breath does not fog the air.

Thomas cannot think of anything to say. He stares at Mr. Hawke, who stares back quite cheerfully, as though this conversation could not please him more.

"How did you get outside?" Thomas asks.

"I cannot think that is the most pressing thing you have to say to me. It cannot be why you have trespassed upon bank property."

It is not, and Thomas manages to snap out of his confusion. "You spoke to Madeline Yardley."

"I did," he agrees in an enthusiastic tone, as though he has just confirmed that they had seen the same delightful play. "She does not have your best interests at heart, I promise you. She only wants to pull you away from your obligations to your family. You mustn't trouble yourself with her. At least for now. Perhaps in the future, but the future is an uncertain thing."

"You sent the Elegants after her," Thomas accuses.

"Why, it is remarkable that you think I have that sort of power. I assure you I do not." He raises a thumb to wipe away a drop of rabbit milk in the corner of his mouth.

"I don't believe you. You are the magician behind everything Thresher's has been doing. That much is clear."

"You give me too much credit, I'm afraid. I am but a mere servant—a simple facilitator. And I am certainly not capable of commanding creatures like the Elegants. But it occurs to me that they are known to set upon whores," Mr. Hawke muses. "I wonder if that tells you something about your Mrs. Yardley."

Thomas feels his hand tighten to a fist. He pulls back his elbow, and he has no doubt that he will strike Mr. Hawke, but his arm is suddenly hanging limply by his side. How did it get there? He does not feel tired, but his limbs are so very languid.

"You are making difficulties where there need be none." Mr. Hawke raises his hands and adjusts Thomas's coat. He pulls the lapel this way and that until he is satisfied. "Mrs. Yardley has nothing to fear while you remember you are promised to another. Perhaps it is best you go home."

"Promised to another," Thomas sneers. He speaks words that pain him. He does not mean them, and he hates himself for pretending to, but if he is to be a banker, he must be willing to prevaricate to drive a hard bargain. "Esther Feldstein is damaged goods. She is pregnant, and I can promise it is not my child. I shall not marry her."

"You have entered into a bargain," Mr. Hawke says airily. "You haven't a choice."

"You know the truth of it," Thomas says. "Your house made her that way. If you can undo it, then I shall agree to proceed."

"You shall agree to proceed regardless," Mr. Hawke says. "And I can do nothing. I am not like these Golden Dawn men, these harlequins with their costumes and silly rituals. I make no pretense that the world is mine to order as I please."

"Surely there is something you can do to help her." Thomas hears the pleading in his own voice and hates it. He will not trouble himself to Mr. Hawke's humanity.

"The world is changing, but one thing remains unaltered." Mr. Hawke's voice is hard and cold. It is the first time Thomas has heard him speak without his breezy tone. "People who meddle with what they do not understand will suffer."

"And shall I suffer?" Thomas asks. He knows he sounds like a little boy, but he keeps talking all the same. "I closed your portal."

"Indeed you have," Mr. Hawke says. "It is very clever of you. And yet what is written in chalk can surely be erased and rewritten. A lot of work, and all for nothing. Good night, young Mr. Thresher."

Mr. Hawke turns around and opens the door. He steps over a pile of dead rabbits, their bodies scattered and broken and bloody.

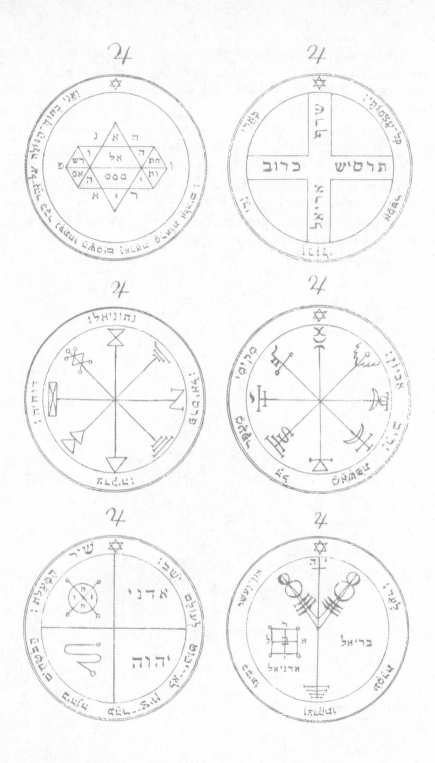

TWENTY-EIGHT

SWIFTNESS

M R. HAWKE NURSES upon rabbits. What can Thomas do with this information? Nothing, he decides. He knew already that Mr. Hawke was a strange and inexplicable creature, bound somehow to the bank's entanglement with the Peculiarities. He is not, however, the designer of the bank's original magic, or so he claims. Thomas has learned nothing new about what the bank is doing or who is devising these operations. He has also learned that Mr. Hawke is unable or unwilling to help Miss Feldstein.

Thomas has, however, closed a portal.

There can be no doubt that Mr. Hawke was correct. Thomas has achieved only a temporary victory. Nevertheless, for the first time, he has some sort of weapon, and if he can damage a portal, perhaps he can also destroy one permanently. Mr. Hawke wished to make Thomas feel powerless, but Thomas dares to hope that he has begun to learn how to strike back.

Thomas must proceed. He has things to do. He has scores to settle. He has a bank to save. In that context, who does and does not suckle upon rabbits is irrelevant.

It is time, he decides, to clean house. To that end, the next day he takes a hansom to a street not far from Bloomsbury Square—the need for walking is over, after all. He has no need to conserve his money. He will either live or he will die. He will be rich, or he will be poor. Pinching pennies now will matter little later.

He finds the Feldstein house to be both more and less impressive than he had imagined. It is not small, but smaller than Walter's, and there is something disarmingly modest about its appearance. The exterior, at least, is tasteful. None of the garish statuary or Corinthian columns of the newly moneyed. Once he is admitted, he finds the interior is similarly restrained. Mr. Feldstein has either hired someone to explain to him the principles of English taste, or he is not nearly so brash as he wishes the world to believe.

He has asked for Miss Feldstein, and he waits for her in the parlor. Much as with his encounter with Mrs. Yardley, Thomas is not entirely certain how he will say what he has come to tell her. He needs to reveal everything, even more than he told Mrs. Yardley. Though he spoke his heart to the widow, his vulnerability made him guarded. There is no vulnerability with Miss Feldstein. There is nothing between them but their shared adventures and hardships, and honesty can only bolster that bond.

It is an odd thing to consider. This woman he hardly knows, with whom he has little in common, an unmarried mother-to-be, should be the one person upon whom he can depend. She simply has no reason to lie to him, just as he has no reason to deceive her. She wants nothing from him but access to the little knowledge he can acquire.

Thomas turns when the door opens behind him, and he sees not Miss Feldstein, but her father. The diminutive man walks confidently despite his bow-legged gait and slouched posture. His bushy mustaches dominate his face in the style of many a slow-witted Englishman, but there is nothing dull in his appearance. His lively eyes miss nothing.

"Eeeeeeh!" It is a glass-shattering East London shriek. "It's the fellow who wants to marry my daughter!"

Thomas forces a smile and shakes Mr. Feldstein's hand, pretending that these vocalizations are a perfectly ordinary greeting. "Good afternoon, sir."

"I told the little miss to cool her heels, I did," Feldstein says with a yellow-toothed grin to show how pleased he is with this power over his daughter. "Thought the two of us might have a little tête-à-tête."

"Certainly." Thomas waits to be asked to sit, but no invitation is forthcoming.

Feldstein pours himself a drink—whisky by the smell of it—and does not offer one to Thomas. He then sits and peers up as though addressing a servant. "You'd better tell me why you think yourself worthy to marry young miss."

Countless times he has stood before tutors and headmasters, asked to explain himself, and the lies and half-truths always danced elegantly from his tongue. Until recently, Thomas has always possessed a certain facility for ingratiating himself with authority figures, but he has no will to do so now. Walter and Feldstein have conspired to make this marriage happen. Thomas will not indulge the fiction that he has come hat-in-hand.

Thomas looks directly at Feldstein. "My brother wishes me to marry your daughter. Similarly, you wish your daughter to marry me. I have been maneuvered to the point where I have little choice but to give in to my family's desires. That is the whole of it."

Feldstein licks his lips and then works his jaw. These tics strike Thomas as nothing but an attempt to stall for time. "You think yourself mighty clever, I expect."

Thomas laughs. "I think myself beaten. But allow me to turn the question upon you. Yes, I am a Thresher, but my brother despises me, and I cannot imagine I shall ever rise above my current position at the bank, which is one of utter insignificance. Walter will feel no compulsion to share any of the family fortune. It is true that he is older than I am, but the difference in years is so little that planning upon his demise—on the off chance he leaves anything to me—makes for a poor strategy. In short, I do not see why you should wish to inflict me upon your daughter."

Feldstein smirks. "If you believe this little speech will alter my thinking, you are mistaken, young fellow."

"I do not doubt that you have your reasons, sir. I merely wish to know what they are."

"If you must know," Feldstein says with an almost childish pride, "I have been promised a peerage."

This declaration stuns Thomas. "Who with the power to grant you a peerage could possibly care who I marry?"

"Who do you suppose? Your brother."

Thomas's laugh is a derisive snort. "My brother? What influence could he have over such things? He knows a member or two of the House of Lords, but I've seen no evidence that he is in a position to dictate events of that magnitude."

Feldstein looks as though he has woken up and cannot recall where he is.

"I hope you've made assurances," Thomas continues. "Were I you, I should wait until you have this peerage, or at least until you see evidence it is forthcoming, before you make any commitment from which you cannot retreat."

"The contract has been signed," Feldstein says. "Should your brother fail to deliver what he has promised, the consequences will be devastating."

Thomas laughs again. "You would litigate your remedy? Walter will have no fear of that. It could take years before you receive any sort of judgment, and at the end of it, my brother cannot be forced to provide what is not in his power to give."

"Litigation be damned," says Feldstein. "Contract-breakers are none too pleased with themselves nowadays. Bad luck and ruin, it is. Your brother's a canny one, but he won't risk trifling with me."

Thomas recalls Walter's words. *All contracts can be broken. They* will *be broken.* "My brother believes he has a means to render agreements moot and the consequences irrelevant."

It is not until he says this that he understands it to be true. The portals all over London that magnify the Peculiarities. The drafting of magicians into his service. The reckless distribution of money as though the future is of no consequence. The only possible conclusion is that, for Walter, the future *is* of no consequence. The world, Walter seems to believe, is on the cusp of change that will make his obligations and difficulties and promises meaningless.

Thomas no longer doubts that Crowley's assumption is correct: the dawn of the twentieth century will usher in an entirely new world—much as the nineteenth did, though in a very different way. Perhaps that is the fate of mankind—to live in a world remade every hundred years. Growing up as he has, sheltered from the poverty and suffering and despair wrought by the previous revolution, it has not seemed so bad. For those whose bodies and souls were harvested for wealth in England's factories, it is another story. The lucky few—let us say, for example, those who are not currently turning into trees or even those not currently carrying rabbit children in their wombs—have the luxury of being equally unconcerned with the next revolution. For those who feed the furnace of progress, however, change is frightening indeed.

"What's he up to, exactly, this brother of yours?" Feldstein asks.

"I haven't a clue." This is the truth. The notion that his brother means to wipe away old bonds has struck him with the force of revelation, but that does not mean he understands the how of it. "It must be something . . . monumental. Something that he believes will, at the very least, make any agreement between the two of you irrelevant. He wants a concession from you now. What he has promised to give to you later is of no moment."

Feldstein remains quiet and thoughtful for a long time. He looks out the window. Then he turns to Thomas. "You would say these things about your own brother rather than marry Esther? You hate her so much?"

Thomas feels his shoulders slump. He has spoken with conviction, even with passion, but he has failed. "I cannot pretend to wish to marry your daughter, but I do not hate her. I quite admire her. Certainly, I like her much too well to see her forced into a loveless marriage."

Feldstein jerks his head slightly as though slapped. Perhaps he took Thomas's words as an insult or a challenge. He blinks away surprise and then pushes himself to his feet.

"I'll look into what you say." His voice is softer now, less grating and more deliberate. How much of his bluster is an act, a public persona that hides someone who mistrusts the world? "I doubt it, young fellow, but it may be you suppose you are speaking the truth."

"I have no reason to lie," Thomas says. "And more than that, I no longer wish to lie to anyone. I am done with deceiving the world, sir."

Feldstein leaves the room without a word and without a glance backward. Now, with no one to think him rude, Thomas finally sits.

A few minutes later, Esther Feldstein rushes into the room, skirts flying, strands of unruly Abramaic hair striving to escape her bun. Her face is flushed, and her eyes are glistening with rage. "How dare you show yourself here? Have you any idea of the position you've put me in? I thought you were—I believed we were united in our resistance. For you to go behind my back, to betray me like this, is unforgivable. You don't expect me to actually marry you, do you?"

Thomas has no wish to marry her, but even so, the vehemence of her question stings. He doesn't think that being married to him would be so terrible, other than the fact that he would no longer be strictly mammalian in too short a time.

Thomas stands and takes her by the elbow. "Please, don't upset yourself. Remember your condition."

She shakes her arm away. "I'll not shatter into pieces if I become angry."

Thomas stands there, entirely unsure what to do with himself. "You have every right to be angry with me. I ought never have agreed to anything without discussing it with you first, but I hope to help you understand why I did what I did."

His gentle tone seems to disarm her. "Very well."

Thomas attempts to find some way to begin this conversation. "There are things about myself I have not told you."

"I should hope so," Miss Feldstein exclaims. "You are not under any obligation to tell me anything at all. We are not beholden to one another, and what happened in that house does not make me dependent upon you. I am not someone to pity, sir."

"Quite so." This business of confessing, of unburdening, is becoming something of a habit. Thomas peers at the open door. "Perhaps we might go for a short walk."

Miss Feldstein understands, and she rings a bell so that their coats and hats might be fetched. A few minutes later they are out the door and circling the block. As he did with Madeline Yardley, Thomas begins to tell her everything, but somehow the words come more easily. He has some practice, though he does not think that is the reason. It is Miss Feldstein. He does not need to impress her. He has nothing to lose, and so he reveals all—the arboreal plague, his reasons for joining the Golden Dawn, Crowley's pronouncement about his poor skills as a magician. He even tells her of the discovery that his friends were never his friends. These seems to shock her more than the fact that he is turning into a tree. Though he is pleased when her pity is replaced with admiration and shock when he tells her about closing the portal and the strange interaction between Mr. Hawke and the rabbits.

"After learning how cruel your brother has been to you, and the monstrous nature of his confidant, how can you then agree to do their bidding?" she asks.

"Because I want him to leave me alone," he explains, hoping to keep the exasperation from his voice. "I want him to give me the freedom to come and go as I please for a few weeks. In that time, I mean to learn whatever purpose he has in all his machinations and to stop him."

"You don't intend to go through with the wedding, then?"

"Please don't be insulted." He offers her a sad smile. "I have come to believe that whatever my brother wants must be corrupt. In any case, I cannot marry you. I have—there is another woman I have in mind."

"Oh," she says. Her face reddens and she looks away. For a terrible moment Thomas wonders if he has misjudged her. Has she actually come to hope for the wedding? He then sees it is not the case. "I understand entirely. I have a gentleman of my own."

Thomas realizes this admission has cost her something. He is touched by her candor. He also feels a strange twist of jealousy, and now he understands her reaction. He does not want her for himself, of course, but no one wishes to be rejected. The loss he feels is more conceptual than personal. In the years to come, he will be gone from the world of human concerns, rooted in his spot, caring only for the movement of the sun and the passing of the seasons. Miss Feldstein and her lover may marry and have human children. They will live normal lives. He envies this unknown man to his core.

Still, Thomas cannot let this moment pass. It is his day to be honest, to confess his heart, and he will do so now. "I am speaking with you, Miss Feldstein, in a way that is not my custom. I suppose it is not the English custom, but I have been particularly unused to revealing my mind. You and I do not wish to marry, and we never shall, but I admire you, damn it. You are a true friend, which is something I have lived without for a very long time. I cannot think of anyone in this world braver and more forthright and honest than you."

"Oh," Miss Feldstein says again. Her skin reddens once more in the wind and cold. "Mr. Thresher, that is most unexpected. I thought you at best tolerated me."

"There was some friction at first," he admits, "but only because my brother was pushing you in my way. But you are unlike any woman I've ever known. You are unlike any person, I should say, for your qualities are rare in either sex. I would never want to put you in any danger, but your insights and understanding are invaluable. I hope I may count on you in the next two weeks to continue to provide me with such help as I might require."

There is a moment when Thomas fears she will take his kindness and discard it like rubbish, but then she flashes a luminous smile. "Mr. Thresher, I am honored. Of course I shall stand by you. It is certainly in my own interest to find out what our families are hoping to accomplish, but I think whatever it is, as you say, may go to the heart of the Peculiarities themselves. I should be furious if you did not invite me along."

Thomas cannot help but notice that she does not speak of an admiration for him as he did for her. Well, why should she? He is a cipher. He has spent all his time with an uncaring family and false friends. Every good thing he might have been he has abandoned. He has been neither friend nor scholar nor mathematician nor banker. He has never been a son or a brother. He has done nothing and been nothing, and he is in the process of transforming into nothing. Yet, he thinks. Yet. *When this is all over, she may see a different side of me. When I have saved my family's bank, when I have thwarted my brother's plans, even I may see a different side of myself. I may*, he thinks, *become something entirely less insignificant.*

It would not be such a bad way to spend one's last months in human form.

Thomas wonders if he should ask about the man she admires, but decides he has no wish to know. It is likely a labor organizer or crusading journalist or some other earnest fellow who is busily engaged in saving the world. Or maybe he is a long-bearded Jew who travels about clutching his prayer book. He is, no doubt, the sort of man to whom she could confess her rabbit pregnancy, and he would believe her story. He would tell her that her magical condition does not alter his feelings for her. It is not Thomas's concern, and he is afraid that if he asks questions, she will mistake curiosity for jealousy. There must be no taint of that sort between them. They are going to betray their families, so they must trust each other.

There is so much more to tell her. He has not spoken of the encounter with the Elegants in the tea shop. Another walk around the block is required. They have circled around and are returning to Miss Feldstein's house when a figure approaches them on the street walking swiftly with absolute purpose. Thomas feels a sharp slap of fear, a primal preparation for violence, before he realizes there is something familiar about this person hidden under hood and cloak.

"Ruby, what are you doing here?" Thomas snaps before the girl can answer. He is angry, though he doesn't understand why.

"How are you feeling, miss?" Ruby asks Miss Feldstein, entirely ignoring Thomas. "Any morning sickness?"

"A bit," Miss Feldstein admits.

The wolf-girl thrusts a package into Miss Feldstein's hands. "Mama said to mix a teaspoon of this powder with hot water and drink it before bed. It will settle your stomach."

"Please thank her for me."

Thomas feels awkward and excluded. This has been his day to speak his heart, after all, not hear about women's tea.

"I don't know that visits upon the street in broad daylight are in the lady's best interest." Thomas does not trouble himself to conceal his irritation. "Is there is something you need?"

"What I need," Ruby says coolly, "is to tell you something for your own good." She peers at Miss Feldstein. "And I was going to give you the medicine to give to miss, but things got all confused. Though this is private business. You probably don't want to talk about what I have to say in front of Miss Feldstein. I hope I don't offend, miss."

Thomas feels himself blushing, though he knows not why. "I cannot imagine anything you have to say, Ruby, that Miss Feldstein may not hear. At this point, I have no secrets remaining to me."

Ruby studies Miss Feldstein for a moment. "If you're sure."

"Out with it," Thomas urges.

"It's that lady, Mrs. Yardley. The one you like so much."

Something electric and jarring happens to his heart. It feels like is shifting and falling inside his chest. "Has something happened to her?"

"Oh, no. Nothing like that. My point is, she ain't what she seems. I knew I didn't like her. Whenever she speaks, you can smell the lies oozing out of her pours. She stinks of it."

Thomas feels like he has wandered into a play in mid-performance. "When precisely have you heard her speak?"

"When you've gone to see her. I've been keeping an eye on you, you know. Always holding back, stealthy-like." She hunches over and swings her arms, a pantomime of stealthy walking.

Thomas feels himself prepared to shout, but something shifts inside him. He does not want to yell at Ruby who, for all her infuriating behaviors, is a good soul.

"People have their private lives." Thomas keeps his tone gentle. "I don't know what your mother has taught you, but it's not right to uncover someone's secrets. If she is not being entirely forthcoming with me, she may well have her reasons. I certainly concealed things about myself until I was ready to speak of them. I will hear no more of this."

Miss Feldstein looks at him appraisingly. "That is a very modern attitude."

Thomas does not feel modern. He feels like the earth beneath him is crumbling. He needs to love Madeline Yardley. He needs to have his imagined life with her. If he does not, is not certain if he will be able to continue. Whatever Ruby knows, he dares not hear it.

"She ain't what she claims," Ruby repeats. "I don't know the sum of it yet. There's more to learn but—"

"That's enough," Thomas tells her in the most moderate tone he can manage. "She must tell me what I need to know when she is ready. Stop following her. Leave the lady be."

Ruby seems confused. Her eyes always appear wet, as though Thomas's kindness has upset her more than any burst of anger. "I'm only looking to help you."

Thomas is having a hard time cutting through the undergrowth of so many emotions at once. "I know you are, Ruby, but I never asked you to follow me about or to spy upon my friends. I never asked you to lurk behind me on the streets. People must make their own way in the world. We need to make mistakes or to learn each other's secrets over time. That is how trust is built."

Ruby nods. "I wanted to do what's right by you, on account of us being so close. Mama won't talk about it, but I know it's true."

Thomas forces a smile. He pats Ruby on the shoulder and steps away from the two ladies. He needs a moment to compose himself. It took all his strength not to demand to know what Ruby has learned about Miss Yardley, but of course he knows already. She has another suitor. A beautiful widow of moderate means—how could she not?

Thomas tells himself he needn't worry. Mrs. Yardley heard him confess his feelings and she did not dissuade him. She spoke of no prior commitments. Let some widow-hunter brings her flowers now and again. When Thomas is done, when he has saved his family's bank from ruin, when he has uncovered the secret of the Peculiarities, we shall see how this doctor or solicitor or grocer, with his box of chocolates and gap-toothed smile, compares to a man who has done battle on the astral plane—or something of that sort.

Thomas turns back to the two women, who are now in close conversation. Ruby says something just outside Thomas's hearing, and Miss Feldstein lets out a roaring laugh. This camaraderie among women makes him profoundly uneasy. In light of all the changes happening around him, he takes comfort in so very old-fashioned a source of discomfort.

TWENTY-NINE
VALOR

THOMAS WALKS THROUGH the main doors of Thresher's Bank and views this building not as a galley slave views the ship, but as something new and alien and majestic. He supposes he must have as a child looked the same way at the marble and high ceilings and gilt picture frames containing likenesses of bloated directors from years gone by. Today he is a new sort of Thresher. Today he is upon business that he hopes will save lives. If it frustrates his brother, then so much the better.

The Elegants have killed and dismembered a prostitute last night. Other than their murder of Arthur Conan Doyle and their attack on Mrs. Yardley, they have been somewhat quiet of late. This is their first attack on a prostitute in months. Thomas does not think it a coincidence. They are agitated. Something is happening, and Thomas is more determined than ever to stop it, whatever it may be. The ruination of his family's bank, the Elegants sowing death and chaos, the portals all about town. He wants to stop it all, and to do that he needs information.

Thomas strides into the documents room as though he owns the place. He wishes anyone with whom he speaks to think he just might. The director's brother, yesterday's clerk, is today's elevated banker. Such things must seem highly improbable to those who do not know Walter as an intimate—a category that certainly includes everyone who works at Thresher's.

Thomas's shoes clack disrespectfully upon the floor as he strides toward the clerk's desk. The clerk's eyes, which are always large, grow larger. His mouth opens to form words, though he apparently cannot think of what words to say.

"Good afternoon, Mr. Handleworth. I'm looking for documentation on buildings recently acquired by Thresher's."

The records clerk studies him with undisguised skepticism. "This is a bank, sir, not a consortium of landlords."

Thomas displays a mirthless smile. "I am aware of that, Mr. Handleworth. I am also aware that the bank does, indeed, purchase buildings from time to time. I should like to see a record of what the bank owns."

Mr. Handleworth shakes his head like a chained dog that cannot reach the man it earnestly wishes to bite. "I'm afraid we do not have those records in this room, sir. This is a place for records of financial transactions. It is a complete record, sir. Very complete. But as for real estate, well, that is another matter, I should think."

"And yet," Thomas counters, "real estate purchased by the bank must be done with bank funds. That sounds remarkably like a financial transaction."

Mr. Handleworth blushes, as though some shameful secret has been exposed.

"I imagine," Thomas opines, "there must be municipal records of such a purchase. Or the major newspapers must know not of the totality of such purchases, but of individual instances. I suppose I should be able to piece it all together. I shall simply explain to those I disturb that you have been unable to help me. They should be surprised, I should think, to learn that Thresher's keeps such incomplete records. I wonder what they would think when I explain that I must go elsewhere for the information because Mr. Handleworth has mislaid his documents."

Thomas turns away but does not manage to take a step before Mr. Handleworth calls after him. "It is your brother, sir. He insists on keeping such records personally. I told him, we must have copies here. I told him, but he would not listen."

Thomas faces the clerk once more. "He keeps them where? In his office here?"

Mr. Handleworth's lower lip trembles as he prepares to say something shameful. "In his home."

Thomas might have considered it strange that he had never before entered his brother's study, but there are many portions of the house he has never visited. He has never been invited, and never thought to explore. He has never felt welcome in the house, and he would no more peek into strange rooms than he would go exploring in other guests' chambers at a hotel.

He is not at all surprised to find the study locked. He asks the maid to admit him, but she tells him that she does not have a key. Only Mr. Thresher does, and she cleans it only when he is present to make certain she does not touch anything.

A small obstacle, he decides. If he is going to put an end to the Elegants attacking people, he must have more information. It is not yet noon, and so there is plenty of time for what he decides must be done. Thomas steps outside to find a messenger and is only partially surprised to be met by Ruby Topping, who is standing on the porch.

"What do you want?" Thomas asks her.

"I come by to apologize," she says. "I shouldn't have snooped in your business without your say-so. Also, Mama says you might need me today. She saw it in the cards."

"So she was snooping in my business as well," Thomas observes.

To this Ruby has nothing to say.

Things seem to shift for Thomas. The swelling of irritation that had been building in his chest vanishes. All his life, the world seems to have conspired against him. He has no wish to turn away people who seem determined to help him.

He finds himself grinning at Ruby. "I was about to call for a messenger. Let me tend to that, and then we can talk while we wait for my response."

"I'll deliver your message," she offers.

"Really, I couldn't ask—"

"No trouble," she says. "I want to be of service. And I like getting about town, leaping from hansom to omnibus. It's great fun."

There is a pause as Thomas tries to think how to refuse this most peculiar of Peculiar creatures, but a sudden realization comes over him. Thomas likes Ruby's enthusiasm. She appears to like him in return. She wants to do things for him simply because of her regard for him. He knows so few people like that.

"You are certain it is no inconvenience?"

"None!"

He is about to ask her to wait outside while he pens a quick note, but then he thinks better of it. Ruby Topping is, he decides, a friend. He cannot ask a friend to wait in the cold. "Please step inside for a moment."

She peers at him. "Really?"

"Of course." He has no reason to fear Walter hearing of this. Thomas can do what he likes so long as he maintains he will still marry Miss Feldstein, so why should he not be kind to his friends? Let Walter rage at him later. It will do no harm.

Ruby follows him inside and, perhaps sensing Thomas's mood, lowers her hood, exposing her wolfen head. The maid comes forward to see if Thomas might need assistance and lets out a little gasp.

"Don't be rude," Thomas snaps. To Ruby, he inquires, "Do you want anything? Some tea, perhaps. I won't be but a moment."

Ruby's large eyes seem to take in more than what is truly before her. Her nose twitches as she draws in the maid's fear and confusion and perhaps the amusing scent of Thomas's mischief. "Some tea would be delightful," she says in an affected, ladylike voice.

"In the parlor," Thomas tells the maid. "A cup for me as well, if you please. And biscuits."

A few minutes later, note in hand, Thomas joins her in the parlor. She stands clutching her cup of tea, admiring a rather shoddy—in Thomas's opinion—rendering of a Parisian café.

"I should so like to visit Paris someday."

"Then you shall." Thomas picks up his own cup and stands next to her.

"Going to another country ain't like skulking about London. I want to sit outside and drink coffee and feel the sun on me like the quality in this picture."

"Things will change," Thomas tells her. "You and me, all those like us, we won't have to hide all our lives."

Ruby continues to stare at the painting, as if searching for a hidden truth. "You can't know that."

"No," he agrees. "But it may be that there is a way to undo what has been done. It is what I am working to make happen."

Ruby does something with her face. It is not an expression he has seen before, but then he does not have much experience with her kind. He thinks it is skepticism.

"How old are you, Miss Topping?"

"Twenty-one," she says with a sideways glance. "Why?"

He'd thought her younger, sixteen or seventeen perhaps, but she is only two years his junior. She is older, in fact, than Miss Feldstein. Still, she is a naïf, and he feels uncertain about sending her out into the world. "I merely want you to be careful. Perhaps you would like to stay here, with me, while I send a messenger. You needn't expose yourself to any discomfort."

"This message," she says. "Has it anything to do with what you say? With ending the Peculiarities?"

He nods.

"I can recollect being a proper girl, you know. The truth is, I wasn't so pretty. Maybe an ugly girl is no better off than I am now. I don't know if I'd want to give up what I get being this way to just be a regular girl, to be despised and have nothing to show for it. The world treats an ugly girl worse than a wolf."

Thomas has nothing to say to this, largely because he knows it is true. He has no notion of what to do about all the world's injustices. He can concern himself only with his brother's. They sit, and they sip their tea in silence until it is time for Ruby to go.

There was no guarantee that he would be in, of course, or that he would even answer the summons. Given the way Thomas had behaved, it seemed more likely than not that Ruby would return alone. Nevertheless, in two hours she enters the house with Aleister Crowley in tow. Thomas is pleased to see he is dressed in a reasonable brown suit, not wearing a dressing gown or a magician's robe or some other outrageous thing.

"You're full of surprises, Thresher," he says as he takes Thomas's hand. If he has any resentment about how their last encounter ended, he does not show it.

"Thank you for coming," Thomas tells him. "Did you bring your tools?"

Crowley, looking pleased with himself, holds up a leather case.

This is followed by a moment of awkward silence.

"Ruby, can you give us a moment?" Thomas asks.

She sniffs at him and nods.

Thomas leads Crowley into the parlor and begins without hesitation. It is the best way. "Look, Crowley, I owe you an apology."

Crowley grins broadly. "What, for behaving like a jackass?"

"Just so," Thomas concedes. For the third time in only a few days, Thomas confesses to being a Peculiar. It is becoming easier each time, and he begins to feel like he perhaps understands Ruby's strange defiance and pride in what she is. Thomas will never be proud to be a tree, but he needn't be ashamed of what is happening to him. He needn't cower from the world.

"I had hoped magic would answer all of my problems, but it seems it cannot," Thomas says by way of conclusion. "I ought not to have unleashed my frustration on you."

"It seems that you are the dolt here, not I," says Crowley, "if you think a few insults can get under the skin of a man like myself. I forgive your weakness."

Thomas feels the surge of admiration and irritation he so associates with Crowley, and they shake hands once more. This man is insufferable, but he is also something quite unusual. He is also a friend, a real friend, and friends must overlook one another's faults.

"Now that that's done," the magician says, "let's see to whatever naughty thing you want done."

"There is something else I wish to tell you." Thomas tries not to look too smug. "I shut down the portal at the house on Cannon Street. No sacrifices, and no vertigo. I altered the algorithm—the mathematical instructions—to render the core value zero. The portal simply stopped being a portal."

Cowley claps him on the shoulder as though Thomas had just said he'd found a smashing new tavern. "Tricky thing mucking about with another magician's circle. You could let something loose or unleash a terrible curse upon yourself. Sounds like you avoided all that, but you know the symbols can simply be redrawn, yes? Sounds like a great deal of risk for little reward."

"Yes, yes." Thomas waves the objections away. "I understand it is nothing permanent, but the point is if we understand the mathematical principles behind their portals, then we're in a better position to defeat them."

"Jolly good!" Crowley exclaims, clearly having heard enough about maths for the moment. "Now, let's talk about your felonious need that prompted you to invite me to this fine house."

Thomas collects Ruby, who is milling about the front hall, and takes them both to Walter's office. The magician unfastens a few ties on his leather case, which folds open to reveal a dizzying number of picks, screwdrivers, files, and other devices designed for mysterious and no doubt illegal purposes. Crowley examines the lock, squatting down to peer into it for a moment, and then lets out a derisive little snort.

"I shall have to teach you a trick or two," Crowley says as he examines his tools. "Half an hour's instruction would make you equal to a lock of this sort."

"I hadn't planned on a career in housebreaking."

"And yet, here we are again." He removes a pick from his case and goes to work. In less than thirty seconds, the lock surrenders with a hearty click. Crowley turns the handle and the door swings open.

There is nothing remarkable about Walter's study. There is a desk, and there are bookshelves and paintings upon the wall. It smells of tobacco and a spent fire. Directed only by a sense of order, Ruby opens the curtains to let in light. They look about, and Thomas spies a vertical wooden cabinet with three drawers. He pulls open one of them and grins.

"This must be one of those American filing drawers I've heard about," he says as he flips through the documents. They are held in leather pouches, cunningly suspended from wooden bars. Each of these pouches is labeled, which seems a handy thing.

Not finding what he seeks, Thomas closes the top drawer and opens the one below it. Here he discovers records of purchases of buildings all around London. He takes out a thick file and sets it on Walter's desk. He removes a piece of paper and begins to take notes. Both Crowley and Ruby start going through the documents, looking to isolate the names of the buildings that Walter, and his father before him, have purchased around London in the past ten years—going back around the time when the Peculiarities first started manifesting. Somewhere in here, Thomas thinks, is the secret to finding out the source of the Elegants.

While they are busy at this work, Pearl appears at the doorway. No doubt she heard a fanciful tale from the maid about how Thomas was in Walter's office with a strange man and a wolf-girl, but she could have hardly credited such a thing until she saw it herself. Now she stares, mouth open, unable to speak.

"Oh, good afternoon." Thomas keeps his voice cheerful as though there is nothing at all unusual in what he is doing. "May I present Miss Ruby Topping and Mr. Aleister Crowley. This is my brother's wife, Mrs. Thresher."

Pearl continues to stare, but Crowley sets down his papers and approaches her with a warm smile. "I am very pleased to meet you." He takes her hand, which she gives up without protest. Her mind, Thomas believes, has temporarily shut down.

Something snaps back into place, and consciousness reappears in her expression. "What is going on here?" She seems, for the first time, to notice Crowley holding her hand, and she snatches it away. "Walter will be so angry. He will blame *me*."

"What, this?" Thomas murmurs, as if someone had asked him about a frivolous book upon his lap. "Just a bit of work in my new capacity at the bank. Walter keeps the records in here, so there you have it."

Thomas notices Crowley's appraising look. The magician seems pleased.

"Did Walter give you permission to enter his office?"

"Oh, I hardly think I need permission to examine records regarding the bank built by my own father and grandfather. Walter wasn't around, so there was no need to trouble him."

"And these people!" Pearl exclaims.

"They're my friends," Thomas tells her.

"Thomas!" It comes out as a hiss. "He won't like it. You know he won't."

Ruby looks worried, like she can sense another orphan who needs saving, but Thomas only smiles. "We'll be done in half an hour. Walter will never know."

"I shall tell him," Pearl announces.

"Why would you do that?" Thomas asks.

"To protect myself. You know why. If he thinks I've taken your side. . . ." She cannot bring herself to finish the thought.

"Why don't you come in and join us?" Crowley asks her. "Have a seat and while Thomas and Miss Topping finish up their labors, you can explain your concerns to me."

"Why should I wish to do that?" Pearl demands, but she sounds less certain.

"Because I think you will enjoy our company," Crowley assures her with absolute confidence.

He leads Pearl to sit on the sofa. He sits very near her, and the two of them talk in low tones. Crowley looks at her as though, despite her overlong and mismatched features, she is the most beautiful woman he has ever seen. He hangs upon her every word. Is this magic, or animal magnetism, or merely Crowley's seductive charisma? Are these simply different words for the same thing?

Within half an hour they have what they need. Thomas looks up to tell Crowley that they are done, that they can begin putting the files back where they found them, but at some point, while Ruby looked through documents and Thomas scrawled down addresses, the two of them vanished from the room.

It is no matter. Thomas now has the list of every property the bank has acquired in the past decade. One of these, he is sure, is the source of the Elegants, and that will be the next portal they must shut down.

They meet the next day at a coffee shop—Thomas, Crowley, Esther Feldstein, and Ruby Topping. Something has changed with Ruby, and she sits with her hood down, seeming not to care while the world looks upon her. A nervous man emerges from the back to hem and haw about perhaps this might not be the best place for everyone in their party, but a look from Crowley sends him scurrying for cover.

"You said you wanted to change things," Miss Feldstein says to Thomas. "You appear to be doing so."

"The credit goes to Miss Topping," Thomas says loud enough for the young lady to hear. Indeed, he takes a great deal of pleasure in the young lady's boldness. She wanted to sip coffee in a public café. They are neither out of doors nor in Paris, but she is not letting the world tell her what she can and cannot do.

"I think you have encouraged her," Miss Feldstein says. "It is nice to see her so at ease."

We have spent so long pretending the Peculiars among us don't exist, Thomas thinks, *even when we* are *the Peculiars.*

"Let's get on with our business," Crowley says, gesturing at the list with a coffee spoon. "Thresher's has acquired ten properties. This includes the Cannon Street house with the rabbits. Given what Thomas has told us, it is likely the portal is open again, or it can be opened whenever they wish it to be."

"That hardly matters," says Miss Feldstein. "I mean, of course it matters, but we must continue to try to find ways to stop them more permanently, but stopping the Elegants, even if only for a little while, will save lives."

Ruby picks up the piece of paper and scans it quickly. Though she has certainly learned her coarse language from growing up in a house with her father, her reading skills have not been neglected.

"Here," she says, pointing to one of the lines with a gloved index finger. "This is the place we must go next. Wentworth Street."

Miss Feldstein nods. "The Elegant killings are all centered around there."

"They are the most violent of the portal manifestations," Crowley says, "but it won't be enough to disrupt that operation. If we are to go there, we must destroy the house, keep it from ever being used for such purposes again."

Ruby gasps. "You don't mean fire! You'll burn down half of East London."

"No, not fire. Something more magical. I shall have to devise a plan."

"The equation in the circle at Cannon Street centered on the value of the symbol omega-alef. I can render it zero."

"Until someone with another piece of chalk comes back and, moments later, undoes our work. No, I keep telling you, maths will not solve our problems.

We need something more magical, and I'll require your help in finding it. You are setting up camp in my flat until we have this worked out."

Thomas nods. He is in no hurry to return to his brother's house. He hopes they can come up with something quickly because the longer they delay, the more people will die.

✦ THIRTY ✦
SCIENCE

THE HOUSE ON Wentworth Street looks haunted.

Thomas isn't certain precisely what criteria one uses to determine such things. In appearance, it is not so very different from all the houses that surround it. Do they all look haunted? He thinks not, and yet there is something about this house. A feeling, one might call it, or more likely simply the knowledge that something terrible lurks inside.

What could that something be? Inside that first house they found rabbits. What is necessary for the summoning of Elegants to this world? And what purpose do they serve? What manner of creature are they when they are not dismembering prostitutes or terrifying women in tea shops? Or is there nothing more to them? Do they exist purely in a state of violent malice? He and his friends are dealing with beings from worlds not necessarily bound by the same laws of nature, which means anything is as possible as anything else.

Above all, Thomas wants to know why Thresher's Bank has arranged for these entities to be in *this* world. The bank seemingly gains nothing from the existence of rabbit children. Thomas cannot see that it gains any more by summoning these killers to haunt the East London streets. Perhaps it is not what they do that matters. Perhaps it is the portals themselves, and what comes through the portals is but a side effect.

"We need to be prepared for resistance," Crowley says while he gazes at the door. "We caught them by surprise at the rabbit house, but they now know that someone has a mind to disrupt their portals." His gaze drifts toward Miss Feldstein. Thomas is, of course, necessary for the operation, as is Crowley himself. Ruby's entire purpose for being there is her wolfen strength. Miss Feldstein, however, contributed much to their planning sessions, but she offers little when it comes to the actual housebreaking. She is also the most vulnerable.

Miss Feldstein will not hear of being left behind, however. She dismisses the concerns raised by the other members of the group not with logic, because she can offer none, but with energy. She has been involved with them from the beginning. She led them to the rabbit house, and she, like Thomas, is threatened with an unwelcome marriage. Even now something alien grows inside her own body. Her expression, her posture, make it abundantly clear she means to see this through to the end.

Thomas is about to offer further objection, but Crowley speaks first. "It is her life. If she chooses to risk it, I for one shall not stand in the way of her will."

Miss Feldstein offers him a nod of her head and a slight smirk to Thomas. The prickly Miss Feldstein whom he first spoke to at his brother's dinner party is not entirely gone.

They approach the front door and find it locked, which surprises no one. The streets here are far more crowded than the residential neighborhood of their last break-in. On the other hand, people of East London are far less likely to call for the police upon seeing bold evidence of crime. Crowley looks about, nods at anyone on the street who meets his gaze, and smashes open the lock. He holds the door while the other three enter.

There is something very wrong with this house. They can feel it the moment they step inside. Like the rabbit house, it is empty of furnishings, and there is the sense of menace, but this is beyond anything Thomas has before experienced. The windows are uncurtained, and though they appear to be made of clear glass, they filter out all light from the outside. It is dark within.

Crowley strikes a match and lights a lantern he has in his pack. Yes, he brought a lantern. What else from his mountain-climbing equipment has he packed? Rope? Picks? Crampons?

Crowley holds the lantern high, for all the good it does. The light is dampened or restrained. A circle of perhaps ten feet is dimly illuminated, but beyond that, all is in shadow.

It is cold in the house, but somehow not temperature-cold. Thomas thinks it is colder than the worst winter day, but he does not feel inclined to shiver or hug himself. His heavy coat does nothing to warm him. The cold comes from within him.

There is a smell, too. Like glass, he decides. Like a glass so clear that you would walk into it, never suspecting something solid stood only inches before you. Thomas did not realize glass had a scent, but he knows what he smells.

"It's glass," says Miss Feldstein.

"And sand," Ruby says.

Thomas realizes she is right. There is sand too. "What does it mean?" he asks Crowley.

The magician shrugs. "We are close to being in another world. An astral realm is touching upon ours, and this place is a little like an embassy, I suppose. On our soil, but also theirs. Basic rules of what is and isn't—such rules as apply for us—may not extend to whatever world we are abutting. The strange smells, the behavior of light, may mean nothing, or they may be important signs that we are simply too ignorant to interpret."

"Such as a warning?" Miss Feldstein suggests.

"Possibly," Crowley says. "Or the equivalent of the scent of baking bread. We have no way of knowing. There is nothing to do but go on or to go back."

They go on.

They move slowly because of the limited radius of the light, but they find the stairs and begin to climb. They all seem to understand intuitively that whatever makes this house work will be found on the uppermost level. Thomas wonders why this is, what power is granted by altitude, but he decides it is not important. At least not for now. Perhaps he will later discover that it is of primary importance. They are so ignorant, he thinks, such hapless blunderers, that they cannot even say what signifies and what does not.

This entire expedition is madness. He knows that. He has no business being here, and certainly there can be no justification in allowing two women to join him in his folly. Even Ruby, with her lupine strength and bravado, ought never to have been permitted to enter, but bringing Miss Feldstein showed an execrable lack of judgment. He wants to turn back, to open the door and tell them to leave. He, who has nothing to lose, and Crowley, who knows nothing of fear, can explore on their own.

"No," says Ruby, looking at him.

"No what?"

"We ain't going back."

"How did you know I was thinking it?" he demands. "Are my expressions so easy to read?"

"Well, yes, generally," she says, "but there is something else. I can hear your thoughts. Yours are loudest, because you were thinking so very clearly, but I can hear all of them." She looks at Crowley. "You are a very disturbed man."

"By Jove, it's true!" exclaims Crowley. "Not about me being disturbed, though I suppose that's true enough to your middle-class sensibilities, but the rest of it. I can hear you all. It takes a bit of focus, like following a single instrument in an orchestra, but it's there."

Thomas tries to concentrate, and he hears an echoing version of Miss Feldstein's voice, and then Ruby's and then Crowley's. It is distant, and it is slippery. It is a writhing eel in his hands. He struggles to hold on to it, but doing so is exhausting, and there are matters of life and death, of the integrity of universes, to which he must attend. He lets it all go, feeling their thoughts burst from his grasp. This is certainly the right thing to do. What the others are thinking is none of his business.

"I don't think this is any place for ladies," he says to Ruby, as though that little interlude of clairvoyance had not interrupted their conversation.

"I know very well what you think," Miss Feldstein answers in Ruby's stead. There is something spritely and knowing in her voice that Thomas does not care for at all. "But you will have to suffer your opinion silently. We are as near to visiting another world as is possible. How can you ask us to turn around?"

"Because I don't want to see you hurt." Had he planned to make her his wife in truth, instead of merely agreeing to do so to relieve pressure from his brother, perhaps he would be able to command her. He has no right to make demands of a sham fiancée. Is that a twinge of regret? Did he, for that one instant, wish he really did intend to marry her? No, he is merely a gentleman, raised to protect women from harm, not lead them toward it. Though, the truth is, being married to a woman like Miss Feldstein would be—no, he will not think about it. It is not the time. The time may not exist. Even so. . . .

"Well, you have no grounds by which to command me," she says with a wicked grin. "You are not my husband yet."

It would be better, Miss Feldstein is thinking, *if he did make me leave. I don't want to be here no matter how much I want to be here. Oh, my lord, he is listening to me?*

She turns to him. "Stop it."

"I am trying, but Crowley is right with his instrument analogy. Once you catch a hold of something, it is hard to release."

"We all have more important things to focus on," Crowley tells them. "Keep your wits about you. We don't know what is here with us."

To no one's surprise, the next floor is empty, much as the ground level. Still, they explore, peering into every room, or what they think is every room because with the diminished light radius, it is easy to be confused. Once they think they have seen all the emptiness this floor has to offer, they proceed up the flight of stairs.

The smell of glass and sand is stronger here, and there is an additional smell—copper. They smell pennies and blood. Or perhaps it is merely copper. Piles of the metal would be no more unusual than anything else they might discover.

Crowley leads the way, down the corridor, and into a large room. It was once, in all likelihood, the master bedroom. Crowley raises the lantern, instinctively thinking to get a better view, though light does not work that way here, and the protective bubble is broken by a face.

It is there, just for a second, leering at them, noseless and hollow-eyed. It is the face of one of the Elegants.

Crowley leaps back, and the face is no longer there. He moves forward again slowly, but he cannot find the creature. It is in there with them, this murderous, monstrous thing, but it stands somewhere outside their sphere of illumination. It moves silently and jerkily. They will not see it until it wishes to be seen. Then, perhaps, it will be too late.

"They travel in pairs," Thomas says. This is something everyone knows, but he is speaking to comfort himself, not to convey information.

Crowley hands Miss Feldstein the lantern. "Hold this." With his hands free, he removes a pistol from inside his coat.

Thomas wonders if, perhaps, the Elegants are immune to bullets. He doesn't know why they should be. They come here through magical means, but that doesn't mean their physical nature defies physical laws. Thomas must remind himself, once again, that things that are magical are not outside the laws of science, simply governed by laws not previously understood. Magic does not mean the suspension of natural law. Magic is the use of natural laws previously hidden or generally unknown. He rehearses all of this as a prayer so he can, at last, conclude that a bullet will stop one of these creatures. Unless, of course, it is protected by some unknown or alien natural law.

They continue to move slowly. Miss Feldstein's hold on the lantern is remarkably steady, which impresses Thomas, who thinks his arm would grow tired. They climb another set of stairs.

At the top, something happens. It is like they pass through an invisible doorway, and all at once the lantern is no longer necessary. They find themselves in a lighted room, but the light is almost as unnerving as the dark. It is unnatural white and sterile and has no obvious source. It smells like wet stone and it emits a faint humming sound. That the light itself is the source of the scent and the sound is true, though Thomas cannot say how he knows it. The light is bright, almost painfully so, and seems to have the capacity to dampen sound. The floor appears to be made of the same wooden boards as the rest of the house, but it feels spongy under Thomas's feet. Or do his feet feel spongy?

The room is long and narrow, lined with what appear to be surgical tables, on which rest bodies in various states of dismemberment and decay. They look wet and glistening, but also lacquered, as though they are somehow preserved. Next to each table sits a small stand containing various surgical instruments, all of them clean and reflecting the sourceless light.

In the center of the room stands a circular, wooden gateway similar to the one found in the rabbit house. It is surrounded by a large circle marked in green chalk, containing within it smaller circles and squares, each of them subdivided, filled with writing in various languages. In several places he sees what looks like a stylized lower-case *h* with a cross through its spine. Thomas knows this to be the astrological symbol for Saturn.

And once again, there is the omega-alef. Thomas has tried to memorize the algorithm from the house on Cannon Street. He believes he can zero it with a few strokes of the chalk in his pocket—except he realizes he cannot. This is an entirely different algorithm, longer and far more complex. Thomas is certain he could understand it, but it would take time, and he would be starting almost from the beginning.

He forces himself to turn away from it. Crowley believes the way to stop the Elegants is not mathematical, and he is the magician. He must remember the plan.

Crowley looks at Thomas. "What do you think?"

Thomas turns to examine the various subsets of circles and squares. He begins to walk around the circle, and at first it appears to be a jumble, like a series of letters thrown together without order or meaning, but then his eye catches a pattern. Then another. There is a theory here, he realizes. If he'd had more time to read Agrippa—months, surely—he would be able to see it all at once, but he feels like he's trying to sound out a foreign orthography with which he is only vaguely familiar.

There are parts, though, that feel less foreign, less unknowable. Thomas begins to see something come into shape. The chaining of summoning symbols, opening doors, propping up archways in the ether. He has an insight about magic itself, about why it is so damned difficult, and then that insight is gone almost as soon as it is fully formed. In mathematics, the best minds can hold on to those notions. Thomas never believed he was among the best, but he was good, and he could grasp these notions longer than most before they turned to smoke. This feels the same.

What he understands with some certainty is that everything Thomas discussed with Crowley about how to corrupt another magician's summoning seems unimportant now. It won't work. Not unless they first zero the omega-alef, just as Thomas did at the rabbit house.

He takes his piece of chalk and steps across the circle's outer threshold. He hears Crowley shouting something at him, but the hum of the light is louder inside the circle, and the words are washed out, as though he is under water, listening to words shouted from the distant shore. He squats and studies and tries to follow the logic of it all, which is deep and absorbing and too large for any one mind. Then he catches a glimpse of it. He sees what is being worked out, and he thinks he can rework the algorithm if only he can keep the various equations in mind long enough. If he'd spent more time with his studies, if he'd trained himself to focus, instead of chasing women and drinks, this would be easy. Easier, at any rate. His mind is soft and lazy, as though trying to read while drunk, but he continues all the same.

Without even thinking of what he is doing, of what the consequences might be, he begins to write. His hand is not so steady nor artful as whoever made the circle. He cannot be sure what he is writing would even be legible to someone who did not already understand the process, but it is there all the same, and in the way of mathematics, it is true. It is absolutely true, across all worlds, in all parts of the universe. If magic is part of the natural world, then it must be governed by mathematics—and mathematics is always the same. Crowley talks about will and imagination and creativity, but what are those things? How can you quantify them? You cannot. But mathematics is a constant truth, here and in the rabbit world, and wherever it is that the Elegants wake up each morning to smell the glass-scented air.

Thomas steps back and surveys his work. He is missing something. Some aspect of the equations has escaped him, and he has not zeroed the omega-alef, but he senses it is diminished. The light feels less bright, its noise less loud. He turns to see if the others sense it too.

They are not paying attention to his triumph, however. Instead, they are facing off against the pair of Elegants who show no inclination to let Thomas finish his work.

Crowley fires his gun. The sound, dampened by the strange effect of the room, is no more than a distant pop. It sounds like something that could do no harm, but the bullet strikes the male Elegant in the chest. It looks down at its wound, and hisses. Indeed, it appears very much like what Thomas would expect a gunshot wound to look like. Torn, smoking fabric. The first appearance of blood. The injury looks quite deadly. The Elegant falls to the ground, twitching like a half-crushed beetle.

"It works," Crowley says with a grin. He turns to the other Elegant, but it has grabbed Miss Feldstein, and there is no way Crowley can shoot without hurting the lady. Meanwhile, another pair of Elegants appears in the room.

"You have stepped beyond the boundary stone," this new male says. His voice is smooth and, well, elegant. The accent is inexplicably northern.

"Be welcome and destroyed," says the female.

Thomas knows they move impossibly fast; they shift from place to place in ways that defy reason. Thomas will have to act quickly himself. Still holding the chalk, he lunges forward and scrawls a few Hebrew characters on the black coat sleeve of the Elegant gripping Miss Feldstein. This is the beginning, the very beginning, of a banishing symbol from the Goetia. Perhaps it is enough. The creature hisses, releases Miss Feldstein, and turns to Thomas.

Another two Elegants are now present. There are six in total, including the one Crowley shot, which is still writhing on the floor, its arm lifting and falling, lifting and falling, like a mechanical thing that is almost wound down. Each pair appears in every way the same as the other, excepting for minor variations in their formal dress.

Thomas, meanwhile, returns to the equation on the floor. If he can zero it out, he can stop the Elegants, at least for now. He tells himself not to get overwhelmed. He must simply follow the logic of the numbers. They always want to go somewhere, like water. There is a kind of inevitability to them. He doesn't know where these numbers are going, but he thinks it is in the opposite direction than the original formulation, and that can only be good. He tells himself it must be so, though he actually has no idea if his conclusions have merit.

The enemy is time. If they cut his throat before he finishes, then the work will be for nothing. He risks a glance away from his work and sees the looming figures all around him.

"Shoot the rest of them," Thomas says to Crowley.

The magician likely has five shots left, which means missing could be a problem. He will also have to reckon with their impossible speed. He moves the gun from one to the other, thinking about where to start, what will be safest, when Ruby states the obvious.

"They're not moving."

The Elegants are indeed still. Other than the one Crowley shot, they stand, quite stiffly, arms at their side. Their eyes stare ahead, unblinkingly. Whatever had been shifting beneath their skin no longer moves.

If Thomas understands his own formula, he cannot yet be finished. Things are happening too quickly. Has he made some sort of error? He cannot be certain because he has no idea what he is doing. He was attempting to work with a combination of what little knowledge he was able to cram and his own mathematical instincts. He may have done something too powerful. He may have done nothing at all. He may have wounded the creatures just enough to make them more dangerous.

Without anyone suggesting it, the adventurers begin moving to the door. The Elegants remain as still as statues in a graveyard. Thomas has to pass near the one he marked with chalk, but it evidences no sign of animation. It appears whatever he did has worked, but he doesn't believe it. He knows this feeling— the formula appears to balance but something is wrong. It is the sort of mistake that disguises itself, but it's there. He can feel it; there is something wrong with the way the numbers move.

"I need more time," Thomas says to Crowley.

The magician looks back at the ladies and then at Thomas. He doesn't say anything, but his point is clear. They have bitten off more than they can chew. They are in real danger.

"Take them," Thomas says. "See them to safety. I'll be there in a moment, but I must first solve this."

He fears Crowley will object, will make some sort of speech about leaving no one behind, but Crowley is not that sort of a man, not that sort of a friend. If Thomas wants to risk his life in the exercise of his will, if he wants to roll the dice to prove his greatness, then Crowley will not stand in his way. He grins in approval. Then he holds out his pistol, barrel first. "Take this. In case maths don't intimidate them."

"It ain't happening," Ruby says. "We all go or none of us."

"I need to be alone to think," Thomas tells her. "I can do this, but you have to trust me. I can close this portal. I can rid London of the Elegants." He reaches to take the gun but his arm does not move.

He tries to lift his arm again, but it is as though it is held in place. Thomas hears Miss Feldstein gasp in alarm, but he does not know why. He cannot quite see. All he can see are the branches, like the first tentative growths of a sapling, that hold his arm to his body. He can see them growing, sprouting leaves while he gazes at them.

He won't be able to see them much longer, because the room is growing darker. The light is fading. And there is something in his mouth. No, not his mouth. His throat. His tongue tentatively probes with strange calmness, and he feels leaves there. They are growing. Always growing. They fill his mouth, and he thinks he should gag, part of him wants to gag, but part of him knows that he does not need a throat at all. He can breathe through his skin, and it is the most nurturing air he has ever tasted.

He hears screaming now, but it comes from so far away that he is sure it is of no importance. Things that are so distant cannot trouble him. His only concerns are right here. His light. His soil. His air. That is enough.

Except he thinks there are people he should be worried about. He cannot quite remember, but that sounds right. Other people. He can almost recall their faces, but they are so hard to distinguish, those things that move so fast, that flit about from here to there. Better to be still. Stillness is all that he requires.

Someone is looking at him, and he thinks it must be one of the Elegants somehow grown close, but it's not. It's the face from his dream—the impossible, hinged face. It studies him now, like it is searching for something though it cannot quite remember what.

Things do not grow dark. They grow light. Thomas is looking at the light that washes out the face, and that is enough. Everything is gone but the light. The light is very, very good.

*

Thomas is vomiting leaves and a thick white liquid that might very well be sap. He is on his knees on the porch outside the house. He can hear Ruby shouting at Crowley, but he cannot make out the words.

The splash of wet leaves before him steams in the cold, and air fills his lungs. It is as though Thomas has broken the surface after nearly drowning. Miss Feldstein is unraveling the thin branches that bound his arms to his body. Thomas feels a snapping somewhere near his hipbone. He doesn't feel pain, but there is a strange sense of loss.

Thomas looks up, and he hears Miss Feldstein say, "Dear God."

Instinctively, he touches his face. There are so many leaves, like a beard. He rubs with both hands. The twigs snap off and fall to the ground. He runs his hand along his jawline to make certain they are all gone. They are, but he can feel the solid flesh where they grew. He is marked now. The time when he can disguise his affliction from the world has ended.

"We need to go," Crowley says. "Can you walk?"

Thomas gets to his feet trying to make sense of the urgency in the magician's voice. Then he understands.

There are Elegants everywhere, moving about the street as if this was their city. Dozens of them. They don't appear to be harming anyone, at least not at this moment. They simply stroll, arm in arm, down the streets, looking this way and that. Admiring shop windows or peering at the sky.

If he'd had more time, he could have closed the gate. Thomas is certain of it. For those brief, fleeting moments, the formula made sense to him. He could see it. He could see how it worked, and he could see his error. The equation has already begun to fade, and he knows that if he goes back upstairs, he will have to start over, try to puzzle it out afresh. He could do it, he thinks, if going upstairs did not mean he would turn into a tree. But he has to try.

"I can stop this," he says. "I must go back."

"If you go back, you will die," Miss Feldstein says. "And likely all of us with you. We must leave here."

Thomas wants to protest, but he is still weak, and he feels himself being dragged along by Ruby Topping. He is halfway down the block before he can even think to try and pull himself free. He looks back and sees Elegants making their way down the footpath, looking at him, and he knows they would not let him pass. Even if he had the strength and the clarity, he would be doomed. He knows this and he lets Ruby pull his hand like he is a toddler dazzled by the dazzling distractions of an ordinary afternoon.

It is all his fault. He might have closed the portal. He could have, but instead he made things worse. Thomas has unleashed a nightmare upon the city.

THIRTY-ONE
CRUELTY

S OME HOURS LATER, Thomas arrives at Madeline's house. He and Crowley have seen the ladies home safely, which has turned out to be less difficult than Thomas feared. The Elegants have confined themselves to the block surrounding their portal house. They have thus far harmed no one, but Thomas fears that is but a temporary condition.

For his part, Thomas worries he has less time. Leaves have grown all over his torso and legs. There is a patch of white bark on his thigh that will not come off. It is only an inch or so in diameter, but he has no doubt it will spread. The leaves that sprouted from his face have left scars. He looks pockmarked, and he will almost certainly have to grow a beard to disguise the discoloration. That is, assuming he can grow a beard of hair, and that he has enough time in human form to concern himself with such things.

Thomas has more important things with which to concern himself than his appearance. The Elegants. He wanted to fix the mess he made, but he hadn't the time. He would have risked his life, even given his life, to adjust his formula, but now it is too late. He cannot even remember what it is he was trying to do. The equation has eluded his grasp once again.

It is the tree in him. It makes him want to do little. To stand still, not sit, and wait. To feel the sun on his face. That is what he desires, but he cannot let himself be deceived by his own body. Thomas has things to do. He must stop Walter. He must save his family's bank.

For whom? The question haunts him. Walter has no children, and trees cannot own property. If Walter is exposed or deposed or—he cannot bring himself to think of what he might have to do to his own brother—or worse, then Pearl would inherit ownership. She is no Thresher. Assuming the bank survives Walter's surfeit of bad loans, sweet, nervous, impressionable Pearl will find herself the target of every fortune hunter alive. He doubts she has the strength to fend them all off, and if she finds someone she truly cares about, why should she? Thresher's will be lost. The Thresher family will be obliterated.

That, however, is a less immediate problem than the ones Thomas currently faces. He must stop Walter. He must figure out a way to contain the Elegants. He must protect the people he cares about.

That is why, with monsters roaming East London, Thomas has taken the train to warn Mrs. Yardley. The Elegants have been unchained, and they have targeted her before. She must leave town at least until Thomas can sort this all out. He will not tell her.

He finds Mrs. Yardley not at home in Chiswick. Her servant must be with her, for she does not answer the door. Thomas sits upon the porch and decides he will wait regardless of how much such an act may impede upon his dignity. His body tells him he must stand, he must face the sun, but he sits, the way a normal person would.

After an hour or two or three—Thomas doesn't know—a coach rolls up and Mrs. Yardley steps outside, accompanied by her serving woman. Her expression is somehow serious and blank, and when she sees Thomas, who has risen to greet her, she frowns at first, but she then forms a concerned smile.

"Mr. Thresher, I did not see who you were in the dark. Is something wrong?" That is when she notices his face. She raises a hand as if to touch the little white scars that pock his jawline, then thinks better of it. She must think it some version of the measles.

"It is not catching," he tells her. "I must speak with you. It is urgent. I don't know how much time any of us has."

That is when he sees a figure rushing toward them. Fear grips Thomas, for he initially believes it must be the Elegants, but it is a lone person, dressed not fashionably, but in a hooded cloak. Thomas does not need to see under the cloak to know who it is.

"She ain't what she seems," Ruby announces as she rushes forward. She breathes hard, and she lifts her hood to give her snout better access to air. She seems to care little that her appearance may shock Mrs. Yardley and her maid. Ruby, it seems, is past such things.

"Why, who is this charming creature?" inquires Mrs. Yardley. Her smile is unmistakably false and calculated.

A terrible feeling of doubt, a sensation of plummeting, forms in Thomas's core. He does not want Ruby to say more. He wants her to go away. He wants her to have never come. Why cannot he not have one thing all his own, even if it is the sadness of a parting?

Thomas feels the need to speak. Manners demand that he introduce the two ladies, but he cannot find the words.

"Yardley ain't even her name," Ruby says. "There's nothing Yardley about her. She works for the Special Branch. It's where she just come from."

There was some confusion. Madeline—for that is truly her Christian name—first affected surprise and outrage, but that did not last long. The game is over, and there is nothing to be done for it. "Well, you might as well know all now," she concludes, and so invites them in.

Thus Ruby sits beside Thomas, who stares uncomprehendingly at the woman he thought he might have perhaps loved, he might have perhaps chosen to marry. It was all a fraud.

"Your friend Robert Yardley is alive," she begins. "He lives in Canada, of all places, where he is, indeed, a designer of railways. We believe in sticking with the facts as much as is practicable. He is also married, but I do not know his wife's name."

"Why did you toy with me?" he asks.

"Thresher's has gone to a great deal of trouble to conceal its activities from the Special Branch. They have employed clairvoyants who are skilled in seeking us out. We knew it was unlikely our agents could infiltrate the bank, to find out what your brother was up to, without being found out sooner or later. The men we employed to befriend you were both discovered, as we knew they would be in the end. What we needed was an agent who did not know himself to be an agent, and so you had to believe you were pursuing information about your friend, not doing the Crown's bidding."

"You planted the letter," Thomas says, "knowing I would find it."

"It was a little more sophisticated than that," says Madeline. "There was a bit of a mutual attraction charm involved, drawing you and the letter to each other. Much the same with the letter that led you to the Topping house. That family has no debt to Thresher's, but it was our hope that Mrs. Topping would point you to the Golden Dawn, and once involved with that organization, you would have the confidence you required to investigate further."

"You used me." Thomas has long feared himself to be blank, to be hollowed out. He wishes he were an empty vessel now. He does not want to feel so pathetic.

"I did not enjoy pretending to be precisely the sort of woman I knew would excite your interest. It is a cruel trick. What I particularly dislike is that had we asked you for your help openly and without deception, I believe you would have provided it, given what hangs in the balance. Sadly, we could not do things that way. Your ignorance was of the utmost importance. For the good of the country—and, if it makes you feel better, for the good of your family's business—we required you to be our pawn."

Thomas feels himself forming his features into a mask of unfeeling to match the lady's. "And have you learned what you needed to know?"

"That I cannot say. I report, I do not analyze. I can tell you that we know a great deal more about what Thresher's is doing than when we first met. As to what all of those activities mean, and what sort of danger the bank presents, others must decide. I do know you kicked the hornet's nest today. It will be hard for anyone to deny the Peculiarities now."

"Is that what you want?" Ruby asks.

"I want nothing but to serve," she says with a smile. "As for our government, there is a general belief that we cannot continue to conceal certain truths from the nation. There is no need for people such as yourselves to live in the shadows. Perhaps this is the world as it is now. We must learn to make use of it. Men with your condition make formidable warriors. There is no reason they should not be able to openly fight for the empire."

"Is this why you have used me?" Thomas asks. "To turn victims into soldiers? To raise up an army of loyal tree-men?"

"We did not create the Peculiarities," the lady says. "Our task is not to stop them or enhance them, but to do whatever is best for Queen and country. Right now, we think that your brother plans something that may put too much power into private hands. That is something that alarms us, so of course we took measures to learn more. You were certainly a part of that effort."

It is the implication of his incidental involvement that stings Thomas the most. He could endure being used and manipulated, tricked into exposing his heart, only to have it shattered. It is her suggestion of his secondary importance that hurts most. Thomas is struck by the realization of how much he has always wanted to matter, and how little he always has. Must he always be parenthetical in his own life?

He ought to say something. He is not sure why, but he feels it is important to demonstrate that he is not content to be so readily discarded. "Is that all you have to tell me?"

"What more can you want?" she asks, though her voice contains not inconsiderable sadness. "In the grand scheme of things, men have suffered far worse fates in order to serve their country. I must ask, however, that you minimize your contact with your brother for the time being. We don't know the extent or the nature of protections he has used against Home Office infiltration, and now that you know, you may give the game away by presenting yourself at his home or in the bank. We can place you in a hotel if you require or perhaps rent you some rooms. I understand you haven't your own means, and your connections are limited."

"He'll stay with me mum," Ruby says protectively, taking Thomas's hand. "He don't want none of your charity. Not after you played him for a fool."

Thomas would have been very happy to have a room in one of the better hotels, but now that Ruby has made her case so definitively, he does not know that he can raise the issue again. Besides, with how he now looks, a house full of Peculiars is precisely where he belongs. He stands and, in a mechanical voice, thanks Madeline for her honesty.

He is busy attempting to think how his failure to return to his brother's house will affect his wedding plans. Of course, he does not want to get married, so perhaps this is the best possible way to thwart his brother. He can simply vanish from his brother's life, just as he will ultimately vanish from the world. He knows that will never work, however. He has entered into a bargain. Something terrible will happen to him if he does not do what he has agreed to do. He almost laughs at the notion. What more could he suffer?

"If you can give us a moment alone," Madeline says to Ruby.

Thomas can see that Ruby looks doubtful, but he nods at her, and she steps outside the room.

"You have been much abused," Madeline says to Thomas. "By your family and now by your nation. I hope—well, I don't know how to say this precisely. I understand that you have been treated your whole life as though you are entirely immaterial, and I'm afraid I contributed to that."

That she has put her finger so precisely on the wound only sharpens the pain. Thomas feels exposed before his tormentor. He can bring himself to say nothing.

"Thomas, I don't care for you as I have pretended, but I do like you. I want you to understand that. There is nothing wrong with you except, perhaps, a certain tendency to glibness that affects all young men of your breeding and age. But even in that, you are no worse than many, and better than most. I cannot fathom why your father and brother discarded you, and I know we have only poured salt in that wound, but I believe—I truly believe—there is nothing about you that led them to treat you as they have."

"Why are you saying all this to me?" he manages to ask in a reasonably steady voice.

"Because despite what you must be thinking right now, I strive to be a decent person. I may have served my country in misleading you, but I have done you harm. I hope you will forgive me, and I hope you will look deeper into yourself. You are more than what your brother thinks you to be."

Thomas wants to be angry with her. He wants to hate her, and yet she has gone out of her way to do him a kindness. "And you are certain I am not the sort of man you like?" he asks.

She smiles and meets his eye. "I do not care for men at all."

He takes a step back, quite surprised. He feels he has uncovered another, perhaps less exotic, species of Peculiarity. "Oh. Oh, I see."

"I thought it only fair to be direct with you," she says, "We are not compatible, I'm afraid, but I nevertheless wish you much happiness."

Thomas steps toward the door, but as he puts his hand on the handle, he turns back to her. "I came to warn you that you are in danger. It is still true. The Elegants will come for you. You should leave London."

She nods. "I have been ordered to do so. I will be gone today. But thank you for thinking of me."

Thomas nods. He will have to train himself to stop thinking of her. The Mrs. Yardley whom he liked, perhaps even loved, was no more real than a character in a play. She is a charming actress paid to make an audience fall in love with an illusion. Perhaps Thomas's heart should be broken, but his heart is becoming a thing of wood.

"She's a slut," Ruby says in the hansom on the way to her house. "A nasty slut."

"No." Thomas can hear misery and defeat in his own voice. "That's what makes it so difficult. She is a decent person who has made me miserable and humiliated and alone."

"You ain't alone," Ruby says. "You've got us."

Thomas looks over at Ruby, at her absurd gray-furred wolf face, and he realizes once again that he quite likes this girl. She is bold, brash, and ill-mannered, and she has been nothing but kind to him. He realizes he enjoys being her friend. He is glad she is here with him, right now, to lessen his misery.

He takes her hand. It is a gesture of friendship, and as she squeezes back, he knows that she understands his meaning precisely. There is no awkwardness between them. It is, indeed, awkwardness's opposite, whatever that might be. Familiarity, perhaps? Comfort? They are, after all, two of a kind. They are monstrosities, and it is right that they should be good to each other. Thomas thinks that now that he has stopped trying to dislike her, there has been something quite agreeable about her from the beginning. This is what friendship feels like. Those jesters with whom he spent half his life, manipulated by his puppet-master of a brother, never made him feel understood and accepted and valued.

"I still don't understand why you have been so kind to me," he says. "I have not always deserved it. Yet, from the very first, you wanted to be my friend. Why?"

"I like your smell," she says.

He knows that, from Ruby, this is all the explanation he should require.

When they step into her parents' house, Ruby announces that Thomas will be staying with them. She is clearly not interested in having a discussion on the subject and does not frame it as a question.

"I'll make up a room, so he can go right to sleep," she announces, seemingly pleased with her own initiative. "He is very tired," she explains to her parents.

"There is no rush. I shall not sleep. There is too much to consider." It is true that he feels wide awake. Is it the excitement and emotions of the day, or has his body moved beyond sleep?

Mrs. Topping has arrived, placing a glass of whisky and soda in his hand. Thomas takes a sip and is pleased to discover he is still flesh and blood enough to take comfort from a drink. Mr. Topping leans in the doorway, gazing at him with begrudging approval. He cannot imagine what he has done to earn their approbation. He has only made things worse. He has ruined everything he has touched.

He finds himself sitting in the parlor, telling them about Mrs. Yardley. It feels distant now, like something that has happened to someone else. He wonders if he is losing his ability to experience emotions. As he gazes about the room, though, he knows it isn't true. He cares for Ruby. He likes Mrs. Topping and her excess of generosity. He even feels a kind of grudging appreciation for gruff Mr. Topping. Now that the illusion has slipped away, he feels he can let

Madeline Yardley go. How much of his attraction to her was aspirational? How much of it was about being the sort of person he imagined his brother wanted him to be? Now he realizes that his brother never wanted him to be anything at all. That was always the problem.

"I must undo what I did at the Elegant house," Thomas says by way of listing his obligations. "I must stop my brother and remove him from the bank, but if I do, what have I gained? My goal was to return the bank to my grandfather's vision, but if I am not around to oversee it, I cannot imagine it will fall into the right hands. If only there were more Threshers. Reliable Threshers."

Mr. and Mrs. Topping exchange a look. Ruby appears as though she is about to say something, but Mrs. Topping shakes her head.

"I think it's time," Mr. Topping says. "Past time."

Mrs. Topping nods. "Things moved more quickly than I imagined."

"They always do." Mr. Topping rises and gestures for Ruby to do the same. The two of them leave the room and close the door behind them.

"What is it?" Thomas asks. He feels like he ought to be anxious, but he is only mildly curious.

Mrs. Topping sits across from Thomas and leans forward, hands resting on her knees. It is difficult to read her wolfen features, but she appears quite ill at ease.

"I knew Walter many years ago," she begins. "You may not believe it, but I was reckoned to be quite beautiful. And he—well, he was a different man then." Her eyes have gone wide and filmy. "Oh, he was not a wit, you understand, but he was more lively, more adventurous. Like me, he was fascinated by the occult, but what we believed was a new frontier of knowledge. There was such an excitement in those days. It seemed like we were on the cusp of a new understanding, that we would be the first generation to touch what had been hidden to all who came before us. We met at a lecture, and I fancied myself in love with him for a little while."

Thomas lives in a world of wonders, a place of miracles and confusion. He is like the mythic Greeks who might, at any moment, stumble upon gods and monsters and enchanted helmets. He has seen portals to other worlds and men become plants. For all that, he has finally encountered something his mind simply cannot accept—this iteration of his brother. Mrs. Topping describes Walter as he would have been a long time ago, of course. Thomas would have been an infant in those days, or perhaps not yet born. She has been vague about the year. Walter might have been entirely different, though it is hard to imagine him as something other than what he's always been.

"You knew my brother? And you never told me?"

"You said that the woman who called herself Mrs. Yardley pointed you to us," she says. "It was not only so that I, in turn, would direct you to the Golden Dawn. I imagine she hoped to create chaos for Walter by digging up things best long buried. When you arrived here, when I learned who you were, I could not know what you intended. I needed time to think. And then, I hardly knew how to speak. But do you see why Ruby took to you at once? She knew. She could smell her connection to you."

"She could smell that you once knew my brother?" The words are hardly out of his mouth before he realizes that he is being hopelessly obtuse. It now appears before him, clear as day. He could not see it not because his brain is turning to pulp but because it is an absurdity. And yet, Mrs. Topping claims that it is true.

"Walter is Ruby's father?" Thomas says aloud, like he is testing out the words, trying to put all the pieces together.

"He was younger, more charming then," Mrs. Topping says. "His father, of course, did not care for the arrangement. Walter kept his love for me hidden— for years he was able to conceal the connection—but his father found out in the end." She shakes her head. "You can imagine what happened then."

Mrs. Topping has always seemed to Thomas like a formidable woman. It is hard to believe she could have found something to love in Walter, even as he is being told that that once, perhaps, there *was* something to love in Walter. When did that vanish? Was it when their father forced him to give up this woman and their child? There is more that she is not saying, but this is perhaps not the time to demand all things be revealed. Thomas feels that quite enough has been discovered for one day.

Ruby is his—it takes him a moment to process this unexpected truth—she is his niece. They are family. This wolf-girl is his family. He has been brought together with her. Thomas's family is bigger, more expansive, more loving than he could have ever imagined.

And Ruby is Walter's daughter.

"Can you prove this?" Thomas asks. "She must be his heir."

Mrs. Topping shakes her head. "That was always part of the arrangement. There could be nothing linking Walter to me—to my family. I signed documents. Thomas, please believe me that I would not have done it if I'd had a choice. I had nothing. Walter grew bitter. He came to hate me for having put him in so awkward a position, but he gave us enough to keep us off the streets. You know what happens to penniless women in London. You know what happens to their children."

Mrs. Topping is crying now. Thomas takes her hand, but she pulls it away. It is as though she feels unworthy of his kindness.

"I am hardly in a position to blame you for whatever arrangement you entered into. I presume you were offered money in exchange for silence."

Mrs. Topping nods.

"Then you did what you had to do to protect your child," Thomas says. "If there is no evidence of what you say, then it is a shame, because as Walter's daughter, Ruby might soon be the only remaining Thresher. As things stand, I have no idea how to secure the bank's future."

Mrs. Topping looks as though she is prepared to say more, like she is steeling herself for something large and more difficult than she has already revealed, but they are interrupted by a knock at the door. They hear Mr. Topping speaking with someone, and a moment later he steps into the room.

There is news, he says. The Elegants have begun to expand their territory. They are spreading throughout East London. And they have begun their slaughter.

THIRTY-TWO

SATIETY

A FAMILY OF three, including a teenaged boy, have been found dead in Whitechapel. Two of the corpses appear unmarked, but one has had its organs harvested. Near that, a fruit peddler has been stabbed to death and dismembered, his legs entirely vanished from the scene. Whatever their previous reason for targeting prostitutes, the Elegants seem have become unmoored, striking at anyone who suits their fancy. They are still quite distant from Mrs. Topping's house, but there can be no doubt the scope of their violence is spreading. The newspapers are no longer talking about hidden killers with blades or scalpels. They are talking about the Peculiarities. Even those papers that have for years claimed there was nothing more at work than some unusual fogs now suggest rogue elements within the kingdom may have unleashed "mechanical forces" that they cannot control.

That is how they are framing it. There is no magic. There is no occult. There is only a new and heretofore poorly understand branch of science. Thomas supposes that they are right enough, but he isn't certain that all this fussing about nomenclature much matters.

The Prime Minister has issued a statement that the public should remain calm. The Home Office is, even now, working to contain the danger, and they will make certain it will not spread to "any areas likely to affect the health and economy of the nation." In other words, for the time being the most obvious manifestation of the troubles is confined to the poorest parts of East London. Do not fear, the better sort of Londoners are told. No one who matters is likely to be harmed.

Efforts are hindered by a particularly thick fog rolling in. The newspapers explain that this makes it difficult for the police to act. As soon as conditions improve, the metropolis will be made safe again.

Thomas takes no comfort from these assurances. If he had not botched things at the portal house, people now dead would still be alive. How many more are going to die because of him? He passes the night in a haze, not sleeping but not precisely awake, feeling the itch and pressure of leaves growing from his skin. It is as though there are insects crawling along his body, but somehow it is not unnerving. It is almost comforting.

After the sun rises, he wanders about the Topping house, milling among various Peculiar children, saying little. He briefly goes outside to visit with Mr. Osgood, the tree man, who says nothing and whose only movement is the occasional turgid blink of his eyes.

Thomas wonders if it will be so bad. Maybe he will be happier when there is nothing to do but spread his roots into the ground and grow leaves and drop them as the seasons dictate. Maybe that is happiness, but how would he know? He has likely never been happy. He has been amused and diverted and giddy. He has had moments of enjoyment, but happiness is of something more than those transient experiences. Happiness, he suspects, must be sustained, if only for a little while, to be something other than an illusion.

Miss Feldstein finds him outside, not wearing a jacket, staring at the immobile Mr. Osgood.

"This is what you are doing with your time?" she asks.

"I take comfort that I am not currently making things worse."

She sighs. "You are indulging yourself, Mr. Thresher. Yes, you've had some bad turns, but are you going to spend your days moping?"

He knows she is trying to goad him, and he will not take the bait. He will not defend his dour mood. He does not have to. She knows the facts. Listing them will not make him feel better, and she won't be shamed by hearing what she already knows.

"I was foolish to think I could make a difference," he tells her. "I never should have tried to stop them."

"Stop them from doing what?" she asks.

"From whatever they are doing."

Her lips twitch. "You still don't know what that is."

"Obviously not," he snaps. "Is there a point you are trying to make?"

"The point is that we still need to find out, and we are in a unique position to do that."

"It is the Home Office's problem," he says. "It is theirs to fix. We are nothing but meddlers."

"We are much more than that," she says to him. "Come inside and I shall explain, but I'll not stand here in the cold."

They step into the parlor, but the faceless child is in there, stacking blocks. Whatever they are going speak of, Thomas would like privacy, so he invites Miss Feldstein to his room. No one will care about the impropriety of it. The Toppings are not moralists.

The room is much larger than what he enjoyed at Walter's house. There is a sitting area with a slightly threadbare sofa and a chair near a little table. Thomas has carefully left the door open, but Miss Feldstein closes it. Thomas raises an eyebrow, but Miss Feldstein gives him such a withering look that he feels ashamed. He offers her the sofa, and he takes the chair. The gloomy winter light fills the room.

"What is the big secret you wish to share?" he asks, perhaps more harshly than he intended.

"I had thought we had come much further than this," Miss Feldstein says. "But here is the old hostility returned."

"Forgive me. I am angry and frustrated and not myself any longer, but it is none of your doing." He gestures toward his face, the marks left by the leaves he has broken off. "I am changing. You have your own burden, of course. I only wish we were not so powerless."

"But that is the very thing," she says. "There is no one less powerless in this. We have all the power. They need us to marry."

"I know that." He winces at the abruptness of his own voice. "I do not mean to snap at you, but I am tired of all of this. We have unearthed secret after secret, but we have still not discovered a purpose."

Miss Feldstein appears to care nothing for his tone or his apology. Her eyes are squinted in concentration. "May I speak freely of your brother?"

"My brother," Thomas repeats. "Do you know what I've learned? That Ruby Topping is his natural daughter, my own niece. It seems that years ago Walter cast her aside like she was rubbish. Oh, I know he was little more than a boy himself at the time, and under my father's influence, but he is a man now, and it would have been no difficult thing to seek her out, if only to make certain she is well. I can set aside all my brother has done to me, the inexplicable ways he has conspired against me my whole life, and still call him a monster for how he discarded his own flesh and blood. You may say of him what you like."

Miss Feldstein stares in surprise. "Ruby is Walter's daughter? And you simply happened to encounter her family?"

Thomas sighs. He had hoped to avoid speaking of this, but he cannot—not in all fairness. Miss Feldstein is his partner in all of this, and it is unfair to withhold facts from her simply because the speaking of them will be painful. He tells her, therefore, about Madeline—about her deception and how she put the Toppings in his way.

To her credit, Miss Feldstein looks aghast. She reaches across the table and takes his hand. "I am sorry you were so abused."

Thomas feels the warmth of her skin through the gloves. The human contact is pleasant, but it is also a reminder of a touch he once hoped for—a reminder that he has, again, been manipulated and discarded. It is a reminder that the love he sought, which would have been all too fleeting in light of his metamorphosis, will never be. Instead, he will live out his remaining animate days alone.

He, therefore, as politely as he is able, takes his hand away. He is not destined for tender expressions. He knows this now.

"You are very kind," he tells her. "But kindness will not help me. Indeed, Miss Feldstein, I think you are quite correct. It is a time for action. We know my brother seeks power for the bank, and that he will use occult means to gain it, but we still don't know why he wants us to marry."

Miss Feldstein's full lips twitch. Does she feel rejected by Thomas's businesslike tone? Very likely not, he decides. There has never been so much as a flirtation between them, and she has her labor-organizing beau out there somewhere.

She removes from her bag what at first appears to be a stack of papers, but as she unfolds it upon the table, Thomas sees that it is a single sheet—a map of London. There are several circles drawn over it. "I believe I know what happens when we marry, what will change."

Thomas nods for her to continue.

She sets a finger on the map, which is a detailed rendering of Central London. She is pointing to the center of Hershel Feldstein's little empire. It is Westerly House, the building that Thomas's father sought to buy.

"I understand my father and Walter both wanted the building," Thomas says, "but how does your being married or unmarried alter the ownership of that building?"

Miss Feldstein smirks. "Because the building is mine, Mr. Thresher. Westerly House belongs to me. It has been since I was a little girl, only I never knew it. I have only just learned that it was left to me by my mother's sister, placed in my father's trust for when I come of age, which will be in half a year."

Thomas begins to see how the pieces have been arranged on the board. In a few months, Miss Feldstein will be old enough to do what she likes with the building, but if she were to marry now, the property would be jointly owned by her husband. If that husband were determined to sell it, it is unlikely she would have an easy time stopping him.

The marriage is about nothing more than putting the building in Walter's hands.

What good it does Walter for Thomas to own the building remains to be explained. Walter has not made an effort to befriend his brother, and he cannot expect Thomas to do his bidding willingly. Nevertheless, for the first time Thomas begins to think he may understand at least part of Walter's plan.

Thomas looks at the map, on which all of Thresher's recently acquired buildings are marked. The properties seem to form a circle. At least, that is the most obvious shape, the one the eye intuitively forms, but it is not the only possible shape. In these circumstances, it may not be the most likely one. His eye shifts from point to point, and he sees it.

"It is not a circle," he says, tracing the points with his finger by way of demonstration. "It is a pentagram."

Miss Feldstein looks at the map. "I suppose it could be, but I don't see what—"

He holds out his hand as he stands. He does not wish to be rude. He is not the sort of person who takes pleasure in silencing a lady, but there is something there, just out of his grasp.

A pentagram. They are everywhere in magical practice, of course. It is a core symbol, so that he has seen them at the two portal houses they've visited does not necessarily prove anything. But those houses were more than just places to put their portals. They were there, specifically there, for a reason, and their use of the calculus—attempting to prove something, to point to something.

To connect something. Somethings.

It is the most brilliant thing Thomas has ever seen. Now that he understands it, he feels himself gasp at its audacity. The movement of the earth itself must be factored in—the sun, the moon, the stars themselves. They are threading a needle when the thread and the needle hurl through space, and they must connect with other threads, other needles, at precise points.

"They want to make a portal," he says.

"In my building?"

"*With* your building," Thomas says. "They will certainly need to construct a portal there, and it will be part of the formula that will link it to the others. The connected properties themselves form a larger portal."

Miss Feldstein looks at the map and then back at Thomas. She repeats this a few times. "A portal that will do what?"

He shakes his head. "I cannot imagine what will come through. Maybe that's not the point. The portals sometimes bring in beings from other realms, like the Elegants, but more commonly, they change things here. Rabbit children and wolf-people and—and the arboreal plague. Women cannot give birth to rabbits and men cannot become trees, but they now do. The portals alter fundamental truths of our world. That is what Walter is trying to do."

Something massive, he thinks. A portal made of portals. Could it alter weather, gravity, the cycles of life and death? There is no knowing what his brother is after, but the grand scale of the scheme promises something that will change the world.

"You cannot sell it now?" Thomas asks. "Put it out of your hands so they will leave us alone?"

"I could petition the courts," she says, "but any legal action would be pointless, since it would be resolved long after I came of age. Besides, once it was sold, it would be out of my control. I would have no ability to control who does what with it. It could very easily end up in the bank's hands. They could buy it directly through a third party, and I would never be the wiser. No, as long as we do not marry, and I do not sell, we hold all the power."

Power to do what, Thomas wonders. They can prevent Walter from advancing his scheme, but they cannot make him close down his portals or release the city from the grip of the curses he has unleashed.

"How did you learn about the property now, at this time?" Thomas asks. "The timing is rather fortuitous."

"Mr. Crowley told me," she says.

"Crowley!" Thomas realizes the name sounds like an accusation.

"Apparently, he reasoned that property transfer might be at the heart of a forced marriage—rather obvious, actually, when you think about it. He consulted his tarot deck, and then wrote me to say that the answers I sought were to be found in legal documents. I sneaked into my father's study and did a bit of reading until I found what I believed I was looking for."

"Handy thing, that tarot," Thomas says dryly. He might as easily have written Miss Feldstein and told her to read through her father's legal papers until she found something illuminating. He needn't have used any divination to see that it was a solid course of action. Of course, he didn't, and Crowley did. Whether or not divination played any role in the matter, the magician certainly seems to have been thinking clearly.

"How do we use this information to advantage?" Thomas asks, more thinking aloud than posing a question.

"That rather depends upon what we want," she says.

"We want to stop Walter," he answers. "We want him to shut all these portals down."

"Then let's do that," she responds. "You believe you were almost successful last time. Perhaps if we bring more men, we can grant you the time you need. Mr. Topping must know locals who are willing to fight for their streets."

"We must send for Crowley," Thomas says. "He'll never forgive us is we leave him out of this."

"I should hate to hurt his feelings," Miss Feldstein says with a twinkle in her eye. "And having the greatest magician of our age along with us cannot hurt."

Thomas feels himself grinning. He feels, at least for this moment, more animal than plant.

The fog makes the London streets as dark as night, so Thomas suspects that it may take some time for a message to reach Crowley, let alone for the magician to arrive. In the meantime, they speak to Mr. Topping, who is eager to round up his friends—already inclined toward skull-cracking, Thomas imagines—to push back against the Elegants. He heads out, no doubt for the nearest pub, to begin recruitment. There is little for Thomas to do but wait.

It is Mr. Topping who returns long before they hear anything from Crowley.

"I don't know if this plan of yours is going to work," he says. "There's men posted at the Elegant house. Six that I saw, but it's hard to be certain in the fog. We're talking real men, not Peculiars, and they're armed. If we attempt to get in there, people are going to die."

Thomas has wondered why the bank did not post guards to these houses if they are so important. Perhaps because they weren't important yet. If there are guards there now, it suggests that either Thomas threatened them more than he realized with his formula-tinkering, or the bank is moving into some sort of an end game.

It is close to four in the afternoon by the time Crowley arrives. It is getting dark, but that hardly matters with the fog, thick as it is. Were they planning on assaulting the portal house, the darkness and the fog would almost certainly work in their favor, but no one is seriously considering the option any longer.

"I went by the house on Cannon Street on a hunch," Crowley says. "There are some rather serious chaps posted there as well. Whatever Thresher's has planned, they require all of these portals to be operational."

"I think I have an idea," Thomas says, and with the aid of Esther Feldstein's map, he begins to explain his concept of the giant portal. Crowley strokes his chin as he listens, touching the various properties as Thomas points to them.

"Nothing like what you suggest has ever been done before," Crowley pronounces when Thomas is finished. "It is beyond anything anyone has ever conceived. It's precisely what I predicted. The magical revolution is upon us, and your brother is leading the way."

"You sound as though you admire him," Miss Feldstein says.

"Oh, I do," Crowley says. "This is brilliant. Now, let's decide how we are going to stop him."

They sit in the Toppings' parlor: Thomas, Miss Feldstein, Crowley, Ruby, and Mr. and Mrs. Topping. The gaslights glow and a fire blazes in the hearth.

"I know what you want is to end this right now," Miss Feldstein says, "but I don't think that is possible. We ought to regard this as a process. We begin by going to Thomas's brother and saying we shall not even consider any further negotiation until they clean the streets of their monsters. If they don't agree, then I will refuse to marry Thomas and swear never to sell the building."

"The problem with this plan," observes Mrs. Topping, "is that threats will not prompt Walter to act. You must offer him something, such as offering to sell him the building if he agrees to your terms."

"You can't let him have it!" Ruby shouts.

"Telling him don't mean nothing," says Mr. Topping. "Offer him what he wants to hear if it will get rid of those creatures. Deal with the consequences later."

"I agree with that," Thomas says. "We must have time to think, to figure out how to undo his damage, but as long as the Elegants are out there, killing innocent people, Walter knows we will be desperate to stop him."

"It is also worth noting," Crowley says, "that unkept promises have consequences. A lie will be more readily believed in the current climate, but that is because your brother knows you would pay for your lie later."

To this, no one responds. Thomas believes it is because they are all thinking the same thing—that Thomas has no future to lose. So be it. He is doomed, so they shall use that. They must use any advantage they have.

Thomas pens a note to his brother, and Ruby volunteers to deliver it, but her parents refuse to let her. Mr. Topping says he knows a dozen boys who will risk the fog for a token of silver, and he heads out to the public house. He is back in half an hour and tells them the letter is on the way.

Thomas understands that the final stage of his confrontation with his brother has begun.

After dinner, Thomas is in the room the Toppings have set aside for him. They are all to stay the night. No one wants to travel if they can avoid it, and they may need everyone at a moment's notice once Walter responds to their letter.

He sits on his bed with the door open. He stares out the window into a foggy darkness, and he has no idea how long he has been there, no idea what thoughts have been occupying his mind, when he hears a knock at the door.

He looks up and sees Miss Feldstein standing there. In the dim glow of the gaslights, she looks almost ghostly. Her features are both softened and sharpened in some way that Thomas doesn't understand but he finds comforting. He thinks back at how he once found her face alien and unappealing. He now can think of few faces he'd rather see.

How had he never noticed how beautiful she is? Not merely beautiful after her foreign fashion, he decides. Hers is a powerful, staggering beauty, all the more affecting because it has taken him by surprise, hidden in plain sight.

"I've been calling your name," she says.

"I didn't hear you." He stands up as she enters the room. "I have been less attentive to physical things of late." He has removed more than a dozen leaves today, though he chooses not to tell her this. There has been no more growth on his face, for which he is grateful, but that cannot last for long. This business with Walter must be resolved soon, or he fears he will be unable to participate in the resolution.

Miss Feldstein sits on the bed. Thomas feels himself blush, but the door is open. He sees no harm in sitting not precisely near her. Neither does he choose to be terribly far.

"I may not—exist, I suppose—in this form much longer. No—" He holds up a hand when she begins to say something contrary. "No, it is the truth. I cannot deny it."

"Whatever is happening to you," she says, "must be a part of what your brother is doing. It is my hope it can be reversed."

Thomas says nothing. He supposes he hopes that too, but hope feels like something very far away. It is the disease, he knows. It makes him content to become what he is becoming. He cannot feel the natural terror and regret. His anger at his brother, however—that is something he can still feel. He must stop Walter. He must rescue the Thresher family from itself, even if doing so leaves no Threshers remaining.

Thomas notices that Miss Feldstein's hand is on his own. She wears no gloves. He can almost feel the warmth of her skin on his, but his skin does not feel the way it used to. Even so, Thomas is suddenly quite aware that they are alone in a bedroom. The door is open, but there is no one in the hall. The sounds of the house are all faded and distant.

She is not the woman he wanted. He wanted Madeline, but Madeline was not real. She was an illusion, a pretense. He never quite told her the truth about himself, and she certainly was not honest with him. But Miss Feldstein has been honest with him from the beginning. She has never withheld anything, and she knows his darkest secrets—that he is despised by his brother, likely never to come into any money, and that he is destined to live out his life as a tree. And still, she holds his hand and smiles at him. Thomas feels seen in a way that is utterly unfamiliar.

"I wonder," he says, "if we need rule out marriage entirely. I do not know what I am to inherit, but someone should benefit from what is legally my due."

She laughs, though not at him. "You do realize that you are suggesting you do the very thing your brother most wants. If you wish for an heir, you should make a will and name Ruby Topping."

"I have thought of that," Thomas says, "but if I am to become a tree, my death may be hard to prove. A wife, however, would have an easier time claiming what is mine."

"That is true," says Miss Feldstein, "but we cannot let your brother win. Besides, I am in no mind to marry. I may never be."

"Not even your gentleman?"

She blushes. "There is no gentleman. I merely said that to make you more comfortable, so that you would not feel I had designs upon you."

Thomas feels something flutter in his chest. His vegetable heart has quickened. "That is interesting."

She smirks. "In what way? Are we not merely friends?"

"I don't know what we are," he says. "Do you?"

"I only know that I am tired of playing by the world's rules." She turns away from him. "I could hear your thoughts, you know, at the Elegant house."

It is Thomas's turn to blush. "A person cannot help his thoughts, Miss Feldstein. I cannot help being drawn to—to certain qualities you possess. At the time, I thought my heart committed elsewhere."

She smiles at him. "And if I could hear your thoughts now, what would I learn?"

He feels himself trembling. He does not know if he should answer her question honestly, but it would feel like a betrayal to remain silent. "Now I think I was foolish not to value you as you deserve from the first."

There is something sly in her expression, and she turns away. "Perhaps it is not too late to make up for your former deficits."

Thomas watches while Miss Feldstein rises and closes the door to his room. She remains within.

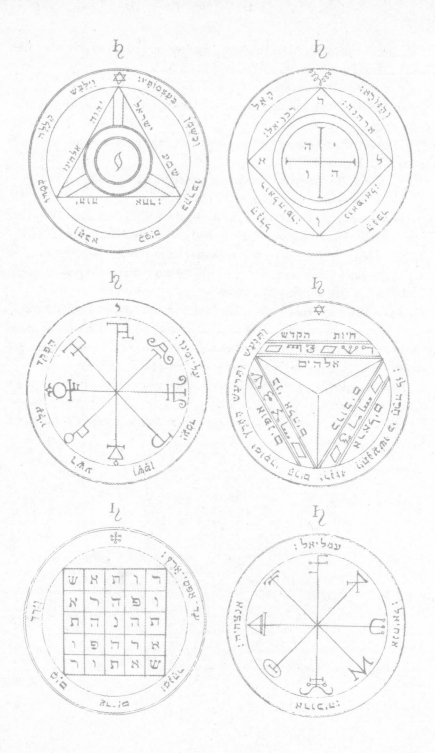

THIRTY-THREE
VIRTUE

CROWLEY LOOKS AT the map. It is spread out for him on the Toppings' dining room table. He stands with his hands behind his back like a general. Thomas sits at the table, holding a teacup. The others will be along soon, he supposes, but right now it is just the two of them.

In the morning they have still received no response from Walter. They have heard, however, that eleven people were killed by the Elegants during the night. Some were mutilated, others simply cut down. The creatures' grip on East London is growing. Most of their victims have been beggars, peddlers, and, of course, prostitutes. They seem to favor the very poor and those out on the street late at night. Four of the victims, however, were sleeping in their beds.

Miss Feldstein—Esther—was not in Thomas's room when he awoke this morning. He slept deeply for the first time in days last night, but he still dreamed of the hinged face, perhaps more clearly than ever. It regarded him with the curiosity of a cat who wonders if the mouse it has been toying with is truly dead.

He had hoped to see Esther at breakfast, but she has not yet emerged at nine o'clock. Thomas would like to believe that she is not avoiding him, but he cannot convince himself. They behaved most incautiously. Now it occurs to him that Esther had no fear of bearing his child. She cannot conceive, surely. Or can she? Thomas recalls that Aristotle believed that rabbits are able to conceive while already pregnant, though he is sure this is nonsense, and gestating a rabbit doesn't make Esther a rabbit herself. He realizes he is thinking in circles.

It was by no means Thomas's first time with a woman, but it was his first time with a woman of her sort. That is to say, it was his first time without there being some sort of financial component. Thomas knows all too well that dalliances with serving girls and poor country lasses might not include the quoting of a price and the delivery of coin, but they might as well. There is always the promise of reward, of access to money or influence or favor, that colors such transactions. This, however, was an entirely different experience.

It was not Esther's first time either. That much was clear. He is not certain how to feel about that. He would rather not have deflowered her, but at the same time, to think of her offering herself up to any fellow who catches her eye—well, it is too much. Crowley would have no sympathy for these concerns. It is a new era. Women ought to be as free as men to pursue their pleasure and so forth. Thomas now possesses an inner Crowley, which cannot be a good thing.

Right now, Crowley is saying something else entirely, and Thomas tries to focus.

"I think you're quite right." The magician gestures at the unfolded paper. "But I don't see any sort of permanent solution. If you thwart Walter now, someone else will come along later."

"Perhaps that next someone will care about lives lost." Thomas rubs his face, trying to stay in the moment, trying to remain an animal and not a plant. He feels the hard lumps of skin under his growing beard. He can no longer think of them as scars. They are tiny bits of bark, and they seem to be spreading. "Perhaps the Home Office will prevent this sort of thing from happening again. We cannot throw up our hands."

"We may have to," Crowley says. "The magical revolution is upon us. Consider how many lives have been crushed in factories over the past century, yet who numbers the dead when we gaze upon Britain's success? It is no longer a new world. It is simply the world."

"I cannot manage the future," Thomas says. "I am burdened enough with the present, and that means negotiating with Walter." He falters at the use of his brother's name. He is no longer an abstract ogre to these people. He is Ruby's father, Mrs. Topping's former lover. Can Mr. Topping see him as a rival? Only if he has never met him. "We have something he desperately needs— Miss Feldstein's property—and we have something he most certainly does not want—a secret heir. He has hidden that truth for a long time, and I think he would be willing to give up a great deal to see that the truth remains hidden."

Crowley helps himself to Topping's whisky. That it is still morning means nothing. He is sufficiently aware of the time, however, not to offer any to Thomas. He does, however, grin lecherously as he swirls his drink about. "You and Miss Feldstein, eh?"

Thomas feels himself blush. "She told you?"

"She didn't have to. I can smell it on you—that animal desire. It is quite potent."

Thomas shakes his head. He doesn't like to speak of private matters concerning a lady, but he needs a friend. "It came upon us unexpectedly. It is so strange, you know. All this time my brother has been trying to bring us together, and in resisting him, we have found that we rather enjoy one another."

"You have shared adventures," Crowley says. "That is powerful stuff. Very erotic. Just be careful, Thresher."

"I hardly think Miss Feldstein is a fortune hunter, nor am I one to be hunted."

"No, not that." He appears annoyed that he has to say it. "I don't like the idea of doing anything your brother wants you to do."

"We are not about to elope," Thomas says. "Frankly, I don't know that she would consent to marriage. She has some very modern ideas."

Crowley raises an eyebrow. "You've a logical mind. Use it at all times. That is all I am saying."

They hear from Walter shortly before noon. The note is terse and unyielding.

Thomas Thresher and Esther Feldstein are to surrender themselves at Westerly House at eight o'clock this evening. No one else may attend. We are in possession of the woman who calls herself Madeline Yardley, and she will die if these conditions are not met.

Thomas stares at the words, trying to make sense of them. Under his brother's supervision, Thresher's Bank has overseen magical portals across London. These have resulted in death and mutilation, lives lost and ruined. Walter has conspired tirelessly against the bank's charter, against his own brother, against all notions of goodness. Thomas has, with the steady and invisible pace of a candle melting into a pool of wax, come to understand that his brother is a bad man. Perhaps one might call him evil. Even so, this threat astonishes him. It is one thing to create a portal from which murdering creatures happen to emerge. It is another to take the life of a human being. A lady.

"I don't believe he would do this," Thomas says, but his words are empty. He does not know what Walter would or would not do.

"Who cares for this woman?" Mr. Topping asks. "What's it to me if they top her?"

"That's monstrous," Ruby says with a gasp. "I don't like her, but we can't let him kill her."

"They ain't ladies and gentlemen that are dying in East London right now," Mr. Topping says, "but they're people just the same. Not a word about them."

"When I go, I shall insist they resolve the situation with the Elegants," Thomas says. "And I shall go alone."

"I can't let you do that," Esther says coolly.

She came into the room to hear the reading of the letter, and it is the first time Thomas has seen her today. Her lavender gown is without crease or wrinkle. Her hair is more orderly than he has ever seen it. She is not looking at Thomas, however. Her comment is clearly to the room at large, not any one person in particular.

"I won't put you in danger." Thomas seeks out her eyes, but she will not meet his gaze.

"It is not your place to decide. What can he do to us? He will not kill us. He cannot force us to marry against our will. They need our voluntary cooperation, which makes us safe."

"I still say we don't dance to his tune," Mr. Topping grumbles. "Let him do what he pleases to this woman. She's nothing to us."

"I can't do that," Thomas says. "I owe her nothing, but I cannot let Walter harm someone in order to prove a point. And while we are calling his bluff, the Elegants continue their murders."

"How does he even have access to Miss Feldstein's property?" Mrs. Topping asks. "It does not belong to him, and yet he proposes to meet there."

"My father has always kept it," Esther explains. "He must have given Walter a key. He oversees the trust and is able to use the building to generate revenue as he sees fit."

"If he can use the building," Ruby asks, "does that mean we can do nothing to stop him?"

"No," Crowley says. "Everything we've seen indicates he believes he must own it. He is no doubt preparing for that day, establishing whatever physical infrastructure is required for his plans, but until the building is his, he will not be able to do whatever it is he wishes to do."

"You are proposing doing everything he asks," says Mrs. Topping. "The time, the place, the conditions—all upon his terms."

"I think Thomas is right," Esther says without looking at him. "Until I marry or agree to sell him Westerly House outright, Walter cannot cross me."

Mr. Topping folds his arms. "Are you certain he can't force you two to marry?"

"Not legally," Mrs. Topping says, as though she has researched this subject at length. Perhaps she has. The issue of patrimony would have been of great interest to her at one point in her life.

"They'll go," Crowley says.

Thomas looks at him.

He shrugs. "The risk is minimal, and it is not as though you have much choice. Whatever else Walter Thresher is, he is a businessman. He will want to negotiate a deal, not clobber these two over the heads and hide their bodies. Remember that we feel rushed. We want to stop the Elegants. Walter feels no such urgency. For him, this may be the first step in a process that can drag on for weeks. Besides, by stepping into Westerly House, you may learn a thing or two about their plans—information we can use against them if we want the Home Office to take action."

"Why can't we go to the Home Office now?" Esther asks. "We can tell them what we know. Perhaps they can force Thresher's to behave."

"The Home Office is a last resort," Crowley says. "The Crown has a long history of siding with the wealthy. For all we know, they could seize the property and give it to the bank, or they could withhold it for concessions they want rather than what we want. It is much wiser to hobble Thresher's and their portal project before turning to the government."

No one can think of a reason why he must be wrong, and so they accept that he is right.

"Now, we have only a few hours to prepare these two," Crowley says. "We must get busy."

"Busy with what?" Thomas asks.

Crowley grins. "With magic."

They've made space for Crowley in the parlor, and he goes to work at the little escritoire. He calls for pen and ink and busies himself for an hour or so. He then leaves the house after telling them not to enter the room, and returns just after five with a large bundle. He goes back into the parlor and shuts the door, telling them that he is not to be disturbed.

Thomas wanders around the house, avoiding his friends, avoiding the other Peculiars. Occasionally he will step into his room to strip and remove the leaves that have grown in the past hour or two. After one such cleansing, he opens the door and finds Esther standing in the hall. Perhaps she was preparing to knock. Perhaps not. He cannot say. She steps inside without being asked and closes the door behind her.

Thomas feels his heart pound. He cannot remember what a person is supposed to do with his hands during a conversation. They hang like heavy pendulums or possibly like tree branches. "Something has upset you. I did something wrong."

Esther forces a smile. It is the most terrible thing Thomas has ever seen.

"Thomas," she begins, in the way of someone who has practiced her words, "what happened between us—it cannot happen again. You mustn't think I don't care for you, because that is not true. I have come to think quite highly of you, but we both know there is no future between us. I do not regret anything, but we must not make more of it than it was."

Despite her words, she clearly regrets it entirely. Thomas searches his memory, trying to find some hint of what went wrong. What had he done? He cannot recall a misstep, a sign that he was too forceful or, heavens forbid, not forceful enough. Were leaves growing on him the whole time? Did he disgust her? She did not behave like a woman experiencing disgust, but perhaps, in his self-absorption, he missed the obvious.

And what the devil can she mean about having no future? He has no future of any kind. Does she not see that? Never before had he been with a woman simply because he admired and respected her, because he delighted in her company. Is that love? Does he love her? How can he know? How can anyone, raised as he has been, possibly know? Only a short while ago he wondered if he loved Madeline. Is that the problem? Is Thomas too fickle in his affections? Perhaps she wants someone more decisive.

Is it a matter of her reputation? Should he suggest marriage? He knows he cannot. Marriage is what their enemies want. Marriage is for people who have their whole lives before them. Marriage is not an option for men with so little time left to spend in the animal kingdom, but to be turned away, at this time, by this woman—well, it is something he wishes were not so.

He takes a step toward her. "Esther. Miss Feldstein. I never meant to take advantage—"

"Don't be an idiot." There is something not entirely kind in her tone. "I am not a child. I make my choice, but that also means I make my own mistakes. What is between us is too complicated, too important, to muddle with emotions. We have work to do, and that is where we must place our energies."

Something has snapped within Thomas, and he does what he has never done before. He speaks without thinking or planning. He says simply what is in his heart. "My feelings for you are real."

Her smile is genuine this time, but even more heartbreaking in its sadness. "All feelings are real, but when this is all over, you will remain you, and I will remain me. There is nowhere we can go together."

Thomas is not sure why that is so. MacGregor Mathers married a Jewess. The world is changing. The world would be changing even if there weren't little boys with lobster claws fighting in pits. There is no reason they cannot have a future together unless it is the most simple of reasons—she does not wish for there to be a future with him.

"I can see it on your face," she continues. "You think yourself responsible for me now. Well, no one is. You have the well-being of the city resting on your shoulders, and I will not have you fretting about me. I know you will not be able to help yourself, so a clean break is best."

He gestures to the marks on his face left by the explosion of growth. "Is it because I am disfigured?"

It is like a film has fallen from her face, and what remains is anger sculpted in stone. "I hadn't dared to hope you would make this easier by being an ass, but you have done so."

She steps out of the room, closing the door behind her.

Thomas sits down on the bed and allows himself to look out the window at nothing.

As for his heart, he tells himself it is no matter. Things are as they have always been, and as they will always be. He is alone.

A few minutes later Crowley calls him into the parlor. The magician's eyes are red and drooping. There is a pile of scrawled papers, and velvet has been unfurled, revealing daggers, a sword, amulets and other trinkets.

Crowley looks miserable but he forces a grin. "Has something happened with you and Miss Feldstein?" he asks once the door is closed.

"She and I have decided that we must concentrate on our efforts here," Thomas says stiffly. "There can be nothing more."

Crowley nods like a man watching a move in a chess match. "These modern women of her class, they don't quite know what to do with the freedom they desire. I also wonder if you are as modern as she is."

"Meaning what?" Thomas demands.

"Meaning don't act as though you really do mean to marry her just because she's—because she has been uninhibited with you." Crowley is making an effort to avoid his usual crass way of speaking. He is trying, it seems, to be a friend. "It can be a balancing act, you know. Don't treat her like she is disposable, but you must also avoid treating her like she has made a binding commitment."

"I admire her," he says. "I don't know how to perform these complicated feelings."

Crowley shakes his head. "No, you may be a bit too earnest for your own good. Keep in mind that the stakes are quite high. People are worried about their lives, their futures, the world itself. Don't pressure her, old man."

Thomas snorts. "For a libertine, you are rather sensitive."

"Which, as it happens, is a necessary attribute for a successful libertine," Crowley says. "Now, let's get down to the life-and-death business."

He presents Thomas with various charms he has written out, a sheathed, consecrated dagger with a bit more of an edge than you find on the magical blade—and a silver ring. "I was wearing this when I seduced Tyche, the goddess of fortune. Perhaps some of her nature rubbed off on it. Certainly some of her essence did." He waggles his eyebrows.

Thomas weighs the ring. It seems no different than a piece of silver jewelry that had never come into contact with a goddess. "Will any of this matter?"

Crowley shrugs. "The portals your brother has created are powerful. We've seen that. These objects may turn a minor point in your direction here and there, but they aren't mighty talismans with which you can expect to slay a giant. You will have to rely on your own abilities to face whatever comes." He then slides a box of chalk over to Thomas. "Be sure to have some of this upon you. You never know when you might have the opportunity to rework a portal."

"It is too bad that I am a shite magician," Thomas says with a sad smile.

"I may have misspoken," Crowley tells him. "Or rather, I believe I may have misread the information in the cards. In retrospect, I think it would have been more accurate to say that you are a shite Golden Dawn magician, but you did things at the Elegant house that I could never have done. You see patterns in magic that are invisible to me, and I am formidable."

"I made a hash of things at the Elegant house."

"I ought not to have rushed you," Crowley says. "I had no faith in what you saw, in what you thought you could do, because it is something new—at least to me. And then, well—you started vomiting leaves, and our opportunity was finished. If you'd had only a few more minutes, you could have done what you wanted to do, and all would have been well. I just couldn't see that. The magical tradition has always been about scholarship, imagination, and will, but that does not mean those things must be the entirety of magic. I think you *are* a great magician, Thresher, but of a new sort—not the kind who unearths truths long ago learned and forgotten, but one who sees new truths in what was always before us. Your brother is also a new kind of magician—or he has one in his service. I can think of no one better suited to stop him than you."

"Perhaps I shall be the greatest magician of our age," Thomas says with a grin.

Crowley looks deadly serious. "No. That will still be me."

"Greatest bollocks of the age is more like," says Mr. Topping. He has entered the room unseen and stands with his arms folded. "A cheese knife, a ring with the cunny juice of a mystical tart, and a box of chalk? That's how you mean to protect yourself?"

"There are things at play that are beyond your experience," Crowley explains as if to a child.

"Thresher is putting himself and that young lady in danger, and he needs all the help he can get," Topping said. "I think I understand things perfectly." He unfolds his massive arms and reveals he's been clutching something in his hand. He slaps it down on the table, and they see that it's a gun, a tiny pistol, so small it looks almost like a toy.

"Asked a chuckaboo of mine to round this up," Topping says. "A single-shot Derringer. Best not to start a ruckus with this, but if you find yourself in a tight spot, it just might answer, and it's easy to hide should they search you."

"I don't know anything about firearms," Thomas explains. "I am more likely to shoot myself than anyone else."

"Then maybe you should practice," Topping says. "Unless you'd rather defend yourself with the chalk."

The Pentacle of Saturn and Saturday.

Alpha et Omega.

A Talisman for the fruits of the Earth

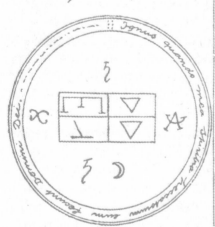

Against charms and Evil Spirits.

THIRTY-FOUR
STRIFE

Thomas and Esther approach Westerly House. The ride over in the hansom cab was silent and slow. The darkness and the fog required the driver to move at an infuriatingly sluggish pace. Esther makes a few attempts at conversation, mostly of the strategic variety, but Thomas feels unable to engage. He hopes she does not think it is because he is angry. He is not. He believes she has made the right decision. Thomas, however, is uneasy about what is to follow. He feels that for all they have learned, for all they have prepared, they are entirely unready for what they will face. Thomas cannot recall an instance of Walter being unprepared. Walter has written the script. He owns the props, has designed the costumes, and hired the actors. Thomas and Esther are merely the audience.

He must master these feelings. He will be made of leaf and wood now. He will be hard and impenetrable and unreadable. They are here to perform a task, and that is what is most important. "Is there anything I should know about this place before we enter?"

Esther shrugs, looking up at the house, so ordinary, linked to its conjoined siblings up and down the street. "I've never been inside." After a moment she adds, "I am sorry I was unkind to you."

Thomas smiles at her. It is genuine, for he finds her concern touching, endearing, even moving. He doesn't need her to adore him. He doesn't even need her to consent to letting him take care of her. All he needs is her regard, and he believes he has it. "You needn't worry about me, but thank you."

Thomas and Esther have arrived precisely on time, but Mr. Hawke responds to their knock with a little pantomime of wondering who it could be. He then smiles his openmouthed canine smile, bows, and steps aside to admit them.

"It is so very good to see you again, young Mr. Thresher. And the lovely Miss Feldstein. A vision of Semitic beauty. A genuine pleasure of the rarest sort."

He helps Esther with her jacket. Thomas removes his own and hands it to Mr. Hawke, who gives no sign of resentment at being treated like a servant. He hangs both on a hook, takes their hats, and gestures toward the stairs.

"Let me see Mrs. Yardley," Thomas says. "Or whatever her name is. I shall proceed no further until I know she is safe, and you set her free."

"She is quite safe, I assure you," Mr. Hawke says. "You will see that for yourself upstairs. Come. Come."

Thomas looks about into the rooms visible from the hallway. They are empty and unfurnished, but not overly dusty. The building, from what he can see, appears like any other unfurnished property. More significantly, he does not feel anything. In the portal houses they visited previously there was the unmistakable sense that they were entering a liminal place. He instantly experienced sensations without references, feelings and smells and sights that made it unmistakable he had entered a place abutting another world. This feels like a musty old house.

"I am confident we shall have a productive meeting," Mr. Hawke says as he leads them up the stairs. "Very productive indeed."

He guides them into a room furnished very much like Walter's study at home. Indeed, Walter is behind a desk. He is writing furiously as though this unwelcome interruption has caught him unawares. Gaslights burn brightly as Walter scribbles away. He sets a page aside to dry and picks up another.

"I have brought young Mr. Thresher," Hawke says, "and his lady friend, the glorious and fertile Miss Feldstein."

Without looking up from his work, Walter gestures for them to sit. They watch while he continues to scribble. Perhaps this is a performance of industry and indifference, but Thomas suspects he genuinely does not care that he is making them wait. As last he sets down the pen and Mr. Hawke whisks the papers away, setting them on a nearby credenza. He then takes a position just behind Thomas.

"Madeline Yardley," Thomas says.

"Not her name," Walter snaps as he begins to scrawl upon a new piece of paper. "She's not here."

Thomas begins to protest but Mr. Hawke puts what he no doubt imagines to be a calming hand on Thomas's shoulder. "We never troubled her. You must see that. Even if you imagine we would engage in such absurd violence, which is not in our nature, then we would certainly not risk the ire of the Crown by abducting an employee of the Home Office. We knew, however, with the fog and the current difficult conditions you would not be able to find that out on your own. It was merely a way to get you here that we might continue to resolve our differences. A rift in family is so unpleasant."

Thomas feels anger and irritation with himself and a sense of having made a fatal misstep. "You never had her, and yet that was the pretense for bringing me here. Then I'm afraid our business is concluded."

"It is not." The voice, hard and clear as a pristine chunk of ice, belongs to Esther. "The Elegants. You must get them under control."

"You spilled the milk, and now you want us to clean up the mess?" Mr. Hawke says with some amusement.

Esther shrugs. "If that is how you would like to phrase it, then yes. Regardless, it is your shrine or portal or whatever it is. You must do something about it."

"It cannot expand much more," Walter says, at long last setting down his pen. "We are not fools. Hawke has run the calculations and believes they are near the outer limit of their ability to maintain territory. I see no reason to exert our energies. They shall feast on the people of East London, but they will go no farther. We never intended that anyone outside the poorest quarters will be inconvenienced."

"By *inconvenienced*, you mean people will die," Thomas says.

"People always die," Walter responds. "It is what they do. They live and die, they breed and decay. It is an endless cycle. A few more deaths in Whitechapel mean little."

"I do apologize that you are under the impression that we are making a request." Miss Feldstein's voice is as commanding as a queen's. "We are not. We are telling you to do this."

Walter smiles grimly. "Do you suppose you are in a position to direct me?"

"We would not be here otherwise," Esther says. "You are not villains in a melodrama. You will not harm us by your own hand. You have no power over us. That said, we have what you need, so let us negotiate."

"What could you possibly have that would be of interest to me?" Walter asks as he makes a few more marks upon his paper.

"You need me to marry Miss Feldstein for her property," Thomas says. "We have deduced that much, though it is not entirely clear how this house will transfer from our control to yours. It is true that I have been ever eager to please you and Father all my life, but you may be disappointed to learn that I am feeling less cooperative these days. Nevertheless, it is a first step, and that step shall not be taken, shall not even be considered, unless you do as we say."

"You think you can issue ultimatums to me?" Walter looks directly at Thomas. His voice is unnervingly calm, but for the first time, he appears to be paying attention to his visitors.

"You have repeatedly *asked* me to marry Miss Feldstein," Thomas answers. "You have never before asked anything of me. You have demanded or ordered or simply acted without my consent. What you need now requires that Miss Feldstein and I choose to do what you wish, and I tell you that neither of us will even consider marriage until all our conditions have been met. Yes, I will suffer terrible misfortune if I break my promise, but I am turning into a tree, Walter. The burden of a little more misfortune does not concern me."

"I see," Walter says. He remains very still for some long time. It is more than a conversational pause. A clock ticks nearby. The sound of Mr. Hawke's somewhat wheezy breath fills the room. Then something happens on Walter's face—a narrowing of the eyes, a hardening of the mouth. "Please follow me," he says.

He stands and steps out of the room, not troubling himself to see if he is indeed being followed. Mr. Hawke looks at them and shrugs slightly, as if they are all equally puzzled by Walter's eccentricities. With no options, Thomas and Esther follow him up the stairs and then up another flight.

At the top floor they find a garret set up as a portal such as they have seen at two other houses now. There is the wooden, circular doorway, surrounded by chalked symbols and markings upon the floor—magic circles full of writing in Latin, Greek, and Hebrew. Thomas is momentarily distracted by what he now recognizes as familiar strings of letters serving as numbers and, of course, at the heart of it, the omega-alef. Here is the algorithm upon which all these portals hinge.

"We no longer require your cooperation," Walter announces with the clipped tones of a vengeful functionary. "Yes, imploring you to assist your family was distasteful, and—as you have your whole life—you refused to please anyone but yourself. Fortunately, things have changed, and now all I require is that you be here."

Thomas and Esther exchange glances. He sees her eyes dart toward the door. Something is, indeed, different, and perhaps they should flee, but not yet. Thomas does not wish to leave until he has learned more. He has not given up on being able to get Walter to stop the Elegants or—barring that—learning how he might stop them himself.

Walter looks at Thomas and shakes his head. "Evidently you have taken certain liberties with this Hebrew slut. Marriage seemed the best way to guarantee what we wanted, but all we required for the transfer of this estate was consummation. We are engaged with much older, more primitive conceptions of marriage and property—notions conceived of before there were kings or cities upon the earth. I could hardly have asked that the two of you rut like beasts, but you have been good enough to do so. The house now belongs to the Threshers, and we can do with it what we wish."

Esther has the strength of character not to blush. She glowers at Walter. Thomas looks at his brother and attempts to figure out what precisely is required to be master of this situation. If Esther can remain unshaken, then so can he. The burden of negotiation now falls to him. "Even if what you say is true and somehow the building is now mine, it is no closer to belonging to you. You will have to deal with me to get what you want."

"This isn't a matter of English law, you ninny," Walter says. "Must you always be so dimwitted? The property belongs to our family or clan or tribe or what have you. As I said, ancient notions of ownership govern these things. The head of the family, who is certainly not you, may use the property as he pleases."

Thomas turns to Mr. Hawke. "This must be your doing. Walter could never have conceived of such a plan. He is too—"

"Dull?" Mr. Hawke proposes. "Unimaginative? Perhaps you are right. It is not in Walter's nature to concoct a scheme this graceful, but you give me too much credit thinking I could manage such a thing on my own. I am but a servant."

"Whose servant?" Esther demands.

A figure emerges from the shadows, more tree than man. Its slow, plodding steps fall heavily upon the wooden floor. Thomas's mind races, wondering what it can mean that there is yet another person afflicted by the arboreal plague. It takes him a moment to recognize that this man is not some stranger. The tufts of white hair, the aquiline nose, the long chin—they are still visible, if hard to discern under the thick plating of bark.

"Father," Thomas whispers.

THIRTY-FIVE
PEACE

"**N**OT SO DEAD as you supposed, eh?" Samuel Thresher's voice is slow and belabored, creaking with wooden strain. Nevertheless, it is much as Thomas remembers it.

Thomas feels Esther take his hand. She understands he needs steadying. He sucks in a deep breath. The arboreal plague that afflicts both him and Walter comes not from either of them, but from their father.

"You are the reason I am diseased," Thomas blurts out. "They say it passes from parent to child, but I never believed you would have had the imagination for magic."

"You have never known me," the old man says. "You know nothing of my abilities or imagination."

Thomas feels himself standing up straighter. He senses time is short. Whatever is going to happen will happen soon, and it is best to say what he must. "If so, it is your choosing. You were the one who wanted nothing to do with your own son."

A crackling sound emerges from Samuel Thresher's mouth. It is wooden laughter, full of hard surfaces and splintered edges. "You are no son of mine. You are Walter's boy."

Walter winces and looks away, as though he cannot bear that a shameful truth should be spoken.

Somewhere something shatters. Words that have never been uttered ring clear in the air, and understanding washes over Thomas, as cruel and forceful as a slap. Mrs. Topping's reluctance to speak more about what she knew. Her evident embarrassment. Her sudden affection for Thomas. He is not Ruby's uncle. He is her brother. Walter, who had not one child with Mrs. Topping, but two, is his father. All at once the mysteries of his life come clear to him. Father did not want him because Thomas was not Samuel Thresher's son. Walter regarded him as a shame. He has felt his whole life like he did not belong because he was explicitly unwanted.

Thomas struggles to gain mastery of himself. These are their cruelties, their disgrace. He has been treated his whole life as though he was a mistake, but the mistake was theirs, not his. He will no longer accept punishment for the crime of existing. "Why did you raise me at all? Why did you not simply send me away, like Ruby?"

"I certainly would have favored such a scheme," Walter says, "but Father thought you might become useful to the family."

"Then why did you treat me the way you did?" Thomas demands. Yes, there are larger concerns than past grievances, but he must know. There may never be another chance to ask. "Why was I not allowed to pursue my own interest, my own friends? If you had but let me alone, I would have taken up mathematics and been no trouble to either of you."

"Ah, but mathematics is at the heart of the magic I devised." There is sadness in Samuel's creaking voice. "You were always more like your grandfather than your father. Even as an infant, you favored me. That was the trouble. I'd have been perfectly happy to see you remain at Trinity, to become Senior Wrangler as I had, but Walter had other ideas."

"And you did not want a rival?" Thomas asks. He still does not understand.

"It was not my decision, but your father's," Samuel says, gazing at Walter. "Though he was young, I made you his charge. I would have been content to allow you to follow your passions. I would have liked another mathematician in the family. Walter had no talents in that regard, and I knew he disliked that you showed abilities he lacked. Walter always had the quotidian mind of a banker, and that was certainly of some use to us. I thought it best he do with you as he pleased. For the good of the bank, you see."

Thomas stares at Walter. "You ruined my life because you were jealous that I could do maths?" He wants to laugh. The key to all mysteries, the reason he was unwelcomed, was secretly molded into a reprobate, was because Walter did not want to be embarrassed by Thomas being good at something most people found impossibly tedious.

Thomas knows this isn't precisely true. Walter hated him before he took to mathematics, but he always feared him, always feared that he was more like Samuel than Walter himself was. *That* was the key to all mysteries.

"You were always lazy and selfish," Walter says. "Father would have seen only the mathematics and ignored the rest. He would have trusted you with too much. The bank needed my steady hand, not your flights of fancy."

"So you conspired to make me a nothing," Thomas says.

"I think that is putting it a bit strongly," says Samuel Thresher, the man whom Thomas still thinks of as Father. "There are many ways to serve your family, and even with your father's efforts to keep you out of the way, I saw that Thresher's would have need of you. I was already preparing for the day I might undo the mistakes written into the bank's charter."

"What good will reworking the charter do if there is no bank?" Thomas demands. "It is bleeding money. Men who can never repay clamor for Thresher's money because they think they will never have to repay it."

"Let them think what they wish," Walter says airily. "The losses are a sacrifice, demanded by that which we serve. It shall be repaid a thousand-fold in the end."

"There is great power in sacrifice," Samuel says. "I have followed your activities in recent months, and while you cavort with fools like MacGregor Mathers, who know nothing of modern magic, I believe you have learned what sacrifice can achieve."

"Sacrifice, yes," Mr. Hawke says helpfully. "But most especially sacrifice of blood. The bonds of kinship contain some of the most powerful magic of all, and the ancient codifiers of these practices evidenced a preference for the male of the species. You ask why you were preserved, and the female cast away. It is because a boy has his uses."

"And the falsifying of your own death," Thomas presses. "All because you wished to hide what you were becoming?"

Samuel Thresher nods as though pleased to be understood. "In order to prepare the final stages, the director of Thresher's required a flexibility that I lacked in my current state. Walter has served me well, and we are now prepared to unlock the final portal. I conceived of this long ago—a linking of portals that shall give me power unknown to any magician since the dawn of time. Raw power. A magical engine with which we can rewrite all rules."

"Rewrite what rules and with whom?" Esther sounds confused, as though this—and not these other revelations—has taken her quite by surprise. "Do you mean to use this portal to—to summon God himself?"

Samuel Thresher wrinkles his face in distaste. "An abstract, formless deity is of no use to me. I wanted something more solid, more—primitive."

"What exactly are you hoping to bring into this world?" Esther asks with what Thomas considers entirely appropriate trepidation.

"Cronos," Samuel Thresher says. "Saturn. The great devourer. His servants already control East London. In exchange for feasting upon the poor of this city, he shall grant me the power to rewrite all contracts, to grow as I see fit."

Thomas understands several things at once. The face he has seen in his dreams, which he has always understood must be connected to the arboreal plague, is Cronos. This is the titan of Greek myth who sought to devour his own children. In the stories, after castrating Uranus, his father, he consumed his own children rather than be overthrown by them. It was Zeus who defeated him and cast Cronos into Tartarus.

Thomas knows the myths cannot be literal truth, but whatever this entity is that Samuel Thresher means to summon, it no doubt has a penchant for mutilation and devouring human flesh. Perhaps it was in truth cast into some distant realm by the ancients, and now Samuel Thresher seeks to free it, to give it the power to devour the poor of East London in exchange for freeing Thresher's from its charter.

"Can you not simply create a new bank?" Thomas realizes he sounds somewhat deranged with exasperation. "Surely this is the long way around. There must be some better way to lend money to rich people than by ruining your finances and then destroying half of London."

"We began by seeking to do just that," Samuel Thresher says in his slow way. "But along the way, we discovered that we could do so much more."

"Once the great magical engine is operational," Mr. Hawke says gleefully, "it will present opportunities of which we have not yet dreamed. Cronos will do as we ask, yes, but we can summon other entities who will serve us in other ways. This is just the beginning."

"Always growing," Samuel Thresher says with a creaking grin. "It is ironic that foolish dabblers like your Golden Dawn made all of this possible. From their efforts to disseminate the once-hidden truths sprang forth thousands of amateur magicians, thousands of insignificant connections to astral realms that were, for all practical purposes, tiny portals. These allowed for bigger, more daring portals. Have you never wondered why the Peculiarities are centered in the most populous, sophisticated cities on earth? It is because that is where the greatest number of magicians live."

"They but laid the groundwork for your brilliance," Mr. Hawke coos.

"And yet you have not used this power to cure yourself," Thomas observes.

"The arboreal plague does not come directly from these portals," Samuel says sadly. "It is something of a cumulative effect of the ambient magic. Most are immune. We, in our family, are not, I'm afraid. Even so, I know that Cronos can cure it. We will be free of the curse."

"You see," says Mr. Hawke. "You have been working against your own interests all along."

Samuel Thresher ignores his factotum. "Ours shall be the greatest magical achievement ever attempted. There are no levers we will not be able to pull. No wishes we cannot grant and no curse we will be afraid to spew. Nations will rise and fall at our command. Wealth will be drawn to us as iron filings to a magnet. Our rituals, our talismans and circles shall no longer be mere whispers, mere nudges one way or the other. Their power will be magnified a thousand-fold."

"You do a great deal of boasting," Thomas says. "But if the power is yours, then why have you not yet used it?"

"We were not yet ready," Walter says. "Now we have the last element."

"Now that the house is ours, the Hierophant must make a sacrifice," Mr. Hawke says, gesturing toward Samuel Thresher. "It must be a true sacrifice, a blood sacrifice, and the nearer in kin to the Hierophant, the more powerful the effect."

"Human sacrifice," Thomas repeats, as if chewing over the idea, as though this were an abstract subject and not something very nearly related to his survival.

"I think you begin to understand," Walter says with a sneer.

Thomas looks at the man he used to think was his brother—but these relations have become a jumble, and so names perhaps work best now—he looks at Walter. He looks at Mr. Hawke, who smiles like a carnival showman. He looks at old, nearly immobile Samuel Thresher. He exchanges a curious glance with Esther, whose expression is a heady mix of horror and skepticism.

It is the skepticism that he latches on to. These men think to spill his blood in a magical ritual. It is hard to imagine how a family could behave more reprehensibly. On the other hand, he and Esther are young and agile. Mr. Hawke may have some unexpected abilities, but Samuel will go nowhere quickly, and corpulent Walter can do little better. "I'm afraid I'm not entirely clear on how you expect to keep me here for such an event. In fact, I think we shall just walk down those stairs and be rid of you."

"You wished to save your family's bank from us, did you not, young Mr. Thresher?" Mr. Hawke asks. "You wished to stop us, though you had no inkling of what it was we were doing. Now that you know, will you now scurry away?"

"I prefer that to offering up my neck on the chopping block." He looks at the door. It is, he believes, time to stop talking and commence departing. "If you need my blood, then I can stop you by leaving." He takes Esther's hand, and they move toward the hallway.

It is then that they hear the sound of feet upon the stairs, dozens of feet, climbing upward. How many? Thomas cannot guess, but many indeed. Enough, he understands, to prevent their passage. If they ever had a chance to escape, it is now gone.

They arrive at the top floor, these men in black robes, hoods over their heads. Some of their faces are obscured, but others are visible, and Thomas recognizes them as men of Thresher's. There are Jenkins and Sullivan and Sherwin from Thomas's own junior clerks' office. It is not only lowly men, however. Mr. St. John, Mr. Minett, Sir Andrew Hyland—all bank directors—are there as well. High to low are present. It is not every man who works for Thresher's, but Thomas does not see a single man who does not. They are brotherhood or cult or order, and Samuel Thresher is the Hierophant who has called for blood sacrifice.

Thomas sets aside his outrage and shock and disgust. It is time to panic.

He can recall wondering, not so very long ago, if he might not be better off dead. Perhaps some of that self-pity seized him when Esther rejected him. It seemed that his life was already over. It had never begun. He no longer feels that way, and if he did, he would not want to die at the hands of his—he thinks for a moment—his grandfather. He has no wish to be killed in order to summon an ancient god that will rewrite Thresher's contract in exchange for devouring the poor. He cannot imagine a stupider end to an unrealized life.

His fear is in no way assuaged when he is grabbed from behind by two of the robed men. He turns and see that Esther has been grabbed as well. Their wrists are bound with rope, and, much to his surprise, the two of them are pushed toward the back of the room, not the front. It seems an inconvenient location for a sacrifice vital to the ritual, but Thomas supposes he is being placed offstage that he might make a dramatic entrance. He has seen enough magical pageantry at the Golden Dawn temple to know how these people like to order things.

Thomas looks at Esther and her expression offers him something that he believes is the equivalent of a shrug. There is nothing they can do right now. They can only wait. If the Threshers are to be stopped, Thomas and Esther must be patient and hope for the best.

Thomas hears the ringing of a bell, and the quiet murmuring in the room ends abruptly. The men around him line up in almost military order into clearly defined rows. This allows Thomas and Esther to peer through the cracks and see to the front of the room.

Samuel Thresher is not wearing a robe, and neither is Walter. Mr. Hawke wears one, but he keeps his hood down. It is he who rang the bell, and he does so again. He steps to one far edge of the circle and rings the bell again. "Purify!" he cries in his nasal voice. He steps to the other side and shouts "Purify!" again. He repeats the process twice more, and then turns to Samuel Thresher. "Hierophant, the circle is pure."

Samuel Thresher nods and pronounces, "Guardian, you have served us well."

From his first exposure, the theatrical nature of magic struck Thomas as ridiculous. He considers the possibility that his evil relations have nothing more sinister planned than a lot of ritualistic hooey. It may well be that this talk of blood sacrifice is purely symbolic. They will pour out a glass of wine or enact the slaying of one of their members.

Thomas hopes it is the case, but he does not believe it. Samuel Thresher does not want the pretense of calling down gods. He wants the real thing.

They perform a ritual Thomas knows well—the Lesser Banishing Ritual of the Pentagram—but then things take an unfamiliar turn. Unfamiliar, but by no means interesting. These are new rituals, spoken in English, clearly written by someone in this brotherhood. They are precisely as compelling as rituals in languages Thomas does not understand. "We harken to the wind, we harken to the dust," and so on. "Spirits of fire, I call to thee! Spirits of earth, I call to thee!" The brotherhood chants along in unison.

Then things become less dull and more terrifying. "Whose blood shall we spill?" asks Mr. Hawke.

"The blood of the Hierophant!" comes the reply from the brotherhood. "Only this shall satisfy Cronos the father, Cronos the son, Cronos the destroyer of fathers and devourer of sons."

Samuel raises a dagger in the air but pointed toward his chest, as though he means to plunge it into his vegetable heart. "I shall give of myself, that my people may thrive."

Then one of them steps forward and intones his line. "I pray thee halt. The Hierophant is the body of the brotherhood. His blood is our blood, and his life is our life. His death would be our death."

Another steps forward. "I shall offer myself in his place."

Then a third brother speaks his line. "I, too, shall give of my blood."

"Your blood is weak," says Samuel. "It is as water. Only the blood of the Hierophant can open the door."

"The door must open," the men chant.

It is now Walter's turn. "Mine is the blood of the Hierophant." He recites his lines as though he has just learned them, as though they are in a foreign language he does not understand. "Mine is the blood that must spill."

Mr. Hawke turns to him. "You give of the Hierophant's own blood? You give of the Hierophant's own flesh?"

"What is his can be given only of him," Walter responds with his usual impatience. "He must command it so."

"Then take the blood of my veins," Samuel pronounces. "Take the flesh of my loins."

Esther goes pale. Thomas stiffens. He believes he knows what will happen next. They have planned and planned and planned. They have pored over Crowley's books and written letters and entered into agreements. They did not, however, foresee that Walter would seek to summon an ancient titan and that Thomas would need to serve as a human sacrifice.

The men of the brotherhood shift their position, creating an aisle that leads directly to Thomas. Mr. Hawke walks down and then stands before Thomas.

Now he understands those dreams, that terrible face. It was Cronos gazing at him across the abyss in anticipation of this moment. This being of unknowable power and designs had been toying with him. It was nothing more than that.

Thomas can offer little resistance. Perhaps, even with his hands tied behind his back, he could smash Mr. Hawke in the face with his head. He might run for the door and perhaps escape into the street. After all, he need not stop them. Delay is enough. Escape would accomplish as much, but escape would require leaving Esther behind. He tells himself that they have no interest in harming her. He tells himself that he cannot help her by allowing these men to sacrifice him. He knows all of this to be true, but he still cannot bring himself to attempt escape and abandon her. His days are numbered, and it is better to die with dignity than live as a coward.

Mr. Hawke puts a hand on Thomas's shoulder. "Here stands the blood of the Hierophant."

Samuel looks down the aisle at Thomas. "The blood," he intones, "is not pure."

Thomas has no idea what that means. Will he have to undergo some sort of purification in order to be killed? More rituals would be adding insult to injury.

Toward the altar, one of the brothers steps forward and puts a hand on Walter's shoulder. "Here stands the blood of the Hierophant."

"The blood," says Samuel, "is pure."

"Wait a moment," Walter cries out. "What the devil do you mean?"

This line, Thomas suspects, is not part of the script.

Members of the order step forward and grab Walter's arms. The large man thrashes, attempting to break free, but there are too many hands upon him.

"It is ironic," whispers Mr. Hawke, who remains standing near Thomas, "that your whole life your family has considered you utterly unimportant, but you are not the one deemed expendable."

"They are really going to kill him?" Thomas asks.

"Oh, yes," Mr. Hawke says. "Most certainly. You have done all you could to disrupt our plans, and you came here with the hope of undoing us. We allowed it because we required that Walter never suspect his true role. From the time you first showed abilities that Walter lacked, Samuel has planned this moment. Yes, you were diverted from your studies, but Samuel Thresher knew you would have all of eternity to make up for a handful of lost years. As his true heir, all you desire will be yours. You and your lady friend will leave this place unscathed. Better than unscathed. You will be free of your disease. Thresher's will emerge in the new era as the dominant force in England and perhaps the world, and you, young sir, are a Thresher. This is your hour of triumph, long planned and hidden."

"But Cronos has been watching me in my dreams," Thomas says. "Why, if not because I am the sacrifice?"

"You are of Samuel's line," Mr. Hawke explains, as if to a child. "In all likelihood, he was attempting to reach out to Samuel and finding you instead. You are so similar, you see. It is why I have always liked you. Cronos was no doubt taking a wrong turn on the way to his true destination. Once again, you mistook something irrelevant for something important. It is common for young men to believe themselves the center of the universe."

The dreams meant nothing. Thomas was merely a blind alley. Is that a relief? Thomas thinks so, but he is not entirely sure. "But what will happen after he comes through that portal?"

"A new beginning," Mr. Hawke says. "You claim you wanted what was best for the bank. Now you shall get your wish. Oh, how I have longed to tell you the truth, how I have imagined your face when all is revealed. You are not the outcast, young Mr. Thresher, but the favored one."

Relief washes over Thomas—after all, he is not about to die—but there is also a rush of anger. Samuel allowed Thomas to be abused so that Walter would not suspect he was destined for sacrifice. And can he simply allow Walter to meet his fate? Thomas cannot quite shake a lifetime of yearning for approval. He does not want his brother or father or whatever he is to die. There should be punishment, yes, and shame. And abject apologies—that much is certain— but death is a bit strong. And then there is the matter of Cronos, whose face Thomas has seen in his dreams. That cruel, hungry face. No punishment Walter might receive is worth freeing that thing.

How much time has passed, Thomas wonders. How long until he can hope to stop this madness?

At the front of the room, Walter is thrashing in the hands of the men attempting to—as Thomas now sees—disrobe him. "Excuse me," says Mr. Hawke. "I must tend to this."

He calmly walks toward the altar forward and when he reaches Walter, he begins to unbutton the bound man's clothing with curiously gentle fingers. Thomas cannot bear to watch.

He turns to Esther. "What do we do?"

"I don't know," she says. "The only tool we have is delay."

Thomas is about to take a step forward. He has no plans after this action, which constitutes the sum of his resistance. Nevertheless, his movement is arrested by a hand on his shoulder. He then feels something cool and his limbs are jarred. He has been cut free.

Thomas turns to see that the hooded man behind him is Aleister Crowley. He holds a knife and is grinning. Meanwhile, Ruby, also—and inevitably— hooded is cutting Esther free.

"Once we broke in, we found plenty of spare robes," Crowley explains. "Disguising ourselves seemed like the obvious approach."

"They are distracted by killing my father," Ruby says. "Let's get you out of here."

Thomas glances toward the front of the room, where the bound and gagged Walter thrashes his head back and forth. Samuel intones some portion of the script, but the words wash over Thomas. He doesn't hear them.

"Don't tell me you want to save him," Ruby says.

"That may be putting it a bit forcefully," Thomas responds. "I'd describe it as not wanting to let them kill him. Let's call it *prevention of murder*. More importantly, we need make certain they don't perform this ritual."

"The ritual will be interrupted," Ruby says. "You can count on that. It's just a matter of when."

Thomas has no idea how long this ritual will take. Perhaps two minutes from now, Walter could be dead, and a yawning hole could open, and Cronos would be free upon the earth. Thomas imagines a giant, plucking pedestrians from the street and biting them in half. He knows this is wrong, but he also knows that it is somehow true. No matter the cost, the ritual must be thwarted.

And there is Walter. Does it make Thomas a bad person that he wants to save him primarily so that Walter will have to live with the knowledge that it was Thomas who did so? That Walter should survive to understand that nothing but his own neglected, abused, conspired-against child saved him from being destroyed by his own stupidity and greed—well, there is a deliciousness to it that cannot be denied. It would strike from the record forever this notion of Thomas's irrelevance.

Also, saving Walter is the moral thing to do. Thomas believes he is certainly motivated by that fact as well.

"Get Miss Feldstein to safety," Thomas tells them. "I cannot walk away from this."

"There's nothing you can do alone," Crowley says. "There's nothing the four of us can accomplish. We have to wait."

Thomas believes there are things he *can* do. If he can get close enough to the circle, he believes he can alter things, make certain that Samuel's plan fails. That won't save Walter, but he can only grapple with one problem at a time. A portal to an unknown realm granting Samuel Thresher great powers is the immediate concern. Written on the circle will be the omega-alef, and if Thomas can zero it, then the ritual will be thwarted, if only long enough to save everyone. There will be no stopping them from attempting it again tomorrow or the next day, but he can only deal with one nightmare at a time.

"I think I can stop them," Thomas says. "If the four of us remain, I'm afraid we will be conspicuous. I believe I can accomplish something alone."

"No," Esther tells him. "I won't let you sacrifice yourself."

He smiles at her. "I can do this without being seen. A few marks on the floor and I'll slip away. Please, go await help."

"Really, Thresher—" Crowley begins.

"You must go if I'm to have a chance," he interrupts, as forcefully as their quiet tones will allow. "No one has ever allowed me to do anything. I haven't been permitted to study, to make friends, to work, even to decide where to sleep, on my own. I am deciding this now. I will stop them. I know how." He holds the magician's gaze.

"Damn it, Thresher," Crowley says with a grin, "I always liked your mettle. Let's go, then," he says to the others.

"We can't just leave him," Ruby protests.

"You heard him," Crowley says. "If he is to succeed, we must leave. And we've already seen they don't mean to harm him. He's right. This is the best way."

Thomas doesn't quite believe they won't harm him if they catch him ruining their sacrifice, but he doesn't point that out. If Esther and Ruby are out of harm's way, he will have the courage to take risks, and if he dies in the attempt, he will die a man and on his own terms. It's not so bad, really, he tells himself. He thinks of Mr. Osgood in the garden. There are worse things than a heroic death.

Esther risks a quick squeeze of his hand, and their eyes meet. "I believe in you," she whispers. Then she turns away.

Thomas is left to pursue what he understands to be a very foolish course of action.

THIRTY-SIX

DOMINION

IT IS LESS difficult than Thomas feared to move to the center of the room. As part of the pageantry of the ceremony, the robed men shift back and forth, turn, bow, kneel, and genuflect. Thomas stealthily creeps from place to place until he finds himself at the front. His hood is pulled down low to make certain neither Samuel nor Mr. Hawke notices him, but they are too caught up with their ritual to trouble themselves with the rank and file of their order.

There, at his feet, is the outer perimeter of the magic circle, its internal boxes and circles meticulously drawn. The omega-alef sits at the heart of its algorithm, and it is not entirely new. It is not the one from the rabbit house, but it is very like the one from the Elegant house, the one Thomas nearly was able to zero. There are so many familiar elements, and Thomas believes that this may be the master algorithm, drawing to itself the power of the other portals.

If that's true, he thinks, he may be able to do more than stop the arrival of Cronos. He may be able to help a friend.

Thomas approaches with the chalk in hand, but he wonders if he needs it. Could he reach forward and simply smudge the nearest portion with his foot? Would that disrupt things sufficiently?

Probably, he decides, but the sabotage would be easily detected. There is no doubt a master drawing readily available, and it would be a matter of minutes to fix the damage. No, Thomas needs to use the chalk to alter the algorithm, to make the effort impossible to find unless one understands all the calculations. Going through each element, looking for an error, would take hours, even days, for the most acute of minds. Samuel could find it. Possibly Mr. Hawke, whose skills are still unknown to Thomas, but likely no one else. How much time would they need to fix the damage? Thomas isn't certain, but he hopes it will be enough.

Then he is given a gift. At some unseen cue, all the hooded brothers kneel. Thomas follows, only a beat behind. The chalk is in his hand, and he is ready.

No one is looking, and he reaches out to alter the nearest equation.

His hand hovers, but he does not write. Thomas begins to see something that he did not quite see before. Rather, he sees with a new clarity how the algorithm directs the omega-alef. It is all about the flow of energy, from outside the portal to within it. He may not understand everything it represents, but this part, this one part, begins to unfold before him.

It is the directional portion that interests him, because Thomas sees—he thinks he sees—the series of symbols that represent either side of the portal. There is something here much more powerful, much more potent, than zeroing the equation. If he could reverse direction of energy—well, he doesn't know precisely, does he? At the very least it would be the sabotage he originally planned. Could it harm the entity traveling between worlds? It could do much more than that. If he does not truly understand what he is looking at, then he will have at least ruined Samuel's scheme. But if he might undo all Samuel has wrought—could it be the end of the Peculiarities? Unlikely. Samuel himself admits he is not responsible for all that has happened. It might, however, be enough to undo the worst of it: the Elegants, the lycanthropes.

The rabbit births.

He could make Esther's difficulties vanish. Has he the right? Is this the sort of meddling with women's lives that she hates so much? He doesn't know. She said herself that she didn't want him fretting about her well-being, but he cannot change who he is. She may, in the inexplicable way of women, resent him for making decisions about her life, but it is his family that put her in her current condition. If he can sacrifice his father's plans to help her, then he will have zeroed a more important equation than any written here.

While considering all this he has used all his time. He must now stand, and he watches as two hooded men lead the naked Walter over to the altar. Walter writhes and struggles, but his movements are subdued, and Thomas wonders if he has been drugged. A leaf sprouts from his pale and freckled shoulder.

One of the men holds down Walter's shoulders. Another seizes his ankles. Samuel waves a dagger over him and speaks lines about blood, about power, about the universe flowing through him. This is all part of the ceremony, however. He makes no threatening gesture to Walter.

Nevertheless, the terror in Walter's eyes is genuine, but Thomas has not entirely ruled out that this is all theater. He does not put it past Samuel to withhold that information. He can be cruel. Perhaps the fear is required for the magic to work. There is no point in speculating, because when it comes to magic as it is generally practiced, Thomas is shite. Anything is as possible as anything else, which means there is nothing to be gained by speculating. He must assume they mean to kill Walter.

Thomas glances up and sees that the Elegants look on with placid faces.

Yes, there are now Elegants in the room. There were none an instant ago, but now four of them—two couples—stand behind Samuel, watching as he performs his ritual. They have shown an interest in Thomas in the past, but they don't seem to notice him now. They are intent on the dagger in Samuel's hand. Their eyes shift as Samuel raises and lowers it, moves it from side to side in some sort of ritualistic gesture.

"Blood begets blood," Samuel says. "Sacrifice begets reward. Cronos, accept my gift." He raises the dagger over Walter's chest, poised to bring it down.

This is not mere pageantry. Thomas can see from the arc of the motion, the look upon Samuel's face that he means to kill Walter. If he acts now, Thomas will destroy his chances of sabotaging the ritual, but if he stays his hand, Walter will die. Walter, his father, who pretended to be his brother, who did nothing for Thomas's entire life but thwart and subvert, and these he did from the pettiest of motives. In this moment, Thomas must choose between the city, perhaps the world, and Walter.

A face appears in the portal now, distorted and unclear, like someone looking up from under water. Its coloring and features are hard to discern, but it has a puzzled expression, and there is a grotesquely hinged quality to it.

It is Cronos or whatever it was that the ancients called Cronos. It is a thing somehow connected to the Elegants, and if it comes through the portal, nothing will ever be the same again. Thomas understands that the rules by which man has lived since he first rose up from whatever primordial source he sprang will be transformed.

He must make a decision, but he knows it is too late for that. He has decided already. He reaches into his robe, into his jacket, and pulls out the little pistol that Mr. Topping gave him. Samuel is distracted by Thomas's quick motions. His eyes grow round when he sees the pistol, but in his wooden torpor, it is too late for him to act, too late for him to dodge. Thomas squeezes the trigger.

The gun pops not so loudly, but in the silence of the room the surprise is enough to make even the Elegants wince. Thomas has aimed for Samuel's chest, but he is no great shot. He misses, hitting his arm instead. The dagger flies free as does the arm itself, broken like an old branch. Blood and dust and a thick white fluid—most likely sap—oozes out of the wound. Samuel stares ahead, stunned.

Then he looks at the floor, sees the dagger, and he reaches for it with his remaining arm.

It has all been for nothing. The Elegants are moving toward Thomas now. They will be on him in a moment.

And that is when the distraction Crowley promised arrives.

Samuel MacGregor Mathers, wearing his Golden Dawn robes, is brandishing a sword. His wife, Moina, stands behind him also in robes and carrying a rifle. Behind them are dozens of other members of the Golden Dawn, all of them dressed as if for one of their ceremonies. Some have firearms, some swords, and some whatever bludgeoning instruments they could find on the quick—cricket bats, broom handles, pokers from the fireplace. The Golden Dawn outnumbers the bankers by at least ten.

More than that, they are there to brawl. The bankers had not been prepared to do much more than chant. Most of them back away. They are unarmed, and by the looks of things, entirely unwilling to die for the cause. A few of the Golden Dawn brothers are overly zealous and begin beating the cowering bankers, but most turn their attention to the front of the room—toward Mr. Hawke, the wounded Samuel, and the Elegants.

Moina Mathers fires her rifle at one of the Elegants, striking the target. The scent of gunpowder fills the room. The creature hisses and staggers but does not go down. MacGregor Mathers, certainly believing his wife will be targeted by this creature, lets loose with a Highland battle cry and rushes forward with his sword.

Thomas decides he must have faith in the chaos around him. Somewhere in the room, his friends will be keeping an eye on him. He doesn't have to see Crowley or Ruby to know they will make every effort to keep him from harm. He rushes forward, taking from his jacket the dagger Crowley gave him, and cuts ropes that have bound Walter to the sacrificial altar. His hands are still tied behind his back, but Thomas has no time or interest in Walter's comfort or dignity. Let him wander around naked and helpless. It is the circle that needs Thomas's attention now.

Perhaps it won't matter. Perhaps with all the chaos that has erupted the ritual is already ruined. Perhaps Samuel and Mr. Hawke and all those responsible for this madness will die, but Thomas cannot depend upon that. He can only count on the relentless ambition of greedy men who wish to make certain Thresher's Bank is always growing.

Pistols and rifles fire. He hears the thud of metal and wood upon flesh. He hears the screams of men, but, thank God, no women. He looks to the floor and gets on his knees below the fog of smoke that is filling the chamber. There it is. He cannot see the whole thing, but he can see this part, how the omega-alef reaches into infinity and pulls, how the numbers dip into and out of sanity and then again into something that will rip his mind to shreds if he considers it too long. It is, for one shining instant, as clear as the simplest of addition, and then it is gone, just like that, leaving a dizzying after-effect like a flash of bright light in the dark. What he saw has vanished, and he does not want to get it back. He is afraid to understand it entirely. But he thinks he understands enough.

Thomas goes to work. It is not so very hard as he feared. He does not have to keep the whole thing clear in his mind at once. He only must understand one portion of it, the directional component. He needn't consider the whole of the map—only the location of certain roads, where they connect, where they come from and where they go.

Maps can be turned around. Numbers can change directions. What if things are moving one way instead of another? He has always enjoyed the dynamic slipperiness of the calculus, and the problem would be amusing, a diverting little puzzle, were people not fighting, perhaps dying, all around him. Still, he must shut out all distraction. He must make himself indifferent, if only for a moment, just long enough to keep the maths straight.

When he sets the chalk down, he is certain he has done what he needs to do. He has no idea how long he was working on the equation. A minute? Several? Much is as he last saw it except the Elegants are holding back, huddling near the portal, entirely unconcerned with what they see all around them. The Golden Dawn brothers and sisters are rounding up the Thresher's lot, who appear to have largely surrendered. Walter, still naked and partially bound, has crouched down in a corner, using his legs to cover as much of his ample flesh as he can. No one has thought to give him a robe, and Thomas is not displeased. Though death is too strong a remedy for his crimes, disgrace is merely a good start.

Near the altar, Samuel stands scowling, his wooden features a mask of resentment. Behind him, Mr. Hawke has his hands raised, as if in benediction.

He grins with the prideful indifference of an adolescent caught in the pantry with a serving girl.

"There is no need for violence." Mr. Hawke's tone suggests that he had not, moments ago, been undertaking the murder of the director of his bank. "We are all hermeticists here. We understand one another, do we not?" He turns to the Elegants, who have been standing still, as though waiting for some unseen cue. "Make no move. Do no harm. We are all friends with one another."

Crowley takes a step toward Mr. Hawke, and for a moment Thomas thinks the magician means to strike him. "Shut up. I don't know what has stilled them, but it is not your words. Perhaps they merely wait to see what happens next. Perhaps they require another ritual in order to act." Crowley looks to Thomas. "What do you think we should do with your brother and the rest?"

"Kill them." It is Ruby. She and Esther are pushing their way toward the front. MacGregor Mathers is close behind, but there is no misunderstanding about who is in charge here.

"Don't be silly," Esther says. "We shan't go about simply killing people. We should deliver them to the Home Office. Let the Special Branch decide what to do."

Mr. Hawke nods eagerly. He sees this as an opportunity to lower his hands. "That is an excellent idea. The rule of law has ever been the strength of this nation. We are a just people. It is what defines us, elevates us above the savages."

"I don't like it," Crowley says. "There's a good chance that they'll simply strike a deal and attempt to recreate what has been happening here. The government will want to master this sort of magic before anyone else does. They'll be worried about the French and the Germans. They'll be afraid of the colonials. They'd rather have Cronos devour half of India than endure another uprising there."

"There is no stopping progress," Mr. Hawke warns in his best schoolmaster voice. "Magic can't remain forever bound to the past. These are modern times. Magicians will practice modern magic. Surely it is better if we pave the way. Think of the possibilities, my friends. I was but a half-starved clerk when Mr. Samuel Thresher plucked me out of obscurity. I have become something akin to a god. Can we deny these benefits to all mankind? I will share my secrets, but for good, you understand. Can we deny the world such bounty?"

Thomas realizes that Crowley, Ruby, and Esther are looking at him. Why should he have the answers? Admittedly, they are talking about his family, the bank that bears his name. On the other hand, it is Ruby's family too. No one is asking her to decide.

Of course, that isn't fair. Thomas grew up a Thresher. He has lived with these people all his life. He has toiled in the bank. He must be the one to decide or, at the very least, put forward a reasonable suggestion. It would make things easier, so much easier, if they could—well, not kill all of them. That would be wrong. But make them disappear, somehow. That is not an option, and he knows that. They cannot lock them in cages for the rest of their lives like they were lions in the park. Whatever the risks, they must turn them over to the Home Office. It is the only rational course of action.

"It is not our place to decide their punishment," Thomas says.

"I am so relieved to hear you say so," Mr. Hawke tells him. He visibly relaxes. Perhaps the entire room does as well because that is the moment he chooses to make his move.

With almost impossible quickness, he pushes Samuel Thresher down on the altar. He raises a dagger that lies unused upon the table and thrusts it into the old man's arboreal heart. It is a nail driven into a piece of wood. It lands with a splintering crack.

Samuel does not scream so much as he grunts. His limbs stiffen in a moment of resistance, and that is how they remain. They are frozen—in death? Is Samuel dead? He does not move. His eyes are open and no more animated than a statue.

Thomas thinks he ought to feel something, but whatever those normal and human emotions might be, they will have to wait. The death of the Hierophant was the last element in the spell. Either Thomas has succeeded, or something terrible, something unimagined in the scope of recorded human civilization, is about to be visited upon them.

Thomas's act of patronicide completed, Mr. Hawke raises his hands again and steps back. He is still grinning. "He would have wanted it," he says, though none of them heard Samuel Thresher make a case for his own sacrifice. "All else was done. The ritual was built around finding a substitute for the Hierophant, but sometimes there are no alternatives. Now, observe my friends as we welcome our new master and see Thresher's triumphant!"

He gestures toward the Elegants, who had been standing statuesque near the portal. They are gone. Thomas did not see them vanish. He did not feel anything change, but the Elegants are simply no longer in the room. There have been no lights or flashes. No vortex has manifested within the portal to draw in evil and chaos. For an instant, he thought he saw the face from his dream, confused, perhaps pained, but then the face dissolved, as if turned to sand. Then the portal is simply an empty frame. Thomas can feel the change in the air, much as he would feel a storm rolling in, or, perhaps, a storm breaking.

Mr. Hawke appears confused. He looks toward the portal and then back at Thomas, whom he somehow recognizes as the cause of this mishap, though it is clear he cannot fathom the particulars. Then his eyes narrow to Thomas's hands, to the chalk stains on his fingers. Mr. Hawke glances from the hands to the markings upon the floor and back again.

Thomas would have preferred to see Mr. Hawke sucked into the portal by some extraordinary inhalation, to see the portal collapse and diminish until it shrinks into a mere point upon a plain, but there are no such theatrics. Sometimes magic is spectacular, but sometimes it is merely ordinary. Magic manifests now in the stillness of the room. There is no sound but the heavy breathing of the men and women who have fought their magical battles with guns and swords and fists. Somewhere someone coughs. A foot scrapes upon the floor. Walter emits a groan and his naked buttocks emit a brief honk of flatulence. It is all so tediously ordinary. It is a moment utterly devoid of Peculiarity.

"What have you done?" Mr. Hawke asks. For the first time Thomas can remember, there is no mirth in his voice, no superior indifference. He appears frightened. "Years of dedication gone to ruin. It should have worked. It was supposed to work. I saw that it would work."

"Whatever else you saw," says Esther Feldstein, "you did not see Thomas Thresher."

He looks at her and smiles. Thomas has the very distinct feeling that he has won. As he looks across the room, he understands that it is a very messy sort of victory, but he will take it, nonetheless.

THIRTY-SEVEN
THE UNIVERSE

THOMAS STEPS INTO the board room of Thresher's Bank. The new directors are waiting for him. They applaud. None of them knows the first thing about banking—about traditional banking, that is to say. They know nothing about how banking has always been done, how it has changed over the past century to value growth above stability or security. They will have a great deal to say, he hopes, about how banking evolves in the dawning century.

That Thomas, who has little banking experience himself, should be the new governor was hardly a matter of choice. Most of the members of the board were taken away by the Home Office. The few who had no knowledge—or claimed no knowledge—of the strange happenings among the directors could only approve of Thomas, the only Thresher neither dead nor incarcerated, taking command of the bank created by his grandfather. That the founder was truly Thomas's great-grandfather is something they do not know. Not all truths need be circulated.

Those remaining men of the old Thresher's board have been dismissed. Thomas does not want them around. They were too obtuse to see the bank was being hollowed out from the inside. Either that or they chose to ignore what was plainly visible. Either way he has no use for them. Thresher's will have to sink or swim without them.

Sinking seems more likely. The bank is burdened with crushing debt. Thomas believes he can conceal the scope of the damage from the general public for a few more months. In that time, he has a chance to turn things around for Thresher's, but to do so will take a miracle worker. It will take a magician.

Thomas looks about the room at his new partners. There are women here—two with wolfen features that mark their unmistakable Peculiar affliction. Another is a Jewess. Some whisper that though she is unmarried she has been pregnant, but she shows no sign of it. And she will not.

There is a gruff laboring man in the room, and a brash young fellow whose only qualifications are his own significant family fortune and a knowledge of magic. These people have no experience in banking, but they can learn. Their only qualifications are that Thomas trusts them. They will seek out new blood, of course. They will find promising candidates to fill their ranks, those with a deeper knowledge of money matters than any in the room, but for now Thomas has agreed to take the reins of Thresher's only if he can work with those he knows will help him set things right the way he sees fit. Thomas must be in the company of his friends.

He wonders what Walter thinks of all this. Does he know? Along with the other Thresher's men who had participated in the ritual at Westerly House, Thomas turned Walter and Mr. Hawke over to the Special Branch. When he went to visit a few days later, he was told that both men had escaped. Thomas doesn't know how to interpret this claim. Have they really escaped? Are they being held in seclusion? Are they cooperating with the Home Office in secret experiments? Have they been executed? Have foreign rivals abducted them for their knowledge? Even guessing is an exercise in absurdity. He thinks he could ask Crowley to consult his tarot desk, but the truth is, after everything that's happened to him, he's not sure he would believe the results.

Thomas has moved back into Walter's house. Pearl continues to live there in theory, though she has gone to stay with her sister in Norwich and has said nothing of any plans to return. It is a strange experience, walking around the house as though it is his own, the servants deferring to him. There is also the matter of Walter's study, which Thomas believes he ought to explore at length. There are papers to read, notes to review.

Not yet. Soon, he tells himself, but he is not ready.

He believes he may have time.

The leaves have not stopped growing, but the rate has slowed. Thomas does not know if altering the equations has begun a process of reversal or merely hindered it. Perhaps his body requires some time to remove the unknowable toxins from his system. One guess is as good as any other. All he knows is that he likely has more time than he had before.

The Peculiarities, likewise, are diminished but not eliminated. No one has seen any sign of the Elegants since the incident at Westerly House. There have been no new reports of rabbit births, but Ruby and Mrs. Topping are no less wolfen than they were before he began. Some things may never reverse, though he has not given up hope that they will reverse slowly. On the other hand, he is simply guessing. The world is now an unknown place. The old rules are gone. The new rules are uncertain. Thomas hopes to play a role in writing them.

As for Esther, she believes the life within her vanished as a side effect of what Thomas did at Westerly House. He has been unable to bring himself to tell her that he knew what he was doing. He supposed he might have done the same thing if he hadn't been thinking of her, but it is also true the idea might not have occurred to him if he'd only been looking to stop the ritual. He does not know, just as he does not know if Esther would praise him for making decisions about her pregnancy or condemn him. He hasn't had the courage to find out.

"Gentlemen," Thomas says to the room. "Ladies. You've examined the reports I've prepared. You know this bank is in serious financial jeopardy. We will have to find lucrative investments to increase liquidity, and we will have to do so at once."

Crowley and Mrs. Topping are sitting next to one another. They both have their files sitting in front of them and, on top of those, they each have their own tarot decks.

"We have some ideas," Crowley says.

Three days after their first meeting, Thomas is in his office much later than he would like. There are documents to read, loans to approve, letters to write. He dedicates the afternoon and much of the evening to these responsibilities, and when he is done, the looming pile of obligation seems no smaller than when he started. He could keep working through the night, and he thinks it would be no different.

He does not work through the night, however. He leaves shortly before eight that he might meet Crowley and Esther and Ruby at a nearby tea shop. When he arrives, the three of them are already present. A seat is open at the table between Esther and Ruby—his sister—and he takes it with some feeling of trepidation.

Since the incident at Westerly House, his conversations with Esther have been of an impersonal nature. They have discussed the events and her new role at the bank, which she accepted only reluctantly. She has no experience and no interest in such matters, she said, but Thomas told her that he needed her— people like her. People he knew he could trust. To that she agreed.

What has happened between them, and what might happen between them in the future, is a topic he has not quite gotten to. He has been busy, yes, but he senses something in her—a regret, perhaps. He does not think it is a judgment upon himself. Rather he suspects she wonders, as does he, if there is any true connection between them. They were thrown together by crisis and circumstance, and in that crucible, feelings of attraction and desire will inevitably multiply. It is its own sort of alchemy. When they met, Esther Feldstein was a radical and Thomas a banker. They have each stepped into the other's role, but the gulf created by their different backgrounds feels yet uncrossed.

Nevertheless, as he sits down, he feels the thrill of energy as she smiles at him. There is something there, he thinks. Perhaps a mere ember that can be fanned to life should he so wish it. Does he wish it? He suspects all three of the people at this table know Thomas better than he knows himself. They know he wishes it.

"Have you forced the great and powerful to their knees?" Crowley asks.

"I've cramped my hand in writing letters," Thomas answers. "I can't say I've accomplished more than that."

"Other than changing the world," Ruby says. She is proud of her new position and proud of her new brother. Thomas considers this odd. He thinks how much happier he would have been to have been raised by Mrs. Topping, utterly ignorant of his father's family. Yet he knows that the Thresher name, and at least the possibility of Thresher money, is not what swells her heart.

Ruby is not the only one of her kind in the tearoom. There is a young wolfen fellow, perhaps a boy—Thomas still finds it hard to determine such things—no more than fifteen, Thomas guesses, eating a piece of cake with his family. He suspects strongly that this is the first time they have appeared in public since the boy's condition manifested. At another table, a man with reptilian skin and a fine suit goes over what appears to be a contract with two other well-dressed gentlemen. The Peculiarities are upon the streets. They no longer hide. Ruby gives Thomas the credit.

This seems a bit of a stretch. Any credit he deserves comes from what he considers to be his most botched exercise—the freeing of the Elegants. That is what made it impossible for London to deny the Peculiarities. That is what drove the newspapers to speak the truth. People died, but people also were freed. That is something. It is also something that the Elegants are gone. That they will never again walk the streets stalking their victims is also thanks to Thomas's band of misfits, his family, his friends. All of the portals have been destroyed. Perhaps they shall not come back, though it may be too much to hope that the knowledge will never resurface.

"Not that I need a pressing reason to see you all outside of work," Thomas says, "but your note made it seem that the matter was important."

"Important, but not urgent," Esther says. "Still, it seems like it will take a crisis to get you away from the bank these days."

"The bank is a crisis, I'm afraid. I have little time for socializing."

"Then you will be glad to know that it is business we wish to discuss," Esther says. "But this setting seemed more fitting."

"We wanted you to see it," Ruby said. "To believe it. Look at that lizard fellow over there doing business like a right gentleman. Who knows what he's up to? Maybe selling something, maybe buying, but it's his first chance, isn't it? Maybe in years. Who knows how much he's got stashed away, but he couldn't go to a bank could he?"

"You wanted new ideas," Crowley says. "Instead we've come to you with an old one. It is Thresher's founding idea—to be a bank for those who are not welcome elsewhere."

"A Peculiar bank." Thomas feels that by speaking it aloud he is testing out the idea, sounding it, measuring it.

"There must be so many people in the city who would choose Thresher's simply for welcoming them," Esther says.

"As you have pointed out," Thomas counters, "The Peculiarities disproportionately affect the poor. And I fear such a policy might drive away current customers—solvent customers."

"And yet serving those who have nowhere else to go was the founder's intent, was it not?" Crowley counters.

Crowley considers another argument. Thresher's has suffered because it has violated its charter. In the Peculiar age, that leads to poor luck. By cleaving to the charter, perhaps they will receive blessings in equal measure. It seems like a worthwhile gamble, but that is not what influences Thomas's decision. He will do it because it the bank's purpose, and if it cannot exist the way it was intended, then why should it exist at all? He will do it because the universe has given him an opportunity to do something that matters, and Thomas wants so much to grasp it.

He looks around the table, at Crowley, at his sister, at Esther. Not for the first time, he wishes all of this responsibility did not fall upon his shoulders. He wished to fix what was wrong in his family's bank, however, and he will not neglect this duty. But it is more than the bank. It is a duty to his country and to his friends. The thrill he feels when Esther smiles encouragingly at him may also play a part in his decision. If he participates in this project, he will be working alongside her. He will feel her approbation.

"Very well," he says. "We will roll the dice."

"Told you he'd like the notion," Ruby said.

Esther is smiling at him with approbation, and it makes him uneasy. He has kept a secret from her, a secret about the most intimate parts of her own life. It was what was done to him, and he cannot endure it any longer. It is better that she hate him than that he hide the truth of his actions from her.

"I must speak with you for a moment," he tells her.

A look of concern crosses her face, but she rises and follows him to a quiet corner of the tea shop.

Thomas looks at the smiling people who sit enjoying their lives. In a few minutes he may take his seat and join their numbers. Or he may watch Esther flee in sadness and rage. He honestly does not know which will happen, but he will live with the consequences. Much as he will do with the bank, he will roll the dice because the gamble is worth taking. He does not know what will happen, but he knows what he does will matter, and that feels like something entirely new.

AFTERWORD

R EAL MAGIC HAS always fascinated me.

By *real* magic, I don't mean the kind people feared might exist and be used against them. I mean the kind people practiced, and continue to practice, believing in its efficacy. This is often magic on a much smaller scale than what is represented in stories of the supernatural. Real-world magicians generally did not believe they could perform miracles, rather that they might nudge conventional reality in a different direction. What constitutes magic, as opposed to religion, can get murky the further back in time you go, and while I have spent some—often frustrating—time with the writings of medieval and early modern occultists, my particular interest is post-Enlightenment magic.

The magicians of the Hermetic Order of the Golden Dawn are fascinating in part because their membership included no shortage of larger-than-life figures: William Butler Yeats, Samuel MacGregor Mathers, and, most infamously, Aleister Crowley, just to name a few. Outlandish people and practices are just the frosting on the cake, however. I am more interested in how this organization of scholars and dabblers, earnest seekers and shifty schemers, changed Western occult practices forever. This was ancient magic systematized, formulized, and rendered accessible to a mass audience. All of this happened at the dawn of the 20th century, a time when reason, industry, and science seemed poised to render organized religion, let alone magic, obsolete.

Yet here came the Golden Dawn, with its origins enshrouded in mystery and not a little chicanery. These were grown men and women, respectable members of society, dressing in robes, wearing masks, and waving around ritual instruments in the hopes of effecting change upon the universe and gaining a greater understanding of things unseen.

Throughout human history, practitioners of magic have always sought to obscure and mystify their art, hiding what they believed to be powerful truths in confusing, circuitous, and deliberately misleading writings. Golden Dawn magicians, on the other hand, wanted to make magic something anyone could practice, which is likely why the order's legacy lives on. The overwhelming majority of people today who engage in ritual magic (I don't have any hard data on this, but my casual research suggests this is a non-trivial portion of the population), practice some form or variation of Golden Dawn magic.

Writing about historical magic presents certain challenges. This is something I've attempted before. My novel, *The Twelfth Enchantment*, dealt with the *early* 19th century revival of interest in magic, but this was more of a literary exercise, an attempt to graft certain novelistic tropes onto the Romantic interest in the supernatural. For *The Peculiarities*, I began with what felt like an intriguing question: What would have happened if the magic practiced by the members of the Golden Dawn actually and demonstrably worked?

I needed to set certain ground rules for myself. I've always been frustrated with supernatural historical fiction that posits the idea that sorcerers, vampires, werewolves, or what you have always been real but have existed in the shadows. That a powerful subset of human beings would spend millennia hiding themselves never sat well with me. It would be like creative geniuses or people with eidetic memories concealing themselves from the general population since the dawn of time. Why would they? If magic worked, everyone would know it and there would be no need to keep it secret. Things that occur in the natural world seem natural. Thus if Golden Dawn magic worked, then the magic of the organization's intellectual forebears would have worked. Obscure magicians like Heinrich Cornelius Agrippa, Paracelsus, John Dee, and Johannes Trithemius would have been among the most powerful people of their times.

If something in the world changed, however, then it might make sense that magic could become powerful and effective at the end of the 19th century. To my thinking, such a change should emerge from the condition of the world as it was at that moment. Thus, the idea in this novel is that the emergence of mass communication, combined with a trans-Atlantic mania for all things occult, could actually effect a change upon the world in a way that would have been impossible for historical occultists working in relative isolation.

The Peculiarities is therefore not a secret history, but an alternative history. I signal this fairly early on in the book when a universally recognized historical figure (I won't name him in case anyone is reading this essay before the actual novel) meets a decidedly unhistorical fate. Having spent most of my career writing historical fiction in which plot points could not run counter to recorded events (which was true even of my previous foray into historical fantasy), this felt like an entirely new kind of project. As I planned out this story, I realized anything could happen.

And then it did.

ABOUT THE AUTHOR

DAVID LISS is the author of fourteen novels, as well as numerous novellas, short stories, and comics. His previous books include *A Conspiracy of Paper* which was named a *New York Times* Notable Book and won the 2001 Barry, Macavity, and Edgar awards for Best First Novel. *The Coffee Trader* (2003) was also named a *New York Times* Notable Book and was selected by the New York Public Library as one of the year's 25 Books to Remember. He is also the author of the middle grade Randoms series. Many of his novels are currently being developed for television or film. Liss has worked on numerous comics projects, including *Black Panther* and *Mystery Men* for Marvel, *The Spider* and *Green Hornet* for Dynamite, and *Angelica Tomorrow*.

He lives in San Antonio with his wife and children.